First paperback edition printed August 2020

Contact the author at natalie@nataliemurrayauthor.com
For updates, sign up to Natalie Murray's newsletter at
www.nataliemurrayauthor.com

ISBN: 978-0-6488059-0-8
ISBN: 978-0-6488059-1-5 (ebook)

For Eva,
my adorable mum

Who welcomed a frankly intolerable number
of books into our lives—especially our car—
and who always talked to the terrifying humans
for me because they weren't Moon-Face or Silky.

But, mostly, for indefatigably supporting every
decision I've made with love (except the one to
play 'When I Die' by No Mercy on repeat, which
was super annoying).
*"And when I die, I keep on living..." *body roll**

Seas have their source, and so have shallow springs;
And love is love, in beggars as in kings.

A Modest Love,
Sir Edward Dyer (1543–1607)

EVERYTHING BEFORE ME LOOKED BACKWARD, like seeing a fractured limb snapped into a surreal angle. After waking up from a heavy sleep, I'd expected to find myself lying on the grubby stones of a sixteenth-century English horse stable. Instead, I sat shivering on the bank of the Connecticut River, its surface a sheet of inky-black glass through the drooping branches of a willow tree.

A few hours ago, I'd dozed off on the sandy river's edge in the arms of my dream boyfriend, Nick Tudor (make that dream *fiancé*), one of my arms awkwardly locked around his horse's bony hoof. So long as our three bodies stayed connected and we all fell asleep—including the horse—the enchanted ring on my thumb should've sent us four hundred years back in time, to where I'd decided to live and marry Nicholas the First, the King of England. *Gulp, no biggie.* But instead of rising and shining in King Nick's court in the year 1580, I'd awakened right where we'd fallen asleep: in Hatfield, Massachusetts, in the present day.

Nick lurched up beside me, his voice thick with sleep. "Good God, we are still in your time."

"I know; I don't get it, the ring's still on." My fingertips brushed the blue diamond's rock-hard ridges again to make sure.

He yawned, moonlight drawing a silver line down the slight curve of his nose. "One of us plainly had not yet fallen to sleep. We must begin again." He clicked his tongue, guiding his horse Stella closer and hooking his broad arm around her leg.

I lay back down on the cold slope of mushy sand. Nick cradled me from behind with his other arm, my quickening pulse like whitewater rapids in my ears. It wasn't me who'd kept us awake: I could tell by my gunky eyes and sticky throat. Nick looked just as groggy, so it must've been the horse who'd failed to fall asleep and kept us all from traveling through time. It was the only explanation.

Nick's soft lips grazed the skin beneath my hairline, stealing my thoughts. I sighed and cuddled into him, finding his mouth with mine. The sighs of pleasure he made as we kissed made my thighs squeeze his, but he pulled away with a frustrated groan.

"I fear that falling to sleep beside you shall never be a simple business," he said through a drowsy smile. "But sleep we must. Lord Warwick is likely awaiting my return and may have already raised the alarm. Christ, what if the men see us appear before their eyes? You must feel favored at court, not mistrusted from the first moment." His beautiful eyes brightened with visible alarm.

I whispered a calming hush into his scarred cheek. "Don't stress. We've got this."

Rolling onto my side again, I shifted to get comfortable.

How on earth was I going to convince four-hundred-year-old English aristocrats to trust me when I had literally no idea how to be a Tudor queen? It had all happened so fast—Nick's 'now or never' marriage proposal and my heartfelt acceptance. I wasn't sure I could really pull off being queen, or even if I wanted to, but I'd lost Nick before, and I had no intention of doing it again. *Ever.*

He tightened his embrace like I'd disappear if he didn't.

The next time I opened my eyes, my body felt like a bag of cement. Had we finally arrived at the Palace of Whitehall?

The world took shape and color around me. A golden blush of sunrise painted the mirrored surface of the Connecticut River, its steady burble like a nature soundtrack. Stella lay motionless on her side while Nick breathed rhythmically into my shoulder, his eyelids fluttering with a dream.

Oh my God, the time-traveling ring isn't working! Which means...

I rolled over to face him, my eyes devouring the dimple that appeared in his cheek when he moved his mouth a certain way, the eyelashes cute enough to kiss, the delicate curve of his lips. Could my treasured King of Pants-Dropping Hotness really be stuck in my time?

I clamped my eyes shut, rising excitement burning away months of chronic anxiety. If the enchanted ring had stopped working and Nick had to stay here forever, I could have my Tudor king *and* my college degree *and* my mom *and* my friends *and* things like flushing toilets, television, and peanut butter! I could also keep Nick without having to follow through on all the scary queen stuff! I shut my eyes and lay still, immobilized with relief so intense that it felt nauseating, when something squeezed my shoulder.

"Hmm?" I muttered, my throat clogged. Nick's handsome face sharpened into view. The air tasted like smoke and straw.

"You must rise in haste," he whispered. "Francis is asleep."

I used both hands to sit up. My eyelids felt glued together. As they came unstuck, objects materialized through the darkness. A pair of misshapen candles burning from iron mounts in a brick wall. Tattered ropes dangling from a low-hanging beam. A flagstone floor brushed with hay.

We're back in the sixteenth century.

My stomach twisted into knots. *I guess Nick Tudor and my mom are going to remain mutually exclusive and I'm going to have to figure out how to be a Tudor queen. Yikes.*

Nick draped an auburn cloak over my T-shirt and jeans and whispered for me to change in the corner of the horse stable. He handed me a smock and kirtle combo that was simple enough for me to tie on myself. I guessed he'd hidden them earlier in the hope that I'd accept his proposal and come back to Tudor England with him.

Needles of hay spiked my bare toes as I hurriedly swapped my old tennis shoes for a pair of satin slippers. I gasped as Nick bundled up my modern clothes and tossed them into the fireplace. Sleepy and disoriented, we silently watched the fabric curl into flames, crackling and sputtering, before he gently guided me through the stable gate. I tightened my cloak to keep warm, my head spinning with the fact that this was really happening—I was back in the Tudor world and engaged to its king! *Mind-blown.* But at least I had Nick by my side, the thought coating me with a giddy warmth.

The sleeping Earl of Warwick, Francis Beaumont, sat crookedly on an upturned log. Stella whinnied behind us, kicking her legs for momentum before pushing herself up onto her hooves.

"Hairbrain!" cried Francis, his ebony eyes flashing open. He jumped to his feet with one hand on his sword.

"Be calm," Nick hissed at him. "Has anyone come? I feared you raised the guards."

Francis shook his head, squinting at me. "But mine eyes heed someone is with you, Your Grace. So all is well then." He exhaled, sliding his hands down his midnight-blue doublet.

"Mistress Grace is in need of rest," Nick said evenly. It was a command to make no further comment about my arrival, and Francis knew better than to disobey. The smells of hay and horse sweat chased us beneath a tall stone archway and out onto a cobblestone road flanked by statuesque trees with sturdy branches. None of this looked familiar.

"You were gone for many weeks, Emmie," Nick explained.

4

"The court is no longer at Whitehall. I have since taken up lodgings at Hampton Court Palace."

I had a zillion questions like, *"Should I act like I've seen Hampton Court Palace before?"* but I kept my mouth shut in front of Francis as the three of us climbed into a waiting coach. With the crack of a whip, the carriage jerked forward, and I avoided the earl's curious stare as I watched the peach haze of dawn illuminate the narrow road through the curtained window. Up ahead, a smattering of smoking chimneys skewered the sky, and a high gatehouse topped with onion-shaped domes emerged. Nick squeezed my hand, his palms a touch clammy. I wasn't the only one who was nervous about this new arrangement.

We bumped across a bridge decorated with Roman busts and passed through the towering gatehouse into a stony courtyard enclosed with redbrick walls patterned with black diamonds. As we stepped out of the coach, my eyes trailed a diving flock of birds to a servant in breeches washing the ground with a broom. He bowed to the king and scampered away with his sloshing bucket. The wall lanterns still glowed with fire, but the rising sun was brightening the courtyard by the minute.

Nick didn't hesitate to make a beeline for the next gatehouse with Francis following a few paces behind us. I hugged myself beneath my cloak. I'd forgotten that sixteenth-century England was cooler than my time.

"You cannot begin to imagine how heartened I am to have you here," Nick said to me as we passed a stone fountain. He nudged my shoulder affectionately.

I tilted into him but sensed Francis's eyes on my back. "How much did you tell Lord Warwick?" I whispered. "Does he know about time travel?" The thought of someone else here knowing the real me would've actually been a relief.

"Heavens, no," said Nick. "I simply informed Lord Warwick of my desire to bring you back to court and that I planned to do it alone, commanding him to wait in the stable for my return." He leaned into me. *"Our* return."

My heart squeezed. Being back in Tudor England, this time by Nick's side, had to be worth all the unnerving parts, like convincing the locals I was queen material.

An imposing building with a gabled roof dominated the next, smaller courtyard. My gaze traced the battlement ridges, searching for archers, although Hampton Court's tall windows made it clear this was a pleasure palace rather than a fortress castle. Behind us, a gigantic gilded clock reflected a ribbon of early morning sunlight. It was bizarre to think that I should've been arriving at college in twenty-first-century London at that same moment. I pushed that thought away.

Nick's face tightened as he turned to Francis. "Lord Warwick, you will see Mistress Grace to her chambers. She may lodge in Princess Catherine's rooms until her own apartments are constructed, for which I favor the south side. You will also nominate a lady's maid until appropriate ladies of the bedchamber are appointed. Inform the Lord Chamberlain."

Francis bowed. "Forgive me, Majesty. You are constructing new apartments? For Mistress Grace." I tried not to take offense at his stunned tone.

"Mistress Grace is to become your queen," Nick said coolly.

Francis's eyes widened, every inch of him stiffening. The opinionated earl wasn't exactly raising the roof with excitement over our decision to get hitched—quite the opposite. A dart of alarm struck my stomach.

Nick's steely voice carried a warning. "You will arrange a feast for this night to present our promised queen to the nobles. I have no patience for any slander about Mistress Grace's attendance at court. I expect the utmost heights of magnificence, of which our lady is worthy in every measure."

"A feast *tonight*?" I said, but my voice didn't cut through the growing tension between the two best friends.

Francis's narrowed eyes met the king's daunting stare. "Your Majesty, may I enquire after Mistress Grace's kin for her presentation at the feast? I will wager her father has not yet visited court."

"Mistress Grace's father has gone to God."

Nick draped a protective arm around me and kicked off an elaborate lie to Francis about how my entire family had just died of consumption in my hometown of Worthing. He explained that it was the reason I'd been called away from court for the past few weeks, and why the Duke of Norfolk—who everyone at court thought was my distant uncle—would formally present me to the nobles on my family's behalf.

My stomach tensed. The Duke of Norfolk was the most powerful man in England, second only to the king. We'd never even met, but Nick clearly trusted the duke to perpetuate the lie about me being his niece.

Francis bowed, but his voice stayed taut. "I am honored to fulfill my king's every command as his most humble servant."

Nick snapped something in French that sent the earl stumbling back a few paces. When Francis was out of earshot, the king cupped my elbows and slid me closer, stilling the quiver in my belly. He was so different here: stressed and almost scary. But when he gazed at me with those devoted eyes the color of a shallow sea, I was liquid caramel all over again.

His forehead touched mine. "It will not be like last time," he breathed, smelling more like a rose garden than a riverbank. "I will build you the finest chambers you have ever seen with a chapel, rooms for music and dancing, libraries—any such thing you desire. With all my heart, I wish for your happiness here."

I ran my fingertips down the knobby gold stitching in his doublet. It was so weird to think that the dirt on his elbows came from the banks of the Connecticut River.

"I love you," I said, the words softening Nick's face. "Even though you just killed off my entire family," I added with a cheeky smile. "I guess that having them move to a tropical island would've been too much?"

His brow crumpled. "Forgive me, I intend only to make less trouble for you. Forget not that your true family has not yet been born."

"Well, by that logic, neither have I."

He chuckled and sighed simultaneously. "I slept but a few hours by a river. Do not make my head sorer than it already is." He pulled me closer, my hips brushing his hard thighs. "You must know that my heart is full to bursting."

My arms glided around his back and squeezed the silky velvet, wanting him to hug me back, but early-bird courtiers were beginning to surface on the edges of the courtyard. Nick unlocked himself from me with visible reluctance and stepped backward.

"I give you leave," he called, a cue for Francis to draw nearer again. "Please sleep awhile," Nick said to me. The boyish smile decorating his face as he backed away liquefied my legs.

Francis called for guards, and a flurry of red coats appeared like a magic trick. They chased after the king through a Gothic stone archway at the next gatehouse.

Francis seemed irritated, and we barely said a word to each other on the way to my new chambers, but it wasn't for lack of trying on my part. The earl and I had locked horns before, and this time I wanted us to get along. But all I could get out of him was that he was now the king's chief counsel after the retirement of Sir Thomas Grey. I swallowed an urge to laugh and fist-bump him at the same time. I wasn't sure Francis had the temperament to help run a country, but his new position as the king's right-hand man was all the more reason to get him back on my side.

The chambers that were usually reserved for Nick's little sister Kit were at the rear of the palace, behind the main chapel. We crossed a quiet, square-shaped courtyard to a three-story building, where Francis used a monster-sized master key to unlock a pair of arched doors.

Stepping inside was like leaving a monochrome world for the Land of Oz. Francis hunted through a drawer for a tinderbox and lit a candle, its glow dancing up the walls draped with vibrant tapestries that disappeared into a ceiling gilded with geometric shapes. After staggering over uneven cobblestones, the woven rush matting felt like clouds.

Francis muttered to himself as he tipped the flickering candle to light the remaining wicks. "Damn orders. Leaves me to sleep on a damn stump while he rides into the damn night. Pay no heed to thieves and assassins, mind."

"All good, Lord Warwick?" I said.

He ignored the question and threw open a cupboard, checking over the pewter plates and cups. "You should have ample provisions. The chambers are regularly made ready for the Princess Catherine."

"How is Kit?" I said, a flicker of fear in my gut. The last time I'd seen Nick's eight-year-old sister, the traitor Mathew Fox had nearly murdered both of us.

"By all accounts, the princess is well. Lodged at Kenilworth Castle and quite safe, grace be to God." Francis stood watching me for several moments while rubbing his trimmed goatee. When he spoke again, his tone was brusque.

"It may be the king's pleasure to seek holy matrimony with your person, Mistress Grace, and I yield myself to the will of our good and gracious king. However, I speak for the Privy Council, and indeed all the peers of the realm, when I say that this union does not come without surprise."

Heat flooded my face. "I think we're all a bit surprised," I said in a small voice.

I instantly regretted the missed opportunity to sound more confident, but Francis was already making his escape.

He offered a small bow before he passed through the oaken

doors. "I shall have a lady's maid sent in haste to prepare your person for the feast. We cannot delay in announcing to the noblemen that their new queen is to be the daughter of a departed physician whom they have not had the pleasure of meeting."

His suspicious eyes didn't break from mine as he backed away, leaving my palms sweaty. I was getting the impression that my old mate Francis would've preferred Nick to marry the frosty French princess, Henriette.

But thinking about Nick's loving words kept me from falling into panic as I explored the drawing-room, warmed by the signs of Kit's previous stay here. A collection of carved horses, lions, crocodiles, and a spiky porcupine was piled inside a toy cart. A play castle stood guard beside it, dressed with wooden figurines of knights and ladies. I made a mental note to ask Nick if his sister could come to Hampton Court Palace so we could hang out again and she could read me poems that she'd translated from Latin.

Smiling at the thought, I meandered through the series of chambers, finding a dining chamber, another drawing-room with pallet beds for servants, a small garderobe with a medieval-style toilet, a dressing room, and a bedchamber with a hand-painted map of England on the wall. It was all a serious step up from my pokey old room at the Palace of Whitehall.

After placing the blue-diamond ring safely inside a jewelry coffer, I stripped to my smock and climbed into the four-poster bed hung with embroidered textiles. The silk bed sheets smelled like orange blossom.

My heavy eyelids closed without effort, sparking an image of Mom watching me. She stood smiling with her back against the laminate kitchen counter, a mug of milky tea in her hand. I'd never have moved so far away from her had it not literally come down to her or the boy I loved. My chest pinched, and I turned over, sinking my cheek into the feather pillow. I refocused my mind on Nick, remembering the way he'd flirtatiously kissed my palm on the rocky sand beside the river…the way his mouth had moved to my fingers, his soft lips skimming them one by one. The memory of his mouth near the blue-diamond ring sent my stomach into free fall. Through all the anxiety about being back in Tudor England, I'd forgotten that the enchanted ring was acting super weird last night! It had never taken more than one try to carry us through time like that before.

I rolled onto my back and gazed at the wooden beams intersecting above the bed. What if something was wrong with the ring? I still knew hardly anything about it, and why it even traveled to my time. What if its magic had finally conked out and I was here for good?

You are here for good, Emmie. You agreed to marry a Tudor king and become a sixteenth-century queen, even though you're an eighteen-year-old from the twenty-first century who has no idea how to do those things. And you've been here for what feels like three minutes, and he's already left you alone.

The thoughts kept coming, and it was a miracle I fell asleep at all.

⚜ ⚜ ⚜

Firm fingers jiggled my arm, stirring me from a restless sleep. My eyes opened to meet a ruddy-faced girl with a tangle of red curls escaping her lopsided hood. She curtsied, silky beige skirts fluffing around her.

"My lady, I am Mistress Bridget Nightingale, here to assist you. With your permission, it will honor me to serve you as a true and faithful subject." Her squeaky voice was cute. She could've been a cartoon voice-over artist.

"Oh, hi, good morning," I mumbled through sticky lips.

"Forgive the correction, but is afternoon, my lady. It is time to make ready for the feast where His Majesty will present you to

11

his most favored noblemen." She heaved me out of bed with the grip of a gorilla before handing me a silk robe.

"Thanks," I said, throwing the robe over my shoulders and trailing her through to the drawing-room, even though the idea of being presented to the aristocrats made me want to hightail it back into the bed.

"I am still to make ready your chambers," said Bridget. "Forgive me; there was no forewarning of your arrival." Her cherry lips offered a nervous smile.

"Oh, it's fine, don't worry." *It's not like you knew a time traveler from the New World was heading your way. It's cool, Bridge.*

She brushed her hands on her skirts and shoved open the oak doors, nearly toppling over. I hurried to help her, and together we struggled to hoist a wooden pushcart strapped with a humungous chest down the stone steps and roll it inside. Bridget didn't want me to trouble myself, but I insisted. Anything to feel like less of a queen-to-be and more of a normal person.

"Would you care for some water?" she said, sounding breathless. "Lord Warwick said that you favor it." She grimaced, accenting the peach rouge on her round cheeks.

"Water sounds perfect, thank you."

Sweeping a ginger curl off her neck, Bridget reached into a shelf at the base of the pushcart to retrieve a pewter jug. After pouring me some water, she guided me into a fringed chair. Next to appear from her bottomless pushcart was a cheese tart, a bowl of sugared strawberries, and a plate of freshly baked macarons. The sight sent butterflies to my stomach. Nick had remembered my weakness for macarons. My skin flushed hot at the thought of seeing him. How many hours had it been?

I sat and chewed the crisp meringues, feeling utterly useless as Bridget guided the pushcart into the dressing room. She soon reappeared, clutching a shimmering silver-colored gown embroidered with falling feathers. Artful slashes in the silver satin revealed blush-pink silk fabric underneath.

"You may choose any cloth you desire for the feast, but I much prefer this one," she said, grinning through crooked teeth. All at once, I loved Bridget and could tell she would be a great help to me in navigating this court.

"It's stunning," I said, jumping to my feet. The perks of becoming a queen were beginning to show themselves.

I ate three macarons in a row while she dressed me piece-by-piece, beginning with several petticoats and one of those ridiculous hoop skirts. The fabric had been warmed by the fire and smelled faintly of lavender.

"How long have you been at court?" I said a little timidly. My instinct to make conversation with Bridget was matched by my fear that she'd ask questions about my life that I wouldn't know how to answer.

"I was blessed to join His Majesty's service in the year last." Bridget tied on my skirts with the speed of an expert. "My father is the king's Master of the Horse."

She began attaching the sleeves of my dress, which felt heavy and expensive. It was a relief to have the company of someone fluent in all things sixteenth century.

"Thanks for helping me," I said. "It's good to have a friend here."

Her whiskey-colored eyes widened. "My lady, it pleased me to no end to learn of your arrival. To speak plainly, when the Princess Henriette of France was in the king's heart and lodged at Whitehall, she had little interest in English ladies for her household. Furthermore, Princess Henriette's French maids were rumored to have desires of the most carnal nature. I wish to become a queen's maid of honour." She blushed. "I may then find a husband of mine own."

"You're looking for a hubby?" I smirked.

She giggled. "Most heartily. Is it just I, or are the noblemen becoming more handsome by the year? The Earl of Warwick steals my breath away." I tried not to chuckle at her crush on the hot-tempered Francis Beaumont. "As does the Earl of Surrey and the gentlemen company he keeps." A blush crept across her cheeks. "And, my lady, I cannot even speak of the magnificence of His Majesty. The king is the most divine person on which I have ever laid mine eyes. You are wedding pure beauty itself."

Our cheeks blushed in unison. "And that's no lie," I said.

She tugged the silk kirtle over my head, lacing it so tightly that I gasped.

"So are there any courtships on the horizon for you?" I teased, trying to breathe.

"Heavens, no, for I am tainted. I fear I will never marry at all." She sucked in a breath. "My cousin, Agnes Nightingale, is a known practitioner of the dark arts. It does not please the king, which is why my cousin was not granted permission to come to court and remains in Buckinghamshire."

"Wow. I'm sorry to hear that." In my time, magic was more of a party joke than a capital offense.

She reached for a velvet box, recovering her smile. "His Majesty had these sent while you were at rest." She lifted the lid, unveiling a necklace of sapphires set in white diamonds with dangling earrings to match. Making jewelry had gotten me through plenty of hard times in my life, and I could've hyperventilated with excitement at the sight of the precious gems.

"Fortunately, our beloved king has never been enamored of ruffs," Bridget said, fastening the cold gemstones around my bare neck. "I find that all ruffs do is hide the jewels."

"And make people look like frilled-necked lizards," I added.

She laughed politely at the joke she couldn't have understood. I was pretty sure that Australia and its creepy animals were still blissfully unaware of European existence in this time.

I stood before a cloudy mirror. As cumbersome as the outfit was, the cushiony swarm of layers felt comforting…like the real me was buried so deep within the dress that I could hide from the nobles while presenting the facade of a Tudor queen. I'd seen how Princess Henriette of France had charmed the English courtiers with her stately Renaissance dances and fluent English, Spanish, and Latin—what would they think of Emmie Grace from Hatfield, Massachusetts? How would *Nick* feel about me if I failed to win over the peers of the realm?

These people are going to eat you alive.

Bridget tore an ivory comb through my hair. "Forgive me," she said, frowning at my knotted curls. Once she'd separated the strands, she wove my hair into a waterfall braid and draped it with a delicate web of diamond flecks. The final touch was a sprinkling of perfumed oil over my head.

"My lady," she said, spinning me to face her. "I am unable to accompany you to the feast, but I must speak my conscience and caution you." Her expression sobered. "There has been much despair at court since Princess Henriette returned to France. While the gentlewomen could hardly bear the princess, the men adored her—a common tale. But mostly because of what Henriette represented...*hope.* For an alliance with France, but more so for an undisputed heir. A royal prince for the people to love." Her kind eyes turned grave. "I admit that I know little of your kin, but I know you are not a blood royal. That puts you in danger of dislike by the noblemen. Do not let them frighten you, and *never* trust them. One alone may seem harmless, but together, they could make you vanish like smoke. Do you understand?"

When my mouth fell open, Bridget sank to her knees. "Oh, I beg your forgiveness, my lady. I have said too much. It is my greatest fault."

I guided her back up. "No, Mistress Nightingale, thank you," I whispered, already trembling.

2

THE LAST TIME a perimeter of guards escorted me to the king's quarters inside a Tudor palace, I'd been suspected of treason. Today, I felt like Beyoncé being ushered to the stage. I caught glimpses of passing courtiers gawking at me in my glittering gown as we ascended a staircase into the more secure areas of court. I swallowed a balloon of nerves. *You got this, Emmie.*

My layered dress swished noisily along an L-shaped gallery before we crossed the Great Watching Chamber and entered the Presence Chamber. A gilded throne with a crimson cushion sat on a dais beneath a golden canopy embroidered with the king's royal arms. It might've looked cartoonish had Nick been perched on the throne holding a scepter, but instead he stood casually beside the smoldering fireplace, inspecting a crease in his palm.

He glanced up and lurched toward me, cupping my cheeks. "I missed you without end," he said, pulling me close. The palace smoke was sitting heavy in my throat, and I gladly breathed in his scent of springtime and roses.

I could barely look at him without blushing. His claret-colored doublet and coat were slashed to reveal contrasting streaks of cobalt blue lined with gold. From the shimmering crown that circled his chestnut hair all the way down to his shining boots, he was a polished jewel in itself. *See, Emmie? Everything's going to be fine...this is why you're here.*

He smirked at me. "Ready to greet the finest nobles in the realm?"

I inhaled deeply. "Being the new girl is kind of my thing."

Our hands brushed, our fingers clinging together as we passed back through the Great Watching Chamber, pausing at a set of double doors crossed with pikes. Guards in red liveries stood stiffly in all corners of the room. Nick released my hand to straighten his cuffs.

"His Majesty the King, and Mistress Emmeline Grace!" cried a herald, followed by a blast of trumpets.

"We will soon bestow upon you a worthy title," Nick said under his breath.

"I didn't know I needed one," I whispered.

The pikes separated, and we stepped onto a platform at the eastern tip of the Great Hall, which would put any grand city cathedral to shame. Its hammerbeam ceiling had to be more than fifty feet high and was stunningly decorated with royal badges and fantastical creatures in vibrant shades of sapphire blue, ruby red, and metallic gold. Hundreds of lit candles crossed the space on wires, illuminating the gold thread in the sparkling wall tapestries and turning the cavernous chamber into a magical valley of light. Gentle music drifted down from the minstrels' gallery as if sent from heaven itself. The country's highest-born aristocrats were like extras in the theatrical scene, bowing to us from beneath the platform in their pearl-encrusted Tudor fashions.

"Okay, Hampton Court officially steals the show," I said under my breath.

Nick's voice exposed a quiver of nervous pride. "Before long, all my palaces will be ours to share."

I squeezed his fingers, but what I wanted to say was: *I only want you.*

The king spoke calmly but held the room's attention. "My dearest lords, it is with every pleasure that we proclaim Mistress Emmeline Grace our most dear betrothed. God willing, this precious lady has agreed to marry your true and faithful king and will make a most blessed queen."

The lively music cut to a desolate silence as the sea of faces gaped up at us. The reaction was so arctic that I'm surprised I didn't freeze solid on the spot. One guy with a pointed beard even glowered at me like he'd caught me double-dipping the ketchup and fries. *What the...?* When Nick's forehead tipped regally forward, however, the nobles clapped politely and bowed. The crisp harmonies of lutes, violins, and oboes again floated from the balcony, and my shoulders loosened as the room's chatter resumed. Had I imagined the icy reaction?

Nick and I crossed the tiled dais strewn with perfumed rushes to take our seats at an ornate table crowned with a green-and-white canopy. Servants washed our hands with rose water while guests hurried into their assigned seats at trestle tables positioned around the hall's edges. Nerves had dried out my mouth, so I threw back a shot of sweetened wine.

After the king said a prayer of thanks, the servers began their parade of dishes, offering slices of roasted eel, porpoise, lamb, turkey, pheasant, and swan. I hunted for vegetables but found only sliced citrus fruits artistically displayed like Chinese fans. A sweaty chef carved the turkey in front of the king and used a two-pronged fork to distribute it smoothly onto our gold plates. Nick grabbed a dark slice of meat with two fingers and slid it into his mouth.

Everything he did was adorable, but I raised my brows at him. "You saw that guy use a fork to pick up the meat to put it on the plate, right?" I whispered.

He licked his fingers. "I believe so."

I leaned closer. "So you haven't joined the dots on what else a fork might be good for?"

He reached for his wine, considering my question. I nearly disclosed the answer to my riddle when it hit me that I might bring the fork's prevalence in England forward by a century or two. I'd changed more than enough history merely by being here. To divert Nick's mind from my reckless question, I dug into the turkey with my fingers and probed him about our audience of stony-faced guests.

He whispered funny stories about some of the men sitting below us, thawing some of my unease. When he began discreetly caressing my fingers in his lap beneath the table, every inch of me fluttered.

While Nick briefly spoke with one of the passing chefs in French, I focused on surveying more of the crowd, nearly choking on my turkey. My old court bestie, Alice Grey, was watching me from the far end of the hall. Beside her sat a courtier with trimmed gray hair—the man I'd seen her dancing with at the Midsummer's Eve feast. I tried to nod hello to her, but she didn't look my way again through four more pungent meat buffets and an onslaught of sugary desserts. A chill blew through the drafty hall. I'd expected at least a smile from Alice.

Nick's warm hand cupped mine. "I will present you to my most favored nobles, and we may then retire. You must be wearied."

I swallowed alarm as the king stood up, guests scrambling to their feet in response. Servants carried away plates of half-eaten marzipan treasure chests as the courtiers left the tables and huddled into groups like a networking event.

Showtime.

The first man brave enough to approach us was the Earl of Dorset, who was the same height as me and shaped like an upside-down egg. He bowed to the king and kissed our hands.

"I have had the pleasure of seeing you at Whitehall, madam," he said to me, subtly tugging at the sash stretched too tightly around his waist. "It grieved me to hear of your family's demise."

"Thank you," I said softly. "It's been a difficult time."

It was a necessary lie, but it still made my jaw clench with guilt. I reminded myself that lying to people in this place was going to become my full-time job.

The conversation had barely begun, but it was immediately exchanged for introductions with the Lords Chancellor, Chamberlain, and Privy Seal; a tipsy mayor of London; and several earls and barons, including Lord Ashley, who I'd once saved from choking. It was all so different from the days of the Palace of Whitehall. Rather than secret trysts with the king behind closed doors, I was now openly by his side, presented to the most important men in the country as his chosen bride. My nervous panic was beginning to feel like motion sickness.

"The woman who has bewitched the King's Majesty," called the baron Lord Wharton in an insulting tone as he approached me with Alice Grey behind him. Beneath a pearled hood, her wavy hair was woven into a cluster of braids pinned with fresh flowers. Alice hated wearing her hair up.

Despite my efforts, she wouldn't meet my gaze and angled her neck past my shoulder like she was more interested in whatever was happening behind me.

The baron's face held a sinister smirk beneath his walrus-style beard trimmed into two points. "Mistress Grace, do I recall your person from Whitehall, when the king proclaimed his betrothal to Henriette of France?" he asked. Bringing up Nick's former fiancée was a clear strike at me.

"I can't say; you're not familiar to me," I couldn't help but reply. My eyes flashed to Nick, but he'd stepped away with the new French ambassador.

Wharton pursed his lips. "I understand that your late father was a physician?"

"That's right. Doctor Martin Grace from Sussex. Worthing, to be specific."

I knew I was sounding like a dingbat, but the baron was already edging his way into the king's conversation as if I'd bored him, rudely angling his back to me.

Alice and I were left alone. "Welcome to Hampton Court, madam," she said to me, curtsying stiffly in her prune-colored gown. "It greatly pleased me to receive the happy news of your betrothal to the king."

"Thank you. It's *so* good to see you." I smiled nervously, breathing in the cinnamon scent that was an Alice Grey hallmark.

She didn't return the smile. "It seems the circumstances of loved ones may change substantially without any caution at all," she added coolly. "As you are quite aware, I have come to suffer this knowledge on more than one occasion."

The smile slid off my face. I'd never seen Alice angry with me before. Her mom once vanished from court without a word—just like I did several weeks ago. Was she pissed at me for putting her through the same thing again?

A pair of arms pierced the tension between us, offering two cups of wine. It was Francis Beaumont in a stark-white coat strikingly draped over a doublet of emerald green. He looked as suave as always, but Alice scarcely glanced at him as she strode back to the baron.

I accepted one of Francis's cups. "Are Alice Grey and Lord Wharton a couple now?" I asked him, taking a large sip of wine. I already knew from Google searches that Alice was destined to marry Francis, at least until I first arrived in the sixteenth century and began influencing their relationship. If she married the snide Lord Wharton instead, she'd die in childbirth. A lump grew in my throat.

Francis huffed into the lip of his cup. "Ask me not about the fancies of Mistress Grey. The lady has refused to speak with me since your disappearance from court." My tight grip on the cup slackened. At least Francis was still crushing hard on Alice. There was hope for them yet.

We watched the king swallowed up by a cluster of fawning men.

"I must rescue His Majesty from this weariness," said Francis, dumping his cup onto a server's tray.

"Are you upset about Nick and me?" I cut in before he could step away. "About our betrothal?"

His coal eyes pinched at the corners. "I take pleasure in anything His Majesty desires."

"*Francis,*" I urged. Maybe it was too much wine making me so insistent, but I didn't care about the formalities or protocols of the court; I cared about Nick, Alice, and Francis. They were my people here, in a place where I had no family. I needed at least one of them to be real with me. "You said earlier that this was all a surprise," I added, a little shakily. "But I'm starting to get the feeling that none of it is a *good* surprise."

His lips pressed together. "Mistress Grace, it pleases me without end to see His Majesty merry, and the affection between you is plainly genuine." Once he'd rattled off the expected statement of loyalty, he dropped his voice. "A marriage, however? That will come at a cost higher than you can imagine. England is closer to peace than she has ever been, and our good king does not hunger for war. I wish not to see our realm come to ruin."

"To *ruin*?" It was hard not to let my offense show. "That's the last thing I want."

Nick knocked past Francis to gently hook my arm in his, drawing the room's attention with his natural magnetism. Was Francis right to be concerned? Had Nick really made a terrible mistake in choosing me over Henriette of France?

"My dear love," the king called loudly. The eyes of nearby gentlemen nearly popped from their sockets. "It will please you to see your *uncle,* the Duke of Norfolk, has presently arrived from his duties in Sussex for this most joyous occasion. His Grace received word only this morning."

A colossal man stepped through the throng in a navy coat trimmed with black ribbons and dotted with seed pearls. His sausage-sized fingers clutched a hat sprouting an ostrich feather.

The duke dropped into a bow and kissed my hand. "My dear lady and precious niece. It pleasures me beyond measure to look upon you again."

I felt like I'd walked into a Shakespeare play, except I'd forgotten my lines. When had Nick had the time to convince the Duke of Norfolk to continue this fabrication about being my uncle? But if Norfolk was as thrown about the sudden engagement as everyone else, he didn't let it show. Courtiers tipped their heads at the duke like he was the King of England himself, and he was legitimizing me to every one of them. I could've freaking hugged the old upper cruster. When the duke rose back to his imposing height, a thick gold chain swung from his chest.

"Will you lodge at court awhile, my lord?" Nick said to him.

"Naturally, with His Majesty's permission."

"On condition that you wash in haste; you smell like a horse's chamber pot," Nick quipped.

Laughter echoed through the hall, Norfolk's loudest of all.

The duke offered me a gloved hand. "A stroll in the courtyard, madam? All these haughty gentlemen...you must be in need of some air."

Nick winked at me, sending butterflies to my stomach, before turning into a circle of waiting courtiers that I knew bored him to tears.

I smiled shyly at Norfolk, mentally latching onto him after his endorsement of me. He boldly took my hand, steering me out of the Great Hall and down a stone staircase that led to a drafty gatehouse. A sword swung from his hip as we strolled outside into the clock courtyard, where a smattering of drunken courtiers lay slumped on benches. I paced away from the stomach-churning stench of barf at the base of the wall.

The evening air felt slightly warmer with Norfolk around, like he really was my only family here. His face was attractive for an older man and sharply angled like it was carved from marble. I hadn't seen my dad in months, but the thought of him still pierced my chest.

"I appreciate you riding all this way to meet me, Lord Norfolk," I said, hoping that was the right way to address him.

"I bid you to call me Uncle Harry."

I knew that Norfolk's real name was Henry Howard and that most Henrys here were called 'Harry' for short. He gazed up at the astronomical clock that presided over the courtyard. My eyes followed his, blown away by the giant disc of gold that was tinted cherry-pink by the last hour of daylight.

"I have no true niece, you know," Norfolk said to me. "Well, until now, I suppose. I will speak plainly; I had not supposed that King Nicholas would marry for pleasure. After the despair it brought to King Harry…to the Queens Mary and Elizabeth. However, I suppose that foolish desire is in the king's blood."

My fingers curled, starting to feel the cold. "It's not foolish desire," I said in a small voice. "Nick and I have already been through a lot together, and this is the right thing."

Norfolk grunted. "How would a girl know any measure of what is right for a king?"

We still faced the clock, the waning light masking the crease of disappointment that crept into my skin. *Please, no. Not you too, Norfolk.*

"I don't pretend to be anything I'm not," I finally said, the hypocrisy of that statement shaming me in my period gown. "But I love the king, and I know he loves me. We just want to be together and make each other happy."

A bark of laughter burst from Norfolk's throat. Before I could form a response, he took a lofty step inside the gatehouse beneath the clock tower. "Have you yet laid your eyes on this?" he called, aiming a thick finger at the stone ceiling.

I steadied myself and gathered my skirts to follow him, gazing up. Among the intricate stone carvings in the vaulting was the image of a crowned falcon.

"The falcon was the royal badge of Queen Anne Boleyn," Norfolk explained, like he was narrating a documentary for the history channel. "When King Henry had Queen Anne executed for treason and adultery, he neglected to have the badge removed."

I'd read up on the Tudors lately. Anne Boleyn wasn't a royal princess like Henry's first wife, Katherine of Aragon, but Henry the Eighth had married her out of genuine, passionate love. When he tired of her and met Jane Seymour, however, he had Anne's head hacked off with a sword.

A burning torch in the wall morphed Norfolk's striking face into that of a monster's.

"The necks of foolish girls in love are highly desirable, Mistress Grace. You would be wise to take good care of yours."

He made a small bow and left me there, frozen solid beneath the relic of a besotted young queen who'd gambled her life on the heart of a Tudor king...and lost her head for it.

3

I HURRIED back upstairs and into the warmth of the Great Hall, but Nick's calming face was absent from the thinning crowd of courtiers. There was also no sign of Alice Grey, who must've called it a night. I asked after the king, and a guard ushered me into the Presence Chamber. Aside from the guards, Nick and Francis were the only men in the room, and were speaking intently beside the canopy of estate.

My instinct was to back away, forever out of my depth on important Tudor matters, but Nick spotted me and ushered me over. Francis had been addressing the king, but when I approached, the earl's mouth clamped shut.

"You may speak freely in front of your promised queen," Nick ordered him. "Inform Mistress Grace what you did me. There will be no secrets between us."

Francis's throat bulged in a tight swallow. "Madam, I have it on good authority that a squadron of Spanish warships was sighted this night in the English Channel."

I felt the blood leave my skin. "Warships?"

My reaction sent Nick stammering like he was embarrassed. "Four ships, which is hardly a fleet. King Philip seeks peace more than I, given the mess he has made of the Low Countries. It is no more than a pretense."

Francis gripped his hat so tightly that his knuckles whitened. "Sending warships as a mere performance? Majesty, Spain has more than a hundred ships like it...the strongest navy in Christendom."

"You need not remind me of King Philip's admiration for his glorious self," Nick said with sarcasm.

Francis gnawed at his lip, unable to conceal his annoyance that I was privy to this discussion. I was more than happy to leave them alone, but I didn't dare move. First the nobles disliking me, and now the threat of war with Spain. What had it been—less than a day since I arrived? Tudor England needed to take the intensity down a notch.

Nick's eyes flashed with anger. "My patience with King Phillip is at an end. That idiot seeks to increase my troubles while we are preparing for a new queen. We shall remain idle no more."

Francis stuttered through his nervous suggestion. "Majesty, before such a glorious occasion as the crowning of your chosen queen, I counsel you to propose a meeting with the King of France. If you sail to Calais in haste, you may yet save the peace treaty between France and England. When King Henry beholds the magnificence of the King of England in person, he will be persuaded. A visit of your sacred person is a pledge of commitment...an apology for what transpired with his sister, Princess Henriette."

Henriette's name felt like a shard of glass in my throat, and Francis probably meant it to have that effect. She was the French princess to whom Nick had once proposed but then ditched for me. Now Spain was taking advantage of the severed marriage alliance between England and France by taking a swing at England. I wanted to disappear for my part in this unfolding disaster, but instead, I stood there, coiling my fingers into tight fists. Was Nick already regretting his decision to leave Henriette and marry me?

The king drew a deep breath and then expelled it. "I will think on it. Inform the Lord High Admiral to examine the forts and make ready the beacons and warships." Francis made a gracious nod as if he was accepting a gift. "My lord Warwick," Nick added, "I am trusting you to see to it that the Spanish withdraw their provocation, or you will answer for it."

Francis bowed as he backed away, sweaty curls pasted to his neck. A flame of sympathy sparked in my chest for his thankless position as the king's right hand, which had eclipsed the cheerful friendship they'd shared until now. Alice's father, Thomas Grey, had the job before Francis and had been only too glad to throw in the towel.

Nick scooped up my hand into his soft fingers. I was well acquainted with how my fiancé could flip from Jekyll to Hyde— the drawback to dating a Tudor king.

"My love, we must part," he said. "I must think on this issue of Spain."

His palm skated up my cheek, and I tilted into his touch. I brought my lips to his fingers and kissed them like they were strips of candy, one by one. A fluttery sigh escaped his mouth, and he turned into me. "Baby," I whispered, wishing we could just be alone.

A moment later, feet thudded, pikes detached, and members of the Privy Council began filing in, headed by the formidable Duke of Norfolk.

Nick drew away from me and ordered the gentlemen to follow him into his council chamber. They disappeared through the Great Watching Chamber like a consortium of high-powered CEOs, leaving me alone beside a candelabrum of polished gold.

A pair of polite guards offered to escort me back to my chambers, and I accepted with relief. I'd had more than enough excitement for one day. The opulent palace corridors and gemstones swinging from my earlobes would never get old, but as we headed downstairs to my rooms, I felt only the terror of Nick facing a medieval-style war. Having him hacked to bits by a Spanish sword was so *not* my idea of wedded bliss.

Eager for sleep, I avoided chatter with Bridget Nightingale about the night's events as she undressed me. I climbed into the warmed blankets and breathed in their orange scent, the oppressive silence clawing at me. At my home in modern-day Hatfield, my mom often left her television on, even when she was at work. Cars sped up and down our street at all hours. Dogs barked at annoying times. Here, the only background noise was a deathlike silence. I blew out the candle and rolled onto my side in the empty bed, my fingertips tracing the pattern of entwined vines embroidered into the curtains. A gentle pattering crept through the window, and I closed my eyes, relieved for the sound of falling rain. Just any sound at all.

At the first blackbird's cry, Bridget heaved open the window shutters like a boarding school mistress, leaving me to eat breakfast in bed and say my morning prayers. I sat up on the mattress and massaged the back of my neck while chewing crispy white bread and pondering the timeline of coffee.

Bridget poured me a bath at my request, and I sank into the water strewn with fragrant herbs and rose petals. My fingers swirled through the cloudy liquid, circling the small scar from the old arrow wound on my thigh, which had healed nicely.

My head exploded with thoughts about how I might help Nick with his war pressures. I wanted to be more than an obedient Tudor queen who decorated the king's court as a silent symbol of piety. That was definitely—and hilariously—not me, but I was kidding myself if I believed I had any advice to offer about sixteenth-century European conflicts. Sir Thomas Grey's earlier plan of a marriage alliance between King Nicholas of England and Princess Henriette of France was sounding more ideal for England by the minute. Now I'd woken up freaking out that Nick would regret his decision and send me on a one-way ticket back to the twenty-first century, where I'd never see him again.

My toes squished the cloth lining the bathtub as I climbed over the wooden edge, landing on a linen sheet. After I'd dried off and slipped on my smock, I dunked the ewer into the bathwater and carried it out to Bridget.

"Where can I put the water?" I said to her. "Is this the best way to empty the bath?"

She swerved away from her sewing. "Oh, my lady, I will attend to it."

"It's okay; I want to help."

She wrestled the ewer from my hands. "Forgive me. I must complete my tasks, or I may be relieved of my duties."

With a sigh, I relinquished the ewer, reminding myself that Tudor folk were comfortable with their rigid master-servant roles. I didn't need to call extra attention to myself by challenging the system.

After Bridget had rubbed my teeth with mint water and a tooth cloth, she dressed me in a pretty ivory gown embroidered with hundreds of tiny botanicals. She fixed my hair into a plaited bun and pinned a pearled hood over the top, before handing me an embroidery hoop, a silver thimble, a pincushion, and a monster-sized needle. I barely restrained a sigh of annoyance. Had I seriously just spent an hour getting dolled up for a spot of sewing in my private chambers?

Good morrow, obedient Tudor lady of the house. Prithee, would thee sew with me?

There were some upsides to the tedium: more than an hour spent stitching the tentacles of a giant caterpillar distracted me from fears about Nick facing the Spanish Armada. I was glad for the company of the chambermaids who flittered between the rooms, changing the sheets and brushing down the outer pieces of my gowns. A French tailor turned up to take measurements for my new wardrobe, nattering to himself while making notches in a long strip of parchment. As the morning progressed, I soaked in as many tips as I could about the protocols of the Tudor court.

Nonetheless, I was ready to toss my mindless needlework into the fireplace when one of Nick's gentlemen of the chamber arrived to request my presence for dinner with the king.

OMG, finally. Presence freaking granted.

We carefully crossed the cobblestones that were still slick with rain and headed upstairs to the heated splendor of the king's Privy Chambers. The gentleman instructed me to wait in the Presence Chamber, so I hung out beside the stone fireplace that smoldered with chalky logs. So much for a normal relationship… things felt even more formal than before.

The king appeared within minutes, sending away a flock of councilors with a flick of his wrist. He strode toward me with his confident gait, his hypnotic eyes sending searing heat to my stomach.

"Forgive me," he said, taking my hands. "The feast last night brought many distractions." He wrapped himself around me like we hadn't seen each other in months, smelling as amazing as ever. *Gah.*

Guards parted in smooth succession as we clung together and strolled through Nick's withdrawing chamber, study, and library before reaching his private dining room. The walls gleamed with cloth of gold, absorbing the rich smells of the roasted meats and pies drowning in tangy sauces—every dish presented with the fanfare of trumpets. There were so many servers fussing over us that I couldn't ask Nick if there'd been any developments with the Spanish conflict. As I forced myself to eat beef pie with my fingers, I imagined fixing him a tuna melt sandwich in my

Hatfield kitchen, which inspired a pang of longing that surprised me.

Nick distracted my thoughts with our usual effortless chatter, and by the time we finished dinner, we were canoodling our way into his drawing-room. He followed my eyes that counted at least six people in the tight space; there were two pages stoking the fire, a long-haired boy blowing into a flute, guards policing each doorway, and a servant holding out a fruit platter that must've given him carpal tunnel syndrome. It felt like the least private living room on earth.

"Now that you are my betrothed, we should be watched when we are alone to make certain there is no question that you are pure," Nick explained, cuddling me from behind. "There is to be no uncertainty about our son's legitimacy."

The thought of falling pregnant at my age tightened my stomach. A son? *Yikes.*

"What if we have a girl?" I couldn't help but dangle. "We can call her Nicky."

He spun me around with a strained smile. "If we are blessed with a daughter, we will make her a suitable match." His knuckle stroked my cheek. "The son of a great king."

"So now our baby is getting married? Holy smokes, I'd like to have at least met the guy first." My gaze flashed across the room, but none of the attendants showed any signs of listening.

"Do not torment me with talk of our babies," Nick said, relaxing into a chair. "I can imagine nothing sweeter." He hooked his boot around the leg of an opposite seat and slid it close, cocking his finger for me to sit with him. "Besides, as much as I yearn for the day you take to your childbed, I also fear it in great measure."

He swallowed tightly and didn't elaborate, but I knew what he meant. Postpartum deaths were common in Tudor England, and pregnancy could steal a woman from the world at any moment—

and the baby. There were no medical hospitals, antibiotics, or nurses like my mom.

With both of us happy to change the subject, we played cards and teased each other with kisses until a gentleman strode in and bowed, clutching Nick's traveling cloak.

"Already?" the king said with dismay.

"The congregation has gathered at the royal barge, Your Majesty," the coat holder replied, his chapped lips trembling. "Forgive me; you wished to be informed without delay. The tides are now favorable." Another attendant fluffed the king's feathered hat.

Nick chugged the remnants of his wine and reached for my hand. His dimpled cheeks had reddened. "Emmie, I have come to a decision to sail to Calais. I shall meet with the King of France at first light on the morrow."

"Oh?" A chill spiraled up my neck.

"Spain is acting in a most provocative manner, and God willing, I must save the alliance, or we risk many men. You know I desire only peace and stability, but if there is to be war, we must have France side with us. We cannot allow Spain and France to unite their faith and mount an offensive."

"Of course." My stomach roiled at the thought of him leaving Hampton Court practically five minutes after I'd moved here. I still had so much to learn about court etiquette, and now I'd be alone. "Can I go with you?" I said.

He ran his palm over the back of my hand. "You must know I desire nothing more. I just won you back, and to part again feels intolerable. But there is no way for you to come; we have not the time to make ready your presentation ceremony. Besides, I must make peace with King Henry about what came to pass with his sister Henriette."

Hearing Nick say his ex-girlfriend's name scorched my chest. He tilted into my line of sight, reassuring eyes of translucent blue holding mine. "You need not feel troubled about Henriette. You know that I love you with all my heart."

I nodded, fingering the silk ridges of his embroidered sleeve. I didn't say it out loud, but I feared that one look at Henriette's royal family would be all it would take to remind Nick how much more suited she was to him than me.

He stood up, cueing the men to drape the cloak over his broad shoulders.

An idea struck me with sudden clarity. "Should I go back home while you're away?" I said, hopping to my feet. "I mean to Worthing," I added for the benefit of all the ears in the room.

The shock in Nick's face was startling. He knew precisely which home I was talking about: Hatfield in modern-day Massachusetts, not Worthing in sixteenth-century Sussex.

His brow pinched with visible hurt. "My palace does not please you?"

"Of course it does, it's just...I thought it might be a good opportunity."

Nick's eyes clouded with the sort of anxious fear that I'd seen before—twice. It was the same expression he'd had after I'd disappeared back to my world without intending to ever return to Tudor England. A few days earlier, I'd promised Nick that I'd never do that to him again.

"Don't worry, we can talk about it later," I said, reaching for his fingers.

His gaze searched mine while the gentlemen fluffed up the feather in his hat. "Enough," the king snapped, and they scurried away.

"With all this Spain business, I have been careless in reporting news of your household," Nick said to me a little shakily. "Suitable ladies and attendants are being appointed as we speak. Construction of your apartments is already afoot. I have instructed the Master of the Revels to keep your person and your ladies merry in our absence. I pray you will come to feel at home here."

My shoulders felt rigid as he wrapped his arms around me. "By God's grace, be safe," he said, nestling his soft lips into my neck. "My heart remains here in your hands."

Tears sprang to my eyes without warning. Nick Tudor was about to leave for France on a primitive sailing ship that could sink at the first sign of a storm. What if he came home with a renewed marriage alliance with France—or worse—never came home at all? Before I could gather my words, he was already striding away from me, the blue-diamond ring glinting from his third finger.

ᗰᗩᗰ   ᗰᗩᗰ   ᗰᗩᗰ

The next day, I woke to the rich smells of roasted meats that reached my bed from my dining chamber, more lunchtime aromas than breakfast. I must've slept late. My toes disturbed the creaky floorboards, and Bridget burst into my room to dress me, explaining that one of my new lady attendants was waiting in the next chamber.

"Oh, you should've woken me."

"I was commanded to leave you at rest," she said, tying on my sleeves. Her tight coral-colored gown accentuated her generous curves.

"Next time, you can wake me," I insisted, a little frustrated that Nick now wanted to control my sleeping schedule. I would've liked to have at least been up before dinner, which—to be fair—was at ten o'clock in the morning in this place.

The dining chamber greeted me with fragrant wafts of cooked rosemary and lemon. I stiffened as Alice Grey glanced up from the circular mother-of-pearl table. She rose to curtsy at me.

"My lady, may I present your new lady of the bedchamber, Mistress Alice Grey," said Bridget. "She is the daughter of the—"

35

"I know Alice," I cut in with a chuckle. But the woman who had been my closest friend at court refused to meet my eyes.

We all sat down, and I appraised the spread of roasted chicken and lamb, a tower of meatballs, at least twenty white bread rolls, and a platter of carrots carved into Tudor roses. The perfect breakfast for a lion, or perhaps a Neanderthal man.

Alice washed my hands in a bowl of rosewater, a nervous tremble between our fingers. "It is rather strange," she said evenly. "Queens usually choose from their own relations for their households. But, then again, Mistress Grace is not yet the queen."

The words hit with the punch of an insult, which wasn't like Alice at all. I dropped a chicken leg onto my plate that I couldn't imagine eating, and not because I'd just woken up.

Bridget's painted eyebrows fluttered with excitement. "According to the Lord Chamberlain, a third maiden has been called to court to attend to your household but has not yet arrived."

"Have mercy on us if the Sackville ladies should be forced upon us," Alice replied, scratching beneath her hood.

Bridget giggled. "Did you hear what occurred this winter last between the Sackvilles and the Lennards?"

Alice nodded with a grimace.

I bit into a peppery meatball, working hard to keep a smile on my face. It was hard to watch Alice and Bridget chat about the upper-class connections they had in common, reminding me how lowborn I was and out of place here.

"I do wonder who the new maiden shall be," said Bridget. "Perhaps somebody with a devilishly handsome brother?" She spun to me. "My lady, may I ask when you came into favor with his most gracious Majesty?" She blinked with what looked like pure envy.

I instinctively glanced at Alice for help, but she rested her chin on her palms, watching me.

"The king and I got together this summer," I replied, my face a furnace. "We kept it on the down-low for a bit."

Alice finally chimed in, but it was far from a rescue effort. "You may recall that Mistress Grace purported to be visiting Whitehall on behalf of her father in the summer," she said to Bridget. "Mistress Grace took pleasure in flirtations with several noblemen—Viscount Hereford was the first, if I remember—before climbing the tallest tower in all of Christendom and snatching the king from the arms of the Princess of France. It is truly a tale for the theatre."

Bridget smiled politely through fuchsia cheeks. My gaze fell to my plate until the browned chicken skin and carrot chunks began wobbling through my swelling tears.

"Excuse me, I just need some air," I said, sliding my chair back and making a beeline for the drawing-room. I shook open my folded coat, wrapped it around my shoulders, and headed outside to the courtyard.

A war with Spain, threats from the Duke of Norfolk, the expectations of becoming an accomplished Tudor queen, and now my best friend Alice Grey turning against me. Coming back to 1580 was starting to feel like a mistake.

4

I KEPT GLANCING over my shoulder to see if Alice had followed me, but only a pair of brooding guards trailed me through the stone corridors bordering the clock courtyard. Most of the courtiers had vanished upstairs for dinner, so I grabbed my chance to explore more of the palace without the constant stares and scrutiny.

Strolling along twisting galleries, I paused to admire paintings of Nick's achievements and magnificent biblical tapestries threaded with gold. I passed a gallery of canaries in ornamental birdcages to reach a library with leather-bound books stacked horizontally. Two men who were evidently late for dinner sat arguing on a bench beneath a stained-glass window. Their troubled eyes deflected to me—probably thinking I was a poor exchange for Princess Henriette of France—and I escaped back outside. Carpenters and bricklayers milled about the courtyard, swinging planks of wooden scaffolding into place. Was this where my new apartments were being built? I shivered. It was too weird to think about Hampton Court Palace being redesigned because of me. How would that change the future?

I breathed through my tense stomach, becoming irritated by

the guards who wouldn't get off my back. They lingered in my peripheral vision like goons from a mafia movie.

Nick! No one's going to attack me in broad daylight.

Ducking into a windowed corridor near the palace entrance shook the guards off my tail—at least until they located me again. Relieved to be free of them for now, I stepped into a smaller courtyard crowded with wagons, pack horses, and servants clothed in cheap leather doublets. The sour stink of rotting vegetables attacked my nose. Horses' hooves clopped along the cobblestones while servants unloaded sacks of sugar and barrels of cabbages and cauliflower. The trademark Tudor opulence was gone, and I'd clearly crossed into an area of court where I didn't belong.

With the main passage obstructed by an enormous cart carrying a mountain of firewood, I proceeded down a thin, doglegged passage that opened into a sunless corridor. Now it was the stench of fish that sent my palm to my mouth. I lurched toward the more bearable smells of roasting meats in the next building.

I felt the intense heat of the raging fires before I saw their furious flames snapping the air, practically searing my skin. A sweaty servant fanned smoke toward the windows as I registered the sequence of blazing fireplaces, each one gigantic enough for me to stand inside. Perspiring cooks in sooty aprons sat beside the open hearths, turning massive spits threaded with chunks of meat.

A man whose pleated coat failed to cover his ample belly slid sideways through the trestle tables to reach me. "Good morrow to you, my lady. May I be of help?" he said, wiping his hands on the frayed ribbon supporting his hose.

"I'm a bit lost," I replied, salty sweat dripping onto my lips.

"If you are unaccompanied, may I call for one of the lords?" he said with a frown. "This is no place for a lady."

"It's okay. I'm just leaving."

Escaping into the next corridor, I tripped over a cluster of men lying on sacks who were either asleep or three sheets to the wind. I knew that Nick wouldn't like me being here. I stumbled my way back into the burning-hot roasting kitchens, slamming into the master cook's burly chest.

Emmie Grace: making a spectacle of herself since the day she was born!

"The lady is here, Your Grace," the chef stuttered with the sort of servitude that made my eyes search for the king. But when the chef stepped aside, it was the Duke of Norfolk who appeared behind him. Wanting to shake myself for losing my bearings, I had to follow the duke's forest-green cape like a naughty schoolgirl back through the stinky warren of kitchen corridors. When I recognized the windowed passage leading back to the western courtyard near the palace entrance, I thanked the duke and glided past him.

"I have more important tasks than chasing after a feather-brained girl," he uttered behind me.

"I was just going for a walk and lost track of where I was," I said over my shoulder. "Is that a crime in your neck of the woods?"

Norfolk cut in front of me, blocking my path. He smelled almost as good as Nick: like sandalwood and vanilla.

"His Majesty has traveled to Calais," he said to me.

"I'm aware."

His prominent lips pursed. "The truth is that I desire war with the cod's-headed Spanish, but our king desires peace, and it may be too late. The French may never forgive His Majesty for disgracing their princess—the daughter of a king—for no more than a common upstart from Worthing. Make no mistake, they are mocking King Nicholas in France as we speak."

Norfolk's glare declared that I was to blame for England's latest troubles, and even though I'd never admit it to him, he wasn't exactly wrong. Yet I had no intention of ever leaving Nick, and my chest crushed with a burning need to win over the duke. He was supposed to be the one to help me. Would he address me this brazenly if the king were still here?

"I trust that the king knows what he's doing," I said, trying not to stammer. "I'm not here to cause any trouble, and I'll do whatever I can to help keep the peace."

"How about serving as the king's mistress?" Norfolk offered like it was a simple solution.

My teeth gnawed my lip. It was a fair question in Tudor times, but I'd genuinely tried to be Nick's mistress before while he had a romantic relationship with Henriette. "I wish I could do that," I replied honestly. "But I love him too much. It would break me."

Norfolk's cool eyes narrowed. "Madam, what right do you have to place your needs before a king's? What dowry do you even offer? No family, no treaty, no land. You say you love His Majesty, but you willingly demean him."

I maintained my stare. "I don't *demean* anyone," I said through my teeth. "For your information, Nick was the one who chased me—begging me to marry him." Norfolk scoffed at the concept. "And you have no idea what I've had to give up to be with him," I added. "So unless you want me to update the king on all the unpleasant things you've said about us in the five minutes you've known me, I suggest you cool your jets and find a way to get over it."

I was sure that would scare him off, but he squatted to meet my eye level, wine and rosemary on his breath. "You are incapable of ruining me," he said. "I am the Duke of Norfolk; I speak my conscience. Furthermore, I have known His Majesty since he was a babe. Our dear king has a known weakness for pretty girls. You may be the only pretty girl in England with a mouth and mind dumber than a pail of rocks, but you are not the only pretty girl in England."

His sharp stare delivered a warning before he shoved past me and continued on his way.

Tears blurred my vision as I wandered back into the western courtyard in a daze, the whir of carts and horses seeming even more foreign than before. I considered the quiet safety of my chambers, but the thought of again facing angry Alice made me want to scream.

Instead, I left the palace proper altogether, crossing the west gatehouse bridge to find a patch of wildflowers sloping its way down to the olive-colored curve of the River Thames. Slippery mud gripped the heels of my satin pumps as I hitched up my skirts and climbed down to the riverbank. White daisies peppered the grass like snowflakes, and I sat among them and hugged my knees. I was still reeling from my intense chat with Norfolk.

For a few minutes, I watched servants offloading bags of grain from barges onto a wooden landing platform. Aside from the wind delivering an occasional odor of sewage, the soothing gurgles and horn-like calls of ducks could have come from the Connecticut River. No wonder Nick liked it here at Hampton Court Palace; it was peaceful.

Thinking about him aroused a twisting heat in my stomach. When jerks like Norfolk weren't trying to intimidate me, I loved being here with Nick. Having him feel the same way about me as I did him was a literal dream come true. But I had to find a way to be happy here when he wasn't around. Aside from learning the customs of the court, I needed a freaking *life* in Tudor England.

I swatted away a bee so that I could snap off the stems of a few daisies. After slicing open their stalks with my fingernail, I wove each flower through the split ends, fastening the daisies into a garland bracelet. When Nick proposed to me, he also promised me a jewelry workshop. Once that was ready, I'd learn how to make the most striking bracelets, necklaces, earrings, and rings that Tudor England had ever seen. Emmie Grace: Tudor queen and jewelry designer. I smirked and slipped the garland over my wrist.

My chest felt lighter as I made my way back to my chambers, surprised to find them empty. After untying the ribbons of my muddy shoes, I sat on a velvet chair and curled my legs up in my silk stockings. I helped myself to a macaron from a silver bowl on the table, already conceptualizing the first showpiece I'd create in my jewelry workshop. I'd seen a noblewoman at the feast wearing a cool chain of pearls tied into knots, and it spawned an idea for a corsage-like bracelet of knotted pearls and gemstones.

While hunting for a quill to sketch the idea, I spotted the black box on my pillow. It was tied with a bow made from peony-pink ribbon—the same color of the knot ring I'd once made for Nick.

Butterflies crowded my stomach as I untied the bow and lifted the lid. On a bed of navy velvet sat the enchanted blue-diamond ring and a folded note. All the air in my lungs escaped in a rush of relief. I brought the ring to my nose as if I could smell the future through its cold surface…my mom, my friend Mia, my schnauzer Ruby…even those hideous alphabet blinds in my bedroom.

I slipped it onto my thumb and split open the king's seal to read Nick's note.

Dearest Emmie, my miracle girl.

My heart is so sore to take leave of you. However, it is made worse by the thought that you feel a prisoner here. You are not. You never will be. Therefore, I commit this ring to your care.

Please know that, no matter where your person shall lie, there is a king, and a man, who desires to be with you, then and now, and every day for all eternity. You have not—in any time or place—a more loving or loyal servant.

Your most true,

NR

I flopped back onto the bed, my heart a racehorse flying at top speed. My season ticket back to my homeland sat on my thumb, ready for boarding. But Nick had trusted my promise not to use the time-traveling ring without him, and I had to be worthy of that. Plus, it had taken a few goes to work correctly last time. What if I used it to pop home and then I couldn't get back here again? It was unthinkable.

What I needed was to find out more about the enchanted ring…like why it sends people through time when they fall asleep and its reasons for acting so strangely the other night. There was so little I knew about it, apart from the fact that it had been cursed by a soothsayer hired by Mary, Queen of Scots. Bridget Nightingale had said that her cousin was a renowned soothsayer in Buckinghamshire—perhaps she could help; maybe she was even the same soothsayer! Feeling the dangers of witchy business in Tudor England creep up my spine, I turned to the map of England on the paneled wall, but I was terrible at English geography. My fingers traced the parchment, searching.

The front doors to my chambers banged shut, making me jump. I slid off the ring and locked it inside my jewelry coffer.

In the drawing-room, Alice was helping Bridget out of her cloak. Bridget fell into a curtsy. "Oh, my lady, Mistress Grey and I searched for you."

Alice tugged off her fringed gloves with her teeth. "We found you not, but Mistress Nightingale did discover the Earl of Surrey making his way to a tennis match."

"His silk shirt was so fine that one could see his flesh right through it," Bridget added, her bronze eyes glinting. "Surrey must have felt the chill. It was no wonder that his handsome tennis partner closed his arm around him as if to keep him warm."

"Never mind that," Alice replied. "It is the king's pleasure to begin your lessons this day, Mistress Grace. The pavan, the almain, and the volta."

Lines of confusion touched Bridget's brow, and I flushed hot.

These were basic sixteenth-century dances, and a queen-to-be should have learned this stuff years ago, if I'd been of this time. Now, if I had a hope of convincing people like the Duke of Norfolk that I wasn't an appalling substitute for a French princess, I needed to become a total badass at all things Tudor, starting with the weird dancing.

"I'm ready," I said. "I'll get up to speed with all the moves, and the three of us can put on a show that'll bring the house down."

Alice laughed, drawing my smile to hers. Her icy expression had thawed a little.

Bridget had to finish her embroidery, so she stayed behind while Alice led the way to the rehearsal room. I fumbled for something to say as we strolled in awkward silence, but it was Alice who spoke first, sounding surprisingly choked.

"I pray you forgive me for my earlier words about your close-ness with the king," she said. "I meant not to upset you. My damn tongue."

I nearly tripped at the apology, my pulse soaring. "It's okay," I said. "Your summary about us wasn't exactly off the mark."

As we turned into the clock courtyard, I gathered the courage to ask Alice the question that'd been on my mind since the feast. "Are you mad at me because I disappeared from Whitehall a few weeks ago without telling you?"

Her lips turned downward. "Well, it was not the first time you vanished from court, and I understand if you are unhappy here; sometimes, I miss Northamptonshire in great measure. But you did not even speak a word of farewell, yet you know what I have suffered with my mother's passing from sight."

"I know." We reached the gatehouse bustling with courtiers queuing to ascend the staircase to the Great Hall. "I'm so sorry, Alice. Please believe me that I've never wanted to hurt you."

She pulled me outside to a streak of graffiti chipped into the brick wall, lowering her voice. "Then why must you lie? I once asked you if you had a dalliance with the king, and you assured me that you did not. We spent every day together, yet you never mentioned your pursuit of His Majesty's hand. Now you return from Sussex as our promised queen?" Her tanned forehead rumpled. "For how long had you been plotting this?"

I'd started to tremble. "I never wanted to keep this from you. There was no plot. I only became close with the king after I caught the one-day fever, but he was still pursuing Princess Henriette...he asked me not to tell anyone. I didn't know what to do."

She exhaled, shaking her head and staring at her feet. I'd never known life at Tudor court without the friendship and support of Alice Grey. I wasn't sure I could pull it off.

"Why does it bother you so much that he and I love each other?" I said, a little exasperated at the constant disapproval.

"It bothers me not!" She spoke quietly but vehemently. "I can think of no one I desire to see His Majesty with more than you. But the last time I saw you, you told me you loved *Lord Warwick.* You were weeping over him. And then you left court without a word—was it not Lord Warwick who drove you away?"

Shock overcame my face. One of my countless lies to Alice Grey was that I was in love with Francis Beaumont, the Earl of Warwick. I'd forgotten all about it. No wonder she was so angry with me!

"Alice, *no,*" I said. "I made the Lord Warwick thing up as part of my cover for being with the king. God, I'm so sorry. I don't love Francis; I never did. The person I'm in love with—the one I was weeping over—is Nick."

There had been so many lies that I didn't know how to untangle them. When tears threatened my eyes, Alice pulled me into a hug, her fern-colored gown silky beneath my fingers. "I have been furious with Francis for driving you away like he did Violet," she said into my hair. "I have not spoken a word to him since."

I pulled back, gutted at my role in this. "Are you serious? I already told you: I think that Francis Beaumont loves *you*. In fact, I know he does. Please don't push him away because of me."

She blanched at my endorsement of Francis as her potential boyfriend, keeping her focus on me. "Emmie, I am happy for you, truly. I am happy for King Nick…for the realm. While the advantages of marriage alliances are plain, I do feel our glorious king is deserving of a love match of the greatest measure."

I squeezed Alice's small hands, the return of her favor lifting a boulder off my chest.

Inside the dance chambers, a stout man with a beard clipped into a triangular point greeted us with a bow. I recognized him from Whitehall as Lord Mayberry, the Master of the Revels. He invited us to sit on the window seat while he barked in French at the quartet of musicians who were warming up their instruments.

We sat down, and I begged Alice to catch me up on any gossip. She beamed, seemingly only too happy to do so, intense relief loosening my shoulders. We fell back into our old routine as easily as slipping on a cloak. She told me that the Dowager Countess of Warwick was still under house arrest for her suspected role in her daughter Isobel Beaumont's plot against the king, and that Robert Fox, the twin brother of the traitor Mathew Fox, had been exiled because of the disgraced family name.

"Yikes. How's your old man, Sir Thomas?" I said. I kind of missed Alice's cantankerous dad, even if he did once try to bribe me to break up with the king.

She smiled. "I am greatly pleased that my father has retired. His mind is calmer now. He has taken to caring for hawks and raising bloodhounds for hunting. It was not a simple decision for me to remain at court without him, but I fear that if I return to Northamptonshire, I may miss word of my vanished mother. Such news would likely reach the king first."

I swallowed the beginnings of a lump in my throat. Alice had no idea that her mom had been a traitor conspiring with Mathew Fox and Mary, Queen of Scots to bring down King Nick. Another Titanic-sized lie between Alice and me.

She twisted toward Lord Mayberry and huffed. "Shall we begin, my lord?"

He glided across the squeaky floorboards like that was a dance move in itself, his slender fingers pressed together. "My ladies, I bid you forgive me for the delay. Mine instruction partner will surely arrive here at any moment."

"*I* am to serve as an instruction partner," Alice corrected.

"You may assist," Mayberry replied with an anxious smile. "A lord of the Privy Council has advised that Mistress Grace's new lady of the bedchamber has presently arrived at court and is accomplished in all the dances...one of the finest ladies in the realm."

Alice's brow puckered. "What does a member of the king's council care about dancing?"

We jolted at the thump of the oak doors swinging open, a tall, feminine figure striding toward us. I thought I'd seen beautiful with Princess Henriette of France, but this was another level.

"Heavens," whispered Alice.

The Victoria's Secret model curtsied at me, her honey-colored skirts rippling with silk cleverly embroidered to catch the light. Her hairstyle belonged in an art museum: the wheat-colored curls styled diagonally across her scalp and topped with a stylish French hood.

"Hi, I'm Emmie Grace," I blurted, my supremely un-elegant voice echoing off the paneled walls.

She dipped her heart-shaped face at me, the letters 'LP' swinging from her pearl choker. "Good morrow to you, madam. I am–"

"Mistress Lucinda Parker," Alice finished, her voice barely above a breath.

Their eyes met in a steely stare, and my mind tore backward.

I'd heard the name Lucinda Parker before. She was Nick's former mistress before I came along...the one who'd been in his bed the way I hadn't. Rumored to have had a child with him. Pain shot through me like a lightning bolt.

"Shall we begin with the volta?" Lucinda offered, smiling playfully at the mention of the seductive dance. "His Majesty always took such pleasure in it."

My head swarmed like a shaken beehive. When Norfolk said I wasn't the only pretty girl in England like it was a threat, this must have been his plan. He wanted Nick to fall back into the arms of his former girlfriend, Lucinda Parker, who was elegance on steroids.

It wasn't just Spain that the Duke of Norfolk wanted a war with, it was also me. And he'd just fired the first shot.

5

DID NICK KNOW that Lucinda Parker was at Hampton Court? Did he want her here? The questions pecked at me like pigeons as I watched Lucinda frolic through dances like a gazelle while I did my best to copy her with my trademark clumsiness. When the torture-fest ended, Alice suggested the three of us return to my chambers so Lucinda could become acquainted with "all manner of our promised queen's needs and wishes." It was a pointed remark to drum into Lucinda that I was the king's girlfriend now.

I slipped Alice a look of appreciation as we wandered back to my chambers, but Lucinda's statuesque shadow trailing us left me a little flat. It'd never been in my nature to be catty or to make a girl feel unwelcome. I'd been a new girl out of my depth enough times to know how lonely it felt. But that didn't mean it was easy to watch Lucinda flooding my drawing-room with her perfume and intimate knowledge of Nick's body. The thought hollowed my stomach.

We introduced Bridget to Lucinda, and the four of us chatted with tedious politeness over mini cheesecakes before Lucinda excused herself to use the privy.

"Mistress Parker is *so* pretty," Bridget gushed to Alice and me like that was all that mattered. "I do wonder if she has a handsome brother. For no other man shall look twice at any other maiden as long as Mistress Parker is present."

Alice shot Bridget a look.

Our dear king has a known weakness for pretty girls.

Norfolk's cruel words crashed back into me. Before Lucinda returned from the washroom, I filled Alice and Bridget in on my uncomfortable conversation with him.

"Should I tell the king?" I asked them. I shuddered to think what Nick might do to him in retaliation, and I didn't fancy antagonizing the duke any further, but Alice and Bridget were quick to school me on the power of Norfolk. Even the king had to be careful about offending the most influential duke in the land. It wasn't exactly music to my ears.

Alice pressed a slender hand over mine. "Norfolk is a pillock and has always been. However, I caution you to trouble the king not with the matters of women. His Majesty is likely to think ill of such things, and we should handle this with discretion."

I nodded through my disappointment, but I knew that Alice was right. Nick wasn't the boy next door. He was a sixteenth-century King of England. He had bigger issues to deal with than any insecurity I might feel over his ex.

"I pray you are not vexed, my lady," Bridget said to me. Her rust-colored eyes radiated awe. "For it is *you* His Majesty has chosen to marry, and you are quite extraordinary." Her gaze brushed over my tweezed eyebrows, my teeth that had been straightened by metal braces, my hair recently softened by a sample from Walgreens.

I squared my shoulders at them both. *Damn straight.* Lucinda Parker may have the demeanor of a Tudor princess, but I had four hundred years of human evolution on my side. I could take her.

Alice smirked at me, reading me like a book the way only Alice Grey could.

ᴡᴧᴡ　　ᴡᴧᴡ　　ᴡᴧᴡ

It was a relief to discover that Lucinda Parker was easy to get along with and a decent lady of the bedchamber. What bothered me was that she was so freaking *good* at everything. Her accomplished presence judged me through my attempts at memorizing the strait-laced almain dance, the bumbling beginnings of my French lessons, and my first wobbly tune on the virginals. She embroidered better than me, danced me under the table, played the lute like the Tudor version of Eric Clapton, and never once looked at me like she was jealous of my relationship with the king. My imagination wasn't nearly as restrained. Without effort, I could see Nick kissing her, whispering in her ear, gripping her tiny waist with his perfect hands. The thought of it hardened my stomach to rock, chased by an urge to barf. When he returned, surely he would see that she was a thousand times better suited to a queen's role than I was.

At least Lord Mayberry had arranged countless amusements to keep us all distracted, and my ladies and I were treated to dance concerts, masques, plays, acrobatic displays, and a four-hour organ recital that was more sleep-inducing than any opiate.

One Saturday after dinner, the choristers of the chapel royal staged a special performance for the peers of the court. The Duke of Norfolk stood at the back, rudely chattering to Lord Wharton through a breathtaking solo sung by a nine-year-old boy. It hit me that Alice Grey hadn't spent much time with Lord Wharton since my arrival feast. I didn't know if it was what I'd said about Francis Beaumont crushing on her, but I didn't dare bring it up. The last thing I wanted was to encourage her back into Wharton's arms, who was about as affable as Norfolk.

After the concert finale, the duke hung out near the Great

Hall's exit like a security guard, bowing to my ladies and me as we passed.

"Mistress Grace, it must please you to have a maiden so accomplished as Mistress Parker join your household," he said, his sky-blue eyes giving away none of his dislike for me.

Fortunately, I'd had a few acting lessons in my day. "Oh, I haven't thanked you yet for bringing Mistress Parker to court," I said to him, offering Lucinda my sweetest smile. Hers was so freaking gorgeous that it nearly blinded me. "I'm delighted to have her in my service."

Lucinda fidgeted with her jeweled belt, blushing at me. She dipped her head at Norfolk. "My lord, I am most thankful for your petition to bring me here. I owe you my gratitude for allowing me to provide for my dear daughter."

My forehead pinched. I hadn't been aware that Lucinda's employment at Hampton Court was helpful to her baby.

"I am certain you shall find a most worthy husband," said Norfolk, ignoring the mention of the bastard child. "You are so fine a lady that there is no man in England who would not desire to court you."

No man in England who would not desire you—including its king. Another strike aimed at me. I made sure that Norfolk heard my bored exhale as I swept the girls away without so much as a polite farewell.

As the days dragged on, I tried not to think about Nick at sea —or in the vicinity of the polished Princess Henriette—while my ladies and I strolled through the privy gardens, continued my lessons, sewed in my chambers, read poems, and attended performances.

"So many merriments even without the king's presence," Alice commented during yet another masque. She smirked at me. "His Majesty is showing the court how important you are."

The sparkle in her eye caught me. I'd never considered Alice much of a romantic, but she was becoming more flushed by the day over my courtship with King Nick. It was reassuring to have her blessing, even though she still had no idea who I really was or where I came from.

The masque concluded with a ceremonial dance, before the Great Hall transformed into a feast of pepper eel, honeyed pigeon, and roasted swan devoured to the bones. While the courtiers danced up a storm, I kept an eye on the arched entrance to the Great Watching Chamber. Alice skillfully averted Lord Wharton's advances, her eyes also glancing toward the king's doorway every so often. It struck me that I wasn't the only one waiting for a cute boy with blue blood to stride through the archway. Francis Beaumont had also been away from court for an awfully long time.

That night I lay awake, cursing myself for eating rich foods to the point of bursting, when images of my mom's kitchen drifted into my restless vision. I'd been so distracted by improving my Tudor skills that I'd stopped thinking about my life in the modern world. It reminded me of when my dad left and I'd started to forget about him—almost like he'd died. I could see that happening to my other life now: having it slip into nothingness like it never even existed. I swallowed the heavy thought and focused on counting how many days Nick had been away: seventeen.

It felt like seventeen years.

Seventeen long nights turned into thirty-four—feeling like thirty-four *years* of waiting—until a blast of trumpets on an otherwise routine Wednesday morning declared that the King of England was finally home.

I escaped the chair where Bridget had been pinning my hood and dashed to the window, pressing my face to the grimy pane between the lattice frames. Alice appeared beside me, but all our looking was pointless because we couldn't see the river from here.

"I think he's back," I said.

"Which means Francis, too," she added, biting away a smile.

We fell back from the window and grinned at each other, nearly laughing. "I knew I should have washed my hair this day last," Alice said with a moan.

"Goodness, and I," called Bridget, still in her nightcap. Beyond the windows, distant murmurs of activity reached us from the adjacent servants' section of court.

"Shall I have a maidservant pour a bath?" said Lucinda she glanced up from her pallet bed. "There is certainly much time until His Majesty will wish to see the ladies of the court. He may not call for us until supper."

I didn't think she meant any offense, but Alice stepped forward. "The queen's ladies are capable of running our baths, Mistress Parker. We need not trouble the maidservants. Furthermore, His Majesty *will* wish to see his betrothed in haste, and Mistress Grace must be made ready for the king. Two attendants should suffice." Alice grabbed Bridget's arm and yanked her toward my dressing room.

"Thanks, Alice," I said quickly. "But I could use Lucinda's help, too."

I'd never called Lucinda by her first name before. Her eyes softened with gratitude. I appreciated Alice's militant protection of me, but I was determined not to freeze out Lucinda Parker because she'd once dated Nick. Even if she had slept with him.

The atmosphere relaxed over a fashion parade of gown options and a bowl of fresh strawberries soaked in sweet wine. By the time we were appropriately blinged up, the three of us were in fits of giggles over one of Bridget's gossipy stories involving an earl and a pair of slippers. The temperature was above average for late summer, and I lugged open the oak doors to let in some fresh air.

I gasped, nearly falling backward. Nick Tudor stood on the front step, taller than I remembered, more tanned—and more beautiful, if that was even possible. For a moment, we both froze with shock before his lips curled into a half-smile. I just about lost my legs. We were being watched, so I sank into a quivery bow.

"Dear God, Emmie." The emotional words escaped his breath as he pulled me close, a stunning whiff of roses enveloping me through his tight hug. A sheathed sword swinging from his waist knocked against my thigh.

"You're back," I said into his freshly washed hair. I could see the claret-colored shoulder of one of the guards behind him, hear the shuffle of Alice's footsteps beside me, but everything drew me to Nick, and I clung tightly.

The muscles in his back tightened as he pulled away, his eyes locked on something behind me. "Good God, it is Lucy," he said, a little breathless.

Lucy?

I swiveled, my heart rising to choke my throat as Nick strode past me to offer Lucinda Parker his hand. She fell to one knee and kissed his bronzed skin. When she rose again, her eyes shone, her body language mimicking his. It was as if I could feel the tight braid that tethered Nick and I snap free and begin frantically unraveling.

"May I inquire after your daughter?" Nick said to her, his voice like ripples of silk.

She beamed. "Elinor is well, Your Grace. We call her Ellie. She is presently lodging with her grandmother, undoubtedly already learning her way around a card table."

Nick chuckled. "Your mother is a dear lady. I miss her on occasion."

The ground felt like it shook beneath me, and I jerked backward, colliding with Alice's bundle of skirts. Regardless of etiquette—or even sanity—I couldn't be in the room one more second. *Lucy? Really?*

"I'm finding it warm in here, so I'm going to head out for a bit," I blurted, sounding hollow. "The lavender is so pretty at the moment, especially with those white butterflies. You guys have seen them, right?" *OMG, Emmie, you mumbling fool!*

I lurched past Nick, but his fingers caught my arm. "My lady, you may first accompany me to dinner," he said smoothly. "I am quite famished after such a journey."

"The king flatters our lady with his personal visit and invitation," Alice said behind me, subtly reminding me that rejecting the king's direct invitation would be unthinkable.

Nick dipped his tousled hair at my curtsying ladies and led me out the doors.

Our arms rubbed together through our silks as we crossed the small courtyard. "So how did it go in Calais?" I said without looking at him.

He sighed. "The alliance is presently secure, and the Spanish appear to have retreated from the channel."

"That's great." Relief loosened my tight shoulders. "I knew you'd pull it off."

I wanted to reach for his hand—to play with his fingers again—but there was the whole 'Lucy' thing; plus, there was something so formal about striding through court with the king. The guards announced his presence at every turn, and courtiers would bow like their lives depended on it, never meeting Nick's eyes or turning their backs on him. I gathered my skirts so I wouldn't trip as we ascended the stone staircase leading to the king's apartments. Sometimes he wasn't my boyfriend, he was just a monarch—so frustratingly untouchable.

"What was the French king like?" I asked him, genuinely curious about the omnipotent sovereigns of sixteenth-century Europe.

"I must say that Henry was rather ordinary," Nick replied.

"Shorter than I remember and quite gaunt. He refused my invitation for a cheerful wrestling match. I suspect because he feared he would lose." I could tell that this pleased Nick. He didn't bring up Henriette, and I felt a touch looser in my shoulders.

The Great Watching Chamber had been reorganized into a dining room for the most important men at court, with competing aromas of savory and sweet dishes. The nobles bowed at Nick from their chairs ordered by rank, with the Duke of Norfolk in prime position. His staring eyes were a pair of daggers in my back as we passed through to the king's private dining chamber.

"Is something amiss, my lady?" Nick said to me as we sat down at opposite ends of the long table. He rumpled his dark auburn hair with his fingers.

"What do you mean?" I replied, my cheeks hot. After so many weeks of craving Nick's return, something felt uncomfortable between us. His reaction to Lucinda Parker had thrown me; I'd felt the chemistry between them, not to mention that I couldn't forget how accomplished she was compared to me. *Another barf.*

He brought a gleaming wine cup to his lips. "You seem not at ease."

"Oh no, I'm fine," I said, the reply an obvious lie.

He cleared his throat, helping himself to a bread roll. "Well. You may wish to hear that, as part of the treaty terms, King Henry has proposed a marriage alliance between his brother and the Princess Catherine."

"You mean Kit?" I blanched. "But she's eight."

"It is a betrothal, Emmie, not a marriage until my sister comes of age." I couldn't believe how delighted he looked. While the idea of French royalty didn't stink, it was still an arranged marriage for an eight-year-old.

"How old is this French guy?"

Nick dipped his bread roll into a saucer of melted butter. "The Duke of Anjou is twenty and five."

I nearly dropped my slice of mustard chicken. "Twenty-five? That's a massive age difference. Don't you want Kit to marry someone she loves?"

Eyes of glistening sea-green flashed at mine. "I must protect England against Spain. A marriage alliance with France is more important than ever. It will bring peace to the realm."

My stomach sank. The political marriage alliance was supposed to be between Nick and Henriette until I came along and refused to play the role of mistress. Was poor Kit to be the trade-off? Marrying an old French duke that she'd never even met?

We sat there chewing in restless silence while servants and gentleman milled about, trumpets blasting beside my ear at the arrival of every deluxe dish. Memories of our private picnics on the grass at Robin House stirred my chest. Maybe being the king's secret mistress hadn't been such a terrible option after all. At least it meant some privacy and no arranged marriage for Kit.

Nick's knife clinked as it dropped to his plate. "For the love of God, Mistress Grace. I beseech you to tell me what vexes you." Lines of concern crossed his brow.

It took me a moment to clarify my thoughts. "This is all so amazing," I said honestly, my eyes circling the overdone extravagance. "I've never seen anything like it. But I haven't seen you for more than a month, and I guess I want some time with my boyfriend *Nick*, not King Nicholas, if that makes sense. It's just... there's always so much pomp. And a heck of a lot of people."

I knew my words sounded foolish. In this world, Nick was a divine creature, appointed to rule by God's hand. How does one even separate man and king?

The perceptiveness of his reply stunned me. "You wish for less formality and more seclusion." He flicked his silk napkin over his plate. "I understand. I have missed four and thirty dinners with you, and I could hardly bear it."

Thirty-four days. He'd also counted.

"Mister George," Nick said without raising his voice. One of his gentlemen appeared through a tapestry that'd been sliced up to hide a secret door. "Pack up some of this. Make certain to include wine, and water for Mistress Grace."

"Pack it up, Your Grace?"

"In some manner of pouch," Nick said with annoyance. He gave an order in French to one of the gentlemen, who dashed off ahead of us.

"What's going on?" I said as we both rose to leave the table.

Nick gestured toward the Great Watching Chamber. "This way, my lady."

The visibly confused nobles rose again over half-eaten platters of meat as we passed back through the chamber and descended the king's staircase to the clock courtyard. A discreet series of twisting corridors spilled us out into the majestic gatehouse that guarded the road entrance to Hampton Court. We crossed the stone bridge to where two saddled horses stood snorting and stamping their hoofs. A groom whose skin was overrun with zits was tying leather pouches to the saddle of Nick's mocha stallion. Another boy gripped a pair of my riding boots.

"You're kidding," I said through a breath, rushing to my favorite horse, Stella, and running my palm across her furry side. "We're going riding?" I beamed at Nick like an idiot.

"Riding and dinner. And, dear God, I have dreamed of that smile." He looked at me in a way that roused a butterfly swarm in my stomach as I tied on my riding boots.

Nick mounted his horse in a single, swift motion while I fumbled with two grooms to clamber atop my neighing mare. The king clicked his tongue, and our horses lurched into a trot past the iron-tinged stench of the slaughterhouses and into the grassy hunting park. The guards who accompanied us kept their distance as we accelerated to canter across miles of wooded fields and swampy meadows, eventually stopping at a thin stream that gurgled contentedly through the wild landscape. A stone wall peeked through the gnarled trees. We must've reached the perimeter of the palace grounds.

Nick helped me climb off Stella, sweat slipping down his brow. He offered me a leather pouch of water before pouring some for the horses. I finally had him all to myself in this secluded space. I was so giddy with happiness that I could've turned cartwheels.

"This is perfect—thank you," I said. "But no picnic blanket, velvet cushions, and golden flasks this time?" I added cheekily.

Nick's lips curled into his dimples. "I thought that surely there would be less mockery if we did this the Emmie Grace way—without the fanfare. Of course, however, mockery *is* the Emmie Grace way."

I bit through my smile as he untied a leather satchel from his horse, whipping out leftovers from our fancy-pants lunch that were wrapped in linen. He unrolled the strips of cloth and laid the portions of bread, chicken, lamb, and beef out on the grass, swatting away a hovering bee. It was like watching the president of the United States make his own coffee.

I forced away an aching desire to have things with Nick this simple all of the time.

But here, alone with him, seeing him behaving so informally, I couldn't restrain myself. A moment later, I was reaching, drawing him into me with both hands.

He sighed as our lips connected like magnets. We kissed hotly, the king tumbling backward as I practically tackled him. For several glorious minutes, I let myself fall into the gooey sweetness of Nick Tudor again, tasting sweet wine, mint, and berries. The perfect Nick-flavored cocktail.

Then the lovestruck eyes of Lucinda Parker flashed in my mind. I fell off him, panting as I hit the wiry grass.

"Are you well?" Nick said, sitting up. His lips were red and swollen.

I wasn't sure if I'd ever get used to the feeling of loving someone so much that the thought of them being with anyone else was like gutting out your own heart with a hook knife. I thought this time would be different. That I wouldn't have to compete with anyone for his attention, even in my mind. But it seemed I'd moved on from paranoia about Princess Henriette's sixteenth-century poise and accomplishments to worrying about Lucinda's instead.

"Should we have a chat about Lucinda Parker?" My words came out strained. "I know that you didn't invite her to court…it was the Duke of Norfolk because he hates my guts for marrying you."

I expected shock and fury, but Nick just laughed lightly. "Norfolk is plainly dramatic. You will come to know his impetuous nature."

I opened my mouth to protest, but Nick continued speaking in that maddeningly authoritative tone. "Your suspicions that Norfolk invited Mistress Parker to court are likely true—she is a cousin of his of some sort, and I can think of no other councilor who would undertake such a deed without my permission. That said, I do understand why you are not roused by Mistress Parker's presence; however, I made a vow to you that I would keep no mistress, and you must trust me."

"I know," I said, feeling uncomfortable. "I don't want this to be a *thing*; I really don't. For a start, that'd make Norfolk far too smug for my liking. But while the thought of Lucinda being here freaks me out a bit, I also think that her having a position at court is good for her baby daughter, right? These aren't exactly the golden years of single motherhood. So I think she should stay. I'm officially okay with it."

He kissed the back of my hand like he was proud of me. I was also proud of myself. Nick had all the power in the world, and if he wanted to hook up with Lucinda Parker, there'd be jack squat I could do about it. But there was no way I was letting Norfolk win. He'd brought Lucinda here to torment me, so I was determined to be okay with it.

Nick tugged me toward him, his lips close enough to kiss. "If only you could see inside my heart," he said softly. "You would know how mine eyes desire you above all things. You would know this to be true, and it would release you from the burden of your fears."

"Well, either that, or I'd see a bunch of blood, muscle, and some of those ventricle things if I could see inside your heart," I said through a straight face.

Rolling his eyes at another wisecrack that we both knew he wouldn't understand, Nick climbed to his feet, indicating for me to stay put. "I have something for you, you troublesome little thing. Well, two somethings." He untied another satchel from his horse and retrieved flashes of purple and cream, hiding the mystery articles behind his back. After dropping to his knees and shuffling toward me, he smirked and nodded at his arms, a mute invitation for me to choose a hand.

I grinned and pointed at his left arm. He produced a petite velvet pouch that drooped with something heavy. I fished out a heart-shaped locket dangling from a delicate silver chain. Clicking the pendant open revealed a miniature painting of Nick that was unlike his usual portraits. There was no crown, no pretend beard, no added weight, scepter, or flat cap. It was simply Nick Tudor wearing a white linen shirt and a chocolate-brown leather jerkin, with his hair unkempt and a slight smirk on his face. Every part of the portrait was the man I loved.

"Will you wear it close to your heart?" he asked a little shyly.

I threw my arms around him. He toppled backward, crying out.

"What's wrong?" I said, scrambling off him as he smoothed out a crushed scroll. "Oh, yikes—sorry."

Nick unrolled the now creased page he held in his right hand.

"This is a royal decree proclaiming that you are to be granted lands and the title of the Marquess of Pembroke."

I covered my mouth with one hand, the humid smell of dirt reaching my nose from where my fingers had hit the earth.

When Nick grinned with flushed pride, I hugged him again, thanking him repeatedly. An alarming thought pierced my swelling excitement: Norfolk and the nobles already thought I wasn't worthy of Nick's attention, and with good reason. What would they think of my free pass into the English peerage? I reminded myself for the millionth time that I was here for Nick and that's all that mattered.

We stretched out on the grass and lay there for as many blissful minutes as I could steal, kissing, and chatting—mostly kissing.

It had to have been early afternoon when Nick finally declared that he had to return to court to deal with a new trade bill. He was straightening his saddle when I spotted his bare finger and remembered that the blue-diamond ring was still in the coffer in my room.

I slid between him and the saddle, the closeness of our hips making his brows rise.

"Hello," he said, looking right into my eyes as he kept tying the leather.

"I forgot to thank you for leaving the ring with me when you went to Calais." The seriousness of the subject tightened my voice. "I didn't use it behind your back, just so you know. I'd never do that."

He swallowed hard. "I am relieved to hear it."

"I've been meaning to talk to you about something, and it's good that we're alone. This won't take long." My fingers drew circles on his muscular forearm. "One of my ladies, Bridget Nightingale, has a cousin who's a soothsayer. She lives in Buckinghamshire."

Nick's hands paused on the leather. "Agnes Nightingale."

"You know her?"

"Certainly not. She is a known heretic and ought to be burned. You must stay away from her."

The harsh words sent me back a step. "Actually, I was hoping we'd go and see her." Nick's brows shot up, and I barreled on, my breath short. "Rather than *burning* her, she could help us with the blue-diamond ring. Maybe this Nightingale girl could tell us why a ring that was supposed to curse you sends people forward in time instead...to twenty-first-century America, of all places. And why didn't the ring work properly the last time we used it? Maybe she can tell us." I scanned Nick's expression for evidence that he was also concerned about the ring acting oddly.

His body stiffened like a statue, before resuming his tying. "I admit that this alarms me."

Relief expelled hot air from my lungs. "I know. What if the ring has stopped working altogether and we're stuck here?"

His face twisted. "I mean to say that your *words* alarm me... your preoccupation with this ring and the dark arts. If the people even suspect that their queen is a heretic, they will petition to have you burned." He tugged the leather to tighten the knot, unsettling his grunting horse. "Furthermore, what you say of being 'stuck'...is that not the purpose of you being here? To stay?" He scraped a hand through his disheveled hair, looking frustrated.

"Of course it is!" I replied, trying not to lose my cool. "But you promised me that I could go back home and tell my mom why her only child has disappeared for the *third* time. When you asked me to marry you, you said that we had to come back to Tudor England immediately, which gave me hardly any chance to think and no time to talk to my mom." I emphasized every word like Nick was a two-year-old.

He brought a hand to his brow, holding it there for a moment.

When he finally looked at me, he could hardly meet my eyes. "Forgive me...you speak the truth. I gave you my word, and I have been too occupied with all manner of headaches since we arrived to think of it." His teeth grazed his bottom lip. "There remains much to prepare for your coronation, but you must see your mother."

He found my fingers. "We will go to your home this night," he said matter-of-factly, like he was suggesting tacos for dinner.

The floor slipped out from under me. "Tonight? *We?*"

"I fear that I will survive not if you return to your time without me. When there is talk of war, a prince does well to remain secure in his chambers. Amid this Spain business, I can make preparations to be confined to my rooms without being disturbed, and we shall take leave to see your mother. God willing, I could get us a day at best. I pray you say it is enough."

"It's enough, it's enough," I cried, folding my arms around him and squeezing with relief so intense that it pinned a smile to my face.

An uncomfortable shiver jerked through me, wiping away the grin. I'd planted myself in Tudor England for nearly two months. How had my presence here affected the path of history? Not to mention my poor mom. Guilt thickened my throat at the thought of what my disappearance had done to her. At least now I could finally tell her the truth about where I went and end all the mystery.

It was time for my mom to meet Nicholas the Ironheart.

6

It was past midnight when Nick summoned me to his chambers, a portrait of cute kingliness as he pored over a scroll in a navy-blue jerkin with teal herringbone stitching. He must've commanded we be given our privacy because the gentlemen and pages swiftly evaporated from sight. Guarding my chastity was evidently no longer priority number one now that time travel was on the agenda.

I crawled right on top of him in the chair, its wooden legs protesting with a creak. He was chewing a mint sprig that smelled like toothpaste, and a gilded wine cup sat on the hand-painted table beside him.

"Sleepy?" he said, planting a gentle kiss on my nose.

"That's me," I replied, drawing my knees up and snuggling into his chest. The room always felt lighter when we were alone.

He dropped his papers onto the side table and shifted to get comfortable beneath me.

It was the first time we'd cuddled this closely without kissing each other senseless, the heaviness of the situation overpowering the intense attraction between us. Plus, all I could think about was whether the ring would fail to work and if I'd never get back to my time again. I shut out the depressing thought, and we stayed wrapped together on a sixteenth-century chair, waiting for sleep to carry us to an uncertain future.

The first time I awakened, Nick was deep in slumberland. The candle beside us flickered lower, and the silk bed sheets were still folded open, prepared for the king's rest.

Please, no. We're still at Hampton Court...I'm never getting home again!

I twisted to relieve my stiff muscles, and Nick stirred.

"The ring's not working again," I hissed in the darkness.

"Fear not," he said drowsily. "Let us move to the bed. Perhaps it is not restful enough here."

Hoping with every fiber of my being that he was right, I followed him onto the raised four-poster bed and crawled into the silk sheets. Maybe that's what went wrong on the uncomfortable riverbank when the ring failed to transport us through time on the first try—perhaps we hadn't fallen into a deep enough sleep for it to work correctly. Nick hugged me from behind, and I nestled into the cradle of his arms, waiting for the tiredness to overcome my body again. Every hour it took for us to get to my world was one less hour I could spend there.

If we get back there at all.

My body had begun to sink into the mattress when I rolled over onto a jagged rock, the humid odor of moist sand overwhelming my nose. My sticky eyelids broke open.

The creamy edges of Nick's linen shirt fluttered in the wind from a few feet away. He stood facing the lapping shoreline of the Connecticut River—right where we'd left the last time. I could've cried out with relief. The sun's position suggested it was mid-morning.

"Good morning," I called, my voice hoarse with sleep. He spun to me and smiled, but his cheeks were drained of color. Still, the sight of him in my time made my chest twist with an ache I felt keenly. He was a Tudor king, yet he somehow suited this place. If only this world could be enough for him...if I alone could be enough for him.

Goosebumps speckled my neck. Temperatures had cooled since we were last here.

Nick climbed back up the bank and took my hand. His shook a little. "What of your cloth...and mine?" He gestured to my white satin stomacher and lush gown the color of red wine.

"If anything, they'll help explain where we've been," I said, realizing how idiotic that sounded. *Emmie. You haven't just been in Maine for the summer.*

We scaled the tangle of muddy roots until the field behind my house emerged through the slouching willow trees. It felt like I hadn't been here in ten years. Something was comforting about the quiet meadow dotted with the tired old horses. If you squinted to shut out the power lines and the glimpses of white fencing from Bayberry Street, we could've been in Tudor England. I hoped that Nick took solace in that as we inched closer to my fence, one petrified step at a time. Were we really doing this?

As the chipped tiles from our roof came into view, my palms dampened with sweat. My fingers slipped on the latch of our fence, and Nick pressed his hand to my back to steady me.

"Are you okay?" I asked him, swinging the gate open. He nodded stiffly, and we pushed through to my yard. The silence made clear that our schnauzer Ruby wasn't home: she'd bark at any sound. Mercifully, the spare key was still wedged beneath the untrimmed hedge.

I unlocked the back-porch doors and took a hesitant step inside. "Mom?" I called, my stomach in knots. Nick must've been sweating bullets as we entered the weathered clapboard house. To him, Carol Grace was more than his future mother-in-law—she was practically an alien from an unknown world.

Silence greeted us. Perhaps Mom was upstairs asleep after one of her overnight nursing shifts. Dishes clogged the kitchen sink, and a trace of coffee circled the bottom of a cup on the counter. A pile of unfolded laundry sat on the living room floor beside a fresh spaghetti-sauce stain on the carpet.

I left Nick on the couch and hopped up the stairs, two at a time. Mom's unmade bed was empty, but her toothbrush felt damp. Prescription pill bottles sat opened on the counter, but I didn't know what they were for. Remorse wrenched my insides apart. Had my disappearance made my mom sick?

Opening my bedroom door revealed the modest space mostly as I'd left it. The only thing different was my suitcase: it sat open on the bed with the contents unsettled. My old jewelry tackle box looked pitiful beside the neighboring trio of new sweatshirts I'd bought for London. All those hopes and plans that never happened. The book Mom bought me, *A Student's Guide to Living and Learning in London*, had been searched through. She must've looked for signs for why I never caught that plane.

Feeling heavy with guilt, I untied the pieces of my Tudor gown and changed into jeans and a pale-pink sweatshirt. After tying on my sneakers, I wrapped my arms around myself, savoring the comfort of cotton.

"Mom's not here," I said, trotting back downstairs. "But she was home recently."

Nick nodded, more color escaping his cheeks at the sight of my modern outfit. "We will wait."

I spent the next half an hour tidying up while Nick tapped his thighs with his fingers, surveying the living room he'd seen once before. I could tell he was trying not to flip out, which I appreciated. His nervous gaze scanned the faded wooden dining table... the threadbare cushions on the couch...the paint-chipped walls... my masculine outfit. He must've thought my time was so drab compared with Hampton Court and his twelve thousand other palaces. Thank the stars he didn't ask me about the black rectangle in the corner; he was *so* not ready for daytime television.

After washing up the dishes, I made us some tea and buttered toast. Nick inspected the neatly sliced bread before risking a bite.

When he glanced at me, it was clear that honey-wheat bread wasn't the heaviest thing on his mind. "Tell me, Emmie; I must know. Is the King of England a Tudor?"

I choked on my crust. Last time we were here, I'd refused to tell Nick anything about the future. My presence in the sixteenth century was bad enough; we didn't need its king editing his decisions to accommodate my version of what was to come. But we were getting married now, and he deserved something. So I explained the current state of the British monarchy and the added role of prime minister. Nick didn't have a conniption or start foaming at the mouth, which was a relief. He then asked me about France and Spain, but all I shared was that Europe was mostly at peace. When I reminded him that America had no monarch but a president who was accountable to the people, his brows practically hit his hairline. "That is madness."

"Actually, a democratic government is infinitely more equitable and fair than an absolute monarchy." When I realized what I'd said, I rolled my eyes at myself. I was talking like him, even while back in my world. All those lessons with my ladies were starting to pay off.

"It defies the will of God Himself," said Nick. "I am pleased that England remains dutiful of its princes." He shook his head, glaring into his teacup, genuinely miffed.

I swallowed an urge to quote some of the Declaration of Independence—especially the part about all men and women being created equal. It wasn't like I had no regard for the royals, but we'd come a long way since the divine right of kings.

Our shared silence was an agreement to disagree, and we finished our snacks with no sign of my mom. I considered calling her, but if she was driving, it might shock her into a car accident.

A distant vibration drummed a ripple across the sky through the screen door.

I stood up and grabbed Nick's arm. "I know what we can do for a few minutes that won't require a car. Come with me."

We headed back to the field where two horses stood flicking their tails and crossed the field to Bayberry Street. Nick gaped at everything in sight, asking me what more things were, and I did my best to explain without freaking him out. We cut away from the street and onto a rustic path behind my friend Mia's farm. It led to an abandoned fire lookout tower on the crest of a small hill.

"It's over here," I said, leading Nick to the tower. I climbed the first few rungs of the ladder, brushing the orangey rust residue off my fingers. "I hope you're not afraid of heights."

"Not nearly as afraid as I am of your coaches bereft of horses," he said behind me. He scampered up the ladder with ease. We paused at the top, my feet hovering a few rungs above his. "I never go onto the balcony," I explained. "It's old wood up there, so I'm scared it'll collapse." I dropped down a few rungs until we were eye level and carefully snuggled close to him without disturbing our footing.

Nick's neck twisted in all directions. "Good God. Is this what you wish to show me? This gray matter?"

I chuckled. "The gray rectangles are roofs. The big ones are probably farms or warehouses. But that's not what I wanted to show you." I pointed to an overgrown strip of runway in the distance. "There's a small airport there...mostly for recreational flying."

"Flying?" His face crushed with a frown.

I grinned. "Just wait. It's a beautiful day, and there's a family with a huge farm out that way, bigger than Mia's. I'm pretty sure I heard their plane already."

I was supposed to be watching for the Cronin family's light aircraft, but the sunlit flecks of green in Nick's confused eyes were hard to look away from. The wind blew a wisp of hair across my face, and he brushed it away, my heart picking up speed. His fingertips drew a slow line down my cheek, his gaze becoming soft and intent. He tugged me forward without losing our balance on the ladder, and our lips and breath melted into one, tasting of heat and love. Despite our precarious position, my fingers instinctively dug into his pants, tugging at his shirt, when the sky growled. Our mouths parted, and our heads jerked up as the canary-yellow plane swooped past the tower with its wings outstretched.

"Forget cars; this is how the well-to-do travel," I said over the wind and distant propeller, a smile of pride in my voice.

Nick blinked at me, his eyes enlarging. *"Flight?"*

"Aye, Captain." I felt my chin lift. "It's another form of travel in my time. In a big passenger plane, we could get to England from here in less than ten hours."

His gaping face wouldn't look away from the sky.

Even while clinging to a dodgy fire tower in rural Massachusetts, it was impossible to deny how much more advanced the world was in my time. It was hard not to look at Nick and feel like I'd beaten him in the Olympics...again. Why was he so sure that he couldn't live here? It was infinitely less tense, and the terrifying nobles were hundreds of years away. Plus, I could be so much more impressive in this place—I knew how to take the twenty-first century by storm, but in the Tudor world, I felt mousy and untalented. Did Nick really want that side of me?

Regardless, his deer-in-headlights expression over the airplane was priceless. I was still giggling about it after we'd crawled back down the ladder, our calves cramping with stiffness.

"It was like you were a kid with every single ice cream flavor on one giant cone," I recalled, pausing to bend over and laugh again.

"What is ice cream?" said Nick, and I howled so loudly that I couldn't breathe.

I knew I was acting insane—losing composure over some-

thing that wasn't even that funny—but the months of unbeliev-
able fear and stress had finally caught up with me. The sincerity
of Nick's dimpled smirk as we strolled back to my house
reminded me of how I'd felt the last time he was here. I'd have
given anything for him to feel this unburdened in his own time.

It turned out that ice cream was already a thing in early
Renaissance Europe, except it wasn't called that yet. The spot-
light shifted as Nick shared more stories about his world,
including the impressive names of people he'd crossed paths with
like Nostradamus and Catherine de' Medici. It wasn't until we
reached my gate that I understood we were engaged in some sort
of competition over whose time was more impressive. Surely it
was a no-brainer who took the title on that one. How could Nick
root for a world that was outdated by more than four hundred
years?

He was halfway through a story about Sir Francis Drake's
voyage around the world when I grabbed his arm. Our back gate
was open, but I was sure I'd shut it. As we watched, Mom's back
appeared through the gap, a phone pressed to her ear.

My instinct was to push my Tudor boyfriend out of sight and
into the elm trees flanking the fence.

"Can I just talk to her first?" I said with a breathless pounding
in my chest. "Please. But you *have* to stay here. Don't you dare
leave without me." We'd been in this situation once before: when
I left Nick alone in the field, and he dumped me for Tudor
England without a word.

He took my hands. "Of course, you must. I will wait here.
Besides, you have the ring, Emmie." He gave me a nod of encouragement. I'd broken out in a cold sweat.

My sneakers crunched the grass as I pushed through the back
gate. Mom spun to look at me, blood leaving her face. She said
something into the phone and hung up before shakily sliding the
handset into her pocket without moving her eyes from mine.

The next few moments happened in slow motion: Mom

pressing her forehead with both palms, turning away and then back to me, before crumbling to her feet and hitting the grass. I dashed over and helped her up while she mumbled that she was okay through pallid lips. Ruby was running in circles nearby, snapping the air with frantic barks.

"Mom, it's okay...I'm here," I repeatedly said as I guided her through the screen door and onto the couch. Ruby was now licking my ankles like they were carved from peanut butter.

Mom squeezed my forearm so tightly that I winced. "Emmie, you're okay." She stared at me with a face I hardly recognized. Had she aged that much over the weeks I'd been away—had I stressed her out that much? Or had I already forgotten the spidery lines sprouting from her eyes, the crooked front tooth that people found so attractive, or the fact that she'd given up using makeup? I wasn't sure I wanted to know the answer.

She was muttering again. "I saw you were here already, but I was—I was taking Ruby to the vet and, I...well, I always knew if you came back, it would be when I wasn't here; it's just my luck, you know? I was saying that to Kevin...Kevin what's-his-name the other day."

"Is Ruby okay?" I asked, sitting beside Mom.

"She's fine. Just her shots for the year."

Guilt grabbed my chest and shook it hard. I usually took care of Ruby's medicine.

The mumbling had stopped, and Mom was now gaping at me. *Man, she looks tired.*

"I'm *so* sorry," I said, the words inexcusably deficient. "I know you must've been so worried."

Her eyes flared wide like they could shoot lasers. *"Worried? I* called the police! There's a case file...they searched for you for days. Mostly at the river." Her voice broke, unlocking a trickle of tears.

"I'm sorry," I said again, this apology no more forgivable than the first. "Should we call them?"

"Of course I will," she snapped like I'd overstepped on something. "As it turns out, missing adults who have taken off before are not considered a critical emergency." She brushed both eyes with her knuckles. "So, where on God's green earth have you been? I truly can't believe this."

The question wrapped a taut rope around my neck and squeezed.

I was in Tudor England, with Nicholas the Ironheart. He's actually a good guy, by the way, and we're getting married. I'm going to be a Tudor queen. Surprise!

When I didn't answer—not sure how to—Mom shrugged. "I know you never caught the plane to London…never arrived at college. Your bag is still here. What were you planning?" She was starting to hyperventilate.

"Nothing. I *was* going to go to London, and college, and to do everything we talked about. But something happened with someone, and I had to go somewhere else for a while. I wish I could explain it all to you, but it's…it's a lot."

Mom's face distorted with disgust. "Something…someone…somewhere. You sound like your dad when he left."

My jaw fell open. My first memories of my dad were of laughter and adventure when the three of us drove through England for his history doctorate. But after we moved back to America when I was ten, he traded Mom—and me—for his coworker within five months. Since then, I'd barely seen him. I wasn't even sure I could call him *Dad* anymore.

"Please don't compare me to him," I said gently, but inside that shot had hit home, like she knew it would.

"Don't?" Mom threw a cushion at me. "You're doing just what he did, except worse—giving up all your dreams to chase some selfish person who is clearly more important to you than your own family! Don't treat me like an idiot, Emmie. The second you walked through that gate, I knew you'd been off with that boy from the summer. I can't believe you would be so stupid!"

I slunk away from her. "I'm not treating you like an idiot. I came back here for you!"

"You've been gone *without a trace* for weeks and weeks! Have you not heard of a damn phone!" Her shoulders shook with tears, a wet tissue balled up in her fist.

"I'm so sorry, Mom," I said through a sob as I reached out to her, but she shoved my hands away. "Believe me, I would've called you if I could have, but there was no phone."

Every part of her face twisted before she cried into her palms, greasy clumps of her unwashed hair falling in front of her face.

"Please, I'm sorry," I begged, forcing her to let me hug her. "I love you, okay? There's a really good reason why I couldn't call." Her arms finally accepted the embrace, and I relaxed a little. "There's so much to explain. I know I haven't been myself."

She pulled away, dabbing her eyes with her soggy tissue. "Then it's time to start because, God help me, I've hit the last straw. You need to tell me everything right now. *All* the someones and somethings."

My stomach folded over itself. I should've rehearsed this conversation. There weren't many ways you could explain the reality of time travel to someone. But Mom leaned back into a cushion and crossed her arms at me, ready for the truth.

I blew through my lips, my sweaty palms rubbing my jeans. "It all started when I found a ring. Actually, I bought it from that old hoarder, Jane Stuart." I wiggled my thumb at her. "This one."

She leaned closer. "I remember it. Very dazzling."

It was hard to speak through my thick throat. "The first time I went missing for a day—when I was at Mia's—I'd fallen asleep at her house wearing the ring. Then I...I woke up in a different time."

Mom barely blinked.

"I was in the sixteenth century," I spurted. "I'm not kidding. This ring is, like, *magic*." As the words left my lips, I heard how side-splittingly ridiculous they sounded. "It makes people travel through time when they fall asleep wearing it...back to sixteenth-century England. Can you believe that? I've been hanging out with the freaking Tudors!" I barked a jittery laugh.

Mom's brow furrowed, and she began rubbing her thumb and forefinger together like a nervous tick. When she finally spoke, her voice was hardly louder than a breath.

"Emmie, what's going on? Are you on drugs?"

"Of course not. Ew."

"What is wrong with you then?" she cried. She slid away from me. "Why would you tell such a stupid and *weird* story?"

"It's not a story. I know it sounds crazy—believe me—but it's the truth." Mom looked like she might barf all over my new sweater. "I can prove it to you," I pleaded, instantly regretting the idea. I couldn't keep shipping people back and forth between worlds like time-traveling tourists. But Mom looked like she didn't even register the offer...she was too busy trying to breathe, her hand clutching her stomach.

I grappled for something convincing to say when I remembered that I had another way to prove my bonkers story.

"Just wait here," I said, before rushing back outside to the field behind our house.

Nick rested against the fence between the weathered roots of an elm tree, his athletic legs outstretched. The strong winds had brought the fishy smells of the river closer.

"Come with me," I said, wrenching him up by his arm. "I told Mom the truth about the blue-diamond ring, and she's freaking out. You need to help me prove it's true."

"What?" Nick exclaimed as he chased me through the back yard. "Christ, to what end? Do not trouble your mother with this; I beseech you!"

I halted at the steps leading to the porch, gasping with tension. "Look, my mom has no idea who I am right now, and she is my only family, okay? You have your people and your kingdom. I have my mom. *She* is my people. Apart from you, she's all I have. I have to make her understand what's going on."

He pressed his lips together, squaring his shoulders. There was a shiver of movement at the screen door. Mom was gaping at Nick through the mesh.

"Mom, this is Nick," I blurted. "He's from the sixteenth century." After grabbing his clammy palms, I walked us into the house where he towered over Mom's petite frame. Her cheeks were colorless, but her eyes expanded with awe as she took in Nick's features. I made a snap decision that the whole Nicholas the Ironheart thing would be a step too far. It would be like bringing home King Henry the Eighth or Queen Victoria.

I threw Nick a look, silently instructing him to listen carefully. "Nick and I met during my first visit back to the sixteenth century. He's a courtier in the court of Queen Elizabeth the First. He can tell you anything you want to know about that time." I reached for his hand, but our sweaty fingers struggled to lock. "He's also the reason I've disappeared a few times—*without a trace*, Mom. I was with Nick, in Tudor England, where they don't exactly have cell phones. And if you don't believe us, well, you'll have to come back and see it for yourself."

How exactly will you do that, Emmie? Will the three of you fall asleep creepily holding each other's hands? Or will you leave Nicholas the Ironheart alone in modern America while you take your mom for a little jaunt back in time? Moron!

Mom gawked up at him, her voice thin. "Go on then, prove to me that you're a friend of Queen Elizabeth the First." She spat a humorless laugh.

Nick rubbed his lips together and fidgeted with his sleeves. I couldn't blame him for being lost for words. How do you prove your identity to an alien from the future? I had to jump in—to get Nick out of this position I'd put him in—but when he found his voice, it was clear that he didn't need my help.

"Madam, it is my sincerest pleasure to be presented to you,

79

the beloved mother of my dearest betrothed. May I humbly prostrate myself at your feet."

He dropped to one knee and kissed Mom's hand before returning to his imposing height. "Most precious lady, what Mistress Grace claims is indeed true. The moment I laid mine eyes upon her—within the Palace of Whitehall—my heart knew two truths. The first: that our lady, most adored, was not of my realm. Her speech, her manner, her inclination was most certainly of another time." His eyes moved to mine. "The second was that Mistress Grace owned every piece of my heart, and I knew that I would love her until my dying breath."

It was dizzying and dreamlike. In my dowdy living room, one of the most famous kings in history was speaking sweet nothings to me. Not to mention bowing to my commoner mom in her sweatpants.

Mom tilted her head at me, a trace of a smile on her lips. "Is this one of those prank TV shows?"

"Sometimes I wish it was," I replied. Nick blinked at us, obviously lost.

She groaned and pressed a palm to her hip. "Whatever. I'm going to figure this out. But for now, my daughter is home, and you, young man, are nothing if not well-spoken." She sidestepped us to enter the kitchen. "Is anyone hungry?" she called weakly.

"We had some toast, but I'm still pretty hungry," I replied.

"Sorry, but I think it's going to have to be sandwiches." She was digging through the fridge. "There's not much else."

"That's fine," I sang out.

For the first time since Nick and I had arrived back in the present, I could exhale without effort.

෴   ෴   ෴

Nick gobbled up Mom's overcooked grilled-cheese sandwiches dipped in ketchup, and his hands had finally stopped shaking.

However, any hope that Mom believed my story about time travel was dashed when she asked if Nick and I had been living in the forest. She'd moved on from the reality television show idea and now thought we'd joined one of those historical fan groups that camped out in medieval costumes.

The weird thing was that Nick and Mom seemed to get along. They chatted at the table for a while: all superficial stuff like preferred styles of cheese and the weather. Anything that Nick didn't understand, he changed the subject to something else. When he said anything loopy, Mom looked at me and laughed, her eyes lighting up in the way only Nick Tudor could inspire. The whole time he sat with his fingers loosely clasped in his lap, breathing easily with a relaxed smile.

Nicholas the freaking Ironheart is sitting at my ketchup-stained dining table, sweeping my mom off her feet. Yeah, nothing to see here, folks.

Amazingly, Mom hadn't picked up on the earlier 'betrothed' comment. Instead, the bigger issue was her evident belief that I was back home to stay. Nick had been away from his kingdom for hours, and we didn't have much time left.

"Where do you live, Nick?" Mom asked. "Do you need to sleep on the couch?" She side-eyed me like I better not consider having him in my bedroom.

"Actually, we were just going to go upstairs and have a chat about that, weren't we Nick," I said, passing him a look.

"Indeed." He rose to his feet, tipping his head at my mom in a Tudor-style farewell. "This has been a pleasure beyond words, madam."

"It was good to meet you." She turned to the window with a dazed expression, and we headed upstairs.

"Your mother is dear," said Nick as he took a tentative seat in my desk chair. It swiveled, and his legs shot out to steady himself.

I chuckled. "And you make one heck of a twenty-first-century boy." I slid into his lap and folded my arms around him. He murmured his delight and nuzzled his lips into my neck. A flash of yearning heated my spine. "You and my mom seem to get along," I ventured nervously. "Why don't we just stay here? There's no war with Spain to fight; no scary dukes, or stressful council meetings. Just you and me. And ketchup."

Nick's laugh was more like a breath, but it cut nonetheless. Why was he so sure the question was a joke? Was the idea of staying in my time that ludicrous? Couldn't he tell how anxious I was about becoming a sixteenth-century Queen of England without making a muppet of myself—or worse?

For a few seconds, neither of us said anything. Awkwardness chewed up the air, and the chair squeaked beneath us.

Nick fingered a lock of my loose hair. "Is there any more you wish to do before we take our leave? I fear you may suffer when we part from this place."

His eyes couldn't meet mine, and I could tell he was picking up on my reluctance to leave my time so quickly. He didn't need to worry: despite how badly I felt for my mom, I wasn't about to let Nick jet off to the sixteenth century without me. *Been there, done that. And it sucked.*

I thought about his question. "There is one thing I'd like to do," I said, fear crawling across my skin like spider's legs. I didn't have a laptop anymore, but Mom's phone had internet.

I led him back downstairs, finding Mom still staring vacantly through the window. She said I could use her phone, and I opened an internet search window. Nick had seen a cell phone before, but his eyes still boggled. He slid nervously into the couch.

My fingers locked up in protest as I typed the words that I knew I shouldn't.

"Queen Emmeline Tudor"

Click.

No results found for "**Queen Emmeline Tudor**".

I frowned and typed a less specific search.

Emmeline Tudor, 16th century

Click.

No results found. Showing results for **Elizabeth** Tudor, 16th century.

The phone hit the table, my stomach splitting. Why wasn't I there? Was this proof that things didn't work out between Nick and me? I couldn't bring myself to type in 'Nicholas the Iron-heart's wife'. I'd already learned that it was too much of a head-trip to try and live in two different centuries. My decision had already been made, and my home was with Nick in Tudor England. If I kept coming back here and Googling myself, I was legitimately going to end up in a psychiatric hospital.

Nick sat tapping his feet, twiddling his thumbs madly. He kept glancing at the clock on the wall.

"Mom, Nick and I have to go now," I said, trying to sound calm. "You know I love you, and if there was *any* other way…"

Her face fell. "Where are you going?"

"Tudor England," I explained again, trying not to sound impatient.

Mom huffed with exasperation. "Enough of this…Emmie!" she cried. "I'm going to have to call your father again. I just can't deal with you on my own anymore."

"No, don't call him," I cried. Mom blatantly still held a candle for the guy and didn't need much of an excuse to contact him. I did *not* want to be that excuse.

I held my forehead with my trembling fingers. I had no idea what to do. Telling Mom the truth had been a mistake, but Nick had to get home.

"I don't know what to do," I said to him. "Should we take her back with us?" In the corner of my eye, Mom's head was in her hands.

"Christ, no," he whispered. "I have enough ladies from the future running around my court. It is not so easy, Emmie." An apology flooded his face, but he was right. I wasn't sure my mom could convincingly play the role of Tudor lady, which could put her in real danger back there. Norfolk would sniff her out like a bloodhound.

Another idea struck me. "Mom, can you come upstairs? Nick, do you mind waiting outside my bedroom for a minute?"

Mom sighed but didn't resist as I ushered her up the stairs with Nick following behind. While he waited outside the bedroom door, I lugged my suitcase off the bed.

"What are you doing?" Mom said in a sharp tone.

"Proving that Nick and I aren't total nutjobs. But first, you have to help me with these clothes."

"Oh my," she breathed as sixteenth-century silk rippled through my fingers. I explained each step so she could help me dress, sparking a sweet memory of her fastening the intricate straps of my prom gown—only a few weeks before I met Nick Tudor.

"You look incredible," she said, pacing backward to take in the full sight of me. "I can see why you like this English history stuff." She flopped into my desk chair and crossed her arms.

I yanked Nick into my room, despite his visible reluctance. When I guided him onto the bed and lay down beside him, Mom hopped to her feet.

"If you think I am going to sit here and watch you two—"

"Ew!" I said. "What you're going to watch is Nick and I going to sleep. And because I'm wearing this enchanted ring that I told you about, we're going to disappear before your very eyes." *Ugh, I sound like a wannabe magician with her own YouTube channel.*

Mom burst out laughing. When Nick and I didn't join in, she sighed. "Fine...okay."

Nick lay as stiff as a board beside me. I willed myself to relax.

It was a moment I knew I wouldn't forget, and not only because it was certifiably insane. The room was silent save for the breathing of the two people in the world I cared for the most. Two people who had nothing in common—apart from me—and who'd probably never see each other again. As I lay with my eyes pressed shut, I imagined the wedding Nick and I could have had here in my time. Something casual and intimate, with Mom and Nick shooting the breeze about cheese and my maddening stubbornness. Mia would be there, and our friend Josh, and *gawd*, maybe even Dad. They'd all think I was on crack for getting married at the age of eighteen.

And while my mom watched my boyfriend and I fall asleep together, her face revealing how uncomfortable she was with this, the soothing vision of a modern life with Nick Tudor lolled me to a peaceful sleep.

7

THE MOMENT I opened my eyes, the spell broke. Nick was out cold with our fingers still tightly fastened. Mom sat drooped in the chair, gently snoring like one of the elderly ladies at the rest home.

"Mom!" I hissed. "You have to look at us."

"Hmm? I know," she grunted, shifting to straighten her back. "I worked last night."

Luckily, I'd become a world-renowned guru at falling asleep on cue. The blackness returned within minutes.

The next time my eyes peeled open, Mom was watching us closely. Both Nick and I had fallen asleep, yet we were still in my Hatfield bedroom. I tried to explain to Mom that the ring had recently began acting strange, and might take a few attempts to make us disappear, but she was already in the doorway.

"I think it's time we get some help," she grumbled. "I can't deal with this anymore."

"No!" I pleaded. Nick stirred and rolled onto his back beside me.

"I won't tell your dad about this," Mom said as if to reassure me. "But, I am going to call a psychiatrist in Boston." She returned to the bedside for a quick feel of my forehead before clomping down the stairs.

I swore at the ceiling, and Nick shifted to face me, cuddling me with both arms. "We must sleep, Emmie," he said groggily. "I am out of time."

I lay there, examining his dozing face. He'd done his best to help me, and my mom wasn't his biggest problem. A Tudor king couldn't melt into thin air without all hell breaking loose, so there were two possible scenarios here: Nick and I could fall asleep and disappear together, leaving things unfinished with my mom—but at least she now knew I wasn't at the bottom of the Connecticut River. Or, I could let Nick travel back to his time alone, and remain here to sort things out with Mom. Before returning to get me later, he'd have to explain the abrupt absence of his bride-to-be to the likes of Norfolk, and potentially be consoled by Lucinda 'Lucy' Parker. *How about no.*

The choice was clear. I wasn't going back to two-timing the different centuries. I'd already made my choice, and being with Nick was still the right decision for me.

"We need to fall asleep again as fast as possible," I said, burrowing into the heavy warmth of Nick's arms. "Carol Grace on the rampage can be a dangerous thing." I was still dopey with tiredness, and the protective cocoon of his embrace soothed me back to sleep.

Hours later, an earthy sweetness tickled my nose. I turned my face away from the rose-scented sheets and onto my back, sighting billowy mounds of black velvet punctuated with red and white Tudor roses. Nick lay beside me, staring at the canopy.

We were back at Hampton Court Palace.

Nick's concerned eyes found mine, his fingers slipping into my hand. "Are you well?" he said softly. Leaving Mom behind in that state had clearly freaked out the both of us.

I tucked my free arm behind my head, letting my jumbled

thoughts crystallize. *I guess I'm not going to see my mom again for a good while.* What would happen to her?

"Emmie?" Nick pressed gently.

"I'm a bit sad to have left my mom that way," I admitted.

He lay still, aside from the fingertips circling my palm. "I share your sorrow. You are fortunate to have a mother who cares for you so."

I twisted to look at him. Nick's capable maturity made it easy to forget that he'd lost a mother of his own. His mom, Queen Elizabeth the First, had died soon after giving birth to Nick's little sister Kit. My finger traced his facial features, many of them gifts from his handsome father, Robert Dudley, the Earl of Leicester. "I bet your mom would give anything to be here with you," I said.

He shrugged. "My mother would yearn for her throne, but to see me not."

"That's not true."

He smiled bleakly. "Elizabeth was born to be a glorious prince. Despite her many troubles—her mother's beheading, betrayment by her father, imprisonment by her sister—Elizabeth yet won the throne with pride and might."

"She was amazing. Just like her *son.*"

His voice drooped with sadness. "A son who snatched his mother's fortune and promise. Elizabeth wedded my father only because she was with child, Emmie…with *me.* If my birth had not come to pass, my mother would never have married beneath her station. If she had not then sought a second heir—my sister —then God would not have called Elizabeth away. When all is said and done, it is *I* who caused Queen Elizabeth's untimely death."

I cupped his trembling face. "No. Your mother loved you and Kit more than anything; I know it. You've had so much to deal with for someone so young. Too much."

He dropped his chin to my shoulder. "We have both felt loss, have we not? But we have one another now, and that remedies my heart in great measure."

"Mine too."

I relaxed a little as his long fingers played with the blue diamond on my thumb. "You spoke the truth when you said that this ring has become strange," he said. "Once again, we awakened no fewer than two times before it carried us back here."

"I'm glad you agree." I inspected the diamond for any signs of change. "I still think a soothsayer could help us out with some answers. Maybe someone like Agnes Nightingale?" I made a pleading grin. Last time we'd spoken about this, Nick had spurned the idea of paying the soothsayer a visit. "If it's too risky for you, we could start with an astrologer," I suggested, remembering what I'd been reading about the more accepted sciences in the sixteenth century.

Nick's teeth pressed his bottom lip. "To speak plainly, Emmie, I bid you consider that we destroy the ring."

For a second, I couldn't process the words, like they were in a foreign language. "Destroy it? Why?" That'd mean never going home again. Never seeing my mom again. *Ever.*

Peach sunlight cast diamond-shaped shadows across Nick's strained face through the leaded window. "If the claims are true, this ring was enchanted to ruin me. Now it has plainly become impaired. We have no knowledge of what its sorcery may yet do. Must we wager our lives on it?"

I could barely speak. "There's no evidence to suggest the ring could harm us in any way."

"But do you not agree that the ring has become fickle?"

"If by that, you mean 'acting a little weird', then yes. Of course."

He leaned away from me. "Then what is to say that the next occasion we travel to your time, we will not become trapped there forevermore?"

It was apparent that the thought of having to stay with me in my time frightened Nick to death, which was impossible not to take personally. "Why would that be so hideous?" I said sharply. Had Nick already forgotten the incredible invention of human flight? How about the peace of anonymity and of being out of the Tudor pressure cooker?

His face read mine and then crumpled. "Emmie. We have suffered through this puzzle enough. I am a king, and one bereft of an heir. If I were to quit my kingdom, there would be unthinkable bloodshed. That vile woman Mary Stuart would come for my sister and the Tudor throne. If mine actions were to surrender England to a Catholic heretic, it would mean the damnation of my soul. Must we even speak of this again?" His voice rose with frustration.

"It's okay, I get it," I said. "You want to destroy the enchanted ring, meaning I can never visit my mom or my home again, because those things don't matter as much as your kingdom and throne."

He made an exasperated huff. "You must know that I do not ask this lightly. This ring has proven itself unstable and may cease to take effect at any moment. Therefore, if we were to journey to your time again, I would have to stake my kingdom on it, for the ring may never bring me back here. If you were to journey to your time without me, then I would stake losing *you* to all eternity if you could not return."

I didn't know what to say. Nick was so used to getting his way, and it showed.

He slid out of the bed. "What is certain is that you made a choice to be my bride, Emmie, so the question is: what are you prepared to give up? When my grandfather wed Katherine of Aragon, that woman never set foot in Spain again. There are many stories of English princes marrying foreigners who were content to live out their lives in their new kingdom. If you choose me, I want you to choose *me*. But if I am not enough—if all of England is not enough—then perhaps you have made the wrong choice." He turned his face away from me.

"Nick, I did choose you, but it was a fast decision, and I didn't think it meant I'd never be able to see my mom again," I called after him, but he'd already tapped once on the paneled wood. The doors opened immediately to the scurrying of boots and a voice crying, "His Majesty the King!" Nick disappeared into the frazzle, leaving me blinking away tears.

It felt like I'd been away from court for a week, but the ease with which I slipped into my old routine reminded me that it'd only been a day. Bridget quizzed me with cheeky questions about why I'd been locked away with the king overnight, but Alice shushed her. Lucinda kept her focus on her sewing like she didn't want to know.

I didn't catch sight of Nick for several days, and he was evidently avoiding me. Our conversation about the enchanted ring festered in the pit of my stomach, and I wanted to clear the air. I was nowhere near ready to destroy the ring without at least trying to learn more about it. Surely he could agree with me on that.

I distracted myself with my snore-fest lessons, took leisurely strolls in the gardens before the weather changed, and sank into the ease of some girl time.

At first light on Sunday morning, one of Nick's gentlemen delivered a message that I'd been requested to join the king at chapel. I still wasn't used to being summoned without notice like the family pet. *He's a Tudor king,* I reminded myself as I waited in the processional gallery upstairs, smoothing my hair and fidgeting with my dress.

Nick arrived swiftly, draped in a velvet coat of forest-green that stunningly contrasted with his blush-pink doublet.

Courtiers and attendants kissed his hand at every turn, and what I thought would be us catching up became a public performance as he formally led me through to his royal pew.

We'd barely spoken to each other before I was ushered into a separate balcony beside his. A thick curtain of crimson velvet separated us. I couldn't even *see* Nick, let alone talk to him.

Tudor king, Tudor king, Tudor king.

I focused on snapping mental photographs of the Chapel Royal ceiling, which I'd never seen from this vantage point. Lifted from the pages of a fairytale, it shone in a cobalt blue constellation of golden arches, stars, and royal emblems. Its majestic beauty was enough to entertain me through the liturgy that was difficult for me to understand. When a choir of boys in white ruffs began singing, their euphonic voices like angels, I gripped the balcony handrail, fully absorbed. *Okay, so maybe airplanes and ketchup aren't all the world has to offer.*

When the service ended, the curtain between Nick and I glided open, and I swept toward him before he could disappear. As soon as we reached the processional gallery, courtiers rushed at the king with scrolls and petitions in their hands. Francis Beaumont had arrived on the scene to field them off, allowing Nick and I to duck into the concealment of one of his private stairwells and have a moment alone. Perhaps Francis was warming to our relationship, which served as a timely boost of encouragement.

"Was the service to your satisfaction?" Nick said to me, his expression hard to read.

"The choir was incredible," I replied, my voice bouncing off the stone walls. "It was probably the most beautiful thing I've ever heard."

His shoulders relaxed a little. "I am pleased to hear it."

He couldn't look me in the eye, clarifying that he was still as uncomfortable with things as I was. He offered me his hand. "I wish to show you something."

I took his fingers, mini fireworks bursting between the heat of our skin. Our argument had done nothing to weaken the electricity that had brought us together in the first place.

We reached the drafty downstairs corridor and continued toward the construction site on the south side of the palace. A supersized canvas tent had been erected to protect the works from the rain. My new apartments were still haphazard muddles of building sites, but Nick led us right beneath the wooden scaffolding. The King of England was clearly endangering himself by marching through an active worksite, but no one dared stop him. Workers bowed in deference before fleeing like scurrying roaches. We climbed a dusty stairwell that smelled recently laid and passed through two unfinished chambers. The third room shone in stark distinction to the others, because it was already complete—a dazzling masterpiece among the uncut timber and grimy bricks.

"Holy crap," I murmured as I spun in all directions, taking in the magnificent jewelry workshop. Wooden trestle tables filled the space, neatly arranged with gilded files, iron pincer-like scissors and smaller cutters, brass blocks and molds, crucibles for heating metals, and other archaic tools I didn't recognize.

"Is this all for me?" I breathed, turning to Nick. He'd remembered his promise to build me a jewelry workshop, and he'd evidently made it a priority.

He nodded. "The gold and jewels are being kept safe, but you shall have as many as you need. Does it please you?"

I exaggerated my pretend grimace. "I guess it'll do."

Nick was accustomed to my sarcasm and finally smiled, closing the space between us. I had to stand on my tiptoes to wrap my arms around his neck.

"Any such thing you desire, tell me, and you shall have it," he said as we rocked together in a standing hug. "I have summoned a fine jewelry craftsman to teach you anything you desire. His name is Mister Andrea Bon Compagni. Call upon him any time you please; he is presently at court. Your maidens will assist you."

"Wow. I don't know what to say, which, as you know, is unheard of." I squeezed him tighter.

Nick's efforts had subdued some of the tightening pressure between us, but we still hadn't agreed on what to do with the blue-diamond ring. He hadn't asked for it back, and for now, it was living inside my locked jewelry coffer. As the king, he could have the ring snatched from my bedchamber and destroyed with a single command, and I tried not to think too much about that possibility.

"I must take my leave," he said, breaking from me and straightening his collar. "I have made time this day to prepare for your investiture ceremony."

I rested against the edge of a wooden table. "Anytime you need me, I'll be here. And if I'm not...nah, I'll be here."

His sparkling eyes held mine as he backed through the doorway, looking so hot with his naturally ruffled hair that he made my stomach twist. "Your new cloth should also be at hand this day," he added, before rolling around the doorframe to disappear.

"My new cloth?" I called after him.

"For the harvest feast of Michelmas," he replied. "This year, I much desire a masquerade. We must also honor your new title."

His voice faded, and I sat there, processing the news. I had to appear at another royal ball with the Duke of Norfolk, Lord Wharton, and the rest of the sullen aristocrats—this time as a new member of their exclusive nobility club. But perhaps this is what it'd take for them to finally accept me. I was going to become the Marquess of Pembroke, followed by Queen Emmeline Tudor...*yikes!* Do or die, this was happening.

Deep in my gut, questions still wriggled about the blue-diamond ring and Nick's desire to destroy it. King Henry the Eighth's first wife, Queen Katherine of Aragon, may have chosen not to sail back to Spain, but she presumably had the option. I was willfully marrying a Tudor king who I adored with every bone in my body, but I was still a twenty-first-century American girl. Freedom was the one thing I wasn't prepared to give up without a fight.

ᴡᴏᴡ　ᴡᴏᴡ　ᴡᴏᴡ

Mercifully, only a handful of Privy Council members attended my investiture ceremony in the Presence Chamber the following morning. My plush ceremonial robes sank into the woven matting as I knelt before the king, and a sacred coronet as freezing as an ice sculpture was placed over my head. As the letters patent were read out, and King Nick formally granted me the title of Marquess of Pembroke, a tremor quaked through me. I could barely look at Nick in this state without feeling like I was making eyes with a living angel. The jewels in his crown splashed prismatic colors across the candlelit wall, and despite my modern viewpoints, I couldn't deny that every inch of him radiated power and glory from within his scarlet robes.

When Alice was washing my hair in the bath afterward, she told me that all the Privy Council members usually attended the investiture ceremonies. There should've been plenty more people there. I swallowed the discomfort that brought. If I continued freaking out about every little thing—needing every person in the realm to like me—my life here would be a misery. I was trying the best I could.

You're the Marquess of freaking Pembroke! I reminded myself as I began dressing for the masquerade feast. Truthfully, I had little idea what a female marquess even was, how she ranked, or what she was supposed to do. I knew I could ask Alice, but I'd have to be careful about sounding like I'd barely heard of the title. At least it would be swallowed up by 'Queen of England' before long, and I was pretty clear how that one stacked.

My anxiety over the Michelmas feast was borderline paralyzing, but the dress that arrived for me from the Royal Wardrobe sweetened the deal a little. The sleeves and gown of scarlet-red satin were draped open to reveal a white kirtle threaded with triangular patterns of white diamonds centered with rose-shaped ruby brooches. Behind me, Bridget and Lucinda chatted at length about the eligible men who'd be at the feast while weaving my hair into elaborate braids. It was a shame that their efforts were entirely concealed by a magnificent ruby-encrusted hood. I usually hated having all my hair covered, but Alice's makeup had turned me into a magazine ad for glowing skin, and she'd accented my lips with the perfect shade of creamy red.

I swiveled from left to right in the mirror, glittering like I was tangled in fairy lights. The ensemble was comically swanky for Emmie Grace from Hampshire County, but at least I looked the part of my new title. I could nod and wave like a real queen-to-be and not have to say much to anyone. I wished I had useful contributions to make, but I'd have to rely on a dignified silence to get me through until I learned enough in this century to be able to offer something worthwhile...if my position even allowed that.

I repressed another pang of longing for my time period.

Alice and I were unhooking our masquerade masks from their storage pouches when a messenger arrived with a letter for Lucinda Parker.

"It is from my mother," she said, hurriedly snapping open the wax seal. "She brings news of my daughter, Ellie." She read a few words before slumping into the table. "Dear God."

Bridget finished clipping on her jeweled belt and dashed to her. "What is it?"

We all gathered around Lucinda. "Ellie has taken ill," she breathed. "My mother believes it to be consumption."

My chest leaped. "You should go to her." I was pretty sure that consumption was what the Tudors called tuberculosis.

"Mistress Parker cannot travel alone," said Bridget. "I will go with her." She threw me a nervous glance.

"Of course," I agreed. "Alice and I will look after each other, won't we, Alice?"

Alice nodded, giving Lucinda's arm a compassionate rub. Lucinda's pendant necklace tinkled as she fell into a chair, finishing the letter. "Mother complains here of the costs," she said. "The king has raised taxes, and now she cannot afford to buy remedies for Ellie."

"For what has His Majesty raised taxes?" Alice griped, like Nick was her frustrating older brother.

Lucinda folded the letter in her lap. "It says here that taxes have been raised to pay for the coronation of the new queen."

I felt my jaw hang. "I can't believe that—I'd never agree to that; I'm so sorry."

Lucinda's silvery-blue eyes were free of judgment as she looked at me. "I shall remain at court. I must petition the king for some course of aid for my household."

"But I can do that," I said. "You should be with Ellie."

Lucinda rose to smooth her skirts. "You are most kind, my lady. However, I would not ask you to do my bidding. In any case, I fear that His Majesty will be less favorable if I do not make mine own case for my daughter."

"The king may not like Mistress Parker leaving court without his permission," Alice explained to me as though she knew I was confused. "She is to become a lady to the queen."

I took Lucinda's clammy hands. "Ask the king tonight then. Apart from the fact that time is clearly of the freaking essence, it's usually when he's in his best mood. And if he doesn't help you, *I* will." I had income from my lands now, even though I had no idea where my lands were.

Lucinda didn't want to write to her mom until she'd spoken to the king, so we tied on each other's shimmery, feathered masks and left for the king's Privy Garden. It was a chilly evening for an outdoor shindig, but that's what the king wanted, so it was happening.

Masked noblemen voiced their admiration and tried to guess our identities as we strode past the avenue of clipped yew trees and into the pre-party zone. Guests hovered in clusters around the low hedges of the knot gardens, drinking wine, nibbling hors d'oeuvres, and dancing merrily in the open spaces. Green-and-white poles topped with heraldic beasts overlooked fragrant beds of primroses, violets, and cherries that masked the river smells. Each square-shaped garden was bordered with an impeccably manicured hedge.

A tall guy with thick, windswept hair sprouting from an ivory mask took my fingers and led me into the volta. I pretended I had no idea it was King Nick, to keep up his charade, and the guests paced backward to give us space. After so many tedious hours of dance practice, I actually didn't make a total idiot of myself and kept pace with the king's smooth movements. Cheers sounded as Nick gripped my waist and lifted me to the sky—practically dirty dancing for Tudor times—before concluding the display by dropping to one knee and kissing my hand. A collective gasp at the kneeling king rippled through the crowd, but within seconds, Nick was back on his feet. *Holy crap, I just pulled off the volta.*

"Do you know me?" he said in a theatrical voice, and I tried not to laugh. Dorky Nick was adorable.

"Are you the Earl of Warwick?" I replied loudly. Alice cracked up—always the first to react over a Francis Beaumont joke.

"Only if I have shrunk by a head," said Nick, tearing off his mask.

The nobles roared with laughter like it was the funniest joke ever told. Nick beamed down at me, affection pouring from his sea-colored eyes. He slid a hand inside his coat that was the Tudor colors of green and white, extracting a sliver of gold.

"For my lady, most dear, and your promised Queen of England!" he cried, draping the glistening chain over my head. I'd expected more cheers, but there was mostly gentle clapping as my fingers clutched the heart-shaped ruby that pressed against my neck. My mind shot back to Nick sitting beside my mom, dipping sliced bread with orange cheese into ketchup. He must've thought my home—my life—was so unimpressive and beggarly compared to this. Enough rubies were hanging off my body to buy a planet. Had he really raised the people's taxes to pay for all this?

The frazzled Master of the Revels hurriedly cleared a larger space. Two armchairs were carried in for Nick and me, and the rest of the guests gathered behind us on foot. A masque unfolded before us—an iridescent spectacle of actors playing unicorns, nymphs, knights, and damsels, accompanied by lively music and primitive fireworks that could've blown us to smithereens. When the performance finished with a lady rescuing the archangel St. Michael from danger, Nick threw me a covert smirk. He'd arranged the surprise feminist ending to impress me. If it hadn't been the sixteenth century, I'd have kissed him right there.

After our chairs were removed, a mob of waiting nobles and diplomats sucked the king inside their huddle like a whirlpool. I waited on the perimeter, peering around for Lucinda. She had to have her chance to speak with the king, and single mothers didn't exactly enjoy priority access in this place.

Alice arrived beside me with two cups of wine.

"You're a good girl," I said, accepting one. It was sweetened with warmed berries.

I winced at the sight of Bridget trying to engage the visibly uninterested Earl of Surrey in conversation. While it wasn't my business who the cute earl hooked up with, I suspected that pretty maidens weren't exactly on his radar. I'd noticed the way he looked at other dashing gentlemen of the court with shining eyes, and his intimacy with his male tennis partner. Not that I'd ever mention my theory to Bridget, or even Alice—this was a dangerously different world to the one I knew.

Just beyond Bridget and Surrey stood Francis Beaumont among a throng of lords.

"How do you think Lord Warwick is going as the king's right-hand man?" I asked Alice, genuinely curious.

She considered her answer. "It appears that Francis has been a good servant to the king, and he has fairly handled the Spanish threat. However, he has become as single-minded as my father: sparing no end in his efforts to please the king and the lords. I suppose his sense of duty is to be commended, but I fear he will end up like my Papa...wedded to his work." The longing in Alice's voice spoke volumes. I'd never have pushed this hard if I wasn't sure that Alice and Francis secretly fancied the pants off each other.

"Okay, enough," I ordered, the effects of the wine relaxing my inhibitions. "You and Francis need to get together, like yesterday."

"What in the high heavens?" she said through a chortle.

"Stop it," I said like she was a naughty schoolgirl. "You and Francis have had more misunderstandings than Romeo and Juliet, but they're all cleared up now. Let's go through this again: Francis was once betrothed to your older sister Violet, but then he called off the wedding, not because he was a jerk, but because he is actually in love with *you*. The second issue was that you thought Francis had driven *me* away from court for similar reasons, but that also turned out to be false. Does that cover everything?"

Alice gaped at me, before spinning to face Francis again, her slate-colored skirts rustling against the gravel. Together, we watched Francis brush sweaty black curls from his temples while he listened to a nobleman speaking with wild gesticulations. Francis patted the man's shoulder before turning to another man who appeared equally as distressed.

Francis's gaze moved to catch Alice's stare. Neither of them looked away for several seconds. The irritated noblemen turned away from him, and Francis swayed on his feet, clearly deciding whether to approach us or not. I took Alice's arm and walked quickly over to him.

"Good evening, and God save you, my ladies," Francis greeted us with a bow like we were two strangers. Alice dipped into a polite curtsy.

Oh, for goodness' sake, you two.

"I am grateful for your timely rescue," he said, guiding us into a quieter space. "Every hairbrain in this palace finds it his duty to make petty complaints without end." I smelled musk on his skin as he brought his wine cup to his lips.

"Much has changed since you were merely in charge of court entertainment," Alice said to him with a wry smile.

A torch flame flickered in Francis's dark eyes. "Make no mistake, my lady, pacifying the nobility is a performance indeed."

She laughed. "Perhaps if this is all to fall short, you may join the theatre. You would make a fine Narcissus."

Ha, typical quick-witted Alice. In Greek mythology, I remembered Narcissus to be the hunter who was physically beautiful but utterly self-absorbed.

"I feel I would be more suited to Achilles," Francis quipped. "And you, my lady, would make a finer Helen of Troy."

Her cheeks tinted the color of cherries, but she held his gaze. "A lady in a playhouse? I have heard there is much kissing to be observed."

Francis smiled. "Well, if there is to be kissing, I would then wish to change my part to Prince Paris."

Biting down on a smirk, I backed away from them. "I'm just going to find the king," I said. "Sometimes he drinks too much wine before he eats."

The truth was that no one could stop Nick from drinking or eating whatever the heck he wanted—not even me. But Alice and Francis were finally flirting like they'd been suppressing it for years and I wasn't going to get in the way.

It was past sunset, but supper couldn't begin without the king's command. I weaved through clusters of guests, searching for Nick, most of the courtiers morphing into horror-movie characters through their strange masks in the dim light.

Looping back around, I ambled past the musicians until I spotted flashes of green and white fabric through the torchlights. I slipped between the flaming lamps, careful to avoid their heat. I curled around to see Nick with Lucinda Parker standing beside a stone dragon fountain, both their masks removed. She must've finally been asking him for money to help with her daughter. Good. *Nick...be nice.*

I leaned closer. Neither of them was saying anything. Was he being difficult? Nick was just gazing down at Lucinda, whose tilted face was a few inches from his. They could've been shooting the cover for a historical bridal magazine.

The gesture was so unexpected—so shocking—that, at first, I thought I imagined it. But no, Lucinda took Nick's hand in hers and tugged him toward her, catching his lowering lips with hers.

8

I DIDN'T KNOW IF—or for how long—Nick kissed Lucinda back. The unfolding scene was too blurry behind the stinging fog of my tears. I tore away from the streak of torchlights and onto an avenue leading back to the privacy of my chambers. I couldn't be here—four hundred years away from home, doing my best to convince myself and others I was Tudor queen material—if Nick was cheating on me. I had to get away...to escape...to be out of this stifling outfit. Its sleeves were so tight that they pinched my skin as I reached up to wipe my eyes.

It was just my luck that the moronic Duke of Norfolk was tucked away on a bench within a coterie of standing councilors, like he was the king holding court. Beneath the cloak of nightfall, the men didn't appear to see me as I scaled a short hedge and landed within a tangle of rosemary in a strip of greenery that ran alongside the pathway. I felt bad for the well-tended garden, but I'd sooner bash my way through rose thorns than have those jerks question why I was fleeing the feast.

The memory of Nick's lips touching Lucinda's plunged a stake into my heart and twisted it. Had she been playing me this entire time? God, had *he*? I squashed the unbearable thought and continued silently along the shadowy garden bed, attempting to sneak past the men without being noticed.

"…His Majesty's private inclinations," one of them said.

"The king's marriage is no matter of privacy," snapped the Duke of Norfolk. My satin heels stilled in the dirt, every inch of me listening. "King Nicholas's decision to marry this feather-brained girl instead of a blood royal will lose him the affections of the people and give cause for civil war."

"I suspect the people may come to love her," argued the first man. "She has some quality of allure."

Baron Wharton grunted. "This marriage is no more than a laughingstock. It does naught to further the realm and may even bring England's standing to ruin." Lord Wharton spoke robustly, and the others shushed him.

"But to petition against your niece," the first man said to Norfolk. "Surely you desire such a match?"

The duke scoffed. "Half the silly girls in England may lay claim to be my niece. My brother was quite the ladies' man."

Rambunctious laughter exploded, chased by more shushing.

"Mistress Grace is no more than a nobleman's daughter," said Norfolk. "You can be certain that she is of little value to me."

Not even a nobleman's daughter, idiot. Plus, it's Lady Pembroke to you. I still wanted to snort at that name.

"The girl has plainly poisoned His Majesty's mind," Wharton said. "He has a foolish devotion to her. She can have any pillock in England; she need not have our king."

Norfolk's voice dropped. "Are we all in agreement that this marriage cannot move forward? We have need for swift action."

I expected some contention—especially from the guy who defended me at the start—but there were only murmurs of acceptance.

A blast of trumpets nearly jolted me into a hedge. Sheathed swords swung from the men's leather belts as they scampered away to the riverside banqueting house to guzzle the king's expensive delicacies.

Backstabbers. I huffed quietly to myself.

We have need for swift action. What did that even mean?

Surely nobody would dream of attacking the king, but it'd only take a single blow from one of those mighty swords to my heart—or Nick's—to end our relationship for good. We couldn't exactly marry if one of us was in the ground.

I'd put the King of England in danger again by being here.

Double damn and all the freaking bad words. I climbed back over the hedge and trudged up the path leading to the banqueting house, feeling the torchlights cast me back into the limelight. A guard buckled almost to his knees at the sight of me and called off his mini search party. It was obvious that Nick had already realized I was missing from the feast and had ordered the guards to find me or suffer the king's wrath. The guard looked so relieved to see me that he made the sign of the cross. Jeez, I'd only been gone for ten minutes.

The banqueting house smelled like a country fair, with rustic parcels of peaches, oranges, radishes, parsnips, carrots, and onions hanging from the candlelit eaves. The king sat on his throne beneath a canopy of odorless deep-purple daisies that wouldn't bother his asthma, with Francis whispering into his ear. Nick's hand gripped the back of my empty chair to his left, his body angled toward it. I untied my mask and braced myself as I approached the dais.

"For the love of God," Nick cried as I slid into my seat. Francis slumped forward with visible relief. He'd probably had to handle Nick's panic over my disappearance.

"To where did you vanish?" Nick huffed as Bridget scrambled onto the platform to help me with my dress like it was my bridal gown. There were too many faces in the stately chamber to find Lucinda Parker's. "Why do you smell of rosemary?" Nick added, studying me.

"I'm fine," I snapped at the fussing Bridget, shame sending heat to my face. She bowed and returned to a table beside the angel's wings sculpted from wheat fronds. There sat Alice and Lucinda, murmuring at each other through cheerful grins. My cheeks felt like they had turned to stone.

"I just went for a walk," I said to Nick, looking at the decorative floral crusts of the blackberry pies on a nearby table. Anywhere but at him.

"Yes?" he prodded.

"I saw..." My voice trembled. Nick's hand had curled into a fist over the purple-and-gold table runner. A cook was shucking oysters before the king, each sticky clack unsettling my nerves.

I saw Lucinda Parker kiss you.

"I saw the Duke of Norfolk with some of the privy councilors, including Lord Wharton," I said under my breath. "They were talking about our marriage, and Norfolk encouraged them to try to stop it."

Nick's face twisted with disbelief as Francis hunched forward, also listening.

"They said they were going to take *swift action*," I continued. "There were five of them, and they're all sitting with Norfolk now." I subtly gestured toward the treasonous gang.

Nick lurched forward and snatched the knife right out of the oyster chef's hand.

"Majesty," Francis hissed, slamming his palm over Nick's wrist. The cook scurried away to safety.

"You are certain?" Nick asked me, his eyes flaming jewels of aquamarine.

"One hundred percent."

"Majesty, it would do well to remain calm," Francis cautioned, sliding the knife away from the king.

Nick's hands were now tight fists of white skin. "No man may question the pleasure of their sovereign king," he said through his teeth. "*All* are bound by God to obey me."

Francis's curls tipped in a gesture of submission. "My gracious lord, I caution you to consider the cause of such plotting between Norfolk and the councilmen before they increase in numbers." He shot me an uneasy glance. "A king's marriage should bring greater power and esteem to the realm. What case have you made for Lady Pembroke, who offers no such benefit?"

Nick slammed his fist down so hard that the table shook. The musicians were trained to play loudly enough so guests couldn't hear Nick's conversations, but nervous faces peeked at the evidently furious king.

"Any man who does not have his king's welfare at heart will be summoned before me to explain himself—no matter his station," he warned Francis in a steely tone.

The earl returned an obedient nod. "You shall continue to find me your most true and faithful servant, Your Grace."

Humiliation scorched my cheeks over hearing Francis still overtly questioning our relationship, especially given how I'd just gone in to bat for him with Alice. No matter how much Nick and I loved each other, it would never be enough for Francis, who wanted his king to be politically secure above all things. But I truly believed that he genuinely loved Nick too much to ever cross a line the way Norfolk had and conspire to stop the marriage.

Nick sat stewing over his wine cup before he smacked it across the table, sending red droplets flying like blood splatter. "I cannot even look at these faithless cod's heads," he snapped at Francis. "You will arrest every member of the Privy Council on the grounds of sedition. Interrogate them all and make ready a warrant of execution for those found guilty."

Francis's face mirrored my own horror. "Majesty, the entire council? I beseech you—"

"You dare question me!" Nick grabbed him by his ruffled collar and yanked him to his feet.

"Nick!" I chastised, and he squeezed the fabric with barely contained fury before releasing Francis.

"No man shall ever speak on matters of my marriage!" Nick bellowed to the chamber of nobles, every face a white sheet. "Those who offend the will of their anointed king will find themselves on trial for high treason." He thrust both hands beneath the dining table and shoved it forward, sending gold platters and cups clanging across the tiled floor.

A moment of chilling silence followed before Nick grabbed my arm and marched me out beneath a procession of arches woven from wheat fronds.

ⅶⅾ   ⅶⅾ   ⅶⅾ

"Let go of me!" I cried when we were safely out of earshot. I was hot with rage at how Nick had treated me in public, not to mention the violent outburst that had Nicholas the Ironheart written all over it.

He was already calmer and halted on the path, but I was just getting started. I continued my brisk pace toward the palace.

"Lady Pembroke, I command you to stop," he called after me. I didn't break my stride. One of the guards stayed close to me, awkwardly passing by the king. I couldn't care less what they thought of us.

"Vexatious girl," Nick huffed before he briskly caught up again. He dashed in front of me, pacing backward while I charged forward. "Christ, Emmie, I bid you to speak your ill feeling!"

At that moment, I just couldn't. Lucinda…Norfolk…Nick's scary eruption and talk of executions…the relentless pressure to become a convincing Tudor queen overnight. *Where do I even freaking start!*

"Blessed girl, I love you," said Nick. He stopped still at my onrush, and I banged right into his sternum. I spun away to face the sundial, my stomach a hollow cave.

108

I could hardly get the words out. "If you love me, then why did you sneak off into a private part of the garden with Lucinda Parker and let her kiss you?"

Nick gasped. "Who said such things to you?"

"I *saw* you!" I clenched away the urge to shove him with both hands. "To be honest, you both looked pretty cozy." His silhouette wobbled through the tears threatening my eyes.

He dismissed the comment with a shake of his head. "It was nothing of the sort. Mistress Parker's daughter has taken ill—a private matter—and she bid me aside to ask for my assistance. As she is your lady, I granted it. Mistress Parker's kiss was no more than a gesture of gratitude."

"A gesture of gratitude?" The words ripped through my bewildered laugh.

He took my shoulders and swirled me to face him. "Do not make more of this than it is. Do you know that it is considered polite in this realm to kiss another man's wife before first entering his home? You stake too much in a chaste kiss. Mistress Parker brought her lips to mine for scarcely a moment, did you not see?"

"Just…please!" I waved my hands to shut him up. I didn't want to imagine any more lip-locking than I'd already seen.

Nick's palms kneaded his forehead. "Christ, I would sooner see Mistress Parker banished from court than have you doubt my devotion to you."

"No." My jaw hardened. "You know that she's got a sick baby, and she needs the money." The memory of Lucinda's plight roused another thought. "She also said that you raised the people's taxes to pay for my coronation…people now can't afford medicine for their babies."

Nick crossed his arms. "And by what means do you expect me to pay for the crowning of your person, my lady? Have you found coin growing upon trees in this realm?"

"Haven't you got something like *sixty* palaces?" I countered, vindictively repeating what he'd once shared with me with such pride.

He paced away from me before circling back with frustration. "I fear that you understand nothing. Not me, not mine intentions, not my wishes, not my kingdom, nor my decisions."

"That's not true," I said, seizing the chance to air what'd been plaguing my mind most of all. "But there is one thing I don't get: why you would ask me to destroy a ring that's literally the only way I could ever see my family again. I'd *never* ask that of you."

He expelled a heavy breath. "Emmie, it is not so much the ring as that I feel you have one foot in this thing and one foot out. This night alone proves this marriage to be a battle hard-won, it is true. I cannot turn any which way in this place without meeting a lord who believes he has the right to interfere in the subject of my marriage. But I am the king, and I will choose mine own wife. That choice is *you*, in spite of the falseness of my subjects and the losses I must endure. Is it not fair that I wish not to lose you, too?"

My throat sealed shut. All this time, Nick had been sensing my trepidation about becoming queen and assuming that it was him that I was unsure about.

"You won't lose me," I said, stepping closer to him. "*You* are the only reason I'm here. But if you need me to destroy the ring to prove it, then I'm not ready for that yet. So I'm sorry, but the answer to that is a hard 'no.'"

The grind of boots on gravel severed the cord of tension between us. Francis Beaumont bowed to the king from the shadows. "Your Grace, the members of the Privy Council have been seized, as you wish, and are being taken to the Tower."

Nick squared his shoulders. "You have pleased your king. Now, I instruct you not to draw Lady Pembroke into this matter any further. My lady has been burdened enough. You will lead the interrogation of the councilors and determine who is to be charged."

Francis offered a stiff, reluctant bow before leaving us alone. Nick shrugged off his velvety coat that smelled like freshly cut roses and draped it over me.

"I don't want those men to be killed because of me," I said to him. "I've never been a fan of the death penalty."

His bottom lip disappeared between his teeth. "A king cannot appear weak, Emmie."

"No one heard their seditious words but me," I argued. "If they're found guilty, can't you keep them locked up instead? You can't behead them just because they don't like me. It'll sicken me with guilt. It's *not* the way things are done where I'm from."

He took my chin between his thumb and forefinger and brought his lips close to mine. "How any man can think ill of you, I will never know," he said, the heat of his breath tickling my skin. His hand slid down to rest on my shoulder. "If it shall please your heart, then I will pursue imprisonment for those convicted of speaking out against our marriage and forgo the scaffold. However, I cannot make the same pledge for those who are found to have plotted against your life or mine."

"That's fair." My fingers found his and held tight. "My only worry is what Norfolk knows about me. He could tell people that you asked him to lie about being my uncle." I hushed my voice so the guards couldn't hear, not that they'd ever speak out.

Nick's eyes shone brighter than the cabochon emeralds sewn into his doublet. "If that dimwit Norfolk would be so foolish as to make that claim, I will heartily refute it. You would have the word of a king to support you, my lady. There is none stronger than that."

॰ৡৡ৴   ৡৡ৴   ৡৡ৴

The next week that passed was eerily quiet at court. Only six members of the king's council had been cleared by Francis to return to work; the rest were embroiled in a trial that I wasn't allowed to witness. Nick assured me that any punishments resulting from the matter would be imprisonment and not execution, but Alice thought that was a fairy story. While she painted on my makeup one morning after breakfast, we debated over how merciful King Nick really was. For every example Alice had of a violent beheading ordered by the king, I had zero rebuttal. My only choice was to trust that my boyfriend wouldn't lie to my face—including about getting snuggly with his ex.

At least Lucinda Parker had taken leave from court to visit her daughter, assuming that poor Ellie was still alive. While the thought of seeing Lucinda still turned my stomach, I'd simmered a little on the whole kiss thing. Alice told me she'd given plenty of men a peck on the lips without any hint of flirtation, and even Bridget thought it was common practice, despite her obsessions with romantic passion.

For now, my wedding and coronation were proceeding like nothing had happened with Norfolk and his treasonous tribe. Nick was full steam ahead on the marriage mission, and I sensed that he was trying to prove his affection for me more than ever after the Lucinda incident.

The week after the Michelmas train wreck, the painter George Gower rode into court on king's orders to compose my formal portrait.

I was never gifted at sitting still for long periods, but posing for a taciturn artist was the break I needed from the pressures of my lessons. I didn't have to pretend to speak Shakespearean to anyone, perform an oddball Renaissance dance, or play an instrument I'd never even heard of. Gower only needed me to sit deathly still, and it took all the mental space I had to keep my feet from falling asleep. I focused on a pretty fringed cushion in the chair behind him, my fingers clasping a single red rose. Nick had sent in a harpist to keep me entertained, and the glittery tune lulled me into a blissful meditation.

Just before supper, the oak doors swung open, shocking me from my trance. "His Majesty the King!" cried a guard.

"Your Grace, the portrait is not yet complete," spluttered Gower in a deep bow.

"I wish to see it not," Nick replied, covering his eyes as he sidestepped the canvas to approach me.

I blushed at him through a tangle of butterflies at the rare sight of him in casual black leather. He glided a scented hand down my cheek, turning my legs so weak that I could've sunk right into the woven matting.

"My love, I come to share news, and I plainly could not wait," he said, the playfulness in his voice divulging that the news was good. "I have made formal the preparations for our marriage rites. Before this, we shall leave Hampton Court on progress. The castle must be cleaned and replenished to make welcome the many men who will wish to behold the wedding of our most blessed queen."

"Progress...isn't that like a king's tour of the country?"

He nodded, kissing the back of my hand. "Occurrences remain of the one-day fever on the roads to Sussex, so we shall travel west, and perhaps north. First to Windsor, then over to Oxford, and God willing, to Kenilworth to meet the Princess Catherine."

"Oh please, yes—can we visit Kit?" Nick's little sister was one of the only people here who felt like family. I ached to see her.

His dimpled smile was infectious. "Kenilworth it is. Kit will be enamored to see you. We shall depart on the morrow." Nick spun to the painter. "You will finish the portrait this day. Our Lady Pembroke will inform you when she is weary and in need of rest."

Gower's oil-stained fingers flew to his goatee as he watched the king leave.

"It's okay," I reassured him. "I'll stay as long as you need."

He tipped his head at me in gratitude, before his hand dashed across the canvas with panicky scrapes. I became a sitting statue again, processing the good news: I was about to travel through sixteenth-century English villages and meet some of the common folk...those who were surely more like me than anyone in this posh court. It would be an escape from the constant unease I felt from not being able to perfect the Tudor protocols quickly enough. A smile tugged at my lips, inducing a tsk-tsk sound from Gower. My cheeks slumped back into somber Tudor portrait mode.

I climbed into bed after midnight, making a stop at the map on the wall in my bedchamber. The route we'd take on progress was northwest, passing right through Buckinghamshire, where Bridget Nightingale's family was from.

My eyes flickered to the jewelry coffer still protecting the blue-diamond ring. This was my chance to show the enchanted ring to Bridget's cousin—the soothsayer Agnes Nightingale—and find out what it was meant for and why it'd been acting strangely. If I could just prove that the ring wasn't going to conk out on one of its journeys to the twenty-first century—erroneously trapping us there—Nick would stop freaking out, and we could even visit there now and then. I wouldn't have to choose between Nick and my mom.

I tugged the sheets to my chin, making a firm promise to myself: before Nick had a chance to destroy the enchanted ring that clearly terrified him, I was going to stop at nothing to get some answers about it—with his blessing or without.

9

SPLINTERS OF SUNRISE through the cracks in the shutters roused me out of bed without my usual sleepy protests. I was fully charged and springy with excitement for my first road trip across sixteenth-century England.

But when I got outside, the number of people lined up to join us was a shock to the system. It was never going to be a couple's escape, but I hadn't expected literally a thousand people to come along for the ride. From the west gatehouse of Hampton Court Palace, hundreds of carts, wagons, and horses queued noisily outside the slaughterhouses and stables before disappearing into the hunting park. Half the court's residents stood in their traveling cloaks, hastily tying last-minute pieces of furniture, bedding, and wall hangings to their horses and wagons.

I clung to the last corner of warmth inside the gatehouse with my three ladies. Lucinda Parker had arrived back at court the night before, giddily sharing news of Ellie's improvement. I was genuinely relieved that Ellie was okay, and nothing was going to dull my perky mood—not even the memory of Lucinda's lips on my boyfriend's. At this point, I was taking everyone's word for it that lip-locking in an age of widespread disease was inexplicably commonplace.

Bridget was bouncing from heel to heel. "My first royal progress," she sang, already on the lookout for rich hotties.

Alice groaned, separating the tangled chains of the brass pendants she'd made for us to ward off bad air outside the palace. "You may come to loathe the progress, with lodging conditions of every which way and no manner of receiving letters." I felt a pang of guilt over my careless excitement—for Alice, our trip away also meant potentially missing news about her mom's disappearance.

"We shall sleep in great comfort," Lucinda argued cheerfully. "We are so fortunate and blessed to be traveling with our promised queen." She tipped her pearled hood at me, finally acknowledging my station over her. I couldn't decide whether or not her kindness was genuine, but I gave her the benefit of the doubt and returned a cautious smile.

"Come then," said Alice, draping the talismans over our heads. "The king will not wish us to ride on horseback so late in the year. We must find our coach."

The four of us edged through whirs of servants securing rolled-up mattresses and trapped hunting dogs yipping from carts but could see no sign of our carriage. Nick emerged through the chaos, a superstar strutting the red carpet toward us as infatuated courtiers bid him good morning from every angle.

"Good morrow, my lady," he said to me, dropping into an elegant bow.

I'd never acclimatize to the sight of Nicholas the Ironheart bowing to me, nor the impact of Nick Tudor in full finery. He liked the comfort of long pants, but today he'd chosen breeches to impress the nobles with his muscular legs. The silk cloth encasing his hips and chest shone with swirls of pearled white, coconut cream, and pale ivory. A thick cloak of jet-black blanketed one shoulder, the bottom half embroidered with snow-colored seashells. The tongue-in-cheek frown I'd attempted was eaten away by an embarrassingly doting smile. Nevertheless, I fired a teasing shot.

"No one seems to know where we're supposed to be," I said to him, indicating my ladies. "The dogs and puffin birds have carts, but we don't. Should we walk to Windsor?"

Nick chuckled with his unflappable coolness. "You are to travel with my person, Lady Pembroke."

Bridget gasped and fluffed out her skirts. "My glorious lord, will Lady Pembroke's ladies be blessed to join His Majesty's coach?"

Nick's eyes didn't move from mine. "I am afraid not, madam. There is not room in my coach for so many beautiful maidens." They all blushed, and I forced my mind away from Lucinda. "I have appointed the Earl of Warwick as your companion."

Alice's cheeks flushed scarlet at the news that she'd be traveling with Francis Beaumont. She was so obviously smitten with the fiery earl that it made me want to squeal, but she'd made clear that nothing had happened between them at the feast. Something was still holding Alice back, and I intended to find out what.

What snagged my attention the most, however, was that Nick not only avoided Lucinda Parker's gaze, but he turned his back to her, offering me an elbow. "Come, my lady," he said.

"Make way for the king!" cried the guards. My shoulder brushed Nick's bicep as we walked, and he tightened his arm around me.

He led me up the stairs of his coach, which was swathed in blue velvet braided with ropes of gold. Before I could take in the lush interiors, we were already kissing. He reached behind me to tug the curtain closed without separating his mouth from mine, his movements heated and urgent. It was a ridiculously inappropriate time to launch into a make-out session, but common sense and Nick Tudor had become an oxymoron. After our recent rough patch, it felt like he hadn't kissed me in weeks, and he feverishly hooked an arm around my waist and tugged me onto his lap. The shout of a commander near the coach was the wake-up call we both needed. I slipped off Nick and onto the cushioned bench beside him, breathing like I'd just run cross-country.

"Forgive me," he said breathlessly, rubbing his swollen lips. "I grow weary of all this fanfare and never being able to see you without the company of others."

The comment caught me by surprise. I'd thought it was just me who craved for it to be only the two of us.

"The king is ready to depart," Nick called before I could reply. Seconds later, our coach shook to life.

He sat back with his hands on his knees, as accustomed to riding in golden coaches as he was to drinking from fountains of wine. I peeked through the gap in the curtain, watching the stables and kennels shrink away in our trail of dust. The graveled road soon melted into dirt tracks as we rumbled along the river dotted with white swans, the crisp taste of the breeze reminding me how stuffy the palace walls had become. Children in tattered shirts and dresses were jogging alongside us, waving with gap-toothed grins.

"God save the king!" their musical voices shrieked. "Long live the king!" A bunch of boys had gathered a short distance ahead, their woolen caps pressed to their chests. I reached through the curtains to wave at them, hearing their delighted shrieks as the coach rolled on. "Can I open the curtains a bit?" I asked Nick.

"If it pleases you." He unrolled a scroll containing trade updates. We'd been out of Hampton Court less than five minutes, and he already seemed more at ease.

I tugged the curtain apart two inches, aware that any more might put the king at risk on the open roads. Our coachman skillfully negotiated the deeply rutted paths as we bumped through acres of dense forest, harvested meadows sprinkled with grazing cattle, rustic cottages bandaged with vines, and colorful constellations of wildflowers grasping the last weeks of spring.

When the road made a sharp curve at the tip of a small hill, I twisted to check out the hundreds of carts trailing us like an ant colony on the move—visual proof that the King of England would never have a private life. He would always be surrounded by his court, his nobles, or his guards.

I shut the curtain and curled into the crook of Nick's arm. The rhythmic bounce of hooves coupled with the security of him holding me rocked me to sleep within minutes.

I woke to the clanging of church bells and the icy touch of Nick's sparkling rings on my skin as he stroked my chin.

"We have arrived at the castle of Windsor," he said gently.

I sat up with a yawn. "What time is it?"

"Time for dinner, I should expect." He helped me climb down the coach steps into the windy and overcast chill. Dinner was Tudor speak for lunch, so I guessed it was before midday.

"Wow," I said, taking in the sight of the fortress castle with its cylindrical battlement towers that dwarfed us. The damp air warned that rain was imminent. Carts, wagons, and horses formed an impatient line down to the river like a medieval traffic jam, waiting for the king to make his exit.

"My lady," he said, finding my fingers beneath the silky ruffles of his sleeve.

We crossed the drawbridge over the castle ditch and stepped inside the windy stone fortress where honking trumpeters broadcast our arrival.

The arched palace entrances were inscribed with royal emblems and the polished initials *NR*, every servant and courtier greeting the king as if he were an angel arriving from heaven. Noble families trailed us into the palace in order of their rank, hunting for their chambers like a flurry of guests boarding a cruise ship.

Nick and I had lunch alone in his royal apartments before he suggested the two of us take a ride through the village before the rain set in.

"It is time my people set eyes upon the lady who has stolen my heart," he said with a smug smile as we mounted our horses.

After everything that had happened with Norfolk and Wharton, I wasn't holding my breath that the villagers would find me as endearing as Nick did. Still, perhaps they'd appreciate my ordinariness more than the nobles. We set out with only the guards accompanying us, clip-clopping down the dirty hill past wild pigs and rabid-looking dogs that smelled like they were already dead. I covered my nose with my scarf, but Nick turned and shook his head at me, and I let the fabric slip back through my fingers—he didn't want us to offend anyone. Market sellers and butchers scurried out of white stores that were framed with wonky planks of black timber, waving and tossing flowers at us. They couldn't have known that the most fragrant varieties aggravated their king's asthma.

"Lady Pembroke! My lady!" cried boys and girls from the roadside, their mothers protectively holding their grimy hands and beaming at me. The people here already knew who I was—even my name.

"We most heartily thank you," Nick called ahead of me.

"Thank you!" I said to my bizarre new fan base. "Bless you all."

If only they knew you're a teenager from Hampshire County who sucked at history at school—yep, smile and wave, Lady Pembroke.

As we guided our horses over a narrow wooden bridge connecting Windsor to Eton, it hit me why I was on a ticker-tape parade through one of the most populated villages in England. Going on progress wasn't just about making space to prepare for the wedding and coronation—this was a national sales pitch. After Norfolk and Wharton's rejection of me, Nick wanted to ensure my success as his chosen bride by parading me directly before the masses. It seemed he'd listened to Francis.

A cold lash of wind from the river echoed the shiver in my chest. I trusted that Nick had all this handled, but the fact that this 'Emmie exhibition' was necessary left me uneasy.

After a week of late-night parties and hunting expeditions in which I refused to participate, our dog-and-pony show carried on through the bustling villages of Brakenhale, Wokingham, and Reading, where lush, warmed manors were always waiting for us. The farther we got from London, the grungier and more rustic the townships became. Potholes riddled the slushy roads between towns, and our lengthy procession had to grind to a sluggish halt more than once: usually when vagabonds were sighted up ahead.

Rain or shine, Nick insisted on parading me on horseback through every village to the unrelenting clanging of church bells. The commoners clearly idolized their brilliant jewel of a king, but my growing discomfort was becoming harder to hide. Not only did it weigh on me that it was apparently necessary to promote me to the people, but showing off our riches like pompous peacocks before the most impoverished people I'd ever seen made my throat thicken with embarrassment.

"What troubles you?" Nick asked me when our coach neared our next resting place, the village of Ewelme. The coachman skillfully steered our carriage through webs of vines and branches that crowded the narrow road.

"Nothing," I replied, absently playing with the tangled strings on my traveling cloak.

"Speak not falsely," he said calmly, reaching over to free the laces with his deft fingers. "I fear you are suffering a temper. Is it the journey? You are wearied?"

"No, I like being away," I said quickly. I was in no hurry to be locked back at Hampton Court. "It's just that…"

"Yes?" His face became alarmed.

"Everyone here is so poor. Of course, I know that things are different in this century, and it's well known that kings in your time had insane wealth, but…it's a different thing to see it in person. Some of the people out here look like they have nothing."

To his credit, genuine compassion stirred in Nick's face. "The plague spared no mercy in its destruction. Grace be to God, no cases have been reported in many months, or we would not be here."

I nodded, but the emptiness remained. Surely it wasn't just the plague to blame for the decrepit streets, the ramshackle sheep farms falling apart, and the bony children. What responsibility did the Tudor dynasty—did *Nick*—take? I then reminded myself that this was how the world worked back then, and I'd have to get used to it like I had chamber pots and beheadings.

We arrived at Ewelme Manor to greetings from a bumbling Lord and Lady Clifford, each as stout as the other. The manor occupants were evidently terrified of their royal visitors, which I found strangely comforting. For once, I wasn't the only one a bit dazed and confused over the constant, jaw-dropping Tudor splendor and the expectations they carried to behave in a certain way.

The king's chef whipped up a lavish feast, which this time didn't include the welcome company of my ladies. By the eighth course, I was fighting to stay awake, until Nick brought the gentle touch of his lips to my ear.

"Can I come to you this night?" he said.

I glanced up at the affectionate plea in eyes, heat streaking up my spine. He was asking to come and lie with me in my bedchamber. We'd fallen asleep together before, but this invitation felt different. Our uncomfortable chat in the coach had left him nervous, and it wouldn't hurt to reconnect and remind ourselves why we two polar opposites were choosing to make a life together.

"Sure, you can come to my room," I replied softly. My stomach began twisting with yearning flutters.

His heavy thigh leaned against mine, and I sensed that he was about to call it a night when Lord and Lady Clifford began a sweet but dithery presentation of gifts. There were pearl buttons and fur-lined hawking gloves that didn't quite fit for Nick, and a painted comfit box and feathered hat for me.

The king thanked them, rising from his royal seat that had—ridiculously—traveled with us from Hampton Court. I was the next one on my feet, fixated on the image of being horizontal with Nick Tudor in a dark room. He'd already made clear that he didn't believe in being together physically before marriage—not with me, anyway—and I was okay to wait for the big stuff, but still...*kissing*. Lots of kissing.

Lord Clifford bowed. "Your Majesty and Lady Pembroke, receiving your divine persons at our home is an honor most sacred. If it pleases you, may we present an entertainment for the king's pleasure: The tragedy of Phaedra by Seneca."

Nick's mouth shot open, and I squeezed the plush velvet encasing his forearm. "Thank you, my lord and my lady," I said. "We would both love to see it."

I steered my bored boyfriend outside to the central courtyard, where a short platform had been erected out of uneven planks of wood with a row of chairs before it. Nick dropped onto one of the only two seats swathed with cloth of gold, passing me a subtle eye roll as I settled in beside him.

The whole play was gobbledygook to me. Some of the roles appeared to be women, but men played them all, and there was something about lust and beasts and topics that made Nick blush. I spent most of the performance's endless hours forcing my eyelids apart.

By the time I slipped into my bedcovers of blue velvet fringed with silver, the sky was as black as the air was silent. When my ladies quietly retreated from the chamber, I knew that Nick was near. A gentle knock sounded from the door, followed by a guard's hushed announcement: "His Majesty, the King."

Nick crossed the candlelight, looking more like a strapping Greek god than an English monarch.

"My lady," said one of the men who followed him, inviting me to leave the bed so he could plunge his sword through the expensive mattress in search of daggers and other dangers. Yikes, poor Lord and Lady Clifford!

I glided into Nick's arms, feeling his bare muscles beneath the cream silk of his feather-light nightshirt. The moment the guards left, he fell into me, our lips fusing with hungry twists as we kissed our way to the bed.

"I love you truly," he repeatedly whispered as if he couldn't tell me enough times. I echoed every sentiment, and yet it still felt like we couldn't get close enough to each other—couldn't quite reach the tip of where we needed to be.

After hours of sensuous kissing and the electric touch of Nick's hands on me, I slept in the cradle of his arms before a crackling fire, paralyzed by a peace I'd never felt before. We'd rarely slept a whole night together without intending to travel through time. It enveloped me with a feeling of being right where I belonged.

ᴡᴑᴍ   ᴡᴑᴍ   ᴡᴑᴍ

Our procession left an undoubtedly relieved Lord and Lady Clifford at Ewelme and rolled on through the emerald blankets of the Oxfordshire farmlands. Wherever we slept, Nick rose early for days packed with hunting, hawking, and feasting, before he'd sneak into my bedchamber after midnight to avoid any whispers about my virtue. We'd snuggle until the crows of the roosters, and then my boyfriend Nick would become King Nicholas the First again: sought-after, pressured, and somewhere away from my company.

Our relationship had begun in a lightning-fast blaze of secret, stolen moments, but now that I'd spent this much time with Nick, I loved him more than I thought possible. And even though I'd willingly given up my world for him, I'd come to realize that I'd only ever be a small piece of his. The truth of that cut a wound into me that I wasn't sure would ever heal.

10

It was a gloomy Thursday at dusk when our train of carts and wagons rumbled up the lonely hill on which Kenilworth Castle stood. Skirted by a midnight-blue lake known as the Mere, the sandstone fortress cut a romantic, fantasy-like figure from a distance. Our coach rattled across a walled tiltyard over the dam, reaching a small figure waiting within the gaping jaws of the portcullis.

"Christ, she not only stands in a draft but waits openly as if to meet the end of an arrow," said Nick, his eyes flared with disapproval. He climbed down from our coach that'd barely stopped.

He marched toward Kit as if to scold her for hanging about so publicly, and I winced in anticipation. Kit dropped into a regal curtsy, but within seconds the brother and sister were embracing, the sight warming my heart. The medieval monarchs were all pomp and stiffness in the history books, but Nick Tudor was as unreservedly loving as he was hot-blooded...just one of the forty-billion things I loved about him.

"Kit!" I called, as I jumped onto the gravel. I felt the smile light up my face.

"Lady Pembroke, I am greatly pleased to see you," she said

into my side as we hugged informally. Her high-pitched voice gave away her age, though she clearly had Nick's height gene.

The wind off the Mere was bitterly cold, and Kit's new governess, the sour-faced Lady Dormer, hurried us inside. Leaving the rest of the procession queuing down the road to Coventry, we crossed over the castle ditch and paced up the sloping inner courtyard. I'd imagined Kenilworth to be a smaller, cozier place for young Kit's household, but with its gothic web of four-story stone battlement towers, it could've passed for a medieval prison.

Kit led us into the Middle Court, her silk slippers embroidered with Tudor roses pausing at the gateway to the royal apartments. "I beseech you: I wish to come back to court," she blurted to me. Even her voice sounded suffocated. "I miss the king and Francis and everyone." She couldn't get the words out fast enough.

"Oh, Kit, make no burden of our lady most wearied from travel," Nick cut in. "You must remain here to complete your lessons. How is your study of arithmetic coming along?"

"You mean fractions and algebra?" She narrowed her eyes at me, making me giggle. I couldn't stop staring at her. Her adult teeth were finally growing in, maturing her pretty face.

"Kit can bring her tutor to Hampton Court, can't she?" I said, turning to Nick. "Why can't she come and stay there? I'll play with her."

He shot me a look that could cut steel. The message registered beyond any doubt: I was to stay out of it. The way he'd shut me down with a single glance pecked at my mind through our tour of the castle apartments. Kit was about to become my sister-in-law—the only sort-of-sibling I'd ever had. Was I allowed to have no opinion on her, especially when she was unhappy? *Cute Tudor king is starting to become frustrating-as-hell Tudor king.*

After an unsettled sleep, Kit and I caught up over a breakfast of sugared pancakes with apple slices fried in cinnamon and butter. I took my chance to gently grill her about her life at Kenilworth. She said she had plenty of time to paint, and her childish optimism was evidently keeping her spirits buoyed, but I sensed that she was lonely. At least I had more time to spend with her than I thought I would. Nick disappeared for days at a time, hunting, boating on the Mere, or playing tennis with Francis and his guy squad. He adored his little sister to the point of obsession, but as long as she was safe, he didn't want her interfering with his fun.

Throughout our six-day visit, Kit spent her mornings translating complicated devotional texts for her tutor before joining me and my ladies in an open-air terrace swathed with vines and honeysuckle. We'd sit overlooking the knot gardens and sew to a soundtrack of twittering birds in the aviary. I loved me some girl time, but the endless sewing and embroidery were becoming a snore—even with the added novelty of having Kit nearby.

"What news of Francis?" Kit eventually asked me, stitching gold thread into an emblem of a portcullis. "I have scarcely seen his person since your arrival."

Alice's chin sprung up, sending her pin into her fingertip. "Ouch," she griped.

"You should ask Alice," I replied with feigned innocence. "She's the one spending all her time with him."

Kit's heart-shaped face fell. "Will you be his wife?" she said to Alice. Poor Kit had been crushing on Francis for years.

"Heavens no," Alice said with a flush. "We are friends, nothing more."

Lucinda snorted, and I laughed out loud. While on the road, we'd all noticed Alice and Francis hogging each other on the dance floor during the evening feasts. In spite of that, I was sure that Alice and Francis hadn't yet crossed the line from platonic to romantic. Something had her heart locked up in a cage, and I suspected it to be the mystery over her missing mom.

Kit brought her embroidery hoop to her nose, sulking for a

few minutes before she spoke again. "In any case, I am truly pleased you are to marry the king, Lady Pembroke. For I have never seen our good and gracious Majesty more merry than when he is with you…it is a love match most true."

The girls mumbled their agreement—even Lucinda. I hadn't realized until then how much I needed to hear those words. Perhaps it *was* acceptable for kings to marry purely for love in this century. When I tried to reply, however, nothing came out. I hadn't stopped thinking about Nick's icy reaction when I'd merely suggested that Kit come to Hampton Court with us.

After celebrating St. Crispin's Day at Kenilworth, Nick announced it was time to be on our way. Kit said she couldn't bear to watch us leave, and this time, there was no tiny figure waving at us from the tiltyard gatehouse. It wasn't until our coach neared Warwick Castle that the tightening coil of my frustration snapped.

"Why does Kit have to stay at Kenilworth Castle?" I said to Nick, stretching my lower back. The bumpy roads were a fast track to a slipped disc.

He didn't remove his hand from mine, but his fingers stiffened. "Must you ask me that sincerely?"

"Did you see her crying when we left? You've always kept her close to you before. Now she's locked up in a glorified cage, a million miles from anywhere. Will she even be allowed to come to our wedding?"

His penetrating eyes focused on me. "You recall not the occurrences of this midsummer last? Of how my sister was snatched from under my nose not once but twice and nearly slain?"

"Of course I do." Both Kit and I nearly ended up six feet under.

"The only way to keep my sister safe is to put her where no devil may harm her again. The princess has her household and all manner of princely pleasures at Kenilworth. There is no reason for her to feel troubled."

"How about the fact that she's lonely? And that she misses you?"

He had no answer for that, returning his gaze to his bottomless mound of work papers. The lack of response dumped more fuel over my burning irritation.

"Is she going to spend the rest of her life in that castle until you marry her off to an old Frenchman?" I pressed. "Did you even tell her about that deal you struck with the French king?"

"Enough!" Nick snapped, both of us lurching as the coach skidded over a pothole.

"Am *I* going to end up locked inside one of your castles when you eventually get bored of me?" I said to his furrowed profile. "You'll throw the blue-diamond ring into a fire like you suggested and then lock me away forevermore?"

He just sat there for a moment, breathing heavily, before suddenly reaching to pull me into him. He didn't want to fight, and I didn't know where to draw the line on Kit. I was out of my depth on royal life, and she was his sister, but if I didn't stand up for her happiness, who would?

"One day, Emmie, you may come to see my home as something other than a cage," he said grimly. "Perhaps it will be the same day that you learn to trust me."

I didn't know how to reply.

Our next major stop was Northamptonshire, where we were to stay with Alice's dad, Sir Thomas Grey, at their family home. The modest Grey manor was across the street from the parish church and overlooked a noisy paddock of bleating sheep and a pen of hunting dogs.

I'd been freaking out about facing Sir Thomas for days. He'd been the king's right hand until he retired in protest over Nick's decision to jilt the princess of France and marry me instead. When Thomas met us in the entrance hall, however, I realized that I'd wasted hours of my life sweating over the reunion. His pale eyes drew me in with kindness, and time away from the pressures of court appeared to have mellowed the old grouch.

"Good morrow and bless you, Lady Pembroke," he said with a bob of his head. He wiped a handkerchief across his brow.

When I replied with a nervous stammer, Thomas patted my hand. His fingers were ridden with arthritis, and he'd slimmed down since I'd last seen him.

His gaze drifted past my shoulder. "My dear daughter," he said, lurching forward to hug Alice. The sight tugged my chest a little. While I'd have given anything to help Alice get her mom back, she was lucky to have a dad who loved her so openly. Everyone in this world believed my dad was dead, and he may as well have been—even if he had been living in the same century.

Another girl stepped into the chamber, a smaller version of Alice, but more mature in the face.

"Violet!" Alice cried before halting at the sight of her older sister's red-rimmed eyes. She put her arm around a sniffling Violet and led her away.

Before I could find out why Alice's sister was in tears, I had to partake in a formal meet-and-greet with a handful of rich, tedious men from the county. Ugh. I itched to get to my room and see if everything was okay. What if Alice's mom had turned up dead? But surely Thomas would've appeared more upset if his wife's body had been found.

When I'd sufficiently impressed the nobles, I was shown to a small chamber adorned with expensive tapestries. My ladies stood gathered around Violet Grey.

Alice spun toward me. "Emmie, may my sister join your household and come to court with us?"

Violet dropped to her knees, her faded satin skirts crushing into the floorboards.

"Dearest Lady Pembroke," she said, her eyes at my feet. "I beseech you to forgive my sorrow on this most merry occasion. It is because I have suffered a great loss. These past weeks, my husband was struck with smallpox and has gone to God. Be assured, I am void of any illness and would be not in your gracious presence if there was any danger of it."

"Oh no," I said, my hand clasped over my stomach in alarm. The mortality rate in Tudor England was enough to send anyone running for the hills. I helped Violet to her feet and guided her to sit on the edge of the bed. "I'm *so* sorry to hear that. Of course, you can come and join us. Please just ask me if there's anything you need."

Violet cupped my hands with gratitude, blinking fast like she was trying to block tears.

"Bless you, Emmie," said Alice.

Despite the bleak start, the feast that Thomas Grey hosted that night was hands-down the yummiest of the trip—even Violet joined us in her mourning gown. By all accounts, Francis Beaumont was doing fine as the king's new right hand, but when the men launched into a political discussion, Thomas offered nuggets of wisdom that sent impressed murmurs rippling around the table. There was no doubt that Alice's dad was a genius, and when Nick commented that he wished Sir Thomas would return to his side, awkward silence swept the space. I'd been around the king long enough to know that could be taken as a formal command. Thomas's cheeks, strawberry-pink from drinking floods of wine, turned chalk-white.

"My father is most merry in the countryside, Your Majesty," Alice said carefully, capturing every eye in the room. "Who would tend to the village sheep, should he return to court?"

Everyone laughed except Francis, who tossed back his last inch of wine.

When Nick squeezed Thomas's shoulder and suggested they discuss the Spanish threats in private, I glanced at Francis. Jet-black curls hung over his face as he looked away, humiliated by the king who also happened to be his best mate. When Nick and Thomas withdrew to the drawing-room without inviting Francis, the earl blasted his way out the back door before they'd made their exit—a classic Lord Warwick tantrum. I sympathized with Francis; Sir Thomas Grey not only cast a long shadow, but from what I could remember, he also enjoyed criticizing the impulsive earl.

Alice excused herself to follow Francis, but Violet was already slipping through the archway. Alice's surprise gave way to a look of distress. I understood why; When Alice and Violet were kids growing up at court, they'd shared Francis as a best friend. Violet soon fell in love with Francis, and he proposed to Violet before abruptly dumping her. He only did that because he secretly desired Alice, but the three of them had never sorted out this triangle. Now Violet was single again, but in the meantime, Alice had also fallen for the dashing earl.

"Want to go outside?" I said to her. "I'd like to see your dad's gardens before it gets dark."

"The gardens belong to my mother, and Father merely tends to them in the hope for her short return," she said a little faintly, but she led me outside to the inner courtyard. Our square heels clopped along the cobblestones as we cut through an archway leading to the walled garden.

Francis and Violet were sitting a stone bench several yards away, their legs so close together that her skirts bunched into his breeches.

"Perhaps wasted hope is a Grey family custom," Alice said to me with a sigh.

"You must be thrilled to see Violet," I said, lightly knocking her leg with mine. "I can't even imagine what she's gone through. You're not going to let Francis get in between you two, are you?"

Francis's jaw jerked toward us. He slid away from Violet faster than we could blink.

"We wished to inquire whether you are well, Lord Warwick," Alice said stiffly. "You took leave of my father's feast so rudely, and as his house guest, no less."

"Did your father not take leave of his own banquet so rudely?" Francis replied, crossing his arms. *"No less?"*

Alice huffed. "Why is your every intention to vex me? I pray to God that we return to larger grounds in haste."

He paced toward her. "That is plainly absurd, given you have not wished to leave my side since Windsor!"

Alice made an 'as if' snort. "And yet, here you are, with your lecherous manner toward my sister, who is in mourning. After you shamed her once already!"

Francis stepped so closely to Alice that they shared the same breath. "Who says I am lecherous! Madam, you offend me as if it is a sport. I will suffer it no longer."

"I will pray for it, then," she snapped. Had he leaned forward an inch, his mouth would've met hers.

"I beseech you both!" said Violet, stepping between them with her arms splayed.

As she launched into an appeal for a ceasefire, I caught sight of a mess so unseemly for a Tudor manor that I zoned out. Edging the pristine garden was a chaotic mound of decaying wicker baskets, tattered saddles, broken wagon wheels, and other junk spilling onto the cobblestones. When I moved closer, I realized it was surplus clutter from a barn so stuffed with crap that you couldn't see into the windows.

"Emmie!" Alice called behind me. "I bid you stay away from that unsightly serpent's nest; there are many dangers."

"What is all this?" I said, the haphazard jumble of broken ladders and planks of wood evoking a memory that felt light-years away.

"Our mother's things," Violet replied in a weak voice. "I have bid Father to be rid of them many a time."

Alice moved beside me. "Father fears that our mother may one day return and feel a stranger without them. It troubled her heart to be rid of anything, but this is plainly a burden."

Blood rushed to my face, leaving me lightheaded. Only a classic hoarder could have this much garbage piled up at home. A hoarder like Jane Stuart—the eccentric lady who'd once lived on Bayberry Street in Hatfield, back in my time. Her garden had been a scrapheap of hoarder's junk, which was where I found the time-traveling ring that brought me to this century in the first place. A cursed ring that was created in Tudor England and last seen with Alice's mother, Susanna Grey, before it ended up in my world.

It just had to be.

I spun toward Alice's face. Her caramel eyes were set with an almost permanent frown—the evidence of too many years of worry and uncertainty. Past her shoulder stood Violet—Susanna's other daughter—who'd lost not only a mother but now a husband.

"Is something amiss, Lady Pembroke?" said Francis, stepping forward.

"I'm okay," I said, short of breath. This family had been through too much suffering.

As I zeroed in on Alice's worn face, I made her a silent promise: I was going to go back to my time to find Jane Stuart and figure out if she really was the missing Susanna Grey.

And if she was, I would bring Alice's mom home.

11

IN THE FEW days we spent in Northamptonshire, I got to know Violet a bit better, who was endlessly polite and unassuming. It felt like a mean thought, but I could see why Violet never had a shot with Francis while Alice was around. Alice was as sharp, witty, and charismatic as Violet was naïve, serious, and hard to make compelling conversation with. I felt for Francis, who'd blown up the romantic headway he'd made with Alice by merely sitting beside Violet on a bench.

When I gently reminded Alice that I was sure that Francis had feelings for her instead of her sister, she insisted that she only cared that he didn't hurt Violet again. I hoped that she wasn't sacrificing her own happiness out of some misguided theory that Francis could be the one to restore Violet's heart—that'd be a classic Alice Grey move.

There was no chance to talk to Nick about any of it. He'd spent days locked in council meetings until the early hours and had stopped visiting me late at night. When our procession departed for Buckinghamshire, I was downgraded from the king's coach to the one housing my handmaidens so Nick could sit with Francis and talk shop. At first, I thought the king was pissed with me about the Kit disagreement, but all his councilors sported the same dazed gazes and unshaven edginess. Something grave had happened, and I prayed it wasn't more war threats from the Spanish.

When Nick's coach ahead of ours made a squeaky turn toward the town of Aylesbury, my stomach clenched. Bridget's cousin, the soothsayer Agnes Nightingale, lived in Aylesbury. Now that I wanted to go back to my time and find out if Jane Stuart was really Susanna Grey, I felt more determined than ever to get some answers about the blue-diamond ring that was still carefully locked inside my traveling chest.

Peasants jogged alongside our coach as it lumbered through the gates guarding the township. Guards used their pikes to block beggars from entering as we were eaten up by swarms of spectators scrambling for a rare sighting of their king. Bored babies fussed on the shoulders of men in tattered hats, while mothers gripped the grubby hands of little girls in tiny coifs. I considered unclipping my pearl earrings and tossing them down to a scrawny street urchin who beamed up at me, but I was worried she'd get trampled for them.

Right after we'd checked into our chambers at Aylesbury Manor, my shoulders slumped at the sight of Nick already behind closed doors in another meeting. For all I knew, we could be torn out of Aylesbury by morning to attend to whatever was troubling the realm. If I was going to try to find Agnes Nightingale, I had no time to lose.

The stifling air in my modest dining chamber was laden with pungent smells from our supper of mutton soup, fried beans, fritters, and aged cheese tarts. Alice, Bridget, Lucinda, and Violet chatted cheerfully while I silently fretted whether to ask them about Agnes or attempt to see the soothsayer on my own. Witchcraft was illegal in Tudor times, and Bridget had spared no mercy when sharing her opinions about her heretic cousin. Even worse

—what if involving Alice or Bridget got them into trouble? Before I risked that, I had to at least try on my own. As for Nick, I could think of a million reasons why I needed to leave him out of this...not least of which was because he'd wanted to toss the enchanted ring into a fire.

The incoming winter had brought some luck by steering in an early nightfall. With the blue-diamond ring securely on my thumb, I told Alice that I was going to see the king, making clear that we weren't to be disturbed. I hated giving her orders, watching her curtsy like a lackey, but I needed to be sure that no one would come and look for me.

In the unlit corner of the corridor outside our chambers, I threw on an unadorned traveling cloak. Draping the hood over my hair and keeping my head low, I waited for the patrolling guards to disappear around the corner and hurried in the opposite direction to the rear staircase that led to the buttery and pantries. The downstairs walls were plain brick instead of expensively paneled with linenfold, confirming that I'd reached the servants' zone.

Getting past the rear door guard was straightforward—none of us were under lock and key, and plenty of nobles came and went from the manor, visiting friends or conducting business in the village. To be safe, however, I kept my head bowed beneath my hood and gave the guard the name "Mistress Grey", mentally apologizing to Alice for stealing her identity for a night. I wasn't planning to get into any trouble, but I didn't need the guard alerting the overprotective king that his fiancée was heading out on the town.

I stepped outside into the frigid night air, my embroidered boots scuffing the gravel as I hurried along the narrow roadside, past wild pigs sloshing in the open drains. I pulled the cloak over my nose to block the stench of sewage and continued down the muddy street, careful not to slip.

When I reached the dim glow of a lantern marking the

entrance to an alehouse, I halted, my throat tightening with fear. I considered turning back to the warmth and safety of the manor, but instead, I pushed open the rickety wooden door, my palms slick with sweat.

Inside the dingy alehouse, hard-faced men huddled over flagons of ale. They watched me as I crossed the earthen floor over a sleeping dog, looking for a bar, but there were only self-service barrels of ale. I caught the eye of a skinny man clearing empty mugs.

"Thy a pretty thing to be out late," he said to me, his lean jaw overwhelmed by a thick blonde beard.

I licked my lips, but they stayed bone dry. "I'm looking for a lady that lives in this town. Her name is Agnes Nightingale."

His bushy brows met in the middle. "I want no trouble here, madam."

"No trouble…I just want to see Mistress Nightingale. Do you know who she is?"

"What doth thee accuse me of?" He stepped back, his gaze roaming down my cloak to the embroidered tips of my costly boots. "Thee be here with the king? Raif!" he called, and a gorilla-sized fellow stepped out of the shadows. "This mistress be maketh trouble. Lookin' for Mistress Nightingale. Best she be on her way."

The bouncer took my arm and walked me to the door like a dog on a leash. My cloak slipped off my head, and a drunk guy whooped at my pearled hood. "Please," I said to the doorman, "I need to find Agnes Nightingale tonight!"

"Thee shall find her in the market square," he said, shoving me into bitingly cold air. The door banged shut behind me, and I darted away from it like ghosts were chasing me. The few crumbling lanterns that actually worked barely lit the street. I hurried farther from the manor until the tangle of black-and-white buildings widened into an uncluttered space that I assumed was the market square. I'd heard of witches leaving markings outside their residences, and I hastened along a row of small doorways, searching for unusual motifs, hanging talismans, or any other signs of black magic. I leaned in to examine a scribble of graffiti on a door when a mangy dog lurched at me through an open window, barking loudly enough to wake my mom in the twenty-first century.

Spinning to escape the alarm the dog raised, I found myself facing the silhouette of a figure hanging by the neck from a wooden frame. My feet dragged me closer in spite of my hammering chest. A young woman dangled from a noose in the dark, her pale face swelled to distortion, her brassy-red curls the only shade of color left in her lifeless body. A picture of a flower within a circle had been scratched into one of her cheeks, leaving streaks of dried blood. The girl hung there in the cold, broken and brutalized, and no one had cut her down.

I backed away, stumbling into a thin figure in a tawny-brown cape. I shrieked, but it was a gentle-faced woman who removed her hood, her startled expression mirroring mine. She smelled like moldy herbs and vegetables.

"They took my daughter," she said to me. "My daughter, they…they took her and they…" Her prominent chin pointed toward the hanged woman. "They hath said it was allowed, that she would not be…you see, they took my daughter."

"I'm so sorry," I stammered. "This is your daughter?" I motioned to the pallid corpse. "Who took her?"

"The king. The King's Majesty. My daughter maketh her dinner this day, and they…they took her."

"The *king* took her?"

"The king's men…the king's men."

"Why?" I cried. Nick couldn't have done this. "Who's your daughter?" *What did she do to deserve this?*

"Mistress Nightingale," the woman replied, gazing over the

girl's body like it was a sculpture she was considering. "They took my daughter."

"*Agnes* Nightingale?"

She nodded. "The king is here, you see…and they took Agnes. They took my daughter."

I should've done something to help the poor mother, but a thousand bricks crushed my chest as I turned back toward Aylesbury Manor, striding toward it with a fury that could've set the whole universe on fire.

He'd *killed* her. I'd been clear to Nick that I wanted to visit Agnes Nightingale—to find out what I could about the blue-diamond ring—and he'd killed her without even talking to me about it first.

I couldn't get up the manor stairs fast enough. I marched through the king's chambers and into the oak gallery, pushing through a luxurious curtain of purple velvet.

Expecting to find Nick engaged in another meeting, I halted mid-stride. He was alone, strumming his lute in a straight-backed wooden chair. His linen shirt was loose and untied, his hair unkempt. Moonlight lit up the blue illustrations in the magnificent stained-glass window behind him.

"You come to complain of my distance," he said without looking at me. "Forgive me. I have been well occupied with matters of importance."

"I just went to see Agnes Nightingale," I replied flatly. There would be no sugarcoating this. Nick gaped up at me as I continued speaking. "I wanted to ask her about the cursed ring, as I told you already. I know you didn't want me to, but it's something I needed to know, and I'm a grown woman, so I went. I found Mistress Nightingale hanging from a rope in the market square. Her mom was there, too shocked to speak properly, but she said that the king did it…that the king's guards came and took her daughter away." I stepped forward as if being nearer to Nick would draw out the truth. "Did you have Agnes Nightingale hanged today?"

For a painfully long moment, he just sat there, blinking at me. When he finally spoke, his voice was stiff. "You would do well not to pursue these discussions, Emmie. You will not question my deeds, nor will you speak to me on matters of business. As for you taking leave in the dead of night, in Aylesbury of all places—"

"So you did do it! You executed Agnes Nightingale, just like you probably killed Norfolk, Wharton, and all those councilors that no one has spoken of since!" I turned away, dropping my face into my hands as I crumpled inside. The stark silence of Nick sitting behind me—doing nothing to console me or to tell me I was wrong—swallowed me whole. The thought came so fast and violently that it sliced right through me: *This relationship is never going to work. We're just too different.*

"Emmeline, look at me," he said, but I refused. "Agnes Nightingale was a known heretic who does the work of the devil," he said evenly. "You may feel otherwise, but in this realm, that is an act of treason against God."

I spun back to face him. "Tell me the truth, Nick. You killed Agnes so I could never prove that the enchanted ring is safe to use and that I'd be forced to never leave this place again."

"Speak not for me!" he snapped, before glaring at a guard who popped his head through the curtain. The guard quickly disappeared, and Nick leaned toward me. "Here is the truth you seek: A villager here made a claim that Mistress Nightingale threatened his person. Days after, the man's daughter died of no known cause. The witch was then justly tried, and judgment passed upon her. When she refused to give penance, I had her die by the rope, rather than the fire. That I did for you, knowing how you despise prolonged death. Yet you remain not gladdened."

I shook my head. "For me? God, Nick, who *are* you?"

Frustration rippled across his brow. "If you do not know that by now, then I am not sure you will ever. Christ, nothing is ever enough for you, Emmie—you wish for only a world and a set of rules that I cannot provide."

I didn't reply, and the room turned silent—the sort of unbearable stillness that I'd only known in the Tudor period. I'd expected Nick to shout at me—perhaps kick something like a petulant child—but he just sat there with his head in his hands.

"Are you okay?" I eventually mumbled. Guilt grabbed me by the throat. All this time, I hadn't considered what my brazen, modernistic views might do to this sixteenth-century king; how they might make him question his own worth and place in the world. Part of Nick's job was to execute people convicted of heresy, and I was laying the guilt trip on thick like he was the criminal.

None of it changed the fact that he'd just had a young girl killed—and one that he knew I'd wanted to see.

"I'm going to bed," I said, my voice hoarse with exhaustion. "You better take some deep breaths, so you don't kick off your asthma."

He nodded, wiping an eye with the heel of his hand. I spun away as fast as I could. I couldn't bear to see him cry. I also didn't want to run into the arms of an executioner. With fists at my side, fighting the urge to turn back, I headed to my chamber and crept over my sleeping ladies and into the bed.

Bridget received word of her cousin's death at first light. I gave her the morning off, wanting her to sleep and not have to think about mindless things like my hair and makeup, but she staunchly refused. The last thing Bridget wanted was to be seen grieving over a dissident, but I could tell she was shaken up. Before we could chat about it any further, the king ordered all the courtiers staying at Aylesbury Manor into the Great Hall after breakfast.

Nick emerged in head-to-toe Tudor glamor, and I questioned whether he was making a point to me that he was still brilliant and beautiful. Gemstones glittered from the intertwined serpents stitched into his jade-green doublet as he announced that we were all to head back to Hampton Court as fast as possible. The French king had soured on the alliance, and—fueled by Spanish support—the Catholic Viceroy of Ireland was now raising an army in the north of England.

Gasps rumbled through the hall, including mine. Nick wouldn't look at me, but I studied his drained face. This was what all the meetings had been about. A Catholic rebellion was looming, with troops already on English soil. I nearly bit through my lip. Was this also because of our marriage?

Not surprisingly, I wasn't invited into the king's coach for the ride home. We made one stop overnight in Hertfordshire, where I didn't even see Nick. By the time we reached the lofty redbrick turrets of Hampton Court Palace, the courtiers were yawning and dragging their feet. Nobles hurried away to the heat of their lodgings, leaving me standing in a windy courtyard, searching for the king. Things felt so unfinished between us. But Nick never appeared.

I returned to my rooms with the girls, grateful for Violet's infectious enthusiasm at lodging in a royal apartment at one of the king's palaces. After we'd all washed, we sat around nibbling cheesecake and macarons. I collapsed into freshly cleaned sheets and didn't move the entire night.

After a long and dreamless sleep, something soft stirred my arm. My eyes fluttered open, before sinking closed again. A soft pat roused me again, and I sluggishly rolled over to meet the source. Nick's angelic face watched me from where he sat on the bed.

"A good morrow to you," he said tightly.

I elbowed my way to sit up, too stunned to consider my bed hair. "What are you doing here?" The pinkish light piercing the shutters had me guessing it was nearly sunrise.

He rubbed his neck, releasing a gentle waft of roses. "The

hour is early; forgive me. I wished not to depart without bidding you farewell, but I cannot delay any longer."

"What are you talking about?" I registered Nick's traveling cloak and the leather gloves resting in the upturned flat cap beside him.

"I must journey to Lancashire to demonstrate support for my troops and to prevent more idiots giving heed to the Irish savages."

I couldn't move nor breathe. The agitation polluting the air we shared had spread like venom, and now Nick was off to a battleground. He might never come back.

"Emmie, I feel this parting may do us good," he said grimly, unable to look at me. "I shall be gone weeks, and it would be a favorable time for you to call upon your conscience and decide whether you trust me…whether you wish to live in a place of war and the necessary protection of princesses…and, perhaps mostly, whether you wish to love a king bound by his duty to punish heretics who refuse their penance."

I waited for my brimming tears to spill onto the sheets. His words were so hard to hear, but he was spot on. I'd been trying so hard to adjust to my new role in this place, but lately I was falling apart, and the Agnes Nightingale incident had been a particularly low point.

"You have to understand that all this has been a massive change for me," I said through a choked voice. "I know that you want me to be happy here, and I *am*—most of the time—but there's a lot to get used to. Frankly, I find the idea of becoming the queen in this place beyond terrifying, and it's not why I wanted to marry you. You have to give me time to adjust to it all. It's not fair to be angry at me when things freak me out—like hanging girls who aren't much older than me."

He slumped forward, looking so tired. "I wish not to beseech you, and I understand the burden of what you have lost, and of what you must now become accustomed. However, Emmie, I must know that I have your hand in marriage most resolutely, for any change of heart—once too late—could bring the Tudor name to ruin."

Tears dripped down my linen nightgown as I tried to unravel my knot of thoughts. While I'd given up my world to be with Nick, he'd also risked his kingdom to marry an unknown like me. I understood why he wanted total reassurance that I could handle it. This was the furthest thing from a normal relationship, and there was more than our hearts at stake.

When I didn't reply, Nick stood up, his eyes glittering with a film of tears he obviously didn't want me to see. "I must take my leave. I am afraid there is no time to spare." He grabbed his hat and gloves.

A robin's piercing cry through the window shook me to sense.

"Nick, I've been meaning to tell you something," I said, chasing after him. He paused near the doors. I quickly filled him in on what I'd discovered at Alice Grey's home…how I believed that her missing mother was living in my time and utterly lost. I left out the fact that Susanna Grey was allegedly once a spy who conspired with Mary, Queen of Scots to destroy King Nick. The Jane Stuart I knew was old, frail, and demented. I could barely imagine her buying a carton of milk, let alone plotting a king's demise. Instead, I reminded Nick that Susanna Grey had a family here and that we both knew what it was like to lose people.

I didn't tell him that a part of me hungered to get back to my home just to give my mind a break from all this.

"What are you saying?" he said, his brows pinched.

"I'm saying that I want to go home for a little bit." Fear seeped into Nick's expression as I continued. "While you head up to the north, I want to go back to my time and find Jane Stuart. If she really is Susanna Grey, I want to bring her back here to where she belongs. Nick, I *will* come back."

Our watery eyes locked together, the conversation silent but clear. We loved each other enough to get this far, but we'd become lost somewhere. We both needed time in our own corners to think, and we had to stop pretending this relationship was working. My chest felt gouged out and torn to pieces.

Bridget Nightingale pushed through the doors holding a fire poker, gasping at the sight of the king. She struggled to lug one of the doors shut, apologizing over and over.

"Leave it," Nick said, and Bridget dropped the heavy iron handle, stumbling. Through the archway, I could hear the rest of my ladies frantically shuffling around.

"My lady Pembroke," Nick said loudly. "I heartily wish you a fine journey home to Worthing and look forward to your short return. Release your conscience from your burdens and look to the light of your kin, so desired and loved by you." Alice was peering at us through the gap in the doors. "I pray you to be merry, and bid you farewell, my love most true," Nick finished, his voice slipping.

Another smooth bow, and then he left, blending into a group of waiting attendants so rapidly that my ladies didn't bother scrambling for their dresses. Through the leaded window, I watched him stride across the courtyard without so much as a backward glance and wrestled away an urge to weep.

"We are to travel to Sussex, my lady?" said Lucinda.

"I do take pleasure in the seaside," added Bridget. After her cousin's execution, she brightened at talk of another getaway.

I could barely speak. "Actually, I'm just going on my own."

"Oh?" said Alice.

"It's been arranged with the king," I added, looking right through her face. Lying to Alice never failed to make me feel hideous. I ached to share the news with her that I may have found her mom, but I gave away nothing. "It'll be a short trip and easier if I go by myself...the guards will keep me safe. You girls have a nice rest. Sleep in, read poems, have parties. But first, I need a bit more sleep."

I offered them a brave smile and backed away, heaving my

bedchamber doors closed. I unlocked my jewelry coffer and slid the blue-diamond ring onto my thumb, sickened by how things had ended with Nick. He'd made it clear that I had his blessing to go back home, but I hadn't had a chance to ask him how he *felt* about it. At the same time, he was heading off to a war zone in the era of swords and cannons.

The image of Agnes Nightingale attacked my vision, her limp body, her dead, bloodshot eyes.

My chest sank. Nick didn't just sanction my trip home so I could potentially help Alice's mom. He wanted me to have another think about where I wanted to be. His heartfelt proposal had happened so fast that only now was he giving me time to decide once and for all if I really wanted all this. If I loved him enough—Tudor king and all—for it to be worth it.

I bid you farewell, my love most true.

Was this the end?

The chilling thought chased me back into bed. I wrapped the covers around me like animal fur. My eyes fell closed, burning for more sleep, but my chest was a raging cyclone. When Alice checked on me a short while later, I pretended to be asleep. She felt my forehead before stoking the fire back to life. A minute later, I heard all the girls departing for chapel.

A vision struck me of Nick's infectious smile and the boyish flush of love that softened his eyes whenever he kissed me. The thought of never seeing him again sent me deeper into the bed until the blanket was right over my head. I shut my eyes inside the cave. I couldn't bear the confusion anymore, the heartache.

Sleep blew in with ease, but I'd forgotten how frustrating the enchanted ring had become—I woke up still in my Hampton Court bedchamber. I tossed and turned, kicked the covers off, pulled them back on, and sat up for a drink of water. I rolled onto my side, meeting a majestic portrait of Nick hanging on the wall. It speared my heart, and I flopped over to face the other way.

When the restlessness passed, I snoozed a little more before a raspy, man's snore penetrated the silence. I rolled over, instinctively searching for Nick's dark auburn curls, but the middle-aged body beside mine had silvery hair, pockmarked skin, and a tiny nose with a curved tip.

I kicked my way out of the polyester comforter, stifling a scream.

1 2

I HAD TO BE DREAMING, hallucinating—anything. My *dad* lay beside me in my bed in twenty-first-century Hatfield, a man I hadn't set eyes on in the better part of a year. I thanked the stars that I was on top of the covers and he was beneath them.

I pivoted off the bed as Dad rolled over, blinking at me through eyes still hooded with sleep. He looked older then I remembered and thicker in the jaw.

"Emmeline?" he said, his mouth a stunned hole. He elbowed his way upright. "Carol!"

"Mom!" I added, rubbing my eyes again like he might disappear. Through all of my traveling back and forth through time, I'd come to know when something bizarre was really happening and when it was a dream. This was legit.

Feet thundered up the stairs, and Mom appeared in her bathrobe, her wiry blonde hair flying in all directions. Ruby scampered over to me, her wagging tail a whir of silver.

"You're back," Mom said to me. "Did you…" She breathed at Dad. "How did you…"

He slid his bare feet onto the frayed carpet, revealing loose cotton shorts, an old university T-shirt, and a round belly. "I'm confused. You said that Emmeline was missing again."

"She was, I…" Mom couldn't speak right, and I felt responsible.

"I *wasn't* missing," I clarified in my Tudor nightdress. Dad gawked at me, but mostly at my face. "I told you that I was in Tudor England," I said to Mom. "Even though you'll never believe me, it's where I was, and I'm not going to lie about it anymore."

Dad scratched his upper back, the side of his nose, and his forearms. It wasn't bed bugs; he'd just never been comfortable in our family. What was Mom thinking when she invited him to stay over?

"Where is your special friend Nick?" she asked me in an apprehensive voice.

"He's back in his time," I replied like that was normal. "The Catholics are planning a rebellion, so he traveled to the north to deal with it. I thought I'd pop home in the meantime."

I fought the urge to burst into raucous laughter. If I wasn't careful, Mom or Dad could have me locked up. They both stood and gaped at me.

"Do you still have your key?" Mom said. "I didn't hear you come in."

"You know that's not how I got here." I sank into the edge of the creaky bed and yawned. I never slept well during a trip through time. "What are you doing here?" I asked Dad in a small voice.

"I told him you'd disappeared again, so he came over," Mom cut in. "We called Paul and Livvy in England to see if they'd heard from you, given this whole British obsession."

Paul was Dad's cousin from Clacton-on-Sea. We'd stayed with him and his wife Olivia back when we lived in England, which felt like a thousand years ago.

"I'd had a bit too much wine to drive," Dad added quickly, his cheeks tinting pink. We both knew that Mom's stalker tendencies didn't need to be encouraged. Instead of escaping home to his girlfriend, though, Dad asked Mom if she could leave us alone for a few minutes. "I'd like to have a talk with Emmeline."

"Oh, okay. I'll finish making tea," she said, a decades-old infatuation still visible in her eyes.

Ugh, Mom.

When she left, Dad flopped into my squeaky desk chair. "I bet you didn't expect to see me in your bed."

"I don't really expect to see you period."

He slumped lower into the chair and crossed his arms. "Your mother has been worried about you. For her to even call and ask for my help, I knew it had to be serious."

I decided to ignore that one. "Did you expect time travel to Tudor England?" I replied lightly, hugging my knees. I was just so over faking everything.

Dad puffed. "It's because of me, isn't it? We don't see each other enough, so you've concocted an absurd history story because you know I admire history." He wasn't smiling, but his eyes twinkled like he'd guessed the stumper in Jeopardy.

The laughter finally arrived, straight from my mouth to Dad's face. "Are you even serious?" I said. "You think I'd go through all this because of you? Just to entice you the eleven miles it'd take for you to visit me once in a freaking while?"

His whole body stiffened. "How could I visit you at this house? Do you know your mother once sent Nina threatening letters?"

"Oh please, do you think I give a toss what your teenage girlfriend thinks?"

"Do not speak to me like that!" Flecks of green blazed through his amber-colored eyes, reminding me of Nick when he was fired up.

More stairs thundered before Mom burst in again. "Is everything alright?" she said.

Dad stood up, snatching his jeans and shirt from the back of the chair. "It seems that Emmeline is back and healthy, which is the most important thing, but I need not sit around and listen to abuse."

"Abuse?" I countered.

My lips pressed together as if it might stop the pressure of my welling tears. This was so classic Dad...to make it all about him. I felt bad about insulting his girlfriend—who was in her twenties and definitely not a teenager—but he needed to take some responsibility.

"Marty," Mom pleaded as he marched to the bathroom and shut the door.

She shot me a fed-up look like this was all my fault, which was ridiculous. Dad throwing a hissy fit over something selfish...Mom acting like she had any power to soothe him—it was all too familiar. I'd seen the same thing a hundred times before Dad left us.

"Why did you even call him?" I said, striding past her to the stairs. I needed water and something to eat that wasn't a roasted animal drenched in rich sauces.

"I called him because you've been acting like a complete lunatic," she replied, following me downstairs to the kitchen. "All this nonsense about time travel disappearing tricks...sneaking away while I wasn't looking and pretending you're some magical fairy."

There were two mugs on the counter and an open packet of chocolate cookies. Dad could only drink tea with something sweet in his hand, even if it was early in the morning. I couldn't help but think my 'lunacy' was the excuse Mom had been waiting for to draw him back into her life. She'd even stocked the cupboards with actual food.

She flicked the lever on the electric kettle and watched me pour myself a bowl of cinnamon crunch. I'd forgotten the euphoric taste of sugary cereal. Yet, while it filled the hole in my stomach, it didn't touch the one in my heart. Had Nick arrived in the north yet? Was he in danger? Was he already missing me, too?

"Your college sent a letter," Mom said flatly, reaching to dig out an envelope from a pile of bills. The 'UAL, Central Saint Martins' logo was stamped in the corner.

It had already been opened, and I fished out the letter, my tummy clenching. It was an approval to defer my first year in the Bachelor of Arts in Jewellery Design course. All the letter needed was my signature and it'd be a done deal.

"A deferral?" I said with confusion, scanning the note for more information.

Mom poured steaming water into her chipped mug. "I spoke to them a few weeks ago about the health challenges you've been facing and convinced them to arrange a deferral for one year. If you sign the form, I can send it back to them."

I stared at her and then again at the letter. A tight coil in my chest that I hadn't even realized was there snapped free. Studying jewelry design at Central Saint Martins had been my dream before Nick Tudor popped onto the scene and derailed me with his invitation to become a sixteenth-century queen.

"You're welcome," Mom said as I grabbed a pen and signed the form. I couldn't see myself ending up at Central Saint Martins now, but a deferral felt less depressing than being kicked out altogether.

I thanked her, and we sat in silence for a while. "Have you heard from Mia?" I eventually asked. Mia Fairbanks had been my best friend in Hatfield, but now she lived on campus at MIT in Cambridge.

"Heard from her?" Mom said, brows lifting. "I must have called her twenty times in the last few months. She's always been polite, but I don't think she's happy with you. Like me, she thought the worst until you came home a few weeks ago. I told her you'd run off with your boyfriend, Nick."

My eyes bulged. "Did you tell her about the Tudor stuff?"

"Don't be ridiculous. I don't think I'd get the words out without laughing. Or crying."

A door opened upstairs, and Mom pressed the boil button on the kettle again before spooning sugar into Dad's mug. I scooped up Ruby for a cuddle and rubbed my cheek against her wriggly fur. It'd be so easy to just stay here for the weekend—to watch television and cuddle Ruby and eat a whole packet of tortilla chips.

But that wasn't why I was here. "Mom, can I borrow your phone?" I said.

"Sure." She sprang up to grab it, obviously glad for my interest in something un-historical.

I took the phone upstairs to my bedroom, passing Dad on the stairs.

"I was just coming down to see you," he said in a tight voice. I could tell he felt guilty about storming out.

"I'll be down in a minute," I replied, offering him a slight, peacemaking smile before slipping into my bedroom and shutting the door.

The last I'd heard about the old hoarder Jane Stuart was that she'd been taken to a Boston hospital for psychiatric evaluation. There was more than one hospital in Boston that handled that stuff, but I'd start with the biggest: Massachusetts General Hospital. Nerves tickled my stomach as I dialed the number.

The lady on the phone from the psychiatry unit was rude but helpful. Her fingernails clicked the keyboard as she looked up the name Jane Stuart. There were two in the system, but the last Jane Stuart had been admitted in June and then transferred to the Cedar Lake Rest Home. She hung up before she could tell me anything else, like how likely it was that Jane would still be at Cedar Lake. Still, I was lucky that this was turning out to be pretty straightforward.

The Cedar Lake Rest Home was in Newton in suburban

Boston, but when I called them, they refused to give me information about any residents unless I was a family member.

Jane Stuart's family is in the sixteenth century dancing the freaking volta! I wanted to shout. Perhaps I'd have more luck if I showed up in person.

Using Mom's travel app, I worked out that I needed to get a bus from Amherst to Boston, and then another bus to Newton. I changed into the same jeans and sweatshirt that I wore last time I was here with Nick, suppressing the twinge of pain that memory drew. Despite all the drama, I wished he was here with me.

After pocketing my phone and a charger, I sneaked two sleeping pills out of Mom's canister, slipping them into my pocket with the eighty dollars I still had in my wallet. My pockets felt bloated, but I had everything I needed.

"I think I'm just going to go see Mia in Boston," I lied as I hopped back downstairs. "It'll be easier if I explain things to her in person." I had no plans to turn up on feisty Mia's doorstep yet after my months-long disappearance, but it was the perfect excuse to head into Boston. I didn't want Dad or Mom knowing about the Jane Stuart stuff.

"You just got back," Mom said, frowning.

Dad appeared from the kitchen, holding a half-eaten cookie. Mom passed him a cup of tea like an obedient sixties housewife. It was a jarring flashback to a childhood that I'd worked hard to forget.

"Are you sticking around, or can I get a ride to the bus station in Amherst?" I said to him, still finding it hard to meet his eyes. "I need to get to Boston."

He glanced at Mom. "What are you doing in Boston?"

"Visiting a friend at MIT."

Dad's chin lifted like that was impressive...like his daughter could be smart by association instead of a loony who thinks she's a time traveler.

"How long until you can be ready?" he said.

"I'm ready now."

He dropped his mug onto the counter and grabbed his keys. The look on Mom's face broke me. Dad wasn't here for her; he was here for me, and now we were both taking off. But this was the way it had to be, at least for now.

"Thanks for everything, Carol. It was good to see you." Dad dropped an awkward air-kiss onto Mom's cheek and hightailed it outside to his car.

She watched him go from the doorway until I wrapped an arm around her. "Bye, Mom." She smelled like she needed a shower.

"When are you coming back?" she said into my shoulder.

"I don't know. But I promise you that I'm keeping safe." I pulled her tighter, telling myself that our separations were becoming easier—even if I didn't believe it—before heading outside to the car that was already running.

After months of riding in horse-driven coaches, Dad's Toyota Camry felt like a roller coaster, but a cushiony one. He turned the heat up and tuned the stereo to a public radio channel, and for the first ten minutes, neither of us spoke. I'd felt more comfortable with total strangers. We'd just crossed the bridge over the river when he spun the volume dial down.

"Will you still be in Boston next week?" he asked. "I'll be there on...uh, Friday I think it is, and maybe we can have lunch." He gripped the steering wheel so tight that blue veins bulged from his wrist.

It took me a second to find my voice. "Maybe." Next Friday was an epoch away. "But, to be honest, probably not."

He drove toward Amherst in silence, before spinning the wheel to make a right turn.

"What are you doing?" I said, watching the town center shrink in the rearview mirror.

"Driving you to Boston. I don't have classes today, and it will give us a chance to talk."

"Jeez, thanks, if you're sure you don't mind."

The car picked up speed, and for a few painfully awkward minutes, we just listened to the hum of the engine.

"Why did you drop out of college?" he finally asked me, checking his blind spot so he could merge onto the highway.

The question felt so heavy, especially from Dad, who'd taken such little interest in my life in recent years.

"It wasn't an easy decision," I replied honestly. "I still regret it sometimes."

He seemed pleased about that. "Your mother said she deferred you, so you can still go."

"I know." I didn't turn away from the bottle-green blur of passing trees through the window. In my view, Dad didn't deserve to speak to me about Mom or my future.

"Why all the interest in the Tudors?" He glanced at me.

I sighed heavily. "Dad, I don't really want to talk about this. I appreciate you taking me to Boston, but can we save this conversation for later?"

He chewed his lip and nodded. "Alright."

I just wasn't ready to talk to him about something so significant as my relationship with Nick and what I'd given up for it. For years, I'd fantasized about long drives with Dad again, his random talk shows playing on the radio, but now that it was happening, it felt too little, too late. Dad had absolutely no idea who I was, let alone why I'd done this. Plus, what was the point of rebuilding our relationship if I was only going to leave again?

After a radio program about the connections between people's desires and brain activity, we resumed light chatter about Dad's pet birds, my latest jewelry ideas, and how funny Ruby was, until we were deep into the suburbs of Boston. He insisted on driving me all the way to MIT, and I had no reason to protest.

He pulled up outside the main entrance and jumped out of the car, stepping onto the sidewalk to hug me. I let him, breathing in the scent of his shampoo that hadn't changed in ten years.

"Bye, Dad," I said. "Thanks so much for the ride."

He squeezed my shoulders, his olive-colored eyes shining. "Let me know when you have a new phone number."

"What do you mean?" I said as he climbed back into his silver Camry. Cars were beginning to queue up behind him.

"I must have tried to call you fifty times in the past few months," he called as an irate driver honked her horn. "I've been emailing, too—I wanted to know how you were settling into London. That was before I knew you never turned up, of course."

I waved as he drove away, grappling with his statement. Dad had tried to call me before he even knew I was missing. Sure, it came after years of neglect, but it was something.

I turned to face the imposing columns of MIT, which reminded me of pictures of ancient Greece, the impressive sight flooding me with hot pride for Mia. The temptation to just walk through the doors and find her residence was eaten up by nerves that upset my stomach. But I couldn't. For now, I had to stay focused on my mission: finding Jane Stuart.

At the bus station, I bought a sandwich and a ticket to Newton and parked myself on a bench, plugging my phone into a socket to charge. A few minutes later, I sucked in a deep breath and switched on the phone. The background selfie of Mia and I beside her swimming pool last summer lured a smirk to my face.

The messages and voicemails arrived in a flurry of beeps and flashes. Tensing my muscles like I was preparing for battle, I opened the texts from Mia. The last message appeared first.

Emmie, I don't understand this at all. If I've done something wrong, PLEASE tell me. Please.

Chewing my lip, I scrolled back further.

You better be dead or I'm going to KILL YOU myself!! Seriously.
WHERE THE F ARE YOU?

I clicked the icon to reply, but my fingers stiffened over the empty speech bubble. What could I say?

Hey babe, I'm SO sorry for the delay, I was back in Tudor England. They don't have cell phone reception there.

My love! I would've been in touch sooner, but I was planning my wedding to Nicholas the Ironheart. OMG, he's so intense.

How are you?? I'm good. Been missing everyone, but Hampton Court Palace is awesome...apart from the Duke of Norfolk wanting me dead, ugh. How's MIT?

My bus rolled into the stop with a strained squeak, and I slid my phone back into my pocket.

Downtown Tudor London was hardly a perfume store, but the buses of modern-day Boston weren't much of a step up. I sank into my seat, tugging the collar of my sweatshirt up to my nose. The city was neat and impressively developed, but I'd forgotten how much hideous gray concrete had been dumped onto the earth in my time. If I shut my eyes and ignored the poisonous smell of exhaust fumes, I could still see the broad meadows and smoking chimneys scored by a steady clop of horses' hooves.

I missed Tudor England already. I missed Nick, and the revelation of how far away I was from him felt blisteringly disorienting. This was so much worse than a long-distance relationship: wherever he was, I couldn't even look up at the sky and feel comforted that he was sharing it somewhere. He may as well have been on another planet. I didn't think I'd ever truly understand a world in which people were executed purely for their beliefs, and our relationship had issues the size of a continent, but nothing felt right in my time anymore. Coming back home alone hadn't been the respite I thought it would be. The thought of never feeling Nick's protective arms around me again turned my whole body cold.

It was early afternoon when I scaled the cement steps of the Cedar Lake Rest Home. There weren't any cedar trees or lakes in sight, just a brick building scrawled with illegible graffiti. The cheerless foyer smelled like disinfectant, and the reception desk sat vacant beside a locked pair of doors. I peeked through the gap like a creeper, watching for Jane Stuart.

A young guy strode into the foyer from the street door, balancing three jumbo-sized packages of toilet rolls on his chest.

"Hey, can I help you?" he said in a friendly voice. His dark hair was carefully blow-dried into a fifties-style pompadour.

"I'm looking for a resident called Jane Stuart," I stammered. "She came here in July. I'm a really good friend of her daughter's."

"Janie has a daughter?" he said with a squinty grin. "I had no idea."

"Her daughter lives...far away. I just came from Hatfield, where Jane used to live."

He dumped the toilet rolls beside the lavatory door. "Janitor didn't show up this morning," he explained with an eye roll. "Come on, I'll take you through. I'm Ajay, by the way."

He waved his ID card over the panel beside the double doors, and they clicked open. I followed him down a short hallway leading to a recreation room that smelled faintly of urine. At the far end sat Jane Stuart in a tattered armchair, her white, wild hair and vacant stare unchanged since the last time I'd seen her. An elderly lady was seated beside her, brushing her fingertips up and down the arm of her own chair.

"You've a friend here, Janie," said Ajay, crouching in front of Jane with a cheerful smirk. "Her name's Emily."

"Emmie," I corrected, pulling up a wooden chair beside her. Jane didn't look at me, her knobby fingers tightly clutching two plastic forks.

The woman beside her tilted toward me. "Hello, Chris," she said in a frail voice, clip-on crescent moons dangling from her paper-thin earlobes. "Look at your pretty face."

Before I could reply, Ajay guided the lady up onto her worn ballet flats. "How about we find that fashion magazine you like, Molly?" he said, throwing me a sympathetic smile.

"Oh good, Chris," she said to him, stumbling a little as they walked away.

Jane Stuart hadn't moved the entire time.

"Jane, do you remember me?" I said softly, leaning forward.

She looked right at me but revealed no recognition. I gave her a reassuring smile, scouring her for evidence of an earlier century. Her polyester shirt and checked pants were straight from a discount clothing store rack downtown. Triangles of dry skin peeped from the sides of her slippers.

"I'm Emmeline Grace from Hatfield," I said clearly. "The nurse Carol Grace's daughter." Jane made a flinch of understanding. The blue-diamond ring was safely tucked away in my pocket. When I mentioned the ring to Jane once, she went ballistic and spurted half-nonsense about evil and heretics. The last thing I wanted was to resurrect that side of her.

Yet, I had to find out whether she was Alice's missing mother, Susanna Grey. It wasn't like I had a selfie with Alice from the

Tudor world to show her, so there was really no choice except to ask point-blank.

My voice dropped to a whisper. "Lady Grey?" I said. Jane's sallow brow crinkled. "Is your real name Susanna Grey?"

Her milky-brown pupils expanded, revealing copper edges. In a flash, I recognized that her eyes were the same color as Alice's sister, Violet's.

"Madam, it is I, wife to Sir Thomas Grey," she said without flinching. "May God save you."

13

MY CHEST EMPTIED OF BREATH. Beside me, in a faded floral armchair, sat Alice Grey's mom, Susanna Grey...the wife of the former chief advisor to King Nicholas the First. I could've hugged her, but I didn't want to freak her out—or break her.

Blankness seeped back into Susanna's face and her knobby fingers fumbled with the hem of her shirt as she watched a man with a walking frame shuffle past us.

Hesitant to push her, I silently helped her eat her lunch, which was two scoops of mashed potato topped with ground beef and gravy. She wanted to hang onto the empty bowl, but the kitchen lady gently pried it from her fingers with a knowing smile.

Ajay glided by again and suggested I take Susanna for a stroll outside in the back garden. She didn't say much as we meandered along a short but pretty path that circled the rear of the rest home. I pointed out the fuchsia flowers, and Susanna seemed to understand—even smiled at times—but she never asked why I'd called her by her long-lost name of Susanna Grey. If I brought her back to Tudor England, would it reverse some of her inertia, or was it permanent?

I wasn't exactly pumped to return to the musty recreation

room with the florescent lights, and Susanna seemed happy enough to sit on a bench warmed by the sun. A plastic straw was impaled in the flowerpot beside us, and she plucked it out and slid it into her shirt pocket.

"You are in need of lodging, dear?" she eventually said to me in a withered voice. Her cloudy eyes had fallen back into confusion.

My chest constricted as the words cascaded out. "No, my lady. I am Mistress Emmeline Grace, the Marquess of Pembroke. I'm a friend of your daughters, Mistresses Alice and Violet Grey."

Susanna's face brightened with clarity. "Lottie," she said. I'd heard her say that name before, but only then did I realize it's what she called her daughter Violet.

I set my hand on hers. Her skin was warm and startlingly soft. "Lottie and Alice are at Hampton Court Palace," I said. "They're both well and are in His Majesty's favor."

OMG, if Ajay could hear this.

Susanna Grey's fingers froze beneath mine, her eyes glistening with recognition. I decided not to mention anything negative, like Violet losing her husband, or any of that stuff I'd been told about Susanna Grey once plotting against the king.

"Your husband, Sir Thomas Grey, is also well," I said. "He has withdrawn from the king's service and is living in your manor in Northamptonshire. I just visited there a few weeks ago on progress with the king, and everything is as exactly as you left it."

Susanna's eyelashes darkened with tears. I patted her hand and watched for any sign of reproach after mentioning King Nick, but her face disclosed only relief. She wiped her cheeks and hunched forward, her papery eyelids falling closed. I'd exhausted her.

We slowly made our way back to the recreation room. A nurse with braids of black hair wheeled a trolley of medicines from one resident to the next.

A protective instinct triggered me to guide Susanna the other way. She didn't need drugs; she needed her family back. When I asked her if she knew how to get to her bedroom, she nodded at one of the U-shaped corridors. We headed down it, past a series of half-open doors that offered glimpses of colorful patchwork bedspreads and framed family photographs. Susanna's bedroom looked more like a hospital ward, with unadorned walls and stock-standard sheets. The number '23' was pinned to the door.

An unexpected shiver of apprehension scrambled up my spine. Susanna Grey was only in the twenty-first century because she'd fallen asleep wearing an enchanted ring that was supposed to curse my beloved fiancé to die. How was it my right to bring a treasonous conspirator back to Tudor England? God, what would Nick do to her if he found out? I could never tell him about Susanna's past.

She sat on the bed and drew her legs inside the thin sheets that smelled like antiseptic. No matter the cause, Susanna Grey was trapped in the wrong century with zero family here. She'd probably live out her days in this bleak rest home, perhaps paid for by the forced sale of her house in Hatfield. I didn't know how she came upon that house or why the previous owner left it to her in his will, but boy was I glad she'd lived there. Without Susanna, without that ring, I would never have met Nick Tudor. The thought of life without him left me feeling suffocated with loss. Why had I let us push each other away so quickly?

"Lady Grey, would you like to go home?" I asked gently. "Do you want to go back to Northamptonshire, to Sir Thomas, Alice, and Lottie?"

A ghost of a smile touched her lips. "Oh, blessed Alice...my Lottie. I pray that God shall bring me to their grace. Have mercy on me, eternal Father." She closed her eyes.

I took that as a yes.

"Then please wait here a moment and don't go anywhere," I said like she'd suddenly lurch up and dance the Charleston out the door. I slipped into the surprisingly spacious bathroom, psyching myself up to steal a resident from a rest home. I swallowed one of Mom's sleeping pills in my pocket and gulped water from the faucet, slipping the blue-diamond ring back onto my thumb. I poked my head around the door. Susanna lay on her side, drawing slow, steady breaths.

Making a split-second decision, I pulled my phone from my pocket and shut the bathroom door. I sat in the shower chair and pressed Mom's number. She answered right away.

"Hey, Mom," I said, already jittery at the sound of her voice. "I'm in Boston. Dad drove me all the way in."

"Oh, did he? How did it go with Mia?"

"Yeah, all good…thanks." I scrunched my face. Mom would probably give Mia a call and ask her for feedback on my mental state.

No more lies.

"Actually, I didn't see Mia," I added, my voice echoing off the tiles. "I chickened out."

She sighed. "Emmie."

"It's cool. I decided that I didn't want to lie to her anymore, and she can't know about the Tudor stuff. Can you imagine if something like that got out? You can't tell Mia, ever. Or *anyone*, okay? Please."

"I won't." The phone rattled like Mom was scratching her ear. "How did things go with your dad?" Her voice always crept up an octave when she mentioned him.

"Yeah, all good. We didn't trade blows, so I'll take that as a win."

"It was nice of him to drive you. And to stay over so we could look into things more, don't you think?"

I didn't reply.

"Did he mention anything to you about Nina?" Mom dangled.

I wasn't exactly a fan of chitchat about Dad's live-in girlfriend, the one he'd left Mom—and me—for.

"No," I said. "Should he have mentioned something?"

"Of course not. I'm just wondering if something's changed there. He's taking more of an interest, don't you think?" She sounded as naïve as a little girl, and I felt sorry for her. At the same time, snakes writhed in my stomach. I just didn't want to see her hurt again. We'd both come so far.

When I spoke, my voice was soft. "Mom, you're way better than him. Don't waste your time anymore, please. He's not going to come back."

"You don't know that! Why do you always have to say things like that?"

I'd hit a nerve. I slid the phone down my neck, blocking out Mom's rapid switch to an ardent defense of her and Dad's failed marriage. If I went back to Tudor England now and never returned, would she drive herself mad over this?

The thought of being cocooned inside Nick's arms again melted my growing rigidity. I had to get back there. Not knowing whether he was safe on his mission in the north felt like torture.

"Will you be coming home?" Mom said after she'd finished her diatribe about her and Dad.

"Not right now. I was actually calling to say goodbye because I'm going away again for a bit." My teeth pressed my bottom lip.

I could've sung the national anthem in the time it took for Mom to reply. Her voice had flattened. "I don't know what to do anymore, Emmie. I am just so tired of all this."

"You need to do something for yourself," I realized out loud. "You know now that I'm okay, right? I'm not at the bottom of the river or in a ditch somewhere. So instead of wondering where I am every minute, why don't you go out and do something fun, like a dance class or learning an instrument? Sewing is actually quite cool if you can believe that. I *will* come back and see you whenever I can. I think about you all the time."

Mom didn't acknowledge my suggestions, but her tight swallow made clear that she'd understood the message...she had to let me go for a while.

"Will you promise to be safe?" she said a little hoarsely.

"Always." I thought it best to leave out the beheadings, burning, and smallpox.

"Oh, and Emmie?" she blurted before I could hang up. "You've always got a home to come back to, okay?"

I nodded into the phone, swallowing the urge to cry. "I love you, Mom."

"You too, cookie."

After hanging up, I sat in the shower chair and breathed deeply through the familiar feeling of guilt. Among other wrongs, I'd officially rekindled the firestorm between my parents—something I'd tried for years to avoid. Now I couldn't even be here to help Mom through it.

Wedging my cell phone under my chin, I carefully dragged the vinyl armchair close to Susanna's bed without making noise. A battle erupted in my mind about what to do with the phone. What if I brought it back to the sixteenth century with me? I could take photos and videos of one of the most famous periods of British history and its key characters. I'd be like scoring footage of Henry the Eighth!

Susanna twitched on the bed, jolting me out of my stupor. Attempting something like that would not only be a betrayal of Nick's trust, but no one would believe the images were real without proof. It would become a conspiracy theory, like Bigfoot or the faking of the Moon landing, and I'd be a laughing stock.

All that mattered was getting back to the sixteenth century in one piece so I could make things right with Nick.

I switched off my phone and opened Susanna's cupboard door, unsettling a mountain of toilet rolls, latex glove packets, dog-eared paperback novels, and a couple of television remotes. The rest home staff were probably unaware of how many missing items their resident hoarder was storing. I slid my phone into the back of the top shelf and shut the cupboard door. Whether someone discovered the phone before I returned was not my biggest issue right now. Susanna Grey could wake up at any minute.

The sleeping pill was beginning to take effect, and I sank into the armchair beside the bed. My breaths eased, and I felt warm and heavy all over. The call of Tudor England tickled the corners of my mind, enveloping me with a crushing urge to be back there in an instant.

I placed my hand lightly over Susanna's, cautious not to wake her. Rhythmic breaths broke through her mouth with popping sounds. She was fast asleep. I inched my fingers beneath hers until our palms touched. Holding my friend's mom's hand was one for the weird book, but I focused on my relaxation, silently begging for the ring to work without a struggle.

After an imperceptible amount of time, my head crashed forward, and I woke to the soft click of my dry lips. Susanna's hand had crept away from mine on the rest home bed, but her eyes were shut. The weight of the sleeping pill coated my bloodstream with lead. If Susanna Grey finished her afternoon snooze and got up to eat a cookie...*please, please, please.*

I'd done this before...I could do it again. *Come on!* I berated myself like a tennis player losing a match. The pep talk worked. After a yucky dream about my friend Mia calmly watching me fall out of a plane, I rolled into the comfort of silk sheets. I was no longer sleeping upright in a stiff chair, I was...my eyes flashed open.

Four walls of pearled netting surrounded me, carrying a stark silence I'd know anywhere. I clutched the sheets to my chest, the gentle scent of orange blossom clarifying that I was back at Hampton Court Palace. I could've kissed the mattress, the gilded ceiling, the paneled walls.

The next thought flung me upward. I'd brought Susanna Grey with me!

She stood at the leaded window, fingertips pressed to the

glass like spider's legs. *Holy crap, she's still in her hideous polyester get-up...and I'm in denim jeans.*

It was evident that no one expected me back this soon—even though it was after lunch, the fireplace hadn't been lit and the room was an icebox. I heaved open the chest stuffed with folded undergarments, hurriedly digging out a smock with a high neck for Susanna, before tearing off my clothes and slipping a plainer smock over my shoulders. I hid my remaining sleeping pill in the tiny compartment within the blue-diamond ring that concealed the miniature portrait of Queen Elizabeth the First.

When I pressed an ear to the crack between the doors, it returned only silence. Thank goodness my girls were out, but they could return at any moment. I had to think quickly.

Susanna Grey's cheeks were paler than milk. "Hi, Lady Grey," I said as I approached her. "You need to get changed right away."

The urgency in my voice clearly frightened her, but she let me help her replace her shirt and trousers with the frilly smock.

I rolled my modern clothes, Susanna's, and that effing plastic straw into a sheet and tossed the bundle into the hearth, coughing at the chalky cloud of ash it dislodged. That was the end of the seventy-two bucks still left in my pocket.

Susanna watched me as I lugged a fresh log onto the mound and lit it with tinder and flint. The fire kindled quickly, and the heat of the flames thawed some of my tension as I watched the clothes begin to disintegrate.

"We need to go over how you came to be here," I said, guiding Susanna into a wooden chair. If she began mouthing off to people about time travel and the twenty-first century—including me in it all—we could both be burned for heresy. After everything that had happened with Norfolk and his gang, I couldn't withstand another scandal at court.

I sat close to her, speaking slowly. "You are back at Hampton Court Palace. Your daughters are here." Susanna blinked away tears. "You have been missing for more than four years, and what's important is that you are back with your family. Everything else: the blue-diamond ring, the time you spent away... *America*...doesn't matter anymore. If you talk about that stuff to anyone, Lady Grey, you could receive a terrible punishment." I reflexively checked that no one was within earshot. "Let's just say that you wandered back into court and that you have no memory of how you got here or where you've been. Just say you remember nothing of your disappearance and go home to your husband and your garden. Okay? Do you understand?"

Eyes of creamy brown scanned me from head to foot. "Have mercy on me and I shall be saved," she said hoarsely, the smock more at ease over her thin shoulders than any modern clothes I'd seen her in.

There was fresh wine in the drawing-room, and I poured Susanna a cup before escaping to the refuge of my dressing room. I dug through the neatly folded silks, careful not to upset them, and retrieved a simple, iris-colored gown with a square neckline that I managed to tie on myself. Weaving my hair into a braid stirred a memory of my first days at Whitehall Palace. It felt like a lifetime ago.

Back in my bedchamber, Susanna hadn't moved. "Where may I find my daughters?" she said with faint confusion.

"They should come back here soon," I replied as my stomach made a hollow twist. Dinner wouldn't be served for hours.

I kneeled in front of her. "Do you think you can wait here while I get us something to eat? You have to promise that you won't go anywhere, please. I want you to see your daughters first."

She nodded, and I trusted that she wouldn't want to be anywhere other than the safety of my fire-warmed bedchamber at a time like this.

Blocking thoughts about Nick's whereabouts that threatened to send me into a panic spiral, I grabbed a cloak and braved the icy air, racing down empty corridors toward the kitchens.

"Do you know where everybody is?" I asked one of the chefs as he piled a pewter platter with cured meats, rosemary meatballs, soft cheeses, and prune tarts.

"There be a wrestling tournament this day at the tiltyard, my lady," he said.

It was a Nick Tudor trademark to stage court entertainments during his absence to keep his subjects occupied and out of trouble. The deserted corridors now made sense as I weaved my way back to my chambers, carefully balancing my tray. Making sure no one was following me, I slunk back to my rooms and bolted the door behind me.

After the mush that Susanna had been eating at the rest home, I wasn't sure she could handle the rich, fatty flavors of the Tudor court, but she scarfed up the spread like she hadn't eaten in weeks. Coaxing light conversation out of her about court stuff helped ease her a bit, and after another glass of wine, she asked if she could lie down for a while.

"Absolutely...I don't blame you," I replied with a yawn, and helped Susanna into Violet's pallet bed. I tried to give her mine, but she balked and refused to take the bed of someone who was higher up in the peerage. She obviously remembered the way things worked around here, which was promising.

An hour into her snooze, I decided that we could be waiting all afternoon for my ladies to come back and swung my cloak back over my shoulders. Sometimes the chambermaids turned up later in the day, and Alice and Violet deserved to see their mom before anyone else.

Anxious about Susanna Grey going missing again—this time on my watch—I hurried to the northern side of court, past the Privy Orchard, and across to the tiltyard. The redbrick arena had morphed into a gambling pit, with eager punters hanging from balconies in the high towers. After a minute of scanning, I spotted Alice, Violet, Bridget, and Lucinda squashed together within the third tower. They were cheering at the sportsmen in the pit who'd tied themselves into a jumble of biceps, calves, and breeches.

As I climbed over disgruntled nobles to reach my ladies in the fourth row, Alice saw me and clapped a hand over her mouth. I'd been gone for too short a time to make it to Worthing and back, and I told the girls it was because I ran into someone on the roads outside the palace.

"Of whom do you speak?" said Alice, handing Bridget her pouch of sugared almonds.

There was no way I was about to answer that in front of hundreds of drunken courtiers.

"Why don't you come back to my chambers and find out?" I said cryptically.

"Emmie," Alice blurted through a laugh, but lines filled her forehead.

"Who could it possibly be?" said Bridget, already halfway off the bench. She couldn't resist a mystery.

"Sorry to be vague and to interrupt the show, but you're going to want to see this," I said, my stomach crunching with nerves. I could've cringed at myself for making it sound like I'd planned a fun surprise. For all I knew, the shock of reuniting Alice and Violet with their missing mom could send one of them into cardiac arrest.

We headed back toward my chambers while they grilled me about this secret person. Alice's curious smile confirmed that she had zero idea it was her mom. The best guess thrown around was the king's sister Kit, and I swiped two fingers across my lips like a zipper, before remembering that zippers were practically as modern as Wi-Fi.

I was relieved to find that Susanna had woken up from her nap. She was sitting in a chair in the drawing-room, playing with her hair. Her eyes flared wide as Alice followed me inside, shadowed by Violet.

"Mother?" Violet said in a flat tone. I might've thought she was unaffected had it not been for her bewildered expression.

"No, Violet, Mother is…" Alice's usually confident voice drifted off.

"She is here," finished Violet.

"Lottie?" said Susanna.

I clutched my side, where I'd tied my kirtle too tight. "I found this lady near to the palace," I explained, the lie burning my throat. But maybe this reunion would finally atone for all my lies to Alice. "She said her name is Susanna Grey."

Alice pushed past me, all her etiquette gone. "Mother?" she whispered breathlessly.

"Alice…sweet Alice," Susanna replied. "By God's grace, I see now that you are a lady."

Susanna rose from the chair, catching both her daughters' hands as they fell to their knees in tears. "Most blessed daughters, oh, how my heart sings at the sight of you. I know not how this has come to pass, but if you are the subjects of a dream, may I never awaken."

A silent cry punched my chest, and I backed into my bedchamber with Bridget and Lucinda, quietly shutting the doors so the family could reunite in private. A silent decision took shape in my head: if Susanna Grey told Alice and Violet about her time-traveling expedition and my involvement in it, I'd have no choice but to argue for her insanity.

After a brief catch-up with Bridget and Lucinda, I asked if they could watch over things while I took a nap. My eyelids had become sheets of lead.

As Bridget and Lucinda sat in the corner and quietly shared theories about where Susanna Grey could have been all this time, I dozed off. When I woke to the distant blast of trumpets announcing dinner, my bedchamber was empty. The robust flames in the hearth said that the fire had been tended, and there was a jug of water and a cup beside my bed. I opened the double doors leading to the drawing-room, bracing myself for what I might find.

Girlish laughter trilled through the comfy space. Shining faces glanced at me from a cluster of fringed cushions on the floor. Alice, Violet, Lucinda, and Bridget scrambled to rise.

"Stay where you are," I said soothingly, crouching beside Alice on the floor. Lady Grey sat in a chair before us, like a librarian instructing an eager circle of children. In just hours, she looked ten years younger.

"Mother was speaking of Hatfield," Alice said a little breathlessly. "It seems the lady has been there these past years, but she keeps speaking of a moving coach with no horses and then laughs and laughs."

The smile slid off my face. Everyone else, however, looked more amused than concerned, including Susanna. There was color in her cheeks, and life had kindled in her eyes.

"Lady Pembroke, we are most heartily pleased to have our mother returned," Violet said to me. "The lady has no memory of how she came to return to court, but we are truly thankful you brought us to her before informing the Council."

"They will wish to question her," Alice added, her mouth tightening. "However, I fear our dear mother has become frantic."

Susanna just stared at her daughters with her narrow lips curled into a frozen smile. It was the face of someone who didn't have a clue what was going on but felt content.

When a single tap sounded at the doors, Lucinda welcomed a wooden trolley packed with steaming pewter serving platters. We arranged six chairs around the circular table. Over dinner, I filled the girls in on my fabricated tale about how I'd come upon Susanna wandering along the nearby River Thames, not only drumming the story into Susanna's head, but also hopefully blocking her from telling more tales about cars or modern inventions.

It was time to experiment with my growing influence around

here, especially now that I felt sure I wanted to stay here with Nick and accept his world for what it was—provided he returned from the north with his head still on his shoulders. I erased that thought as soon as it came.

"Alice and Violet, I'd like you to take Lady Grey home to Northamptonshire," I said, sinking my knife into a poached pear. "As you say, there will be interest in her whereabouts for the past four years and how she ended up at court with no memory of anything. However, that's an issue that should be discussed with her husband, Sir Thomas." Susanna's fingers curled into a knot as I continued. "Bridget and Lucinda will be here to attend to me in the meantime; just come back when Lady Grey has settled in. We need not trouble the king with this, and who knows when he'll be back. You can take one of the coaches."

Alice and Violet looked at each other, eyes gleaming. "Bless you, Emmie," Alice cried, abandoning her chair to hug me from behind. It was probably an outrageous way to treat an impending queen, but I'd encouraged a relaxed closeness in the privacy of my chambers, and I was thrilled to see it in effect. I was never a fan of being at court without Alice, but as one of the future queen's maids of honour, she wouldn't be allowed to stay away for too long. Besides, getting Susanna home safely was more important than me having my best friend at court.

"I shall write to Father," said Violet, twisting toward the desk.

"Don't bother with that; just go tonight," I said quickly. "While the king is away." I looked at Alice. "While the Earl of Warwick is away." Her toffee eyes met mine for a moment long enough to reveal regret. She hadn't yet patched things up with Francis.

Both the Grey girls were apprehensive about leaving court without permission or planning, but I insisted. Within a few hours, Alice, Violet, and Lady Grey were bundled up inside a swaying coach bound for Northamptonshire.

I slept deeply that night, waking late and spending a contented few days tucked away in my jewelry workshop. The craftsman that Nick had summoned to court, Andrea Bon Compagni, schooled me on the equipment with cheery patience. I felt instantly comfortable around his gentle face that was pock-marked with smallpox scars.

In the afternoons, Mister Bon Compagni would leave me with the company of neighing horses through the window or the muted crunches of boots crossing the graveled courtyard below. I'd file and pummel the silver until my wrist seized, crafting a simple thumb ring with a hammered pattern for Nick as a thank you present for the studio. It was going to be a total snore-fest beside his blingy Tudor jewels, but I had to start with something I could handle. There weren't exactly online video tutorials on this old-school equipment. Plus, I had years ahead to perfect my craft here, and for the first time, the thought of a long life in Tudor England excited me more than it freaked me out. All I needed now was my boyfriend back, but imagining where he might be—or if he was being skewered with a bloodied sword—sent my lunch into my throat. I forced myself to focus on what-ever else I could to intercept my catastrophic thoughts.

With the absence of Alice and Violet, I became closer to Bridget—and even Lucinda, who was a shining example of a queen's lady, making sure my chambers were never short of macarons. When she received word that her daughter Ellie had fully recovered from her bout of illness, the three of us held a small dessert party.

Two weeks after the Grey girls left court, a letter from Alice arrived. She wrote that her mom was doing okay, but her father, Sir Thomas, had been called away on the king's business. I wanted to kiss the letter. Surely it meant that, somewhere out there, King Nick was alive. I knew that I would've heard about it had he not been, but communication in Tudor England made a snail look supersonic. It was hard to relax without knowing anything for sure. I wrote back to Alice and urged her to stay on in Northamptonshire until Sir Thomas returned home.

With so many letters coming and going from court, every tap on the door sent me flying toward the handle, hankering for one from Nick. Every day brought disappointment and a reminder of how unfinished things were between us. I wanted to tell him how I felt—that I was ready to make things work with him here. Why wouldn't he write?

The calendar had reached mid-November when another knock sounded an hour after supper.

"I'll get it," I cried to Lucinda and Bridget, and threw open the doors to find Francis Beaumont clutching a feathered cap. After greeting me, he ran a nervous palm down his espresso curls that reached his shoulders.

My throat locked, and I couldn't breathe.

"His Majesty is well, but not yet at court, my lady," Francis said, reading my fear. He glanced past me.

"Oh, you're here to see Alice?" I blurted through my relief. "She's gone back to Northamptonshire with Violet." Francis's face fell, and I explained. "Their mother is back, can you believe it? Lady Grey was found near here and seems well enough, but she has no idea where she's been for the past four years. Isn't that great news?"

Francis's mouth was agape. "Tell me everything."

I invited him inside the warmth of my chambers, but he politely refused. Any man who hung out behind closed doors with the king's fiancée had a death wish. Instead, I asked Bridget to pass me a shawl and sat on the front step beside Francis, filling him in on everything I could reveal about Alice's mom. Nick's name didn't come up again until Francis mentioned that the uprising near Lancashire had been quelled for now. I'd been too scared to ask, so I was grateful that he'd volunteered the news.

"Where is the king now?" My voice was a nervous puff of smoke in the frosty air.

Francis rose to his feet and knocked a boot against the step. "That is why I am here, my lady. His Majesty received word that you had returned from Sussex in haste. He desires to speak with you on a great matter but wishes to do so in private."

"What great matter?"

Francis rubbed his lips together like he was ill at ease. "The King's Majesty is expecting your person without delay at Robin House."

"Robin House?" I said with confusion. The humble manor in the countryside with the thatched roof was the king's most private place that most people didn't even know about. Nick clearly had something to tell me that required secrecy, and anxiety slid into my stomach. Perhaps he'd decided the opposite of what I had these past few weeks: that our engagement was a mistake and the smartest thing for him to do would be to marry Princess Henriette of France after all. Wouldn't that solve all his problems?

Francis surely knew what the deal was, and I tried to read his face, but it was concealed by winter darkness.

"You will consider this matter not to be delayed and will make ready to leave, my lady," he advised briskly. "You may bring your ladies." He bowed and marched away before I could press him on the topic any further. The earl was clearly keeping any opinions on this mysterious matter to himself—perhaps by order of the king.

I rubbed my clammy palms up and down my thighs, my mouth dry. Not only was Nick's great matter urgent, but it came after our unspoken agreement to reconsider our engagement. I felt like I might be sick on the damp cobblestones.

After all the troubles we'd already been through—Norfolk, Lucinda, Agnes Nightingale—what did he have to say to me that was so important? I wasn't sure I wanted to find out.

14

HEAVY RAINS MADE the roads dangerous for travel that night, so I slept at Hampton Court Palace with my mind in overdrive. What was Nick's 'great matter' that prevented him from riding to Hampton Court to face me in public? At first light, I yanked the shutters open, gaping with trepidation at the clear sky through the diamond-crossed panes. Was this the day that I would find out that he wanted us to go our separate ways after all? The thought stole any appetite I might've had for breakfast.

Bridget gnawed her fingertips for most of the slushy coach ride through the mud to the king's secret hideaway—thrilled for another adventure—while Lucinda gazed silently through the open window. Did she know about Robin House? Had Nick taken her there for a cheeky couple's weekend during their fling? I pushed the jagged thoughts away.

The moment our coach swung onto the stone pathway leading to Robin House, I watched for Nick through the window, my stomach a tropical storm of butterflies. I wasn't ready to go through what could be the most heartbreaking day of my life.

The modest manor's front yard looked desolate except for a couple of discreet guards in plain clothes. The main house with the thatched roof was even smaller than I remembered—perhaps because Hampton Court Palace had become the benchmark by which I now measured all royal residences.

A stocky guard with strong hands helped me to the ground. "His Majesty will see you inside, my lady," he said as our short procession of carts and horses clopped toward the stables. A gust of wind bit my neck as I approached the house. I inhaled a steadying breath and pushed through the thick wooden door.

The sight was so unexpected that it sent me back a step. Around the modest dining table sat Alice's dad Sir Thomas Grey, the wrinkled Bishop of Winchester, and King Nick in a doublet of navy velvet, his white peekaboo collar centered with a blood-red ruby. When he glanced up at me, the urge to move toward him was so intense that my thighs clenched.

"Lady Pembroke, I give you good morrow," he said formally, his glittering eyes giving nothing away.

I found myself curtsying, a searing flutter in my stomach. The other men rose to kiss my hand.

"You may sit with us," Nick added, like I'd just joined a corporate meeting.

A page slid a chair in for me beside the king. My elbows brushed Nick's as I sat, sparks heating my skin through the fabric. I wanted to kiss the sweet-smelling space beneath his ear, but that would've been weird. Being this close to him always offset my balance in a way that I never wanted to end.

"It is time for your king and the Marquess of Pembroke to be united in holy matrimony," Nick stated without looking at me.

I nearly choked on my breath, needles of shock prickling my cheeks. *I'm sorry...what?*

The only sound was the king's commanding voice. "The Bishop of Winchester will conduct the proceedings, and Sir Thomas Grey will serve as a witness."

Wrinkled skin sagged beneath Thomas Grey's wearied eyes as he took note of Nick's continuing instructions like his life depended on it. So, this was the 'great matter'...Nick had decided to push forward our wedding without even speaking to me about it. I gaped at my boyfriend's frustratingly perfect profile as he continued issuing orders without looking my way. "Lady Pembroke, you may take your dinner and then dress, and thereupon the service will begin."

"We're getting married *today?*" I sputtered, unsure whether I was more relieved or aghast about the lack of notice. I was getting used to the opinions of women being an afterthought in this place, but surely I got a say in my own wedding day.

The king rose quickly, and the rest of us scrambled to our feet, bowing as he strode out of the chamber without a backward glance. As relieved as I was that he wasn't breaking up with me, I could've throttled him in that handsome doublet. We were going to have words.

I excused myself to Sir Thomas and the bishop and picked up my skirts to dash up the narrow staircase leading to the upstairs bedchamber.

There was no sign of Nick, however—only Bridget standing before the fireplace, warming her fingers. She danced toward me as I entered. "Lady Pembroke, we hear there is to be a wedding—oh, blessed day!"

Lucinda scooted over from the clothes chest and dropped to her knees, pressing her soft lips to my hand. "My lady, if you find the heart to forgive my past actions and permit me to attend to you as Queen of England, you will find me a most loving and loyal servant."

It was the first time she'd openly alluded to the kiss with Nick, but that seemed pretty far down the scale of bombshells right now.

"Why would he want to get married in this small house?" I asked them, genuinely gobsmacked.

"To hide it," Bridget answered plainly.

"Because he loves her," Lucinda argued. "It is the pleasure of the king to keep his more tender inclinations private."

My stomach rolled over itself. I had to find Nick and ask him what planet he was on. The girls looked startled as I rushed back out to check the washroom before clomping downstairs, where four cooks bustled in the tiny kitchen, bumping hips.

"Where is the king?" I blurted to no one in particular.

A guard with imposing shoulders stepped forward. "Mister Joseph Blackburn, my lady," he introduced with a bow. "I believe His Majesty is in the guest lodgings beyond the garden."

"Guest lodgings?" I didn't know there were any here. I thanked the guard and headed outside to a grassy courtyard, where Thomas Grey and Bishop Winchester hovered in their billowy black cloaks like two stage magicians who'd popped out for a smoke.

"Lady Pembroke," said Thomas, stopping my stride. His pale eyes fixed on mine. "When I once bid you to leave the company of the king, I admit that I had mistook you for little more than a lovesick girl. But, madam, I see now that you are nobody's fool." He tipped his head with a short nod. A hot flush of embarrassment crept across my cheeks as I made a thankful curtsy for the vague apology. Thomas had once offered me money to break up with Nick, and I'd not only done the opposite but ended up becoming the future Queen of England. "I also understand that it was you who helped return my wife to her home," Thomas added, a peace offering in his eyes.

"Uh, yes, you could say that."

When he made a nod of thanks and turned away again, I knew this was the closest thing I'd ever get to the old man's blessing.

Before he could leave, a nervous question spilled from my lips. "Why Robin House, Sir Thomas? Why would the king choose to marry me here on this small property—away from everybody?"

I'd expected him to warn me about rebellions and what the

nobles really thought of me, but his cheeks blushed fondly. "Your dear betrothed may have the heart of a king, my lady, but he also bears the heart of a man."

As I glanced over the stony courtyard that clung to visibility within invading thickets of wildflowers and rose bushes, it came together. A part of Nick—a bigger share then I'd have guessed— envied the simplicity of the quiet farmer's life. It was the reason he enjoyed visiting Robin House so much, where I'd seen him tending the roses and picnicking on the grass. Despite the countless times that I'd butted heads with Thomas Grey, he knew layers of Nick that'd take years for me to peel away. He was the father that Nick had never had, which was why he'd been asked to witness the wedding—even above Francis Beaumont. That gave the old grump a stack of cred in my books.

"I'm really happy your wife is finally home," I said to him with a wary smile. "I hope you can get back to her soon."

A film of tears brightened his eyes. He bowed in gratitude and stepped aside for me to pass.

Wedged into the back corner of the courtyard was a tiny cabin built from hand-sawed planks of wood. The door was so stiff that I had to shove it with my hip to get it open. Inside, I found Nick sitting on a wooden stool beside a square hole for a window—a jewel swimming in mud in the ramshackle space.

"Oh, sorry," I said quickly. "You're praying."

He looked up at me, his lips falling open a little. "Lady Pembroke. You are to be preparing your person for the ceremony."

I felt my forehead crease, but this time, I promised myself I'd stay calm. Nick would never be a modern guy, and he'd always think like a dictatorial Tudor king, but I still deserved a voice in this relationship. I'd never stop fighting for that.

"What's all this about?" I said gently. "The last time I saw you, things were weird between us, then I went home for no more than a day, you were away *forever*, and now you announce a sudden wedding without even speaking to me about it?" I shook my head, bewildered. "That's really different to how things are done in my time and definitely not how I imagined our wedding day to be. We haven't even had a chance to say a proper hello to each other."

He twisted back to the window, sunlight tinting his chestnut hair a lighter shade of caramel. "Emmie, I cannot bear the uncertainty of this matter any longer. I love you so truly that it makes me ill to consider that you have had a change of heart about us. But I must know—you may speak your conscience now, I beseech you to."

"When do I ever *not* speak my conscience?"

It was my attempt to lighten the atmosphere, but his cheeks didn't move. I grasped what was happening: despite the show of command in front of Sir Thomas and the Bishop, Nick was giving me one more opening to back out of this thing and return to the twenty-first century if that's what I wanted. I sensed that he wouldn't try to stop me this time.

My voice broke on the truthful words that drew me closer to him. "When you were away, I went home to my time and brought back Susanna Grey—as I'm sure you've heard. But the whole time I was there, I couldn't wait to get back here to you."

He looked back at me, his tormented eyes softening at the edges.

"Do I always agree with you?" I continued. "No. Will I ever completely understand you? Maybe not. Do you make me insane? One hundred percent. But do I seem to love you more every day, rather than less, for some irritating, inexplicable reason? Completely."

His voice was a whisper. "So you do wish to marry me?"

"Didn't I already say yes?"

His full lips puffed with relief, and my heart swelled. For a moment, we just drank in the sight of each other, before his mouth curled into a teary smile. He tipped forward to wrap his arms around me, and I fell into his light like a sunflower. After so long apart, our embrace quickly escalated to deep kisses that made my head spin, before we broke apart, remembering ourselves. Nick dropped back onto the stool and tugged me down into his lap. His lips burrowed into the crook of my neck.

"If you weren't sure that I still wanted to get married," I said, "then why did you go ahead and try to force it? Why plan everything without me?"

"Is it the custom in my time for the man to make ready the marriage rites, even though most assuredly I would have stopped it, had I not had your consent." He skimmed his palms down my arms. "I also feared that mine idleness was causing you to drift away. I should have wed you in more haste. I have taken too long…been too consumed with the Spaniards, and the French, and all manner of duty." He cupped my cheeks and gave them an affectionate squeeze. "You mean more to me than aught, and I wish to wait no longer to marry you."

"Who's Aught?" I said with mock horror. "She's not another one of your ex-girlfriends, is she?"

He breathed a cute laugh, and I tilted into him, kissing the dip in his crinkled brow. "Then let's do this thing, Nicholas Henry Edward. Make me a Tudor, too."

᙭   ᙭   ᙭

Upstairs in the bedchamber, Bridget and Lucinda had laid out a pretty pale-yellow kirtle sprinkled with diamond dust and embroidered with a trail of silver wildflowers that wouldn't irritate Nick's asthma. After dressing me in the gown's myriad pieces, they pinned a medieval circlet of fresh wildflowers over my loose hair and clipped on a necklace of white diamonds. I appraised myself in the hand mirror, my fingers shaking. If only Alice was here to keep me calm with her steadying words. I couldn't believe that she was about to miss my wedding, but I didn't have time to send for her, even if I'd been okay with dragging her back from her mom's side.

Lucinda and Bridget gathered my tissue-soft train and followed me down the narrow staircase and outside, my feet slipping around in my satin pumps that were half a size too big. My heart sank a little as I caught sight of the overcast sky. It hadn't looked that grim when I went upstairs. The next to meet my vision was Thomas Grey, also wincing at the clouds before he spotted me and dropped into a gentlemanly bow.

Nervous excitement hummed low in my belly at the sight of Nick. He stood before the Bishop of Winchester in a coat of marble-colored satin pinned with solid-gold buttons, an affectionate smile adorning his regal face. Tufts of tousled hair peeked from beneath his crown of glittering crosses and fleur-de-lis.

Smiling so wide that my cheeks could've touched my eyes, I strolled toward him to a gentle rendition of "Lady Greensleeves" performed by a flutist. I halted beside my fiancé and gazed up into the blue-green stare that possessed every part of my heart.

Bishop Winchester delivered most of the service in Latin, and I copied Nick when he knelt on a cushion and read from a prayer book, the somberness of the ceremony surprising me. In my time, weddings were cheerful expressions of love and commitment, but in Tudor England, it was a deadly serious vow before God that I felt could never be undone. That might've freaked me out had I been marrying anyone else, but with Nick, the assurance that he'd always be mine made me feel safe and warm all over. We were halfway through the ceremony when the skies made good on their threats and freezing raindrops began spilling from the clouds. At any other time, I'd have shrieked and run for cover, but I just giggled as Nick made an adorable scowl at the sky.

"A most glorious day indeed for the wedding of God's chosen king!" he cried with mock anger, and we all laughed before the ceremony was sped up.

Thomas Grey quickly presented matching gold rings carved with the entwined initials *N&E*. Nick slid mine over my fourth finger, and a taut balloon burst inside me, releasing a euphoric feeling of calm. My fingertips brushed the ridges of an inscription on the inside of the ring, the Latin words *Ne Dimittas*.

Nick smiled at me, reading my thoughts. "It means 'do not let go,'" he said under his breath. I beamed, kissing the gold band circling his fourth finger. It was the phrase I'd whispered to him when we first traveled through time together.

Do not let go.

Ne dimittas.

Thunder whipped the sky, and Nick hurried me inside to where the cooks had squeezed a feast of dishes onto the circular dining table. There was just enough space for our small wedding party, and we dug into platters of duck, quail, and swan, enjoying the closeness and chatter that reminded me of Thanksgiving at my friend Mia's house. Between courses, Nick held my hand beneath the table, our thumbs caressing in a way that made my thighs press together. In all the excitement, I'd forgotten that tonight was also our wedding night.

The moment I remembered what that meant, I could think of nothing else. My eyes locked on Lucinda Parker as she chatted politely with the bishop between small bites of violet-flavored marzipan. Lucinda knew what to do—she'd been with Nick before. I chugged an entire cup of water, but it didn't cut through the drought in my mouth.

"The hour is late, and our lady is undoubtedly wearied," said Nick, dabbing his lips with a silk napkin. "We are grateful for your service and bid you retire to bed." Everyone rose to bow to the king, and Nick walked me toward the stairwell. He paused there, my heart beating into my throat.

"You may expect my short return, my lady," he said a little huskily, pressing his lips to my hand.

Despite my nerves, a thrill danced through me, low in my

stomach. A moment later, Bridget and Lucinda arrived to take me upstairs. Bridget couldn't contain her glee at the idea of a wedding night, which only escalated my jitters. They drew me a bath scented with fragrant herbs, washed and combed my hair, and helped me into a silk nightgown that I noticed could be easily untied. Candles danced light up the walls, my throat sticky with anticipation. Bridget offered me a knowing grin as they left me alone, and Lucinda wouldn't look at me for the first time in weeks. I tried not to let her obvious envy affect me as I climbed into bed and pulled the fur covers to my chin. Despite the fire hissing and cracking in the hearth, I couldn't get warm.

Several minutes later, the distant song of a flute rapidly gained in volume until it was right outside the door. I sat up to a gentle knock and men's voices. Nick strolled into the dim room in his nightshirt, followed by Bishop Winchester, Thomas Grey, and three of Nick's gentlemen of the bedchamber.

OMG, has war broken out or the plague arrived on our doorstep?

Winchester launched into a benediction in Latin, blessing Nick, me, and the bed. A gentleman carried in two dining chairs and angled them toward the mattress, and Bishop Winchester and Thomas Grey sat down in them. Servants carried in a buffet table before dressing it with wine and bread.

Nick sat on the mattress beside me, smelling delicious in his silk nightshirt. A thick fur blanket still separated us.

"Nick," I said quietly, my cheeks hotter than the flames in the hearth. "What is going on?" The flutist trilled a little louder.

"My queen, this is our wedding night," he said with the same breathy emphasis. "You know not what is required to sanctify our marriage before God?"

"I *know* what's required, but with an audience? Is this some kind of creepy Tudor joke?" I hissed.

Nick's mouth opened and shut like he was lost for words. I spotted Thomas's jowly face beyond Nick's shoulder and yanked the covers a little higher.

"The men are here to bear witness that the marriage is consummated," Nick explained to me.

"Yeah, I'm catching on to that." The shiver returned to my skin.

Nick's gaze considered me for a moment before he twisted to face the cluster of men. "You may leave us and remain beyond the door."

Mercifully, the lot of them bowed and scurried out the hallway, shutting the door behind them.

"Did I screw everything up?" I said to Nick, my fingers splayed over my face.

He pulled my hand away to kiss the tip of my nose. "It is plainly not the custom in your time. The men may *hear* the consummation of the marriage, which will suffice."

A sigh of relief burst from my lips, and Nick smirked like I was cute. Our fingers were twisting together again, touching and swirling with focused strokes. There was so much excitement churning inside me that I almost felt faint. I brought his irresistible fingers to my mouth and began kissing them one by one. He watched me closely while combing his other hand through my hair, strong and steady. I rushed forward to kiss his parted lips, unable to hold back any longer. He sighed into my mouth as we fell together, the blanket still bunched between us. The weight of him on top of me made my back arch with the desire to be even closer, and I wrapped my legs around his hips, deepening our kisses.

As I tugged the silk nightshirt up over Nick's muscular shoulders, he whispered something in my ear. "With the men near to verify consummation of the marriage rites, Emmie, I cannot promise to be silent."

Something rumbled low in my abdomen as I guided him into a gentle roll off the blanket and kicked it to the floor.

The few times I'd woken up beside Nick in Tudor England, he'd almost always disappeared before dawn. The next morning, however, there was no squawk of the cockerels, and the light filtering through the leaded window had no golden tinge. It was late, and the king still lay beside me, his bare skin tangled in linen sheets. He stirred at my movements, and I froze so he could sleep longer, but his eyes had already flickered open.

At my insistence, we helped each other dress in our complicated outfits and ate a leisurely breakfast of manchet bread rolls, hard cheeses, and stewed fruits in the privacy of the bedchamber. Thomas Grey, Bishop Winchester, and my ladies had already left Robin House to give us some time alone, and, at last, Nick had nowhere more important to be but beside me in a simple bedroom. It felt like heaven.

Given how short the days had become, he suggested a walk outside while the sun was still high. With plain-clothes guards trailing us, we set off past the jumble of rose bushes becoming dormant for the winter and down the slope of wild lavender. We reached the clearing where we'd once shared a picnic and nervous glances, pausing to take in the memory with our arms entwined. And now we were back here as a married couple. The thought was almost insane.

The wind whispered at us through the fruit trees as we strolled farther from the house, coming to the curve of a small hill. We hiked to the top, catching our breath as we took in the bird's eye view of a honey-toned meadow interrupted by a village that was too small to be walled. In the distance, a handful of residents milled about in their veggie gardens like toy figurines. A girl in a white coif tilted her face up toward us.

I instinctively stepped backward. "Do you know that village?" I said to Nick.

He was snapping pink wildflowers off at the stems. "The hamlet? They are all about the place. Hardly more than farms and cottages." He presented me with a bundle of fuchsia blooms. "For my queen."

I brought the fragrant petals to my nose, feeling my coy smile stretch my cheeks. Nick's casual leathers clung to his legs in all the right places. It was still so long until bedtime.

"Shall we make our return?" he said, heat stirring in his eyes. "I am feeling rather in need of rest, my beautiful wife." His forearm pressed mine.

I switched the flowers to my opposite hand so I could tug him down the hill. "I'm also beat from all this walking," I said. "I could use a lie down." We headed back for the house with flutters of anticipation that made my legs weak. Being married was wonderful.

Later that afternoon, I sat wiping off my makeup with a damp cloth, buzzing with happiness. While Bridget and Lucinda had become my beloved girl crew, I didn't ache to have them back in my company at all times with little privacy. I imagined Nick and I never returning to the palace, just living out our lives at Robin House while I learned how to grow vegetables like the villagers from the hamlet and he tended to his roses. *This* was what I came back for. This was the life I craved with Nick.

He dropped to one knee behind me, swiping my hair to the side. The touch of his lips sent a ripple of goosebumps across my skin. "We must soon determine your royal badge," he said. "I propose a swan."

I reached behind me to glide my hand up his neck, warming my fingers in his soft curls. "A bit graceful for me, don't you think? Do you really see me as a delicate little swan?" I fluttered my eyelashes.

"An elephant?" he offered, sliding into a chair beside mine.

I whacked his arm. I'd actually been thinking about this. "A phoenix," I replied. "The bird that rises from its ashes to be born again. A bird that begins a new life."

His tender smile fired another love-dart into my chest.

"A phoenix is fitting." The soft tips of his fingers stroked my forearm. "We must also settle upon your household, your patronages, your council. Do you enjoy your ladies? We will appoint them in greater numbers."

A mild-mannered knock tapped the door. Nick rose to his full, imposing height. "Come," he said.

A skinny attendant with acne pustules bowed from the doorway. "Your Majesty, a messenger brings urgent news."

Nick stepped closer to me. "What news?"

When the kid glanced at me and hesitated, Nick commanded, "Speak, boy!"

"The Duke of Norfolk has escaped capture by night and is believed to have made for Dover, Your Majesty," he stumbled. "There is word the duke is planning a revolt on the grounds of your betrothal to the Lady Pembroke."

Nick grabbed the boy by his stiff collar. I cried out, scratching at Nick's arm to let go. He obliged, and the kid dropped to the floorboards.

Nick leaned over him, speaking through his teeth. "The Duke of Norfolk has been stripped of such title. On pain of death, you will refer to his person only as Henry Howard, the traitor."

The boy hunched forward and begged for forgiveness, his bony shoulders shaking.

"Make ready the horses and coaches to return to Hampton Court at once," the king snapped at him. The poor kid couldn't get out the door fast enough.

Nick dropped into the chair, catching his head in his hands.

My voice wavered with both shock and guilt. "You didn't kill him," I said, the memory crystallizing. "I accused you of executing Norfolk and lying to me about it, but you didn't. You did send him away...I'm so sorry."

Nick's chest swelled with tense breaths. "That is true. I killed him not, Emmie, but I should have. For now, that traitor Henry Howard is intending to kill us."

15

NICK and I rode back to Hampton Court Palace at first light, leaving the cherished privacy we'd shared at Robin House behind in a cloud of dust. Our honeymoon was officially over now that a disgraced former duke was raising an army to bring us down.

From the moment we returned to court, the king disappeared into secretive council meetings for hours on end. When I did get to see him, I expected the dark moods and outbursts that were his trademark in tough times. Instead, however, he adorned me with jewels and gifts, spoiled me with fancy feasts, staged private performances in my chambers, and issued a wedding announcement across the country. While behind the scenes Nick may have sent soldiers to find Henry Howard—the man formerly known as the Duke of Norfolk—publicly, he was playing every kingly card he had, flaunting his wealth and power to me so I would feel protected rather than afraid. I didn't want to muddle things further by telling him that all I needed to feel safe was to have him close to me.

But instead of privacy and seclusion, the king had put every aspect of our public life on fast-forward. He ordered the commissioners in charge of my coronation to work quickly, and my crowning as queen was scheduled for the first week of December in a flurry of dress fittings, practice ceremonies, and etiquette coaching. I missed Alice even more, who would've kept me calm with her wry jokes and explanations of things I didn't understand. As pleased as we all were for her to be reunited with her mom, it wasn't just me who felt the pinch of her absence. Francis Beaumont didn't dance with anyone at the court feasts, and his usual wayward spirit had simmered, which I suspected was also because Nick had gone ahead with our wedding, despite Francis's misgivings. Fortunately for the both of us, a letter soon arrived from Alice that announced she'd be back at court in time for the coronation. *Yes!*

Whether Kit would join the festivities, however, was another battle between Nick and me.

"She didn't even get to come to our wedding," I pleaded to him over our supper of roasted fish in his dining chamber.

His face made it clear that his sister traveling was still a sore point. "The roads are too dangerous for the princess to travel such a distance, especially with that traitor about. You know that I had wished to wait for a summer coronation, but now that Henry Howard intends to turn the people against us and bring my kingdom to bloodshed, we must delay no longer. As it is God's will, I will see my wife become queen, and I will thereafter crush that spawn of the devil and make an example of him."

I moped over my salmon fillet, hating the idea of Kit missing out on the thrills of the coronation that were right up her street. Still, I had to face that Nick was the expert on the safety of princesses who'd once been destined to die. Kit and I would just have to share a private celebration when I could return to Kenilworth. I planned to ask Nick if we could spend the next summer there—just us and Kit. I couldn't think of a better newlywed vacation.

December arrived, bringing fewer sunlight hours and a cloudy coolness that promised snow. Nick's distracted mood made it clear that Norfolk was still at large, yet the king remained defiant about the coronation plans. In keeping with tradition, we were to spend the night before the ceremony at the Tower of London. Our flotilla of barges sailed along the curvy Thames, carrying hundreds of attendants, courtiers, ladies, and guards. It took nearly a day for us to reach the Tower's sloshing water gate, where I had to hide my nose to obscure the stench of fish and sewage.

We were to lodge in the medieval tower of St. Thomas that overlooked the river, its stained-glass windows offering glimpses of the slanted red roofs atop London Bridge. I didn't want to leave the safety of the spacious bedchamber with its own chapel, and it dawned on me just how nervous I was about the coronation ceremony. I would've swapped the pomp and splendor for the intimacy of our simple wedding a thousand times over, but Nick's enthusiasm pacified my bursts of blind panic.

The city's curfew bells clanged at dusk. The blacksmiths and carpenters halted their hammering in the alleyways below, and an eerie, silent, blackness descended over London. I slept surprisingly soundly beside Nick, and we both rose early to take morning prayers in our chapel. After a lingering kiss goodbye, he slipped away to prepare for the big day in his own chambers, and my heart rate skyrocketed again with nervous jitters.

Lucinda and Bridget arrived after breakfast, sending my squeals of relief bouncing across the brightly colored tile floor.

"Mistress Grey has been caught up on the roads," Bridget said with an apologetic grimace, sending my stomach into free-fall. I'd have to cope with all this pageantry without Alice after all.

But my spirits lifted again as Bridget and Lucinda dressed me for the ceremony in an outfit too beautiful to be believed. My scarlet-red kirtle and stomacher were stitched with sapphires amid golden wing patterns that broadened as they descended to the floor. The gown draped over the top was made entirely of snow-white fur. It made me ill to think about what animals may have been slaughtered to construct the silky cloak, but it would at least keep me warm. My hair hung loose in combed waves, the top of my head left bare in readiness for my crown. The final touches were a sash woven entirely from white diamonds, plus the jewels of the Queens of England which Nick had given me when he proposed to me—a magnificent necklace of glittering blue diamonds with matching earrings.

When I faced the full-length mirror that Nick had installed for the occasion, I appreciated why Bridget and Lucinda were blushing at me like I was some sort of magical creature. I was the living image of a glorious Tudor queen, missing only my crown and scepter. *You go, girl.*

The intense day that ensued was mostly a blur to me. Six of Nick's most loyal courtiers, including Francis Beaumont, led me on foot to Westminster Abbey beneath a mobile canopy of purple velvet fringed with gold. We kept to the broader streets, but the surrounding alleyways with their narrow timber-framed buildings and overhanging balconies were jammed with chanting spectators. When we reached the gothic arches of Westminster Abbey, I could barely feel my face, but I wasn't sure if it was because of the sharp wind off the river or the nerves attacking my gut. The constant clanging of bells from the city parishes amid the grimy city smells were overwhelming my senses, and I began to feel suffocated and weak at the knees. By the time I stood inside the abbey before the Archbishop of Canterbury, I was ready to puke all over his fancy robes. But one look at Nick when he strode into my view in full Tudor regalia, a proud smile echoing the glimmer in his eyes, and I stabilized.

You can do this, Emmie Tudor.

The ceremony unfolded precisely as we'd practiced, except a thousand times faster. Before the High Altar, the Archbishop of Canterbury bestowed on me a ceremonial crown, an ornamental mace, and a scepter. Hymns were sung, and then it was over in the blink of an eye. I was officially the Queen of England and would go down in history as a member of the Tudor dynasty. *Take that, Henry Howard, and your backstabbing gang of conspirators. You can all bite me.*

The king took my hand, and we emerged from the abbey into blinding light and a full-fledged street party. My protective husband sat beside me in a golden chariot, and the commoners cheered—some even wept—at the sight of him. The coronation parade was to lead us down to Westminster Pier, where a feast would be held aboard the royal barges because there hadn't been enough time to spruce up Westminster Hall.

Our glimmering, sunlit chariot moved slowly to the harmonies of a walking choir, its gentle volume swallowed by the rising chants of the crowds. A gigantic sculpture of a rising phoenix loomed over a moving constellation of fire-breathing dragon puppets, acrobats, and dancers with scarves and bells tied to their limbs. I'd never seen anything more spectacular or more expensive, and I tried to put the impoverished peasants we'd seen on progress out of my mind.

Nick snapped at a string of grimy-faced men standing without caps on their heads—a sign of disrespect to the new queen. As we continued past a classical fountain that poured wine, a tall man with an ostrich feather in his hat appeared in the swarm of spectators, and I stretched my neck to make him out. I could've sworn it was Henry Howard glaring right at me. Another guy with a face like thunder looked just like Viscount Hereford, the stuck-up nobleman who Nick had once expelled from his court. As we passed the men, however, I realized my eyes were playing tricks on me—seeing monsters that weren't there. As our chariot tilted toward the pier, a rush of bodies chased us down the hill. By the time we'd reached a standstill beside the stone water gate, I was clambering to get out of the chariot and away from the stifling crowds. There were too many of them.

Guards jostled with forceful revelers as I stumbled down the carriage steps in my ridiculously oversized farthingale. I stepped forward and jerked to a violent halt. My dress was caught on something. I spun to face a mob of wild-faced spectators, their grubby hands clinging to my skirt folds, preventing me from moving.

"What are you doing? Let go!" I cried in shock, but there was too much noise, too many fingers clawing at me. I couldn't see Nick, but I heard him shouting my name. The more the guards pushed to get through to me, the more the wall of strangers pulled at my skirts until I was crushed into a pit of deafening blackness.

My heart was beating a hole through my chest, and I couldn't breathe through the web of bodies closing in on me. My arms, flailing in panic, were seized and ripped upward, nearly popping from their sockets. My legs and shoulders were being violently tugged in all directions, and I screamed in pain until my throat was raw. I was about to be dragged through the streets of London and torn apart, limb-by-limb! I had to fight, but there were too many grabbing hands, before incredible power gripped me and hoisted me toward the sky. Two beefy guards had got hold of me and were carrying me out of the swarm like a crowd-surfer, a dense blanket of clouds swinging over my head. Nick was still yelling behind me—at whom, I couldn't tell—before I was dropped onto a bundle of plush cushions. In seconds, the clawing fingers had vanished.

"Make haste!" roared the irate voice of Francis Beaumont, and the ground beneath us glided forward with two sturdy arms holding me steady.

"Shush," Nick whispered soothingly into my ear. I clutched him tightly like a terrified cat, whimpering.

"What happened?" I said, orienting myself so I could sit upright. Nick and I were inside the cabin on the king's royal barge.

"The people set upon you," he said grimly. "This is why I

shun the city as I would the plague. The people love you so greatly that they could have suffocated you for it." He nuzzled his cheek into mine. "Dear God, if something had happened to you."

Nicholas the Ironheart would split this country apart. That's what would happen.

I gripped my quivering knees, finding a tear in the delicate fabric of my gown. The men and women who'd mobbed me hadn't looked in love with me. I didn't want to break it to Nick that their expressions had held nothing but hatred. Just because I'd come around on the concept of Emmie Grace, Tudor Queen, didn't mean the rest of the country had.

Through the curtains, Francis Beaumont was speaking gravely with the king's security team. I shut my eyes and curled into my new husband, fighting to forget the feeling of a thousand enraged fingers on my skin. We were supposed to enjoy the coronation feast on the river outside Westminster, but our barge continued gliding farther from London. Cannons blasted salutes as we passed with our procession of boats drifting close behind. Nick announced that the coronation feast was to move closer to Hampton Court Palace, which subdued my thumping heart. It'd be safer and quieter there.

The wharves of greater London were soon replaced with fishing villages and lush parklands. The oarsmen swept the murky water as we coasted along the river's edge to the cries of swooping birds finding a home for the night. Trying to forget the nightmare at the water gate, I watched a heron land on a grassy river island, its beak digging into its wing. By the time we made our way around the windy bend to Hampton Court Palace, the sky had blackened.

"We shall feast here," Nick commanded, and our fleet of barges formed a line outside the palace. A crewmember dropped anchor, and a slow barge three times the size of ours drew up beside us, holding feasting tables that were hurriedly being checked and redressed. Sweet herbs were lit to mask the river smells as we climbed on board.

A second boat delivered the senior nobles to the feasting barge, as well as Bridget and Lucinda, who were freaking out about the pandemonium at the pier. Nick left us alone so they could cheer me up, and we sipped wine inside the barge's cabin while a musician gently strummed his lute. Already, I felt the terror of the mob at Westminster withdrawing from my bones.

Through the cabin window, I spotted a girl in a grape-colored gown standing at the Hampton Court Palace water gate, her waist-length, wavy hair making me sit higher on the cushion. She said something to a guard and pointed at our barge.

"That's Alice; she's here!" I cried, jumping to my feet. I leaned out of the open window, waving, but Alice didn't see. When she climbed into a small boat that began rowing to the furthest barge containing the dullest nobles, I cupped my hands around my lips and called out to her.

"What in the devil?" Nick said, pushing through the curtain. When I explained, he ordered his attendants to retrieve Mistress Grey and make her a place setting on the king's feasting barge.

"She'll sit beside me," I instructed, trying out my new authority. Nobody dared argue with me.

Minutes later, Alice climbed aboard, grinning with a healthy glow. She flew toward me but then remembered herself and bowed, praising me as her new queen. Francis Beaumont tipped his tousled curls to her in greeting, and a deep blush coated her cheeks.

"Can you believe it: I left Northamptonshire a week past, but we were stranded in Aylesbury," Alice moaned. "We rode so hard that one of the horses came up lame, and we had to acquire a new one." She gave both Bridget and Lucinda an energetic hug.

Grateful for the heat of the torches in the chilly night air, I caught up with Alice over a sprawling supper of roasted lamb, pheasant, venison, peacock, swan, dolphin, and seal.

As we nibbled on edible marzipan phoenixes with gold wings dressed in rose petals, Alice updated me on her mom. She said that Susanna Grey recognized her former home and appeared happy to be reunited with Sir Thomas, but there was a change in her. Susanna had become frail and unable to look after herself properly. My mind tore back to Massachusetts, where Susanna—as Jane Stuart—had lived in a state of helpless confusion. Alice trembled a little as she asked if her sister Violet could stay in Northamptonshire and care for her mother. Her smile returned when she said there was also a man of three-and-forty years, a Mister William Cornwallis, who had proposed to marry Violet.

"Of course—if Lottie is happy with that, then so am I," I said, licking cream off my spoon. "I'll miss having her around, though. She's a sweetheart."

Alice's knee bounced nervously. "I may also wish to return to Northamptonshire to find a husband so I may be of more help to my household."

I nearly coughed up a coral-colored rose petal. The Alice I knew had mostly shunned the idea of her own marriage. Plus, how would I pull off my new job of Queen of England without her?

She couldn't look at me. "I wish not to leave your household, my lady. However, I remain but a maiden, and if I find not a husband, I fear that I may end up forever dependent on my sister. If any ill should befall her, I could become destitute and as frantic as my mother has become."

"I would never let that happen," I said, sensing the blue diamonds weighing down my earlobes that could probably buy Alice her own house and then some. She had helped me so much already; I would gladly share everything I had with her.

Francis had turned silent beside the king, and I could tell that he was listening. Now if he would just *do* something about it.

A glittering water pageant abruptly commenced in front of our barge, shutting down the conversation. An artificial island that was tied to the wharf erupted in a shower of fireworks, before entertainers dressed as mermaids dived off the island to perform a synchronized swimming dance with coordinated tails flapping. Before they could catch hypothermia, the swimmers returned to shore, and dancers in glittering unicorn costumes began prancing across the island. A breathtaking performance of sung verses followed, before a 'wild man' actor draped with moss and ivy dramatically professed his love to a nymph played by a young man, who suggestively unwrapped his greenery to reveal a suave knight. It was hard to believe that, only a few short hours earlier, a hysterical mob had nearly ripped me to pieces. Now, beneath a blanket of stars and surrounded by people I loved, I was having the best night of my life.

When the pageant ended in a second spray of fireworks, Nick rose to his feet, cueing the courtiers to follow. "Let us dance!" he said. "May I present your queen, Emmeline of England!"

Cheers resounded as Nick took my hand, leading me to a small space in the heart of the barge. Thank goodness for the bit of wine I'd had because he launched me into the volta without a heads-up, stepping and hopping to the lively music. He gripped my waist and lifted me over his hip, and a thrill shook through me that rippled through the audience.

When the song ended, Lord and Lady Ascot were the next couple to dance, followed by Lord and Lady Snell, who were clearly keen to upstage them before the king. Nick and I stood aside with his arm curled around me, politely watching the dances unfold. I glanced over at Alice and Francis. They both sat at the head table like statues, neither looking at the other.

Oh, FFS.

"The Earl of Warwick and Mistress Alice Grey!" I cried out, enlivened by the wine I'd had. Alice's mouth dropped open, and Francis shot to his feet, his olive skin turning pink.

"Naughty girl," Nick chuckled in my ear as Francis led Alice off the dais and into the dance zone. She shot me a 'you're in trouble' look as they passed by, but she couldn't hide her smile. Francis and Alice laced their fingers and hopped together before he grasped her waist and spun her high in the air. Each time they repeated the move, their bodies pressed closer together, their dark eyes fusing. I leaned closer into Nick, and he rubbed his jaw against my hair. Love was blooming, and it wasn't just ours.

The song ended too soon, and Francis folded into an elegant bow like Alice was the new queen. I adored every second of it. Nick announced a change to a more subdued tune, and the harpist took over. The metallic glitter was the perfect backdrop to gentle chatter as Nick pulled out his pocket watch. I could tell he was getting tired.

When we all returned to our seats to formally conclude the night, Francis leaned close to Nick. "Majesty, may I share a short speech?" he said softly. Nick frowned, and Francis dropped his voice to a level I couldn't hear.

When Nick whispered his response, the earl rose and stood before Alice, speaking quietly. "Mistress Grey, may I inquire whether you are in need of the privy at present?"

Privy was the Tudor word for bathroom, and the question was weird. Why would he ask her that in public?

"I beg your pardon?" she said, her voice taking on an edge.

"The privy…a lesson on how to hunt without every error under the sun…another sudden departure to God-knows-where…I mean to know if I may have your full attention for a moment?"

Alice glanced at me, jaw open. "Lord Warwick, does taking no heed of your tedious questions pass as an activity?"

Francis just laughed, looking more than handsome as he strutted to the center of the barge, rubbing the heels of his palms together.

"Gentlemen and ladies of the court, the King's Majesty has agreed that I may have your attention on a matter of great importance!"

Nick snorted lightly beside me.

"Good God, what is he doing?" said Alice.

Francis wavered on his feet, tipsy but coherent. "This night, I wish to honor a lady of true eminence." Every guest on the barge glanced over at me. "I believe it makes me more of a man, and not less, to say that there are certain ladies I cannot bear to live without. This day, we celebrate the Queens of England!" The guests cheered and raised their glasses. I could feel Alice beaming at me. Nick placed a hand over mine and squeezed my fingers.

Francis kept going, his natural charisma holding the barge's attention. "For me, the queen of my person—and my heart—may be slow to believe, but I beseech her to understand why my mouth can be so shy to speak when my heart is in such a roar. Our gracious Majesty has awarded me his blessing to speak it now, so I may show mercy on my soul and share what I can no longer burden with the weight of silence."

When Francis approached Alice and dropped to one knee, we all gasped, Alice loudest of all.

He gazed up at her, his pitch-black eyes soft at the edges. "Mistress Alice Grey, I cannot pleasure in anything anymore without the hope of your love. For you have mine—above all things—you have my love. Dearest lady, would you do me the honor of becoming my wife? I beseech you, for my heart can hide no longer from what is plainly true."

A rush of whispers broke out; it was unthinkable to steal the king's glory at such an event. But Nick looked anything but bent out of shape and threw his best mate a supportive smirk. I wasn't sure I was breathing.

Time slowed as Alice Grey stared down at Francis Beaumont, his eyes blinking up into hers. The electricity between them could've powered a kingdom.

In one swift step she stood up and came to my side, crouching to whisper in my ear. "Emmie, may I have your permission to accept? It would mean I could remain in your service, which would greatly please me."

I wanted to shake her but in a good way. Silence swept the barge as I replied under my breath. "First of all—hell yes! Secondly, you'll never have to ask my permission for anything that makes you happy...*ever*. Got it?"

Her moist eyes gleamed at mine before she hitched her skirts so she could descend the dais to the trembling Francis. Alice pressed a petite hand to the cherry-colored lining of his gray coat —a scandalous but exhilarating move in Tudor England—and slid her palm up to his ruffled collar, sinking her fingers into the black curls of his hair to cup the back of his neck. Francis sighed as Alice pulled him close and kissed him with a conservative sweetness before the king, but one fueled by visible longing.

When their lips separated, Alice whispered in Francis's ear. His smile was teary.

"The lady agrees!" he cried, and the barge roared with cheers. The love scene before me blurred through the tears that skimmed my cheeks. Nick flicked a hand to cue the harpist again, and a hum of contented chatter fell over the barge. The boats behind us glittered with lit candles, none of them able to return to shore before the king.

Nick let Francis and Alice share some time alone in the secluded cabin before he commanded to have us returned to the palace. We climbed aboard the royal barge, which made a sluggish turn toward shore, commencing its glide. I hugged Alice with a squeal. Francis stood back with the Lord Chancellor, still on duty as the king's right hand, but he couldn't stop smiling despite the chancellor's dull tone. I hoped that maybe the genuine love between Nick and I had inspired Francis in some way, despite his early reservations about us.

Our barge rocked as the tip grazed the water gate. Nick gripped my elbow to keep me steady.

"His Majesty, the King!" cried a guard on the platform. Nick and I took a step forward, and a whiz of wind exploded past my ear.

I grabbed the soft folds of skin there. "What was that?" I said, but was cut off by loud yells.

"Duck! Save the king!"

A sudden force tackled me to the ground. I screamed in shock, my chin banging against planks of wood. Fingers clawed at me to roll me over, and I spun into Nick's shaking arms. Shouts and screams tore through the air above me.

"We are being ambushed," Nick hissed as my eyes searched through the wall of black-leather boots surrounding us.

"Stay back!" a guard shouted above us. "Protect the king!"

Two more whizzes sounded, followed by a thud. A woman screamed, and a heavy weight dropped onto my leg, nearly crushing it. I cried out, but my calf was pinned.

"Every man down!" another guard cried, and bunches of fabric sank over boots and heels as people crouched all around us. Nick kept my torso pressed tightly to his. His heart hammered like a bass drum where our bodies pressed together.

The barge fell silent, amplifying the sloshing of waves against the side as our boat rocked in the water. Male voices bellowed in the distance. Footsteps rushed toward us and then stilled before the *thwicks* of releasing arrows began in fast sequence. Nick gripped me tighter.

Endless minutes later, boots thundered closer to the wharf and voices shouted, briefing our guards that the assassins had been apprehended. The guards gave the all-clear for the king to rise within a funnel of men that offered a complete circle of protection.

"Is everyone okay?" I said hoarsely as Nick helped me up and shoved away a guard who tried to touch me. My chin stung, and my lower leg ached.

"We must make haste," Nick said, wiping my chin with his sleeve. The damp spot hurt, confirming that I was bleeding. The barrier of guards escorting us off the barge made it impossible to see, but a woman moaned behind me, and a commotion of people tried to help her.

A second later, Francis's unmistakable voice cried out. "No, no, *no!* By God's grace, no—I pray you!"

I spun around with my heart in my mouth. "Where's Alice?" I said to Nick.

"Make haste!" he said again, pulling me close as we climbed onto the landing stage. Nick appeared unscathed, but his eyes flamed bright green with a blinding rage that I'd rarely seen.

A coach waited on the road behind the king's water gate. Guards with crossbows sat poised inside each window as Nick and I were speedily ushered onto the opposite bench. Perhaps walking up the slope to the palace would be too dangerous.

"Was someone hurt?" I said through the bile in my throat as I angled to see past the guards. People were still huddled over someone on board the barge.

"Who took the arrow?" Nick snapped at a page outside the coach window.

"I believe it was Mistress Alice Grey, Your Majesty," the boy said, his crooked teeth chattering. "I saw the arrow strike the lady in the chest."

The noise that blasted from my lips sounded inhuman. Nick took me in his arms, catching me as I howled into his side.

16

I WAS TRAPPED INSIDE A NIGHTMARE, worsened by the sickening jolts of our coach tearing across boggy ground. I sat up, absorbing the passing blur of tangled woodlands and farming cottages. Hampton Court Palace was long behind us.

"Where are we going?" I said in a choked voice.

"Robin House," Nick replied. "Hampton Court Palace is no fortress."

"But neither is Robin House."

"Few know of the manor's existence," he explained. "You shall be more safe there."

I slumped against the window, watching the brave bowmen on horseback riding alongside our carriage, ready to strike at anyone following us.

Alice was shot in the chest with an arrow. Francis was howling. Alice is dead.

My throat constricted until I couldn't breathe. There was only one reason the king's barge would be ambushed on the eve of his wife's coronation: no matter how well I played the part—no matter how much I tried to fit in—the people didn't want me as their queen. The same way the Duke of Norfolk, Thomas Grey, and even Francis Beaumont hadn't. Would this ever end?

"They are having bonfires in London," Nick said, pointing at a blush of light haloing the horizon. Given the circumstances, I was pretty sure they weren't fires of celebration.

The memory of Alice's face pushed into my mind again—her smitten smirk melting into Francis's—and another sob convulsed from my throat. Nick squeezed me tightly, his breaths deep and heavy.

We held each other until our coach slowed along the mossy pathway leading to Robin House. The guards rushed ahead to check over the manor and light the fires, but Nick and I barely saw them as he ushered me upstairs. We said nothing to each other...the creaking of floorboards as we moved was the only sound to penetrate the unbearable silence.

Not wanting to see anyone, we untied each other's intricate coronation outfits and climbed into the bed, grasping for each other's warmth. Exhaustion sent me to sleep without effort, but I soon woke to an inky-black sky through the leaded window-panes. Nick lay sleeping, a peaceful silhouette of a troubled angel. I knew he loved me—he wouldn't have risked everything to be with me if he didn't. But for Alice to die before she was meant to...just because Nick and I had defied the path of history to be together? The thought tasted like bitter poison.

Emmie, what have you done?

When the thoughts turned so cold that I shivered, I tugged the fur blankets to my chin and took slow, focused breaths so I didn't end up with an asthma attack on top of everything else. I twisted every which way to shake off the despair in my heart, but there was nowhere to hide.

By some miracle, I slept a while longer until my eyes twitched open to the relief of daylight and an empty mattress beside me. The memories of the night before resurfaced, and I dodged them by dozing for as long as I could. Before long, however, my mounting concern about Nick's whereabouts pushed me out of bed.

After sluggishly dressing in the simplest kirtle I could find in the clothes chest, I headed downstairs. Nick was in the dining chamber, huddled over a hand-painted map with four of his privy councilors, but there was no sign of Francis Beaumont. He must've stayed with Alice while she...I swallowed a sob. One of the earls was addressing the king about war taxes, but when Nick saw me, he excused himself, guiding me outside to the courtyard.

"Are you well?" he said, surveying my injured chin. "I wished not to awaken you."

I tumbled into his arms, my stinging eyes locked on the patch of ground where, just a few days ago, we'd married each other with nothing but hope in our hearts.

As I struggled to speak, Nick pulled me to look at him. "Emmie, my lords brought word from Hampton Court. Mistress Grey is alive."

Tears rushed to my eyes. "Are you serious?"

"The lady was shot in the shoulder, not the chest. Doctor Norris says she will be well." He exhaled like he still couldn't believe it. "Mistress Grey is being tended to at court, and Lord Warwick will remain with her."

The hopeless, heavy mass inside me exploded into a burning ball of light. I wanted to cry and scream and shout from the rooftops.

"When can we go back?"

Nick cleared his throat. "You shall not return to the palace, my lady. However, I will take my leave from here this day."

I didn't know how to reply. Why would he leave me here?

Nick took my silence as an objection, and his eyes pleaded with me. "It is much too dangerous for your person to be at court during this time. My council has gathered news throughout the night." His cheeks reddened, his jaw tight. "Fires of high treason are blazing across London in protest of your coronation. Henry

Howard's rebellion against you is spreading, and we believe he sent the archers to the coronation feast. Fear not, my lady; when I find that devil, I will see him dragged through the city alive, and then hung, drawn, and quartered, with his innards fed to the street dogs."

My stomach rolled with nausea. Hopefully, Norfolk didn't feed *me* to the dogs first.

"Just tell me what to do," I said, shaking away the terrifying image. I couldn't believe this was happening—that people actually wanted me dead for marrying the king.

"You will remain at Robin House under close guard," Nick said firmly. "You may keep a maidservant, but no one must know you are here—not even your ladies; do you understand? Few know of this place, and there is nowhere more safe for you to be while I crush Howard and every traitor who seeks to defy his sovereign king."

He began detailing a play-by-play about arrests and burnings and beheadings...the words right out of a textbook about Nicholas the Ironheart. His hands balled into fists so tight that his knuckles whitened. I wanted to calm him down—to talk him out of this merciless spiral—but my lips wouldn't open. Not only did I need Nick to continue being honest with me, but I was no longer sure that kindness and mercy were the best ways to govern a sixteenth-century country. Norfolk's allies had just tried to assassinate me, nearly killing Alice in the process. I had to stop acting like we were living in the twenty-first century. If this fight came down to Henry Howard, the traitor, or Nicholas Tudor, the reigning King of England, I would support my husband, regardless of how much blood was spilled.

"Please be careful," I whispered, my body weak at the thought of losing him. For all I knew, harming the king was part of Henry Howard's plan to get back at me.

Nick caught the fear in my face and tried to hug it away, a tingling heat coursing through our connected bodies. When we parted, he twisted the blue-diamond ring off his finger and slid it onto my thumb.

"What are you doing? I uttered.

He pressed his lips together, steadying himself. "My dearest love, it is time for you to make me a most important promise."

I froze, hanging on every word that Nick struggled to say.

"Emmie, if your life is in danger—at any moment—you will wear this ring and do everything in your power to use it. Wait not for me. Do you hear me? If your life is at stake, you *will* go home to your time without hesitation. I must have your word."

I couldn't grasp my whirring thoughts. The enchanted ring had acted strangely for so long now that I wasn't sure how many time travel trips were left in it. What if I did what Nick asked, and then I could never get back here to him? I'd made my choice —it was to stay here with Nick. We were married now, and I wasn't going anywhere.

A sheen of tears glazed his restless eyes as they searched mine.

"I don't want to use the ring any more without you," I said. "When I went back to my time to get Susanna Grey, the ring was struggling to work again. I woke up in Massachusetts, like, four times. Now that we're married...now that we've *been* together... I–I can't be that far away from you. We have to figure something else out."

He stepped forward, threading our hands together. "Let us then make one more vow. Should your life be at stake, you will use this ring to journey home without me. I beseech you to give me your word on that. But for *any* reason other, we will use this ring only together."

I squeezed his fingers. "Only *together*," I affirmed. "I'm never leaving you again unless it's to literally save my life."

"Only together," he repeated in a strained voice. "We will swear it."

We sealed the vow with a prolonged, distraught kiss, and I cried into his chest, dreading letting go.

Our goodbye was quick and heavy with despair. We couldn't even look at each other for fear of it being the last time we ever would.

Tears streamed down my face while I watched from the upstairs window as my husband climbed aboard his coach. It careened away from the house in a fog of dust.

My back slid down the stone wall until my bottom hit the floorboards. I rested there for a while, listening to the reassuring sound of the guards' footsteps pacing the manor downstairs. A scary number of people wanted my head on a stick, and I was pretty sure that Robin House didn't have a panic room. I had to come up with a hiding place where I could fall asleep in case the assassins figured out where I was and stormed the house—*if* the enchanted ring even worked properly. I slid it onto my thumb and curled my fingers over the smooth stone.

So much had changed in a handful of months. I'd gone from arguing with Nick over my right to use the blue-diamond ring whenever I wanted to hating the idea of traveling to my time without him. Things had become worse here than I could have imagined, but what mattered most to me now was that we stayed together.

Only together.

As long as Henry Howard doesn't jam Nick's head onto a pike and parade it through the city of London.

A descending curtain of dread sent me to my feet. I had to dig myself out of my grisly thoughts before they buried me alive. I moved to the cloudy standing mirror and sized up my appearance, straightening my lacy sleeves. After dragging an ivory comb through my knotted hair, I braided the unruly waves and pinned a hood over the top. Despite being under glorified house arrest, I was still the wife of the King of England.

My young maidservant Clemence entered with a buttery-smelling custard tart and a bowl of winter berries. I wanted her to stay and chat with me, but she didn't dare impose, and I was too slow to request it. The door shut behind her, and I ate in gloomy silence except for the soft slurps of my lips savoring creamed sugar.

Those sounds—alongside the clink of pewter plates, the thud of oak doors closing, and the shuffling boots of guards on patrol —became my life for the next few weeks. I stopped counting how long I'd been at Robin House after seven days because time was moving agonizingly slowly and keeping track only made it worse.

During our breathless farewell, Nick had explained that we couldn't write to each other and risk the letters being inter-cepted. He kept to his word, and no news came. Knowing nothing about his efforts to capture Henry Howard was like living in purgatory. One minute I'd be dusting the bookcase and imagining the former duke spearing Nick with a ten-foot sword; the next, I'd be perked up by a vision of my king in a parade of victory. Which one was it to be?

To release some of the nervous energy bubbling up inside me, I asked the chief guard, Joseph Blackburn, if I could jog along some of the wild pathways around the house if I took a body-guard with me. He agreed with visible reluctance, and I set off in my leather boots down the slope to the birch trees and back again, with four plain-clothes guards trailing me. On day two, a painful blister had formed where the knot of my garter held up my woolen hose. Without any gym shoes, I was going to have to make do with brisk walks instead of jogging. I fell into a favorite route that ended atop the grassy hill overlooking the hamlet, where chirping birds rollicked in the rustling trees. I'd sit there for a while and watch the villagers tending to their winter gardens, taken by the simplicity of their lives. I ached to go down there, not only to see a sixteenth-century farming settlement up close, but to feel less alone here. Aside from Clemence and the guards, I hadn't seen a human face in weeks.

When I asked Mister Blackburn if I could visit the village, he declined with a physical recoil. Later that night, I overheard him arguing with one of the younger guards. The kid warned Blackburn that refusing the queen's request could be a shortcut to the Tower of London—or worse—if the king learned of it. The next morning, Mister Blackburn apologized and offered to take me to the hamlet himself *if* I agreed to avoid the villagers, in case any of them had been in the city for my coronation—as unlikely as that was—and recognized me. Shadows circled his bloodshot eyes. The poor guy hadn't slept a wink over this thing.

I borrowed some clothes from a confused Clemence, noting the relief that blew across Mister Blackburn's face. No one would guess that I was the persecuted queen in a tawny woolen kirtle and a plain apron and coif. I wore no jewelry but kept the blue-diamond ring close to me, hiding it on my thumb inside a pair of woolen gloves.

Four guards hid on the hillside as Joseph Blackburn and I approached the village on horseback, disguised as father and daughter out for a ride. The hamlet was no more than a dirt path lined with single-story wattle-and-daub cottages with few windows. We tethered our horses to an iron ring in a wall and strolled down the dusty track on one side, clinging to the last strip of sunlight. A trio of grubby-faced girls in knitted dresses were feeding scraggly lettuce leaves to a goat beside the pigsty. When they saw us approaching, they scampered to hide behind a man tending to a crop of onions with a hoe.

Mister Blackburn's horse grunted from the wall a few feet behind us. The poor steed had trodden into a tangle of sheets hanging from a wooden frame. Joseph paced back to untwist the horse, apologizing to the farmer. The man stopped weeding and rested on the handle of his hoe, giving us a slight nod of greeting that also delivered a message: we were being watched, so we'd better not be here to start trouble.

Mister Blackburn moved us on, and we ambled past a pen of

undersized sheep and healthy bed of spinach and cabbage, before reaching what looked to be a small alehouse.

"Shall we make ready to return?" Blackburn said, chewing the inside of his lip.

The sight of a marking scratched into the wall beside the alehouse interrupted my response. It was the shape of a flower within a circle, which I'd seen before—carved into the cheeks of the witch Agnes Nightingale.

A man stumbled out of the alehouse holding a flagon, and Mister Blackburn stepped between us. I shifted closer to the dwelling, scanning for more mystical signs. A fur that hung over a small, glassless window jerked sideways. A girl's face gazed out at me with ebony braids of hair that were partially covered by a dirty coif. Her wide-set eyes darted to where the blue-diamond ring sat on my thumb inside my woolen glove. She reached an arm through the hole and cupped her fingers, calling me to her.

I stepped back and tripped over a flock of chickens, sending them into flustered squawks. The girl in the window burst out laughing.

"I'm ready to go," I blurted to Mister Blackburn, my cheeks burning.

He was too fixated on the drunkard from the alehouse to notice the girl, and he led me away from the man with obvious relief. Just a few feet behind him, the dirty-faced girl stared at my gloved hand again with a look of recognition. She'd detected my enchanted ring right through the woolen cloth like it was a flashing lightbulb. She had to be some kind of witch.

As she watched me, the girl's lips curled upward into a strange smile before Mister Blackburn hurried me away.

17

THE FIRST SNOWFALL forbade me from considering going to the village again, which had its upsides. I was still mad with curiosity about the enchanted ring that the witch had sensed—what it was all about, and if it could be repaired—but I wasn't sure I was ready to face any more dangers. As long as the snow was this heavy, there was no decision to be made.

The first few days hiding inside by the fireplace felt peaceful and cozy, and I managed to make sense of the first few chapters of *The Canterbury Tales* by Geoffrey Chaucer. I also added *The Chronicles of England, Scotlande, and Irelande* to my reading pile, given that the rest of the books on the shelf looked even more tedious and mostly devotional.

However, as the days became shorter, I spent more time lying in bed thinking about that witch. What if I was wasting my only chance to find out more about the mysterious ring? But, unlike Agnes Nightingale, I knew nothing about the girl from the village. What if she was dangerous or tried to steal the ring from me? What if she wasn't a witch at all and reported me for my interest in the dark arts? The questions kept circling, but no clear answers landed.

It was a Thursday afternoon when one of the patrolling guards shouted out from the front yard. Joseph Blackburn had been feeling off-color, so one of his sidekicks thundered through the front door to see what was going on. I sprinted to the window. The guards had apprehended a girl with flowing hair the color of dark chocolate who'd pulled up in an unmarked coach. *OMG—it's Alice!*

Fortunately, the guard recognized her, and she hurried inside to where I was waiting.

"What are you doing here?" I cried, throwing my arms around her petite shoulders before remembering her arrow wound. I jolted backward.

"Fear not," she said, reading my thoughts. "My shoulder is healing without trouble." She took my hands in her gloved fingers that were powdered with freezing snowflakes and bowed. "Oh, Emmie, I am surely pleased to see you well! I have waited for news of you for weeks, but I then I thought to see if you might be here. Mistress Bridget informed me of this secret place of your marriage."

Every inch of me iced over at the question that I knew I had to ask.

"Any news about the king?"

Nothing in Alice's face suggested catastrophe, but her brows dipped as she led me into the library so we could sit down. I pushed aside the washed linens that were drying before the fire, making space for us.

Alice clutched my hands with freezing fingers. "I bring no pressing news, my lady, but the latest word I received was that His Majesty is far in the north. Lord Warwick is with him." Her lips tightened at the mention of Francis, but she continued steadily. "Henry Howard has raised an army of many hundreds of men. They have horse and armor in great numbers." She played with the lace circling her wrist, unable to look at me. "The heralds bring terrible stories to court. They say the king has not yet found Howard and has burned villages in search of him. Men have been hanged by the rope, and I have heard of many rains of arrows." Her slim palm clasped her forehead. "Oh, Emmie, I suffer many fears. I fear that the king will summon my weakened father to his duty; I fear our countrymen will come to despise our king for his deeds. I fear that Francis will stop at naught to protect His Majesty and that Francis will…" Her voice caught, and I reached out to touch her hand.

"Don't go there," I said. "We can't think that way."

Alice nodded and pressed the corners of her eyes with her fingertips to wipe away tears while I tried to process her words. Nick was still trying to catch Henry Howard, who'd raised an army with every fighter prepared to go to war and potentially die in protest of our marriage. That wasn't even the hardest part to stomach; the boy I knew to be gentle and loving was nose-diving into a future I'd worked so hard to prevent. In his furious search for Howard, Nick had been burning villages and hanging men, possibly without the time for proper trials. He was becoming Nicholas the Ironheart—violent and vengeful—all because of me.

Alice reached across to rub her injured shoulder, sending guilt to my throat. "Alice, I'm so sorry. That arrow was meant for me."

"Oh, I pray you, Emmie, speak not of it," she said, cupping her ears in protest. "I cannot bear to imagine the loss of your person. I am heartily pleased that we are both well."

Clemence carried in a thrown-together platter of cheeses, manchet bread, and wine. Alice took a grateful sip, and we shared a withered smile. I didn't know how to cope with the news she'd brought. Nick was still in danger, villages had been reduced to ashes, and men were being put to death. I wrapped my arms around myself as if I might fall apart if I didn't physically hold myself together.

"How long can you stay?" I said weakly. "There's a ton of pie in the pantry."

Alice glanced at the window. "The weather is surely worsening, and my place is with my queen. I wish to remain here as long as it pleases Your Highness. We may pray together."

I beamed, my fatigued body roused by the thought of Alice staying. "Of course, I'd love that," I said. "But you should know that we get no news here...the king didn't want any messengers to know where I am. You'll hear more about Francis if you go back to court." I understood the weight of that as much as anyone.

"Perhaps I could ask my coachman to return with any urgent news from the north," Alice offered. "He now knows that I am here, so there can be no harm. Fear not; he is most discreet, my lady."

"That's fine by me," I agreed, relieved to have an avenue for some news. Alice and I shared a smile. At least we had each other now.

Winter at Robin House became infinitely more bearable with Alice Grey there. We played card games, embroidered, read poems aloud, and waited for news that never came. On the Twelfth Night, we welcomed in the new year of 1581 with blessings, fruitcake, and sweetened wine. Poor Mister Blackburn was back in bed with a headache, but I had some cake sent up to him in the hope he could enjoy a slice.

The entire household was passed out after the celebrations when a fist banged on the downstairs door in the dead of night. I thought I dreamt it until two more urgent thumps sent the outside hens into confused cackles. I shot upward in bed, finding Alice's silhouette facing our doorway. She turned to me, her moonlit expression sharing my thought: was it news about Nick and Francis?

Alice draped a shawl over me before we dashed down the stairwell. The guards on night duty stood gathered in the entrance hall, where a young girl in a blood-red cape waited on the doorstep. The wind that blew through the open door was shockingly cold.

"What mischief is this?" one of the guards snapped at her.

"Forgive the hour, my lords," she said in a mature voice that didn't suit her childlike face. "I am in search of herbs in great haste. Mandrake, wormwood, chamomile...any such thing thee may 'ave."

I gaped at her thick braids of black hair. It was the witch from the hamlet.

"What do you need the herbs for?" I said, stepping forward. Had she come looking for me?

"There is a plague of smallpox in the village," she replied without emotion.

"*Smallpox?*" a guard cried with horror.

"I 'ave not enough remedies for everyone," the girl added quickly. I emerged into the light, and her eyes shot to my bare thumb where she'd once detected the blue-diamond ring. "Does thee keepeth the ring safe, my lady?" she said to me. Alice grabbed my arm and tugged me away from the girl in case she was carrying the dreaded pox.

The guards formed a wall that pushed the young villager outside into a bank of snow, cursing at her. She twisted her neck to meet my eyes as the heavy wooden door swung shut in her face.

"How troubling," said Alice as our bare feet padded back upstairs to the bedchamber, leaving the guards arguing over which one had allowed in the villager exposed to smallpox.

My bed was cushioned with blankets and furs, and yet I couldn't relax through the images of the girl checking for the blue-diamond ring on my finger. She was more than a witch—she had to be some sort of clairvoyant.

As Alice gently snored, I watched the strips of moonlight peeking through the window shutters. It was perilously cold outside, and somewhere out there was Nick—risking his life to defend our marriage that should technically never have occurred. Less than a mile away lived a girl who might know something that could help make sense of how I'd even come to be in this time. After the loss of Agnes Nightingale, I couldn't get past the fact that another witch had been dropped into my lap—almost like a miracle. *Like it's meant to be.*

I sat up, sweat seeping into my nightgown. Visiting a witch during the daytime was out of the question. But could I actually sneak out of Robin House at night without being seen? The snow wasn't a deal-breaker—I had a thick cloak warm enough to cook an egg in and fur-lined boots. Smallpox, on the other hand, wasn't a disease I was keen to catch, nor did I want to risk giving it to anyone at Robin House or—heaven forbid—reintroduce it to the twenty-first century. However, having a nurse for a mom had made me pretty savvy about avoiding viruses: if I didn't get close to anyone or anything in the village, and I washed my hands thoroughly as soon as I got back, the chances of getting sick were low. I was more at risk of giving Alice a panic attack if she woke before I returned. Sneaking out at night in midwinter was dicey, even for me, but it was also my best chance—maybe my *only* chance—to finally get some answers.

I made up my mind. I was going to attempt it.

Downstairs, the guard on night shift sat hunched over a book in the library. I slid into the pantry as silent as a cat, ready to declare the munchies as my excuse if he caught me. Beside the cellar door at the rear of the house, bundles of herbs were hanging upside down to dry. I tore off a few sprigs of each and slipped outside with two gold sovereign coins jingling in my cloak in case I needed to bribe the witch.

The air was arctic, and I didn't have a lantern, but the moon hung full and brilliant, and I took it as a sign to keep going. I found the pathway, kicking up powdery snow that spilled into the collar of my leather boots. I sank knee-deep into banks of snow as I descended the side of the hill, my cheeks already numb.

Down in the hamlet, the tiny house where Joseph Blackburn and I had come across the kids and the farmer was boarded up with hand-sawed planks of wood. Keeping away from it, I hastened along the dirt path toward the witch's cottage beside the alehouse, hugging my chest. Knifelike icicles hung from the home's thatched roof like monster's teeth. With my gloves protecting my skin, I banged on the decaying door, feeling no hesitation. More than anything right now, I had to get warm.

Time slowed before the narrow door parted from the frame a crack. The girl's eyes peeked out at me for a moment before the gnarled plank swung wide open. I rushed inside to where a gentle fire sizzled on a mound of stones in a central hearth.

"My lady," the girl stammered, falling to her knees.

"Please, you can get up," I said through chattering teeth. She stumbled upward and tightened her shawl while I took in the primitive space faintly lit by rushlights. The uneven ceiling of crudely cut wooden beams was so low in places that I had to duck.

"This was all I could find in a hurry," I said, pacing across the earthen floor to offer her stems of purple and green, careful not to make skin contact.

Her eyes flashed wide as she took them, her bony fingers skimming the foliage. "Lavender...mint...marjoram. Not any I hath asked for, but the lavender may help the head pains. I thanketh thee."

She separated them into bundles on an uneven beam of wood resting on two stumps. It was the closest thing she had to a table. Hanging above her were charm-like knots of animal bones, snakeskin, herbs, and strips of hair.

"Is there smallpox in this house?" I said, unsure if I should move.

She shook her head, ebony braids flapping. "The pox plague is bound to the Blacke lodging at present. Down the street. Four 'ave did perish thus far."

"*Four?* I'm sorry to hear that." Man, I hoped that didn't include the little girls who'd been feeding the goat when Joseph Black-burn and I visited the village.

I looked for somewhere to rest my frozen legs, but the only vacant space was a bed made from a pile of straw with a wooden log for a pillow. The girl moved a bundle of knitting off a stool and dragged it over to me.

"May I speaketh plainly, my lady?" she said as I sat down on my cloak.

"Please do." I shivered.

She crossed her legs on the dirt floor to sit beside me. "Thee cameth here to seek answers. Let us speaketh them now. Thee may asketh me anything."

For some reason, her frankness wasn't a surprise. My throat closed up as my eyes welled with tears. It wasn't easy to get the words out. "Can you please tell me if my husband is okay? He's fighting a battle in the north."

The girl's eyes fell closed, and she sat there a while, rocking. "The king shall be nay more."

I gaped at her, waiting for more words, but was met by silence. "What do you mean the king will be no more?" I stammered, hot tears burning my eyes.

Her gaze drifted to where my hand buried itself inside the heat of my cloak. "Thee 'ave an enchanted ring. Yet I feel thee doth not understand it. And thee wishes to...most sorely."

My fingers shot out of the cloak, the blue-diamond ring glittering in full view. She already knew I was married to the king, by either snooping or magic, and I took it as a sign to waste no more time and speak freely. "You're right, this ring is enchanted, and I don't understand it at all. Can you tell me something... anything?" My voice shook with urgency.

The girl presented an upturned hand to me, her calloused skin so white it was nearly translucent. A lump grew in my throat. If I gave her the ring, she could refuse to hand it back, use it against me, or even disappear in time to the twenty-first century. I braced myself and dropped it into her palm, ready to fight tooth and nail at the first sign of trouble.

Her hand jerked as she brought the sparkling blue diamond to her eyes, her brow tightening. She glanced back at me with her lips agape. "Thee wanteth the king dead."

"What?" My belly hit the floor. "I don't want the king dead!"

"This ring is under enchantment to take away King Nicholas," she explained, rolling it around her palm with the tip of her finger. "'Tis weak, though. 'Tis power shall last not long." The girl's voice was smooth, but disgust clouded her ageless face. "This be the devil's work. He shall come for thee. *Lex talionis*, mistress. Thee hast been up to nay good...changing things that should not be hath changed. *Lex talionis.*"

I was sure the phrase was Latin, but she didn't say what it meant. The heat of the flames from the fire licked my knees, but I couldn't stop shaking.

"Can you tell me where the ring came from?" I said.

She nodded, a smirk creeping onto her face. "'Twas Joanie, I can see...cunning wench." The girl leaned forward so I could listen carefully. "Joanie hath passed on; she caught the deadly sweat. She was a cousin of mine. I met her but once, when I was a child and she cameth to visit. Joanie was the one who toldeth me I had the sight in mine own eyes and hands." Her fingertips drummed lightly on her torn woolen kirtle. "Joanie lived up Cumberland way. She be a maidservant in the prison where Mary Stuart lodged, who thee calleth the 'Queen of Scots'. Mary's eyes were nay good, and she did want Joanie to read to her, but nay one hath taught Joanie to read. Instead, Joanie did teach Mary Stuart all manner of alchemies, and they becometh cousins of heart. Mary Stuart had commanded Joanie to enchant this ring to curse the king." The girl touched my hand, her skin startlingly cold. "Before she cameth to Mary Stuart's prison, Joanie hadst been a maidservant at the Palace of Whitehall, mistress. Joanie did love the king with all her heart. His Majesty was all Joanie hath speaketh of when we met. Joanie was a defender of the true faith and despised Papists. If it be true that Mary Stuart gaveth Joanie a ring of the king's to curse, Joanie would 'ave made some trick to maketh it seem like the king was dead, but in fact *save* the king in secret."

She smirked with pride for her cousin's wit as I fought to decode her words. This witch believed that her cousin Joanie—who was also a witch—once worked at the Palace of Whitehall and adored King Nick. Joanie then moved to work in one of the castles where the treasonous Mary, Queen of Scots was imprisoned. Joanie became close to Mary, who learned about Joanie's powers of sorcery. Mary, Queen of Scots then commanded Joanie to curse King Nick's ring to destroy him. But instead of doing that, Joanie came up with an idea to curse her beloved king to disappear—*literally*—yet continue to live on elsewhere.

But even if that whacked-out theory was true, why was the ring cursed to send the king to Hatfield, Massachusetts, in the twentieth century? It was so random.

"Would thee taketh some pottage?" the girl said, gesturing to a steaming pot hanging from an iron frame over the fire.

"No, I have to get back, but thank you," I said hoarsely, standing up. I opened my palm in a request for her to return the ring to me.

She slid the gold band down her middle finger, sending panic quaking through me. Before I could react, she'd slipped it off again and passed it to me. "'Tis losing its power," she said again. "The ring was not meant to carryeth two persons, and for so many journeys, as thee hast done. My lady, this ring was enchanted for one use: to sendeth the King of England so far from here that his person would be safe from harm, but of nay more threat to that vile Mary Stuart." Her wide-set eyes leveled with me. "The ring shall work nay longer soon, if not already. The ring will stop soon. I hope thee hast chosen well, Your Highness."

Her last two words were pointed, reinforcing that I'd taken my time-travel fortunes a little too far and written myself into sixteenth-century history as its queen. *Yup, that whole thing, Emmie.*

I psyched myself up to face the wintry night and fished out the two coins from my cloak.

"Thank you so much for this," I said, leaving the gleaming discs stamped with the king's insignia on the wooden beam beside her. She drew in a sharp breath before sinking to her knees in a deep bow.

I said goodbye and stepped outside into the bone-chilling blackness.

When I was a few paces away from the cottage, the girl called after me, her voice a faint line beneath the rising wind. "'Twas thee, Your Highness."

"I'm sorry?" I called back, lifting my fur collar over my mouth.

"Thee wanteth to know why the ring would 'ave brought the king to thy time," she said from the door. "'Tis because of thee. It mattered not where the king went, as long as the place was far and as long as his heart was full and merry. The king would hast been most merry there, with *thee*, mistress." A smile of encouragement unfolded across her face before she swung the door closed.

He would have been most merry there...with you.

The meaning of the sentence replayed in my mind as I began the grueling climb through slushy snow back to Robin House. The reason why the ring was cursed to send Nick to my time—bringing Susanna Grey instead by accident—was because the witch Joanie wanted to send the king somewhere he'd be truly happy...which was with me.

It sounded side-splittingly bonkers, and yet, amid a myriad of unfathomable experiences this past year, something about it felt spot-on, like everything had finally fallen into place.

"*Lex talionis,*" the girl's singsong voice whispered on the curve of the wind. I still had to find out what that meant.

I rounded the final bend to Robin House—thirsting for the warmth of my bed—when I spotted a shiver of candlelight from the upstairs window. *Crap, I've been found out!* I rushed up the pathway that clung to the side of the manor. In the front yard, a huddle of guards clutching lanterns hovered around one of the watchmen who sat on a tree log beside the stables.

"The queen is here!" Alice yelped from behind me, and a guard separated himself from the pack to escort me to where she waited on the manor's front step.

"I'm *so* sorry," I said to Alice, who asked, "Where did you go?" at the same time.

"I–I just popped outside for a few minutes because I couldn't sleep, and I was so sweaty inside and couldn't get away from the heat of the fires," I said.

Her palm hit her open mouth. "Heavens, no…not you, Emmie."

"Not me, what?"

Alice's alarmed eyes darted to where the guards had gathered.

"What's happening over here?" I called, striding back to them, my boots crunching the dense snow. "It's the dead of night." Their lanterns bounced flickers of light as I approached.

"Step back, Your Highness!" snapped the young guard, blocking me from getting any closer. I could see that the seated guard was Joseph Blackburn. Why was his face covered with bees?

I gasped, nauseated, as the truth broke over me. They weren't bees: they were hundreds of pus-filled welts.

"He has smallpox," I said, clutching my sickened stomach. That's why he had been suffering from those awful headaches.

"You must take leave inside, Your Grace," said the guard. "We shall keep Mister Blackburn here for now."

"Outside? In this freezing weather—are you mad?"

"We cannot chance spreading the pox to your person, your

highness. The servants' attic is above your chamber. Mister Blackburn may sleep in the stables."

I was so stunned that I couldn't speak properly. "Don't be insane! Alice and I will stay downstairs...or in the cabin outside."

Alice had appeared beside me, snow flurries landing on her cheeks. "Be calm, Emmie. I have sent word to my coachman to come for us in haste. The pox is terribly contagious, and it is no longer safe here. The guard is already riding to Hampton Court, and the coachman should be here by morning." She gently urged me toward the house.

"He is *not* staying out here," I said through worried tears. Joseph Blackburn hunched forward, his head hanging into his knees. Inflamed blisters speckled the back of his neck. I'd learned enough about smallpox to know that the lesions didn't appear until the person had been exposed to the virus for weeks. He'd most likely caught it when I took him down to the infected village. It was my fault that he was sick.

Alice huffed at me, her face torn with distress. I didn't want to be difficult, and I was the queen now and had to be protected, even if I hated being put on a special pedestal above everyone else.

"Mistress Grey and I will sleep in the guest lodging this night," I said loudly enough for everyone to hear. "It's not likely to be contaminated, and there's a small fireplace in there. Mister Blackburn can come inside the house at once. If Alice and I are leaving the manor anyway, he can use my bedchamber."

"Clemence and I will make ready the guest lodging," said Alice. She scurried back into the manor.

"Please, somebody help him with food and water, or I'll do it myself," I ordered the guards. "If you wash your hands constantly and thoroughly—and stay well clear of any coughs or sneezes—I can't see why you wouldn't be fine. I'll send a doctor back here as soon as I can."

I hurried upstairs to scrub my hands and the blue-diamond

ring in a pail of soapy water before changing into a fresh night-gown. I tossed every piece of fabric I'd worn to the village into the fireplace to be safe.

The moment I met Alice in the cabin out the back, she pressed a hand to my forehead. "Do you feel the heat even now?" she said with a pinched brow.

"I'm not sick," I said in a reassuring tone. "I swear that it was just a hot flush. I get them sometimes."

You mean you were in the smallpox village, chatting with a witch about time travel and curses on the king. Things they kill people for around here.

I secured the blue-diamond ring inside the toe of one of my riding boots. Once Alice and I had built a fire, we both stretched out on the single mattress after I refused to let her sleep on the floor. There had been so much commotion that I hadn't really taken in that we were returning to Hampton Court Palace in the morning. It was hard to lie still and not disturb Alice through my overwhelming relief. I didn't give a toss that some of the men who wanted me dead might be at the palace, lying in wait. I was ready to go home, where I could call for doctors to help Mister Blackburn and I could be among the first to receive news about King Nick.

Nick, who wasn't meant to be in the north of England in the dead of winter, putting his life on the line for a twenty-first-century girl who'd muscled her way into his world. The witch had studied the ring and said it herself: Nick was supposed to be living in *my* time, with me—that was the point of the blue-diamond ring coming into his life.

The problem was that we'd already made our decision to stay in the sixteenth century, where we'd been in near-constant danger. The enchanted ring was nearly out of juice, Nick was at war with a murderous former duke, and the peaceful happiness that the witch Joanie had tried to bring Nick—and me—had slipped right through our fingers.

18

GIVEN that the king was away battling a violent uprising, I braced myself for a spiritless and somber court. The moment we arrived back at Hampton Court Palace, however, it was clear I was way off the mark. A merry clash of lutes and oboes bled jubilantly from the stained-glass windows of the Great Hall as Alice Grey and I climbed the stairs in our traveling cloaks. With trestle tables stretching through the hall and into the neighboring Great Watching Chamber, men and ladies of the court sat giggling and chattering over jugs of ale and steaming platters of roasted halibut and turbot—as lively as I'd ever seen them.

That was until they saw me.

Lord and Lady Snell spied us first, followed by the Earl of Dorset, the sneering Ascots, and the remaining courtiers as a wave of awkward silence devoured the space. Nobody rose to bow to me—their new queen—and there was a severe shortage of smiles. I hadn't missed the glacial temperatures of the Tudor court, and I wasn't talking about the weather.

"It appears our arrival has made good time for supper," Alice said. "I could eat a swine."

Her comment barely registered over the ocean of accusing

eyes still glaring at us. Alice made an unsettled murmur about the queen dining in private, and we continued through the Great Watching Chamber, nearly colliding with a servant boy grappling with a platter of fish from the servants' stairs.

We made our way down the stone stairwell in our bulky farthingales. "Such merriment while the king is at war," Alice castigated. "It would not please His Majesty."

I wanted to reply, but the words wouldn't form. In my eagerness to return to Hampton Court, I hadn't considered how the courtiers felt about my role in their king's troubles. The looks of hatred on their faces made their meaning plain: they blamed me for it. All at once, any excitement I had about returning to the palace evaporated.

Alice heaved open the doors to my chambers and shrieked with delight, nearly sending me out of my skin. Bridget and Lucinda glanced up from their shared platter of turbot, salmon, and pickled herrings with melted butter, yelping at the unexpected sight of us.

"We missed Your Highness above all things," Lucinda cried, leaping from her chair to curtsy at me.

"Oh, thank heavens, you are safe. We received no word of your person," said Bridget, dropping to her knees. She kissed both my hands.

"Alice and I were in hiding and couldn't write," I said apologetically.

Alice frowned, gripping her hip. "When I took my leave from court, I cautioned Mistresses Nightingale and Parker that I would be unable to write with news of the queen." She shook her head at Bridget's escaped memory, but her eyes shone with gladness that we were all back together.

"Well, we are surely pleased to see you both back and free from harm," Lucinda said, her cheeks glowing.

I'd actually missed Lucinda's bright company, and Bridget's hilarious sagas over the single guys at court, which she was already beginning as we sat down to eat. Their hair was plaited so intricately that they must've been bored senseless in our absence.

Their warm reaction to our arrival was enough to restore my appetite and distract me from my dark thoughts about Nick's safety—at least for a few hours. His upper council chamber was visible from my courtyard, but the gilded window shutters remained fastened shut, intercepting any signs of life up there. I could've skewered Henry Howard myself for making so much trouble and putting my husband in danger. I wasn't sure I'd sleep again until Nick arrived home in one piece.

January continued to shroud the palace in clouds of chimney smoke, and the girls resumed my dance and music lessons to cheer me up. We received no status updates about Nick or Francis, but word reached me that the guard Joseph Blackburn had survived the smallpox virus—just not the unsightly scars. I could've screamed with relief. It'd be difficult to face him one day and see the cost of that in person, but I hoped I could apologize to him for my part in it.

⚜   ⚜   ⚜

The calendar welcomed February with a fresh dumping of snow, and claustrophobic courtiers had begun tattling on each other about petty things to keep themselves amused. Likely fearful of what might be said about him, the Earl of Dorset arranged a public swordfight between two renowned fencers in the Great Hall.

My ladies and I rushed in to the performance a few minutes late, my cheeks hot with embarrassment as we searched for seats at the rear. Four vacant stools sat beside the dreamy Earl of Surrey, and Bridget snorted into her fist with glee. The rest of us swallowed giggles as we settled in beside him. Sour-faced nobles twisted to glare at us from the front rows where the swashbucklers were already dueling. Lord Dorset scowled at me with those sugar-spoiled teeth of his that he was so proud of. He whispered to his neighbors, who curved around to shoot me death stares, before—one by one—the men rose to their feet. They tipped their hats to the swordsmen in apology before striding right past me and out of the hall. The exodus continued—row by row—until the only people left inside the Great Hall were me and my ladies, the swordfighters, the Earl of Surrey, and a handful of nobles who were permanently paranoid about the king's temper.

"Emmie, let us take our leave," Alice said quietly, her slender fingers touching my wrist.

"Did they all just walk out because I'm here?" I said.

"Heavens no, there must be some other cause," said Lucinda, but Alice's ashen face confirmed that I'd hit the bullseye on this one. The walkout was a public demonstration against me, the troublesome new Queen Emmeline.

"I bid you excuse me, my ladies," muttered the Earl of Surrey as he squeezed past us as modestly as possible. His athletic form sailed past our noses, but none of us were laughing now.

Alice gathered her skirts. "Come, let us take leave to Your Highness's chambers. We may make a note for the king and record the names of all who took part in this act of treason."

"His Majesty will be sorely vexed," added Bridget, but she could hardly look at me. I felt bad for her. It wasn't her fault she'd been aligned with a dud queen.

Feeling like the excluded kid at school again, I trailed the girls downstairs to my chambers, where nothing but embroidery hoops and sewing needles awaited me. A swell of dread erupted in my chest where it'd been festering since the coronation attack.

"I'm going to go over to my jewelry workshop," I said, halting. The swishing satin of our dresses fell silent beside a giant mural depicting the Battle of Bosworth. "Provided it's still there."

"Why would it be not there?" said Alice with a forced chuckle, moving closer to me. "We shall come with you."

"No, thank you...I just need a bit of alone time." I managed a reassuring smile, turning away as I blinked through the pressure of tears.

Three concerned faces watched me go. Alice, Bridget—and even Lucinda in recent months—had been nothing but loyal to a queen who was clearly going down and who'd dragged Alice's fiancé into a civil war. Had Henry the Eighth's ill-fated wives Anne Boleyn or Catherine Howard had such faithful friends when they were slated for the executioner's block?

With that grisly thought, I kept my head bowed so I wouldn't have to meet any more reproachful eyes and made a beeline for the workshop where I could fall apart in private.

ཝ྄ཁྭ   ཝ྄ཁྭ   ཝ྄ཁྭ

I hung around the studio until suppertime, putting the finishing touches on the hammered thumb ring for Nick. I'd just lit the candles when Alice, Bridget, and Lucinda arrived with a beef pie, a fragrant bowl of herby soup, and a generous slice of ginger cheesecake. I reassured them that I was doing okay and picked at the meal after they left, keen to polish the silver ring one more time.

The dimly lit palace courtyards were desolate by the time I slung on my cloak and headed back to my rooms, passing the stairwell leading to the king's Privy Chambers. It was unguarded —a sad reminder that the king was away from court. The square heels of my pumps scraped the hand-painted tiles as my feet turned right instead of left, scaling the stone staircase.

A chamber attendant spotted me inside the Withdrawing Chamber, tripping over his gangly feet. "Your Highness," he said with a bow, his cheeks colored scarlet. "May I be of help?"

"The king is away from court," I said, like Captain Obvious, "but I'd like to lodge in his chambers this night. I'd also appreciate it if you could get a message to my ladies that I am here and safely lodging alone."

The boy's bow was hesitant, but he led me through Nick's series of ornate rooms until we reached the king's private bedchamber. The sight of Nick's four-poster bed with its black quilted canopy was instantly pacifying. Despite every terror that had come our way, my love for Nick Tudor still felt absolute. I couldn't imagine that ever changing.

Tension began withdrawing from my bones as servants scampered through the space, lighting the fire and fluffing the silk pillows. The lanky attendant offered me food and wine, but I declined, thanking them all for their help. When the paneled doors finally closed, I stripped down to my smock and slunk beneath the fur-lined blankets. A glimpse of a smile touched my cheeks, and I rolled over, breathing in any traces of Nick's scent. I said my bedtime prayers like an exemplary Tudor wife, asking in earnest for my husband to be kept safe.

From that night on, I slept only in Nick's bed. The invaluable company of my ladies still filled my days, and Alice was the only one brave enough to bring up my change of sleeping habits. I could tell that it was more out of concern than anything else, and I explained that being in Nick's chambers was my only respite. There, I could still feel him all around me.

"I am certain our dear men shall return in haste," she reassured me for the zillionth time while stitching a serpent into the cuff of one of Francis's shirts. As she reached for more thread, her shoulder caught the corner of the hard-backed chair and she hissed through her teeth.

"Is that shoulder still bothering you?" I said, my chest constricting.

"It troubles me only at certain angles." She offered me a don't-worry-about-it smile, but her eyes had that same sunken look that I'd seen in my own. The lack of news about Nick and Francis…Alice's shoulder injury that was my fault…the relentless snow…it'd become harder to get out of bed in the morning.

I was stitching the corner of a tablecloth for the poor when the doors swung open, inviting in a gust of wind and a pewter platter that smelled like a bakery at first light. Bridget and Lucinda had gone to the kitchens for some sweet snacks, which had become our mid-morning ritual.

"Heavens, at last!" said Alice. She rushed up to help them unpack the load. I reminded her of her bad shoulder and took over the task.

"Fresh macarons for our devoted queen," said Lucinda, biting into one. Her nose scrunched with exaggerated joy as she chewed.

I retorted with a playful scoff and appraised the spread of sweetened almonds, custard tarts, stewed cherries sprinkled with sugar, cookies with warmed dates, and my favorite: fluffy macarons. I reached for one, but Alice's hand snatched my arm to hold me back.

"Ouch," I said and then realized Lucinda was coughing. Her skin had paled in seconds, and her nails clawed at her neck. She hacked up a glob of chewed macaron, spitting it onto the rush matting. Strings of saliva dripped from her mouth as she hunched forward.

"Are you okay?" I said, the breath sucked out of me.

Bridget screamed as Lucinda slumped to the floor. I dropped to catch her at the same time as Alice. Our heads knocked together, but I felt no pain, my heart beating out of my throat.

"Touch no more food!" Alice ordered, as Lucinda rolled onto her back and vomited violently, almost choking. "I have seen this before now," said Alice, rolling Lucinda onto her side. "This is poison."

I couldn't speak, my eyes shifting between Lucinda's pallid cheeks and the clump of spewed-up dessert on the floor.

Someone had poisoned the macarons, which were famous throughout the palace for being my favorite snack.

Alice was delivering instructions to Bridget, but I couldn't make out the words. Bridget nodded, hitched up her skirts, and ran outside to the courtyard.

Sweat poured from Lucinda's brow, and she kicked with agitation. Alice slipped two fingers into Lucinda's mouth in an attempt to induce more vomiting.

I leaped forward. "Don't do that!" I cried. "That could make her worse." A girl from my school in Hatfield had overdosed at prom, and it's what the paramedic had said to the guy trying to make her barf.

I crouched to feel Lucinda's pulse, asking her to look at me. Her eyes rolled backward, and both hands clutched her stomach. Her pulse felt weak.

Alice squeezed my shoulder, and I realized I was sobbing.

"It was supposed to be me." My voice slipped on the words. "It should've been me. They poisoned the macarons, and now Lucinda will—"

"Stop that," Alice snapped. "You are our blessed queen; we pray to God, day by day, for your health. Better any one of us takes our last breath than you, my lady. The king would never forgive us should any ill befall you."

"I'm no better than her; I'm just *Emmie!*" I said, shocking Alice. I scrambled to my feet, hunting for something, but I didn't know what. "I don't want this…I didn't want any of this," I stammered. "First you…Blackburn…now Lucy. I–I can't hurt anyone else…I don't know what else to do." Tears poured down my cheeks, and Alice rose to comfort me, but I shook her away. "We have to help Lucy," I said. "She *can't* die. None of this was supposed to happen."

Alice's face was grave as she crouched back down beside Lucinda.

Two hard knocks shook the doors, and I darted to open them.

Doctor Norris was on the front step with Bridget, kicking snow off his slippers. He bowed to me from beneath his black hood.

"We think it's poison...please help her," was all I could get out.

Norris strode over to Lucinda and crouched. He dropped his nose to her mouth and cupped his hands around her lips, smelling her breath and then her puddle of vomit. Lucinda was beginning to shiver.

"Can we move her to the bed?" I said. Norris nodded and climbed off his knees with a groan. "She can have mine," I added in a don't-argue-with-me tone, opening the doors to my bedchamber.

Norris and Alice hoisted Lucinda up by the shoulders, and Bridget and I caught the weight of her hips and legs. Lucinda gasped painful breaths as we lugged her through the doorway and settled her onto the mattress. I dragged a stool to her side and pasted wet strips of linen over her forehead to cool her while Norris fussed over her. Not only did I want to help Lucy in any way I could, but what awaited me outside the safety of my chambers frightened me to my bones. I hadn't forgotten the sickening Tudor torture devices that I'd read about in history class. How much did the people here despise me that they would be driven to poison me? Were they so unafraid of Nick's wrath? Was it a member of Henry Howard's rebellion or just another rich courtier who detested me? How much further were they willing to go to get rid of me? Boiling people alive came to mind.

Bridget had began hyperventilating and needed to lie down on her mattress. While Alice came and went from our chambers, monitoring the investigation that'd already begun, I stayed with Lucinda. I changed the sheets when she puked on them and offered her water, but she shivered so much that it was hard for her to ingest. Norris tried to catch her urine in a tin vessel, but few drops came. I had to bite away my frustration when he laid rows of leeches across her arms to "balance her humors". That had about as much effect as the weird gallstone-looking thing he kept dipping into water before making her take sips of it.

Shortly after dawn, a barber-surgeon arrived with a strong lisp and fierce eyebrows. He pulled a knife from his cloak that looked like a nail file and sank it into Lucinda's forearm, holding up a brass cup to catch the draining blood. I had to leave the room, furious at the archaic treatments that surely had little benefit.

Bridget was trying to write a letter to Lucinda's mom, who was looking after little Ellie, but her dripping tears kept smudging the ink.

Soon after the barber-surgeon left, Lucinda stopped responding, and her breathing was shallow. Doctor Norris asked if we could have a word outside. I spooned a little water over Lucinda's lips before following him into the drawing-room. Alice and Bridget gathered behind me.

"Your Highness, I pray you forgive me," Norris said with his head bowed. "There is no more that can be done. Mistress Parker is likely in her last hours. May I send for a minister?"

"I'm sorry...what?" I mumbled. "She threw up this morning. Isn't that a sign that her body's still working through it?"

My words drew no relief to his face. "I regret that I am quite certain she is dying, my lady."

A cry spurted from Bridget's lips, tears brimming over her heavily made-up eyelashes. Alice's breathing was heavy with grief.

Miraculously, I didn't fall apart. In fact, I'd never felt so strong or sure of anything.

I knew what I had to do to try to save Lucinda Parker's life.

19

I SWUNG my riding cloak over my shoulders while Alice chased me outside onto the front step.

"I'm going to go home and try to find some medicine to help Lucy," I said without looking at her. "My father, Doctor Grace, always had good remedies."

She returned a sympathetic frown. "Your father is with God, my lady."

"But he never threw anything out. The remedies will still be there."

Alice's lips parted. "Will there be time? It shall take days to reach Worthing." She grimaced at the silvery sky. "The streets will not be safe...there may be wicked men about. My lady, I cannot in good conscience let you do this."

"Let me? I'm going," I said, stronger than I intended. "There's no talking me out of it. I'll organize some guards to come with me. Please stay with Lucy while I'm gone. Can you do that? I don't want that barber-surgeon stabbing her with his scalpel again."

Alice dropped her head, her cheeks reddening. "Most

certainly, Your Highness. God be with you—always. I will bid the grooms to make ready your horse."

I thanked her and hung there for a second, hating myself for using my position to intimidate Alice into submission. "I'll keep safe and be back as soon as I can," I said gently. "Please tell the grooms that I'll be at the stables soon."

The look on her face made clear that she didn't approve of my impromptu excursion, but I knew she'd obey.

Drawing my hood over my hair, I legged it toward Nick's chambers, bursting into the fire-warmed bedchamber where I'd left the blue-diamond ring inside his magnificent jewelry cabinet that was hand-carved from bone. I'd hardly slept all night as I sat beside Lucinda, so it was easy to fall asleep in the king's luxurious bed with the enchanted ring on my thumb. I didn't have time to panic about what the witch said about the ring being drained of power. Whether the time portal worked or not, I had to try. I couldn't let Lucinda take a bullet for me without doing everything I could to save her life.

I slept and roused at least three times, my drowsy eyelids letting in enough firelight each time to confirm I was still at Hampton Court Palace. I smacked a lump out of the pillow with the sort of irritation that only panic can inspire. Begging for sleep, I slowed and deepened my breaths.

Without warning, my butt plunged to the floor and slammed into cold linoleum. It took a minute for the contemporary room to materialize through my foggy brain...I was on the floor beside a vacant hospital-style bed. A familiar vinyl armchair sat empty in the corner. The number '23' hung lopsidedly on the peach door, and the toxic smell of disinfectant overcame my nose.

OMG, I'm at the Cedar Lake Rest Home! I left from here last time with Susanna Grey.

That meant I was in freaking Boston—not Hatfield, where my mom was a nurse and might have some medicine that could help Lucinda. A rush of nerves sent my stomach into free-fall as I flung the cupboard door open, stretching from my toes to reach for my cell phone. Polished metal met my fingers, and I exhaled with relief, sliding the phone down my bodice until it chilled my bare skin.

Bleary, starving, and looking like a period movie character in a sixteenth-century kirtle, I made it past a few stares from elderly residents to the front exit, mercifully escaping any sign of Ajay, the care worker who'd helped me last time, or any other staff in the home. Outside on the Boston streets, I paced down the road, dialing my mom's number from my cell phone and ignoring the eye rolls from people who saw my period outfit.

Thank the stars, she answered, but her voice was hoarse. I must've woken her up after one of her night shifts.

"Emmie!" she said and cleared her throat. "Where are you?"

"In Boston. Sorry to wake you. How are you doing?"

She sighed deeply enough to inflate a hot air balloon. "I don't know. Surviving. I'm glad to hear your voice." She sounded exhausted.

"Yours, too. Mom, I need to ask you a medical question. If someone has been poisoned, what kind of medicine should I give them?"

"Who was poisoned?"

"No one you know…a friend. She can't get to a hospital, but I think she could be dying. Well, she *is* dying, apparently." The truth of that gripped my throat.

Mom sucked in a sharp breath. "What did she take?"

"I don't even know; it was something put into her food." I described Lucinda's symptoms from the ingestion of the macaron until now.

Another heavy sigh. "We'd have to know what toxin she ingested because the treatments vary. She'd need a toxicology report, possibly a ventilator if her respiratory system is depressed. Her liver or kidneys could be in trouble…I'm not a doctor, Emmie. Why can't she get to a hospital?"

"What about that black stuff—I forget what it's called. One of the girls at school had it when she OD'd at the prom."

"You mean activated charcoal? It can help for certain things, but it's usually given within hours of the poisoning. It sounds like your friend has been sick for a while."

"Less than two days. And I'm happy to try anything that might work."

Mom didn't reply. I heard her climb out of bed and a talk show playing in the background. She always slept with the television on.

"Well, do you think the activated charcoal's worth a try at least?" I pressed.

She sighed. "It's really unlikely to do anything. I've never seen it given after two days."

"*Less* than two days. Please, Mom, I have to try something."

Her television cut to silence. "You'd need hospital grade. Don't bother with the pharmacy. I should have some stored away at the rest home."

"Really?" I was already calculating. If I hopped on a bus to downtown and caught a connecting bus to Amherst, I could be in Hatfield before the day was out.

"I don't have any money on me," I realized out loud. It'd been so long since I'd had to think about my wallet.

Mom made a frustrated huff before swapping the phone to her other ear. "I'll get some of the charcoal and drive in to see you. Where in Boston are you?"

"Oh my gosh, Mom; are you even serious?"

"Emmie, one day, you'll learn what it's like to be a mother. Then everything I do might not surprise—or annoy—you so much."

Her words tore at my heart. In choosing a life with Nick in Tudor England, I'd all but abandoned my devoted mom. I wished that I'd never had to choose between them.

After she assured me that her car hadn't acted up in ages, I said I'd meet her at the library up the street. While reminding her of the time urgency, I asked her to chuck anything edible into her bag and to give our dog Ruby a massive cuddle from me.

It was a relief to enter the library, its warm atmosphere wrapping around me like a hug. I settled into a comfy armchair, flicking through a fashion magazine. *Holy smokes, I've missed fashion magazines.* When their garish colors and stories about celebrity spats became overwhelming, though, I dropped the dog-eared booklet back into the rack and scanned the nearest bookshelf.

It was the boring language section, and I went to move on until the thick spine of a lime-green tome caught my eye. It was a dictionary of Latin words and phrases, and I flicked through to the 'L' chapter, scanning for the phrase *Lex talionis*.

There it was, in black and white.

Lex talionis: the law of retaliation, e.g. 'an eye for an eye'.

An uncomfortable feeling slithered into my gut, settling there. An eye for an eye—why would the witch say that to me?

I tried to distract myself with an old crime novel that someone had left on the table, but three chapters in, I felt like I hadn't absorbed a word. I was eighteen and married with a husband at war, my friend was dying, and I was trying to read about a celebrity murderer who took out predatory men with her stilettos.

A middle-aged woman with scraggy blonde hair pushed through the library doors. It took me a second to recognize my mom. Her cheeks were sunken, and she'd lost weight. She hugged me without saying anything.

"I missed you," I said into her shoulder. She squeezed harder.

She shook her head at my billowy kirtle with bell sleeves but said nothing about it. I dragged two armchairs closer together, and Mom uncoiled a knitted scarf from her neck.

"I gather you don't have long," she said, handing me a crumpled shopping bag. Inside was a white plastic bottle labeled 'Activated Charcoal: Poison Antidote' alongside the directions for use and a bunch of medical jargon.

"Thanks so much for this," I said, the stiff plastic bottle unlike anything I'd seen in the sixteenth century. I should've brought an apothecary jar to transfer the contents into. "Unfortunately, I can't stay long," I added, my voice cracking. "My friend's really sick."

Mom had also brought me a packet of trail mix and two yogurt-coated granola bars. I downed the lot in a few bites, gulping water from her bottle. She tried to give me money, but I insisted that I didn't need it. US dollars didn't buy much in Tudor England.

"Is the charcoal for your friend Nick?" Mom said carefully. Her eyes were roaming all over me, searching for signs of injury or perhaps unhappiness.

"No, it's for a friend of ours...her name's Lucy." I left out the part about Lucinda having a baby daughter who'd just survived a form of tuberculosis.

Mom's hands twisted together, fidgeting. "If you take me to her, I can administer the medicine properly. It should really be given through a nasogastric tube, but I assume you don't have one of those."

"Yeah, we don't have one of those."

We do have leeches, though, and bloodletting. Oh, and that gallstone thing.

"It'll stain her teeth black if she drinks it," Mom warned. "Possibly permanently."

"It's okay. A lot of people where she lives have black teeth. It's actually kind of trendy there."

Mom frowned. "It's also critical that your friend doesn't aspirate this. That would make everything a heck of a lot worse. I also told you the charcoal will probably have absolutely no effect after this much time, right?"

"Yeah. But you never know…I have to try."

She paused, her fingers still fidgeting. "Can I come with you?"

My face fell. "You know you can't."

Mom wound her scarf back around her neck. "I know. Time travel and all that." Her posture stiffened.

My voice cracked with exhaustion, but—as usual—I had no time to lose. I stood up and gave Mom another hug that signaled it was already time for me to head off.

"Your dad wants to see you," she said as we pulled away, my hands sliding down to her bony wrists. "He asked me to call him as soon as you got back in touch."

"Is everything okay?"

She nodded, a blush creeping across her skin. "He just wants to catch up with you. It's a shame that it took all this for him to wake up, but I think he finally has. Can you believe it?"

My teeth dug into my bottom lip. After a decade of Dad being largely a no-show, I'd expected my mom to give the guy a tougher time about wanting a free pass back into my life. The problem was that Mom had zero sense when it came to my old man, and this time I wasn't here to help her handle his miraculous comeback.

You can always visit your mom now and then, Emmie. That's if you can find some medieval charger-cable thingy for the blue-diamond ring so it doesn't conk out.

"I have to go," I said tightly. Mom's hollow cheeks blurred through my tears.

She wrapped her arms around me again. I wasn't the only one crying. I reminded myself that college-aged kids across America were living apart from their parents. This was normal. If only Tudor England didn't feel so many centuries away—literally.

Mom brushed her nose with her knuckle. "Can I drop you off somewhere?"

"No, thanks...I'll just be here for a little bit longer." I eyed the quiet corner with the comfy armchairs that were out of view of the security cameras. With any luck, I could fall asleep there without ending up on a paranormal reality television show about mysterious vanishings.

Mom nodded at the blue-diamond ring on my thumb. "Ah, right. You have to disappear." She waved a hand magically.

I clutched her delicate fingers one last time. "Thank you so much for driving all this way. I know it was a big ask, and I'm *so* grateful."

"You didn't ask; I offered," Mom corrected. "And I'd do it again tomorrow if it meant I got to see you, even for a few minutes."

"Mom," I pleaded, reaching toward her as she stepped backward. She nodded like she was going to be okay, but her crumpled face betrayed the gesture.

I watched her stop at the book display by the entrance, grabbing a title that caught her eye. She held the book up in the air and smiled at me before returning it to the shelf. After blowing me a tear-stained kiss, Mom slipped away from me through the double doors.

I felt like the worst daughter who'd ever lived.

I crossed to the window display and picked up the hardcover text she'd waved at me. It was called *The Tudors: England's Most Notorious Royal Family*. My stomach wound into a painful ball. Mom was trying to connect with me on something she could never understand. I flicked to the section about Nicholas the Ironheart, deliberately squinting to blur my vision as I braved a few words, jittery at what I'd find.

The marriage of King Nicholas I and Princess Henriette of France was divisive and gave rise to civil conflicts that spilled across the border.

I snapped the book shut, every inch of my skin burning.

Why did it still say that King Nick married Princess Henriette and not me?

A woman bouncing a toddler on her knee kept scoping out my kirtle like I was some sort of matinee show. I blocked the offending book from my mind and hurried into the quiet corner of the library, relieved to find it vacant of prying eyes. After settling into a cushy armchair, I wedged the activated charcoal bottle beneath my arm and wriggled into a position comfortable enough to sleep in. Even if someone did see me vanish, at least it wouldn't be caught on camera. I jerked at the memory of the sleeping pill still sitting in the ring casing—I'd completely forgotten it last time! My fingers reached for the tiny latch, but the pill would make me groggy when I arrived back, and I needed to be fully charged to help Lucy. I decided to try to fall asleep without it first.

It turned out that I didn't need the pill: it took less than thirty minutes of meditating to send my shattered body into a power nap, but I woke back in the library in a disoriented spiral of nausea. I'd never regret pushing the ring's limits to try to save Lucinda's life, but if I never saw Nick Tudor again, I'd never get over it. The pattern of dozing off and waking in the library chair repeated on loop until the sky outside had darkened and the library had begun to empty. The woman with the toddler was long gone. If I didn't time travel soon, I'd be sleeping in a snow-bank and probably waking up in a Boston emergency room.

I kissed the glassy tip of the table-cut diamond and slid my hand into the warmth of my bodice, my palm resting over my heart.

Come on...please. Take me home. I want to go home.

I smelled the sublime scent before I even saw him. My sluggish eyelids cracked open at the familiar aroma of rose oil and the heat of a crackling fire. I scrambled onto my elbows, searching the dim candlelight. It was nightfall at Hampton Court, and my husband, Nick Tudor, was sitting right across from me.

A gasp of shock shot from my throat like I'd been punched in the stomach. The love of my life was home safe!

But Nick didn't even move, let alone speak. He just sat in his gilded armchair, blinking at me with a lifeless expression.

Something was terribly wrong—something even worse than Lucinda's poisoning.

20

"You're back," I said with a high-pitched cry. "You're okay." I rolled out of the bed, tripping over my skirts, which had twisted around me. My head ached from the malfunctioning time travel, and my balance was off.

Nick stayed frozen as I fell onto him. I folded my arms around his pearl-colored doublet, breathing him in. My skin throbbed with heat, and the world spun. *My Nick.*

He didn't respond—not so much as a flinch. I pulled back, searching his face. There were no signs of injury. "Oh, thank God," I said, clinging to him again. "I was freaking out."

The bedchamber was as quiet as a graveyard, except for Nick's steady breathing.

"Babe?" I said, pressing my hands to his cheeks and angling his face to look at me. His seawater-colored eyes were blocks of ice. Was this PTSD? Or worse—had he come back from his war as the implacable Nicholas the Ironheart?

I climbed off him. "Why aren't you saying anything?"

He aimed a finger at the plastic bottle protruding from the bed sheets. "What is this?" he said evenly.

All the air fled my body as I remembered. "It's for Mistress

Parker." I reached for the bottle. "It's medicine from my time. She was poisoned."

"I am acquainted with Mistress Parker's condition."

"Is she still…is she alive?"

"To my knowledge."

His eyes flickered to mine, and our gazes fused like magnets. After a moment, he looked away, climbing out of the chair to distance himself from me.

He poured himself a cup of wine and waved the flask at me, but I shook my head. When he took a long swig, still not showing either happiness or relief at seeing me, I felt like throwing the bottle of activated charcoal right at his head.

"Is something wrong?" I said with deliberate terseness.

Nick didn't reply. He just turned toward the elaborately carved shutters shrouding the lattice window.

"Nick!" I snapped. He spun to me and glared. "What's wrong with you?" I said. "We haven't seen each other in *months.* I didn't even know if you were alive, and not a second has gone by that I haven't wished that you were standing here right now. And now that you are, the only thing you have to say is about this freaking bottle?" I shook it at him.

I expected fireworks in response, knowing my husband's temperament, but he just silently poured himself more wine.

I exhaled through my teeth and reached for an empty cup. Nick watched me from the corner of his eye as I filled it to the brim. I took a giant sip of the sweet liquid before unscrewing the cap from the plastic bottle and emptying as much activated charcoal powder into the wine as the instructions directed.

Nick whirled to face me, both brows raised.

"Mistress Parker has to drink this immediately," I explained without looking at him. "It's a remedy for poison from my time, but it might not work. It's probably too late. Still, I'm going to try. It has to be better than bloodletting and leeches." I slid the plastic bottle beneath his bed, hiding it from the chamber attendants.

We could get rid of it later. I grabbed the cup containing the medicine and headed for the doors. Nick seized my wrist to stop me, swiping away the cup of charcoal-infused wine with his other hand.

"You are my wife; you are not an apothecary," he said, dropping the cup onto the oak table. Before I could blink, he dug out the plastic bottle from beneath the bed and tossed it into the burning hearth.

"Nick!" I chastised, covering my mouth. It didn't take long for the licking flames to consume the plastic, sending up a disgusting, lethal stench.

Nick paced away, coughing into his armpit. When he'd settled his throat, he called for a page. A sweaty-faced boy arrived within seconds.

"See to it that Doctor Norris administers this remedy to Mistress Lucinda Parker without delay," Nick commanded with a rasp, handing the boy the cup containing the activated charcoal. "The queen is in need of supper," Nick added while facing the carved stone mantel, swirling red wine in his cup. The page bowed and scampered away.

"I wanted to give that to Lucinda myself!" I exclaimed as Nick shut the bedchamber doors.

"I will have the linens made ready so you may wash," he said with his back to me. "You may then take supper."

A dumbfounded laugh spurted from my lips. Hundreds of words I could've shouted at him gathered on my tongue, but none fired. He picked up a scroll from a side table and began leisurely reading it. I couldn't stand being in this room another second. The smoke wasn't the only toxic thing.

"In case you didn't know, I missed you like crazy," I said without looking at him. "All I've done is wait for this day, longing to see you back home and safe. But, once again, this is not at all how I imagined it to be. I don't know what I was thinking."

I felt the heat of his eyes burning my back as I barged through the doors.

Smearing away tears with my fingertips, I power-walked to my chambers while looking any passersby dead-on in the face. I was officially over mentally apologizing for upsetting the nobles' ambitions by marrying the king. *Come at me, trolls!* I wanted to shout. *I've seen the freaking future, so yeah—I win.*

My chambers smelled like the stinky herbs my friend Mia's mom used to boil, but at least Lucinda wasn't alone. My crepe-pink bell sleeves brushed past the sunken cheeks of Alice, Bridget, and a few other well-wishers as I made my way through to Lucinda.

Doctor Norris was seated beside the bed, dabbing black liquid into the corners of her mouth. It pooled there before oozing down her chin. The gold wine cup beside him confirmed that the liquid was my wine-infused activated charcoal. I moved closer to appraise its effects, but there didn't seem to be any. Lucinda wasn't even able to swallow the stuff. Her eyes were closed, and her skin was an unearthly shade of gray.

Norris grunted as he straightened, a blackened cloth hanging by his side. "I shall call in the minister," he said, vacating the stool for me, but I felt too unsettled to even move.

Mom had warned me that the charcoal would be too late, and she was right. I'd had one chance to seek out help from the modern world and returned with something totally useless. Was there more I could've done?

I blinked away tears. Alice slid beside me, falling to her knees and clasping her hands together. Bridget slipped beside Alice, weeping again, and my legs buckled. I sank to the woven mat and joined them in prayer. I didn't come from a religious family, but as I sat there hearing nothing but Lucinda's shallow breaths, I outright begged for her life.

My eyes sprang open, meeting the silky edge of the bed sheet. This wasn't the first time I'd pleaded for the life of an innocent girl in this century. Nick's sister Kit had been destined to die in Tudor England until I manipulated things to stop it from happening. I'd literally inserted myself into a world where I didn't belong *and* saved the life of a girl who was fated to die at the age of eight.

My stomach crashed to the floor. Did *lex talionis*—an eye for an eye—mean that another life now had to be taken? Was Lucinda's life an exchange for Kit's?

Velvet slippers scuffed the matting behind us. The minister had stepped into the room, motioning for the rest of us to vacate the chamber.

"Are you wearied from your journey, my lady?" Bridget said to me in the drawing-room. Her eyes were so puffy from crying that it was a wonder she could see.

"Hungry?" added Alice, touching my sleeve.

I shook my head. I didn't know why they were so worried about me—all I could think about was the brilliance of Lucinda's smile...of her sitting on her usual stool across from me, stitching tiny butterflies with perfectly arched wings.

An abrupt stiffness swept over the chamber, everyone gasping and bowing.

I glanced behind me into Nick Tudor's heart-stopping stare. He towered in the doorway like the embodiment of kingly presence, a black coat elegantly draped over his doublet.

"Emmeline, will you share a walk with me?" he said. He'd never called me by my first name in front of so many people.

For a few moments, I didn't move. I was beyond furious with him.

His light eyes softened as they lured mine, his cheeks crimson where his dimples deepened. He felt guilty about earlier, I could tell. Plus, we had an audience, and publicly challenging the king in this world was a fast-track to even more disgrace.

I rose to accept his outstretched hand, my fingers folding into the tingly heat of his skin. We strode right past the guards with the untouchable authority that only the king enjoyed.

The snow had finally melted, but the air remained icy as we began to cross the courtyard. I dropped Nick's hand and folded my arms over my chest. He shrugged off his ebony coat embroidered with gold stars and crescent moons and laid it over my shoulders. I was too cold to resist, but I didn't let him see how much the touch of him soothed me. My heart still hurt over how he'd treated me in his bedchamber after having being parted for months.

"Aren't you cold?" was all I said as we strolled in the direction of his private gardens.

He shook his head. "Here feels a great deal warmer after the wretched north."

While the days had become longer, I noticed a sandy-yellow light haloing the exterior palace walls, like extra torches had been lit tonight. Nick looked only at his feet.

"Where did you want to walk to?" I said flatly. I wanted him to know that I was still fuming.

"Perhaps you might tell me, Emmie; you appear to be in command nowadays."

I paused at the gatehouse leading to the privy garden. "Okay, you need to tell me what's wrong," I said, already trembling. "Because it's been pretty horrible here these past few months, and you being cranky with me about something is *not* helping."

He crossed his thick arms. "Cranky?"

"Pissed off," I explained. "Angry…mad…rude. That's it—the way you've been toward me today is *rude*. And I don't care if we're married or that you're the king—you don't treat me that way."

"You left me," he blurted, his voice carrying over the wind. He opened his mouth to say more, but his lips shut again. He looked away like he was too upset to speak.

"When?" I said, dumbstruck. "All I've done is sit here and wait for you like a dutiful Tudor wife!"

He seemed to tower over me, a pillar of strength, but his face held the wounds of a child who'd been abandoned. "For many weeks, Emmie, I have suffered in ways you would believe not. The high north is a place of utter lawlessness, rife with savages who deny the will of their king and willingly seek the fate of high treason. The villages are infested with the pox and plague, and there were complaining soldiers and apostates at every turn. Then the traitor Henry Howard retreated, and I knew not where he was until he was sighted on the roads toward Robin House. All I could think of was you being there without me, and how Howard wishes us both dead. I made straight for Robin House until I received word of your return to Hampton Court. You cannot imagine my relief when I learned that you were safe here at the palace, and well—"

"Yes, actually, I *can* imagine that relief," I cut in.

"However, when I arrived here," Nick continued, "I found you to be gone entirely, with no letter or word of any kind and no sign of the enchanted ring. When my gentlemen informed me that you had been lodging in my bedchamber, I sat there in wait for countless hours, believing with every stroke of the clock that you would not ever return to me...and perhaps with my son and heir in your belly!"

My mouth hung open as I processed his barrage of words. "There's no son—or daughter—at least not yet. And that's why you're pissed off? Because I went back to my time to get medicine that could save Lucinda's life?"

He raised a finger. "You swore an oath to me that you would never take leave to your time without me unless your life was at stake. *Only together.* Did you forget our vow in such haste?" He looked like he might grab my shoulders and shake me, but clenched his fists at his sides. "What if that ring, so utterly fickle, had failed in its enchantment and you could never return here?

You wagered everything we have for a maiden that you do not even like!"

"No, I *do* like her," I said, stepping forward to find his face in the shadows of the courtyard. "All Lucinda Parker ever did to upset me was love you—the same way I do. How am I supposed to hate her for something I do myself as freely as breathing?" My breath shook, a quivery puff of ice. "The poison that Mistress Parker took was meant for me. So was the arrow that nearly killed Alice Grey. There was a fencing show at court while you were away, and almost everybody got up and left in protest when I showed up. The people hate me here!"

A blast fired somewhere west of the palace, chased by the muffled shouts of men, but Nick didn't move. He gripped his forehead with one hand, holding it there as we stood in a deadlock.

An alarming crunch behind me turned out to be the approaching boots of Doctor Norris. "Your Majesty," he said with a bow. "You may wish to be informed that, moments past, the queen's lady, Mistress Lucinda Parker, succumbed to death. The minister shall make preparations in haste, so the queen may return to her chambers."

"What?" I cried, tears obscuring my vision. "Mistress Parker died?"

The doctor's reply was an apologetic bow.

I should've gone to my chambers to comfort Alice and Bridget, but my feet burst into a stride toward the blackness of the Privy Garden—as far away from the death scene as I could get. It didn't matter that I was racing into ice-cold darkness; I couldn't get what the witch had told me out of my head. Her warning blazed through my brain, burning away every other thought.

"This be the devil's work...He shall come for thee... Thee hast been up to nay good...changing things that should not be hath changed. Lex talionis."

"Emmie!" Nick called behind me, but I kept going, chased by the bouncing light of his lantern.

When I reached the dragon fountain, I dropped onto the stone bench, searching for an end to the nausea choking my insides. My fingers were like icicles, but the blue-diamond ring burned hot on my thumb. I'd had no idea what saving Kit's life would do to this world, not to mention marrying its king, otherwise destined to wed Henriette of France. Now, because of my decisions, a kindhearted girl with a baby daughter would never open her eyes again and little Ellie would grow up without a mom.

"Why must you be out here in the chill?" Nick scolded when he caught up to me.

"It's an eye for an eye," I muttered, rocking back and forth to keep myself from freezing. "Lex talionis."

He sat beside me and wrapped an arm around my back. "Again?" he said, short of breath.

"Mistress Parker's death," I stammered. "It's payback for saving Kit's life when she was meant to die—or for me being here; I don't know. Maybe both."

"Payback?"

I searched for an older word. "Retribution."

Nick's arm slid off my back. "How can you speak of saving the life of Kit with regret?"

"I don't regret it," I said, tears dribbling down my cheeks. "The truth is, I'd make the same decisions all over again. But that doesn't mean what we did was right." I gripped my neck, feeling like I was choking, needing air. "You know as well as I do that none of this has been right."

Nick jumped up and crouched to face me. He collected my hands in his, desperate eyes finding mine. "Emmie, no. No, you cannot do this. You cannot lose heart now. We have come too far."

I looked down at him through my swelling shame. How could

I have ever believed that loving him this much would justify changing the path of history? How could I have been so selfish?

"I need to tell you something," I said to his stricken face. "I visited a soothsayer while you were in the north. There's one who lives near Robin House. She's poor and harmless; *please* don't do anything to hurt her. But I showed her the blue-diamond ring, and she recognized her cousin's work in the ring's magic. Her cousin was called Joanie—she worked for you once at Whitehall Palace as a maidservant." It didn't shock me that Nick demonstrated no recollection of the chambermaid, but his eyes hung on my every word. "This maid then went on to work for Mary, Queen of Scots when she was imprisoned. You know that Mary wants the English throne, and she made the witch Joanie curse the ring to get rid of you. What Joanie did, though, was curse the ring to take you far away from this world—not to kill you, but to save your life. She enchanted this ring to send you somewhere far away from here, where you'd not only be safe but *happy*. Do you get it? You would've been happy there...in my time...with me."

A flush drifted into his cheeks. I wished there wasn't more of this story I had to tell.

"But Nick, the witch also said that we'd been up to no good... changing things that shouldn't have been changed. She said the phrase: Lex—"

"Oh Christ, may we have not a moment alone!" Nick interrupted, spinning to where Francis Beaumont drew closer with four guards.

Beads of sweat gleamed from the earl's forehead, even though it had to be zero degrees. "Your Grace, the-the palace is...under siege," Francis stammered like he couldn't quite believe it. Nick and I gasped in unison. Francis continued his explanation, his voice dazed. "There is arrow fire beyond the west gatehouse. Horsemen in the hundreds have mounted an assault. They are armed with all manner of force and say hundreds more are at the ready. Henry Howard is leading them."

Nick's jaw hung open before he lurched up at Francis and grabbed his collar with both hands. "Are you damn certain?"

Francis nodded, his body rigid with fear.

Nick released the earl and pressed his palms together at his chin. "Go now and arrest every traitor that dares rebel against their king."

"But the numbers of m-men, Majesty. There are beyond—"

"Make haste!" Nick spat, and Francis hurried back toward the palace, trailed by the guards. I got up and leaned on my tiptoes to see over the hedges. The glow of the lanterns had drawn nearer, and the air hummed with distant voices. Enraged men were attacking the palace, like something out of the French Revolution. I was shaking like a tree in a hurricane.

"You must be hidden," Nick said faintly, spinning in all directions like a cave might magically appear before us. "Perhaps in some place within the kitchens."

He went on, muttering about hiding spots and priest holes, but his voice drowned beneath the volume of my realization. The nobles' uprising was no longer against me; it was against the King of England himself and the Tudor dynasty as I knew it.

"No," I stated, my heart drumming through my ears. "Hiding isn't going to solve this."

"Only until it is over," Nick said, tugging me toward the path that wound past the sunken fishponds toward the kitchens.

I wrestled free. "This will never be over!" My breath was wild...jagged...but I kept speaking. "This is the end of the road, Nick." I couldn't see through my escalating tears. "I've loved being with you, and even here in Tudor England—believe me, I have loved you more than I ever thought possible—but we can't do this to the world anymore. I have to leave and never come back."

He shuffled back a step like my words were bullets. He shook his head with a slow dread, his startled eyes pinned to mine. "No, Emmie."

"The world doesn't want me here," I pleaded, tears spilling from my eyes. "I don't belong in this time, and the world knows it. It's like it's spitting me back out. People are dying."

"*I* will die without you!"

I stretched out a shaky hand, the blue-diamond ring like a lightbulb on my thumb. "Then come with me. It's what the curse wanted. I was never meant to be here; you were meant to come to *my* world. That's what was meant to happen." I gestured at the palace's stifling redbrick walls. "I *know* you want to escape all this pressure you constantly feel…it's why you love going to Robin House, where life feels safe and simple. It's why you chose to get married there!"

"Enough!" he hissed, folding an arm around his back like I might physically yank him into the future against his will. "You will not do this to me. We made our choice."

A cannon blast made us both jump. Nick gaped up at the palace wall, his forehead creased with distress. But when he stared back at me, his expression had hardened with resolve.

"You will not dare give up on us, Emmie. You know I can never abandon my kingdom, leaving my sister to civil war and bloodshed. When I asked for your hand in marriage, you made a vow that you would never take leave of me again. I have wagered all I have for you and given you everything in return…I made you a queen! God willing, you will be the mother to a king—why is it not enough?"

"You still don't get it!" I implored. "I don't want the kingdom, the riches, the pressures. I didn't want to be a queen…I only came here for *you*. That's all I've ever wanted out of this."

"So, it is I who is now not enough," he observed, tears clouding his eyes.

"Nick, look at what's happening here!" I pointed toward the screams and shouts floating from the palace. The way he was looking at me—the absolute heartbreak in his face—hacked me to pieces. "Nothing lasts forever," I said, the agony in my chest making me curl forward.

"*We* do," Nick said, struggling to speak. "We last forever." He gripped the sleeve over my wrist, finding my bare skin with his fingers. "Do not let go," he pleaded. "Ne dimittas."

I plucked the gold wedding band off my finger and slapped it into Nick's palm. I knew he loved me, but not enough to trade his kingdom for it. He'd beg me to stay, but he'd never come with me and leave Tudor England…and every moment I stayed, I put him further in danger.

I wanted to freeze time so I could memorize every speck of him—a man I couldn't imagine living without—but he'd become a fuzzy silhouette through my weeping eyes.

When Nick lurched forward, begging me once again to hide with him, I exhaled with frustration and pressed my hands to his silky doublet, physically shoving him toward the court.

"If you're not going to come with me, then *go away*," I ordered. "Go home. This is over now, do you understand? We tried, we really tried, but it's done, okay? Pretend I died…pretend I drowned in the river. You'll be free to marry again. Someone the people accept; someone right for you. Maybe you can still have Henriette."

I couldn't look at him but heard him crying—a sound I never wanted to hear again. I couldn't listen—I needed to leave before he broke my resolve.

"Just get away from me!" I screamed.

Nick jerked back a step, shaking his head like he was flicking away flies. He then cleared his throat, his tear-stained voice barely his own.

"If you wish to take leave of my heart so resolutely, then so it shall be. May God be with you, Emmeline."

With those abrupt words, he spun and disappeared toward the palace like he'd only ever been a figment of my imagination.

I sank to the gravel and shuddered with sobs, hating myself for every mistake I'd made. How could I have ever thought I could be the fierce girl who became a queen and ruled the world like a badass. If only this was a fairytale instead of the real world, where girls like me didn't get to become Tudor queens.

I stepped over the knot gardens until I reached a patch of earth concealed by a row of manicured hedges. Grateful to be protected from the bitter wind, I lay on the freezing soil and shut my eyes.

"I'm so sorry," I whispered, curling up into a fetal position. I lay there in a quivering ball, repeating my apology to Nick, Alice, Bridget, Kit, Lucinda—and everyone who meant something to me here. I begged for the oblivion of sleep to free me from my pain before it carried me home to where I truly belonged.

When footsteps neared, I froze, unable to breathe. Multiple pairs of boots were marching along the path nearest to where I lay.

"She hides here!" shouted a commanding voice that I knew too well.

My terrified gaze rolled upward to recognize Nick's broad silhouette through the glimmer of a lantern. The wobble of light moved, revealing a massive, familiar figure beside the king. I scrambled up, trying to edge away. Henry Howard stood beside Nick, a swarm of unkempt men gathered behind them waving pitchforks and hammers. My chest tightened with so much fear that it hurt to breathe.

Howard lifted his lamp to see me better. I crouched to escape it, but the light followed me. I was a mouse in a cage. Why was Nick just standing next to him like the two were old mates? Why weren't they tearing each other to shreds? Why wasn't Nick protecting me?

"Let the king speak!" spat Howard in his bullish tone. "Majesty, what say you? Will you persist in your offense of our gracious God by once more naming this heretic as our queen?"

My gaze flew to Nick, who looked down at me with a face absent of life. For the first time, he looked like the man in the terrifying portrait with the dead eyes and the cruel mouth. He was the embodiment of Nicholas the Ironheart.

"My lords," he said loudly, "I swear on my soul that this girl before me, who once bewitched your devoted king in a manner most vile and depraved, is a monstrous traitor to both king and God."

My head shook wildly, gratified men smirking down at me from all directions. Henry Howard glowed with smug victory, baring his teeth at me like the animal he was.

"By order of the king, bring her to the Tower to await trial on charges of heresy and high treason against the King's Majesty," the former duke bellowed.

"God save the king!" the men called in response.

"Nick, *please!*" I said.

The sky blurred as my husband bent over me, the scent of fresh roses finding my nose. I searched for love in his eyes but found only storms of anger. He took hold of my thumb and yanked the blue-diamond ring right off it.

"No!" I shrieked.

"Take her to the Tower," Nick snarled without looking at me. "This witch dares enchant and humiliate the King of England. She has attempted to consort with the devil and extort from His Majesty a bastard child. She will stand trial to suffer a traitor's death."

"God save the king!" the orchestra of voices repeated. "God save His Grace!"

Their cries overwhelmed my screams as a hundred filthy fingers dug into my skin, stripping me of the rest of my jewelry and lifting me to the raven sky.

21

THE FURY TEARING through my veins obliterated any physical pain as I was manhandled back across the gardens, through the snaking redbrick corridors, and into the gusty west courtyard. The shadowy square teemed with raging men brandishing home-made weapons, their shouts of treason striking me like gunfire from all directions. A subhuman scream cut through the noise, and when my throat burned from the pressure, I realized the roar was mine.

Nobody tried to help me as brutal hands shoved me through the battered gatehouse, across the windy moat bridge, and down the grassy slope leading to the River Thames.

"How could you do this to me!" I howled at the palace wall in the absurd hope that Nick might hear me.

Silence.

My teeth ground together, and my hands balled into fists. Was it possible that his public condemnation of me was just a trick? But it couldn't be. The chances of Nick openly accusing me of treason and heresy as part of some secret plan left me empty. If he cared about my safety, he would've just let me go back to my time. No, it was obvious to me what was happening here: Nick had aligned himself with Norfolk— allowing violent men to haul me away—because I'd wanted to end our relationship for good and leave him. He was never going to let me just walk away, leaving him brokenhearted and humiliated. I'd rejected the vengeful Nicholas the Ironheart one too many times, and now he wanted me to suffer for it. I'd been so stupid to think I was immune to his notoriously unforgiving nature.

"I hate you!" I screamed into the infuriatingly silent sky of stars.

The tides were too low for a barge to dock at the pier, so the rioters pushed me right onto the slippery mudflats. I covered my nose as they marched me across slimy mud soaked in sewage to reach the deeper water.

Somewhere inside the palace, Nick was probably sharing a flask of warmed wine with Henry Howard before an open fire, brown-nosing the former duke to win back the trust of the nobles. I'd been told how dangerous a dissenting duke can be to a king—especially when that duke had won the support of other aristocrats. Despite the risks he had taken for our relationship, Nick had always put his kingdom first, and now he'd handed me over to his enemies to save himself from being dethroned and dishonored. I hoped the guilt of that chewed holes in his insides for the rest of his life.

Another cry of anger burst from my lips as I lost my footing on the slick dirt and face-planted into the putrid sludge.

Two guards hoisted me up by my shoulders and threw me over the barge's edge, my legs tangling in my skirts caked in mud. As I clung to a bench seat, the barge glided away from the sparkling lanterns of Hampton Court Palace.

Away from Nick, and any hope I had of him intervening in my arrest.

Two guards sat between the oarsmen and me, gripping their swords with both hands. They shivered within their fur wraps.

My adrenalin rush was fading, and the freezing air began to pierce through Nick's filthy coat.

"Ugh!" I grunted as I shook it off my shoulders like it was woven from the webs of spiders. I hurtled the slash of midnight velvet out into the middle of the river. Black water swallowed the costly fabric in seconds.

"Christ in heaven!" spat one of the guards. He reached out and smacked me on the back of my head. I swore at him, using all the modern curse words I could think of.

"Let her freeze," snarled the other one.

A guard wouldn't dare strike a queen unless he was sure her fate was already sealed. Whatever Henry Howard had done to poison the country against me was beyond repair, and now I didn't even have the blue-diamond ring so I could disappear. If only I'd told Nick what the witch had said about the enchanted ring losing all its power. Maybe then he wouldn't have bothered jerking it off my thumb, and I'd still have been able to escape.

I wrapped myself into a tight ball and shivered into my knees, praying that the journey would pass quickly. When the temperature dropped, the men on the boat ceased their chatter, leaving only the eerie soundtrack of oars cutting through the frosty river flow. My mind doubled back to the last time I'd been imprisoned at the Tower of London—the lecherous jailers and threats of torture—and I pushed each terrifying memory away.

One minute at a time, Emmie. Just live through this next minute.

I was so cold that I considered begging the guards for one of their furs. But determined to hold on to any dignity I had left, I instead refocused my mind by picturing a sun-swept beach speckled with palm trees. It got me through the time it took to reach the onion-shaped turrets of the Tower that dominated the skyscape. As if waiting for us, the Traitor's Gate portcullis stretched open its sharp teeth to swallow us whole. A single pigeon flew low, swooping past my ear. I envied the bird's freedom, its uncomplicated life. It'd never dream of trying to live four hundred years back in time with a capricious Tudor king predestined to become a tyrant. *Nicholas the Ironheart*—it wasn't like I'd never been warned about his vindictive nature.

"I need water," I grunted as the boatmen tossed the ropes over the wooden posts. Ignoring my request, the guards shoved me onto the rotting deck that did little to improve the rancid, decomposing stink of the river.

I gazed up at the impossibly tall fortress of the Tower of London with its stone battlements, menacing slit windows, and double defensive walls. The death site of three sixteenth-century Queens of England.

You're not leaving here alive, Emmie.

The crippling terror in my body glued my short heels to the cobblestones, and the guards had to drag my weakened legs up the jagged slope. At the base of the stone stairs leading to the gardens, a man waited in a cap and black cloak with silver buttons. It was Master Carey, the Constable of the Tower, who'd handled my imprisonment here last time—back when this time-traveling mess began.

"Hello again," I said to him, followed by an abrupt chuckle. I was becoming delirious, which was probably a symptom of hypothermia.

Master Carey said little as he gravely escorted me upstairs to the royal lodgings inside the tower of St. Thomas, where I'd stayed the night before my coronation. I hid my surprise—and relief—that I wasn't being led downstairs to a cell. For a second, I thought Nick might be waiting in the royal apartments for me, ready to reveal that this was nothing more than an off-color joke —the worst prank ever played. But then I berated myself for giving him that much credit: the chambers were devoid of any kingly splendor, the priceless furnishings and wall tapestries stripped away, leaving only a barren, drafty space.

Instead of the spacious bedchamber I'd slept in last time, I was steered into a smaller room and left alone, the stark clang of an iron lock bolting shut behind me. Tugging on the rigid handle assured me that I was a prisoner here. I marked the length of the space with thirteen short paces along the tiled floor that reached a small fireplace. The rest of the modest room held only a single bed, an oak desk, and a standing candelabrum that I momentarily considered stabbing a guard with in an effort to escape.

I tugged the woolen blanket off the bed and wrapped it around me, crossing the tiles to peer through the two narrow stained-glass windows. So much had happened since I'd last seen this view of the Thames from the neighboring bedchamber. The jumble of turreted buildings looked so short compared with twenty-first-century London—like a top layer had been sliced off the city. Despite the darkness of nightfall, ships and cargo vessels sat waiting for moorings near the north bank of the river. I opened the window for some fresh air, but a freezing gust of wind slapped me in the face, bringing the fetid stench of the castle moat directly below, and I wrenched the windowpane shut again.

I wished for a fire, but there was no wood.

A memory of Nick and I wrapped up in silk sheets at Robin House drifted into my vision, and I forced the image away. As I lay down on the hard bed, my thoughts turned to the monster Henry Howard. During our first meeting at Hampton Court, he'd reminded me of the fate of Anne Boleyn—the girl that King Henry the Eighth had married for love, only to execute her when she upset him one too many times. My stomach twisted into a sickening knot. As hideous as Howard was, he'd seen this coming before anyone. I was ending up just like Anne Boleyn, except I'd been a Tudor queen less than a year.

I crawled beneath the blanket and tossed fitfully. Did Nick really have the stomach to put me through a grueling trial—let alone a beheading—out of pure anger and spite? Or was this all part of a terrible plan to scare me, to force me into following his command and staying in this century? He'd sprung our wedding day on me without so much as a conversation—that was proof of his tyrannical nature that I'd willingly overlooked. Or else, perhaps my arrest was a symbolic gesture to appease the raging Duke of Norfolk and his army, and Nick planned to release me once things had cooled down. If that were so, though, why wouldn't he have just let me escape using the blue-diamond ring? If he wanted me safe, why would he publicly condemn me and risk my life? There was no coming back from a king's damnation in a place like this.

The endless questions chased themselves through my mind until, in the early hours of the morning, I drifted off to sleep, but it was shallow. I jerked awake at every small sound, my terrified mind convinced that each one was the executioner coming for me.

⚜ ⚜ ⚜

Counting blood-red sunsets told me that I spent an agonizing eleven days locked in that silent chamber with zero visitors or word from the king. At every waking moment, I was ready to fight in case someone burst in with a torture device or an executioner's axe. Meager bits of food were brought to me, but nothing else. There was too much time to think, too much time to cut open every moment of my relationship with Nick and dig through the tender wounds to unearth the mistakes I'd made.

Our love had exploded like a meteor that had fused us together so fast that I still hadn't caught my breath. He'd felt like home—like my *person* in the world—so incredibly quickly that it had colored every decision I'd made, even the one to try to save him from his dreadful fate as Nicholas the Ironheart. Before we met, I knew him only as the sixteenth-century king who ruthlessly ruled his nation. When I figured out that was because his little sister Kit had been murdered by one of his most trusted subjects, I'd had only one goal: to save Kit and to stop the boy I loved from becoming that tyrant.

Sunlight on the leaded windowpane reflected my stricken face like a mirror as I faced one truth after another: I adored Kit, but saving her life was perhaps the biggest mistake of all. I'd tried to change the path of history, Lucinda's life had been taken in exchange, and then I'd pushed Nick toward his hideous destiny anyway. I had been such an idiot to believe that I could insert myself into the past and live in it as a queen. It had proved almost impossible to convince the most accomplished people in the land that a twenty-first-century girl had the makings of a Tudor queen. Maybe the only chance Nick and I ever had was if he'd chosen to stay with me in my time and disappeared from the Tudor world. Surely life could've gone on here with Kit as the rightful new queen. For all this time, we'd been fighting an unwinnable battle, and while Kit may have been saved, Nick had been lost to darkness the way the books had always said.

I was still brooding over the timeline when, on the fifteenth day of my imprisonment, an unexpected tap sounded on the wooden door. I froze with fear as it opened slowly with an unnerving creak. Alice Grey looked so pasty and gaunt in the doorway that I almost didn't recognize her. She gaped at me, and I realized I must look as awful to her. When we both recovered from our shock, we fell into each other, hugging, and I stifled the urge to sob into her soft hair, which smelled like cinnamon cake.

"I was not permitted to come before now," she said, helping me to sit on the bed, treating me as if I was fragile. Tears pooled in her molten brown eyes as she searched my face. "My lady, are you greatly sore of heart?"

"I'm terrible," I replied honestly. "I've lost everything." Speaking the words aloud shattered my soul. It wasn't just my life here that was over. Unless Nick freed me, I'd never see the twenty-first century again: my mom, my friends—even Dad, with his stuffy Camry and boring public radio programs.

Alice was rubbing my shoulder, her other hand catching her escaping tears.

"What's happening at court?" I said faintly. I couldn't bring myself to ask about Nick.

She settled herself with a deep exhale. "The palace has calmed. The king has reformed his council, and Francis speaks in a manner most heartening. There have been feasts, and merriments, and the courtiers are making ready for the Easter celebrations."

I nodded, staring at my lap. Now that I'd been booted from the palace, the Tudor court was thriving again. I was right, I'd been nothing more than a parasite here, a plague. An alien from an incompatible world who did nothing but delay the king's malevolent, self-serving temperament by a year at best.

"Where's Bridget?" I said.

Alice sighed. "Mistress Nightingale has taken leave to Buckinghamshire. I fear her heart has become much troubled these past weeks."

Shame crawled up my throat. When I'd met Bridget, she'd been so chirpy, so excited about becoming a maid of honour and meeting a rich husband. Another thing that had been lost because of me.

Alice placed a hand over mine, a cold band of polished gold surprising my skin.

"Francis and I are married," she said.

"Oh my gosh, that's amazing!" I hadn't smiled in so long that it nearly hurt my cheeks. "Where did you do it?"

"At court." The flush in her cheeks exposed the happiness that she was trying to hide. "My lady, that you could not be there has caused me much sorrow. After everything, Francis wished to wait not."

"No, of course not, it's brilliant news." I managed another smile of encouragement. At least Alice's life was falling into place, even if mine was crumbling to pieces.

The conversation dropped to silence before I summoned the courage to ask Alice if she knew anything about my fate.

Her lips trembled, her eyes meeting her lap. "Your trial will take place on the morrow."

All the blood fled my face. A sort of darkness overcame the room, and I lost all sense of myself, like I might pass out. Alice steadied me with both hands, and I could tell that she was fighting not to break down. "I wish I could help you," she stammered through more tears.

"I know," I said, leaning into her. The urge to tell her the truth about me—about where I came from—was so intense that it crawled onto my tongue, begging to be set free. This could be my last chance. But if I told Alice Grey that I was from the future, it'd put her at risk of being complicit in my alleged sorcery. I wanted her to enjoy her wedded bliss with Francis, not to have to testify against me at my trial. I had endangered too many people in this world already. So I sat there and clung to her hands, blessing her over and over in my heart for having been my one rock in this place.

She glanced up at me, sensing something.

"I love you, Alice," was all I managed through my choked voice. "You might be the best thing in this entire world. I will *never* forget you."

Her words were breathless whispers. "You are my queen and lady most dear, and I will love you forevermore."

The depth of her sobs as we hugged one last time made clear that she believed I didn't stand a chance at tomorrow's trial. I'd admired Alice Grey for so many things: because she was spirited, feminist—for a Tudor, anyway—sharp as a tack...and almost always right.

I really was doomed.

With no hope of sleep that night, I lay awake, piecing together a plan. Surely Nick would be at the trial and would see how weak I'd become in just two weeks. He was a vengeful and merciless man—I knew that now better than anyone—but I still believed he'd loved me as completely as I'd loved him. It made me sick to my stomach to think that I could still imagine kissing him deeply —and even hunger for it. It was beyond shameful, like doting on a serial killer or the devil himself, but I guessed that love just didn't switch off that fast. And maybe I could use any feelings still between us to my advantage: at the trial, I would do whatever I could to convince Nick Tudor to set me free. I'd mouth the words "I love you" to him—even scream them if I had to.

I wasn't too proud to beg him for my life.

22

—————

AT FIRST LIGHT, I was marched downstairs to the Tower of London's aging Great Hall, where hundreds of men jostled for space in their flat caps and showiest coats. I braced myself for the appearance of Nick, but I couldn't catch sight of him anywhere.

The guards ushered me up a short ladder and onto a wooden platform. On a table before me sat my three judges in somber black cloaks—the Baron of Wharton, the Earl of Dorset, and Henry freaking Howard. I wanted to hurl all over his infuriating smirk and dumbass ostrich-feather hat. He'd launched a rebellion against the king and queen—how was he judging *me* and not the other way around? However, Howard's presence confirmed that he and Nick had officially kissed and made up. Bile pooled in the back of my throat.

Late-arriving spectators shuffled in from the sides of the hall to watch the proceedings. I searched for Alice, but there wasn't a single female in the room apart from me. And still no sign of Nick.

Coward.

Lord Wharton's grating voice flooded the cavernous space. "Queen Emmeline, you are arraigned before this commission on

277

charges of conspiring to procure the death and destruction of His Majesty, the King of England, through means of malice, witch-craft, and adulterous incitations. How do you answer the charges?"

I pressed my lips together, trying to decide what to say. I'd been given no legal counsel or preparation of any kind.

"Not guilty," I said, clearing my hoarse throat. "I am innocent of the charges."

The baron then launched into a ridiculous story about me pursuing an adulterous affair with the Earl of Warwick—purely because I'd made a joke about him being in the king's disguise at the masquerade feast. It was the first of countless testimonies about how I'd bewitched the king without genuine love in my heart while secretly plotting against him. Hilariously, I was even accused of trying to seduce Mister Andrea Bon Compagni behind closed doors in my workshop, which was also the place where I apparently experimented with recipes of witchcraft. The young maidservant Clemence from Robin House was summoned as a witness and stood shaking before the jury. Unable to look at me, she testified that I'd regularly met with a village witch, and appalled cries exploded from the sidelines. I had no idea how she'd known about my visit to the witch in the hamlet, but I didn't blame her for her testimony. For all I knew, Clemence had been forced to speak out against me; plus, she was right—I had met with the witch, even if it was only once. More outrageous lies were outlined in excruciating and humiliating detail before the accusations turned to my family origins. With nobody able to verify the existence of the Grace family from Worthing, and Henry Howard arguing that I wasn't his niece and that I'd bewitched him to believe it so, the deceit became overwhelming. At no point was Nick implicated in anything; the all-powerful King of England was evidently so unimpeachable that he didn't even have to bother showing up for the trial. So much for begging him for my life.

I clenched my eyes until they were dry. There was no way these men would see me cry.

My thighs were aching after standing for so long before Lord Wharton finally called for silence. While his voice was grave, his eyes twinkled beside the equally as smug Henry Howard.

"This day, Queen Emmeline has made a plea of not guilty to the lords stood here as councilors to our sovereign lord and king, Nicholas of England, and the peers of the realm. After being examined here, each lord has said, one and all, that Queen Emmeline is guilty of all the charges brought against her."

An icy gust of wind blew through me, and I thought I might topple over.

Lord Wharton focused his fierce eyes on me. "Madam, as you have been found guilty, I shall proceed in judgment. You are hereby sentenced to die. From here, you will be taken to your prison in the tower of St. Thomas, and on the morrow at the strike of dawn, you will be executed by beheading, burning, or hanging as shall please His Majesty the King. Your marriage to King Nicholas of England is now null and void. You have no crown, no land or title, and you shall henceforth be known as Mistress Emmeline Grace."

A cough—or perhaps a chortle—burst from Henry Howard's haughty mouth. I wanted to drive my fist through his heart. Fortunately for him, I was swiftly escorted from the hall and back upstairs to my locked chamber. A stale cheese tart sat waiting for me on the table, but I could hardly breathe, let alone eat.

Nick didn't even come to the trial.

He couldn't pay me the freaking courtesy of turning up.

I smacked the pewter plate holding the cheese tart off the table, covering my ears at the brassy clanging. My fingertips slipped into my hair, and I grabbed the dirty clumps and tugged hard, wishing the pain would overwhelm my thoughts until I couldn't hear them anymore.

Why couldn't he have just let me go? Neither Nick nor I had to go through any of this—if he'd just let me travel back to my time and pretended that I'd drowned in the river, we'd both be safe. Did he really prefer the option of slicing off my head?

I fell onto the bed, lying flat and motionless like a corpse.

No matter how I tried to make sense of it all, my thoughts always circled back to the same place: this was my fault. Nick couldn't let me go because he believed that I'd abandoned him. I'd known about his monstrous vengeful streak since the beginning—what he was capable of if he felt betrayed—and I'd willingly walked right into the firing line.

Way to go, Emmeline Eleanor WTF-have-you-gotten-yourself-into Grace.

Now, because of my mistakes—and my deluded, naïve belief in love—the wrath of Nicholas the Ironheart would make sure that I wouldn't leave Tudor England alive.

Nightmares invaded any sleep I managed that night, filled with horrific sounds and images of wild spectators howling for my head at Tower Hill. If only it was still winter with a delayed sunrise to bless me with a few more hours of life. But spring had arrived and dawn would come quickly, bringing with it my execution.

As soon as the inky-black sky through the stained-glass window began to lighten, there was zero chance of more sleep. Frail with terror but determined not to be dragged outside in the nude, I tied on my plain, mint-colored kirtle and sat on the end of the bed. I lowered my head into a meditative position and tried to switch off my mind. I'd seen movies where criminals were in such a numb daze by the time they climbed the gallows that they didn't look afraid anymore.

No such luck. When a key twisted in the lock, and the

wooden door swung heavily toward me, my anxious stomach surged and heaved, emptying bile onto the painted floor tiles.

"Wash that in haste," a velvety voice commanded the door guard.

I glanced up into the sunlit features of Nicholas the Ironheart. Immediately, I slid away as if looking directly at him would kill me right there. I felt his brilliant, deadly eyes assessing me.

"Go away...just go away," I whispered lifelessly. I resisted the urge to puke again as the guard scrambled in with a bucket and cloth. Nick stood with his arms crossed, glaring at the guard, who gave the spot a token cleaning before escaping again. The king charged at the door, heaving it shut before twisting a key in the lock.

I finally found my voice. "Get *OUT!*" I screamed. How dare he show his face to me? I was so physically livid that I could feel my skin burning and my teeth grinding.

Nick held out a shaky palm. "I bid you to be calm." It took me back in time to the similar words he'd said when we'd first met, when I was a prisoner in the Tower of London last time. *"Be calm,"* was the first thing he'd ever said to me. We'd officially come full circle.

I opened my mouth to reply, but the torrent of abusive things that I wanted to yell became confused in my throat. My jaw clenched until it hurt. Even if Nick had sorted out his messed-up head and was here to issue an eleventh-hour pardon, it was too late. I'd been publicly shamed and sentenced to die as a traitor, a witch, and an adulteress. Not even the king had the power to turn back the clock on that.

"How could you do this to me?" I eventually gasped. I wanted to shout the words, but my throat was too choked, my eyes too thick with tears.

"I pray that you hear me," said Nick, sinking to his knees until our faces were level. "You must know the cause of mine actions." His visible regret flooded me with more rage.

"You *do* feel bad," I realized with horror. "You feel guilty about what you did to me in one of your insane tantrums, and now you want me to forgive you so you'll feel better after it's over. You're off your freaking rocker!"

When he opened his mouth again, I cut in first.

"Why didn't you just let me go?" I pleaded, my voice shredded. "No one would have looked for me in the gardens at night. I'd have just fallen asleep. I'd have disappeared. There were so many ways you could've swept my memory under the rug and moved on. I gave up everything for you—my entire life! *Why* would you punish me like this?" My face crumbled with more stinging tears. Worse than the punishment itself was the thought that Nick had instigated it…that had always been the most painful part.

"Forgive me…I bid you to cry not," he said throatily, reaching for me. I jerked away so violently that his hands shot up in defense.

"Don't you ever tell me what to do," I spat. "And don't you *ever* touch me again. Just get the hell away from me!" I crossed my arms over my knees, forming a tight ball. I'd stay that way until they dragged me down to the executioner's block. I was no longer human. I was ready to die.

A thundering of raging voices surged from a distance below, wafting through the window that was slightly ajar.

The crowds are already waiting for me. My nightmare is coming true.

I tried to shut out the hideous chants with my hands over my ears but to no avail.

Nick had moved to the window. "Do you hear that?" he said.

I threw him my most colorful foul-mouthed response.

Despite the modern language, I could tell he grasped the sentiment. He bit his lip and edged the windowpane further open with his elbow. "Listen closely," he said, watching me.

He actually wanted me to hear the bloodthirsty Emmie-haters crying for my head. What kind of sicko was he? Before I could reply, the drumming of feet from afar was chased by three cries of "God save the king!"

Nick swallowed tightly. "It is now done," he said.

"What's done?" I could've slapped him.

"The traitor, Henry Howard, has been beheaded."

"What?"

I didn't think I'd heard right. The room was whirling in all directions.

Nick stepped closer to me, his voice thick. "Last night, Henry Howard was tried, charged, and convicted of high treason against the King of England for launching a plot of rebellion and for plotting the poisoning of Mistress Lucinda Parker."

He took a shaky seat beside me on the bed. All I could do was gape at his ashen face, his soft scent of roses infuriatingly close to my nose. I hated myself for how much I still wanted to touch him. *Why* couldn't I be free of that at least before he killed me?

A shimmer of tears coated Nick's eyes. "Emmie, I did not permit you to vanish from the garden the night of your arrest because I was in need of time. I had to make new a record of my last will and testament so I could make no error in naming the Princess Catherine Tudor as my successor. Kit was plainly my heir apparent, but I needed to make the line of succession certain if I am to surrender my kingship. I was also in need of time to gather the evidence to ensure that Henry Howard would be convicted of treason." His distressed eyes could hardly meet mine. "I pray you will forgive me. You needed to believe it to be true as much as my subjects or their faithless army may have killed you in haste. I had to make certain there was no suspicion of any plotting between us."

I lowered the arm that had covered my eyes as if it could protect me from Nick's insane words. My voice was a faint line. "What on earth are you talking about?"

He glanced up at me, and our eyes seared together, drawing heat to my cheeks. Nick's breath wavered as he spoke. "The instant that I learned of Howard mounting his assault on the castle—meaning to take you from me—I was certain that I would boil alive every last one of them. Not only the men, but their brothers…their fathers…their sons." His cheeks reddened with shame. "I cannot bear to handle this beast I have inside me. You know there is true darkness in me. But the blacker the darkness, the brighter the light that shines upon it." He slid closer, his presence rattling me from the inside out. "I have tried to forget you, more than once. I did consider removing you from my world that night in the garden—bidding you to leave with my blessing—but all I see without you is intolerable darkness." His forehead tilted so close to mine that I could taste the mint on his breath. "Therefore, if you must take leave of this kingdom and I cannot bid you to stay, then—with your consent—I will leave with you."

He dug into the folds of his coat and presented a flash of brilliant blue. Both our fingers trembled as he gently glided the blue-diamond ring down my thumb.

Without letting go of my hand, Nick laced his warm fingers into mine. "I bid you take me with you, Emmie. Can you forgive me for these past weeks? I have thought of naught else but the countless errors of my judgment through all of this. My lady, I beseech you to forgive me. The loss of your person would truly put an end to my heart. Forgive me for all my sins." His head bowed with shame and torment, his long fingers sinking into his messy curls.

I could hardly speak through the boulder in my throat. The last few weeks had been the most chilling of my life. Nick's secret plan to condemn me so he could freely orchestrate his departure from Tudor England was shockingly dangerous, hideous for me, and thrown together in a moment of panic, but he'd done it all to save our relationship.

I'd been wrong. He never wanted me to die, he wanted to come with me…to give up his kingdom for my small life in modern-day America. That's why he didn't let me go when I was in the gardens; he needed time to defeat Henry Howard and ensure that his sister Kit was safe.

He wasn't Nicholas the Ironheart, he was just...Nick. He hadn't stopped loving me at all.

"What about Kit?" I said, still spinning. The thought of all this being another trick was too much to bear.

He squeezed my fingers tightly. "Lord Warwick and his wife will heartily care for my sister, which I have made clear. Francis shall be a worthy Lord Protector, and when Kit is of age, I have full belief that she will be as gracious a queen as her mother Elizabeth."

"And you?" I added, tears dripping onto my cheeks. "What about all this? You said you could never leave this place." I shook my head at the Tudor world that surrounded us from all sides... his kingdom, his duty.

"I will learn to live without it," he said in a strangled voice. He nodded with assurance, but I could feel his heart breaking.

"But Nick, I'm—I'm no royal." I thought of the decadence that followed him at every turn. "You've seen where I live. We eat cheese on toast; we—we clean our own houses. Well, unless you're my mom. Cleaning isn't her strong suit."

"Say not such things," he said, his hands finding my cheeks and pulling my face close to his. He wrapped both his legs around me in a protective circle. "You have you. You are my choice. *You.*" He dropped his forehead to mine again, and I breathed him in.

Nick's heartfelt words filled me with shame. At one time, he'd been *my* choice before things went south. I'd then tried to break off the relationship and go home. Surely he deserved the same chance: to try living in my time but be able to come back here if things didn't work out.

"I have to tell you something," I said as he pressed his soft lips to my tear-stained cheek. "The soothsayer that I saw also told me that the enchanted ring was never meant to be used more than once, especially by two people." Lines appeared in Nick's brow as

I delivered the bad news. "The ring barely functioned when I went back to get medicine for Lucinda Parker. When I tried to use it in the garden the other day—before I was arrested—I already had a plan. If the ring failed, I was going to go back to that soothsayer to try to get her to re-curse it."

Nick's shoulders had stiffened. "What are you saying?"

My fingers loosened in his, preparing for the worst. "I'm saying that this ring might not work anymore. And if it does, and we travel to the modern world to live there, the chances of you getting back here could be *zero*. If you come with me now and you don't like it there…if you regret it and you want to come home—you might never be able to."

Nick leaned backward with a heavy sigh.

My mind was racing. "Could we just go to that soothsayer near Robin House now?" I suggested. "Maybe she can curse it again—like, recharge it—before we even try using it."

Nick's fingertips tugged at his bottom lip in thought, but he soon shook his head. "I cannot reverse what occurred at your trial. I could assuredly pardon the execution in favor of another punishment, but I cannot be seen to be taking you from here. Men would believe it to be the makings of a plot between us. At such a troubled time, the Privy Council may move to depose the Tudor line. Kit would be imprisoned, or worse. It is too dangerous."

"So to disappear is a better option? You think it's better for the king to just *vanish* with the former queen on the day of her execution?"

"Not to vanish…to die."

I stared at him. "Come again?"

Nick nodded at the window. "I have the key to open the bars, and the Council will come to determine that we have willingly plunged to the bottom of the river. Kit will not suffer if I am thought to have taken my life, but she *will* pay for it if I abandon the throne and go into hiding with a queen convicted of treason and heresy. I have prepared a letter which declares that I could not live without you after all, and I will leave it in this room." He produced a folded piece of parchment from his coat. "The lords may wish to see our bodies to believe it completely," he added uneasily. "To that end, there shall remain suspicion over my fate, but I can think of no better alternative."

All the pieces slotted into place like a puzzle. Nick wanted us to feign a double suicide so the crown could pass to Kit.

I paced to the window, considering the plan. When the frame was open, the space was just wide enough for someone of Nick's size to slip through at an angle. The towering outside wall was impossible to scale. If we both disappeared from this locked chamber, and the window was left wide open, people would possibly believe that we jumped.

My voice was barely audible. "What are we waiting for then? If you're really sure."

Nick leaped forward to hug me tightly. I squeezed his shoulders, burying myself in his embrace as he used his free hand to unlock the window and swing the frame of bars out into the biting cold wind. There wasn't enough time for us to make up properly now. In my heart, I also knew it'd take time to get the image of Nicholas the Ironheart forsaking me out of my head. But in my world, we'd have plenty of time to talk through what had unfolded and set things right.

"We'll fix the ring," I assured, holding his forearm. "We'll find a soothsayer in my time, and we'll have it enchanted again. You *will* be able to get back here if you want."

A sad smile touched his lips. "Self-murder means the damnation of the soul, Emmie. If I am believed to have taken my life before God, I can never return. Once I leave this way, I am finished with this world."

"And Kit?" I reminded him again, tightening my hold on his wrist. After all that he'd done to protect his sister...could he really just abandon her?

He shook his head at me, his despairing face shutting the question down. He couldn't talk about it. A new wave of pain engulfed my heart. Kit was going to be Nick's most difficult sacrifice of all. But the last few months had proven that he couldn't keep both her and me, and now he was choosing me. Except that, unlike when I'd been given the same choice, Nick knew there was no way back. His sacrifice would be irreversible.

I wrapped my arms around his neck again and held him, feeling his heartbeat merge with mine. Surely becoming Queen of England would be a better fate for Kit than having married that French aristocrat. That had to be an upside. Nick leaned into me, stroking my arms with the tips of his fingers. A flock of seagulls squawked as they glided over the Thames, signaling the full break of dawn. Through the window, the rallying calls of the Tower Hill spectators gathered in volume, ready for the second execution of the day…mine. We had to hurry.

Nick unfolded the note he'd written and placed it on the chipped floor tiles near the door.

"Come in haste," he said, sliding into the bed. I was curious to read what he'd written in the note, but we both had to fall asleep before the guards came knocking, and I didn't want to waste a moment of time. Plus, I'd come to Tudor England ready to don my best pair of rose-colored glasses and make the most of it, but now, I couldn't wait to get home to the modern world.

I lay beside Nick and slid into his waiting arms. He took one sniff of the blanket and pushed it away, removing his black leather coat and draping it over me instead.

He wrapped an arm around me, clasping my hand wearing the blue-diamond ring so we were securely connected.

"What do we do if the ring doesn't work, and we can't get out of here?" I whispered into the linen pillow.

After a pause, he nodded at the window. "I suppose we will have to jump in truth."

Fear crushed my stomach like a soda can as Nick tightened

his embrace. The heaviness of his arm soothed me like a weighted blanket.

I shut my eyes and prayed silently for sleep and for the ring to work.

"I'm wide awake," I hissed with rising panic. The executioner was waiting for me, and if the guards came in and found us in bed together, both Nick and I could end up headless.

A sudden memory shot me upward like a bullet. I clicked open the enchanted ring's hidden compartment. "I forgot that I've got one sleeping pill left!" I said, wanting to kiss the little blue tablet. I snapped it into two halves.

"What is this?" Nick said as I dropped one piece into his palm and swallowed the other half.

"It's medicine from my time that will help you go to sleep quickly."

He brought the pill closer to his face. "A sleep remedy such as the poppy-seed or lettuce in the milk of a lady?"

I tried not to chuckle at his old-school lactation therapies. "I'm not exactly sure what this pill is, but it *will* work...you can swallow it, it won't hurt you."

"I trust you with my life," he said nervously before downing the pill and wincing at the aftertaste. He lay back down beside me and took my hand, lacing our fingers together.

After a few moments, he spoke quietly, his nervous breath tickling the back of my shoulder. "Emmie, you know I will have no manner of princely splendor in your world. I will have naught to give you: no jewels, no cloth, no horse, no feasts, no lands, no—"

I silenced him with a gentle shush. "I don't want those things," I said. "I want to make my own jewelry, with wire and pliers, just like I used to. I want to make dinners for us...to learn how to cook properly. I just want *you*."

I tugged his arm closer, butterflies hatching in my stomach at the thought of having Nick Tudor all to myself in a regular house. Could we actually have a normal life?

To push away the terrifying thought that the ring might not work and we would have to jump to our deaths after all, I tilted back to look at his calming face.

"So what are your final words?" I stammered lightly. "In case the guards break in, or the ring fails and we have to jump...it's kind of morbid, but do you have any dying words, Your Majesty?"

We lay for a quiet moment before Nick spoke, his breath a soft kiss on my skin. "No matter where we shall travel, my lady—to the future or to God in heaven, I wish to be by your side. For I shall be a king no more, but merely a man, and I will worship and love you as such until the last breath of my immortal soul." He kissed the skin behind my ear, sending a rush of sweet love through my veins. "Can you love me not as a king, Emmie, but as a man?"

My eyes watered with a rush of tears. "That's all I've ever done."

My stomach and my chest twisted with hopeful anticipation. Maybe now, I could finally prove to Nick that his wealth and power meant nothing to me, that all I wanted was an ordinary life with an ordinary Nick. Even though it made me uneasy to think what stealing him away from the sixteenth century would do to the Tudor dynasty as I knew it.

I cuddled into him. "Let's go to sleep," I whispered. "Ne dimittas. Don't you dare let go of me."

The last words I heard Nick Tudor say were a warm murmur against my neck. "As you love me, my lady, I wager my life and kingdom on it."

ACKNOWLEDGMENTS

"Love what you do and you'll never work a day in your life." Sorry, but bollocks. There's nothing easy about writing a book, even when my soul consistently clarifies how much I love it and that stopping is not an option. While writers are often imagined as quirky, reclusive creatures (which we completely are), it's not a solitary experience but a two-way contract between writer and reader that says this is a journey we're going on together. Without readers, my stories and characters would be eternally lost at sea, and I must thank you—the reader—for keeping Emmie and the Tudor Queen on course. To every excited reader who messaged me after finishing Emmie and the Tudor King, asking for more, I humbly offer this work to you. Thank you, thank you, thank you for your support. It means everything to me.

To my wonderful editor, Arielle Bailey, the magical ring to my storytelling: thank you for guiding me out of the ghastly pit of the passive, whiny character and up into the light where Emmie yearned to be with her good-hearted and perceptive nature. Also, endless appreciation for your hilarious comments that pulled me into line when the sixteenth-century dancing became too steamy or when Emmie willingly exposed the modern world to smallpox (Emmie, how could you!).

Thank you to Shaela Odd from Blue Water Books for another perfect cover, and to the woman of many talents, Brookie Cowles, for your interior files. I love working with you both.

I couldn't believe that I had to fly to England to visit Hampton Court Palace, Windsor Castle, and Kenilworth Castle—among others—for this book (such a drag!), and said research trip wouldn't have been the same without my Tudor tour partner-in-crime, Darren Waters. Thanks for keeping me company, Mr. Waters, and where are we researching next? May I also offer immense gratitude to my Hampton Court Palace tour guide, the lovely Sandy Rhodes, and to historian Tracy Borman for more critical questions answered via email (the fangirling hasn't stopped). To Matthew "Matty J" Johnson (again, not The Bachelor one—the original): thank you for allowing me to drag you around London to gawk at so many Tudor heads and bizarre implements! Yes, you have a weird friend.

Thank you to the divine Kathleen Pasqualini for being my beta reader, my book cover consultant, my Australian slang fielder, my source for random US facts, and for thwarting Emmie and Nick's attempts to wake up in the library without their kit on, LOL.

Thanks also go to my fellow author and friend, Lisa Buscemi Reiss, for helping me stay afloat and motivated during some difficult days in this writing process. I truly value your friendship. To the gorgeous bookstagrammer Jen from @bookbookowl for the stunning cover reveal, and all my wonderful ARC readers and book tour bloggers—I adore you! Please accept my heartfelt thanks for your time. I also owe my gratitude to my 'twinnie' writer friend Nicole Webb and her agent Bernadette Foley for the sage advice during the trials of publication.

Once again, to the brilliant Martha Wells: your medical advice regarding poisoning helped ensure that one of my characters died appropriately—that is sincerely a gift in this context (*grins*). Thank you, clever Martha!

In the Hearts & Crowns series, Emmie Grace spends a great deal of time living away from her family, and it's a twisting pain that I have lived and understand—even if my family will forever feel torn in two with the beautiful Canadian side so far away. But to every treasured member of my family, both near and far: from the bottom of my heart, thank you for being my people. I can't not mention my parents and my sister: you are my rocks.

Speaking of my people: Brent, Brady, and Aubrey, while I feel like I disappear into another world every time I write a novel—a world I feel sublimely content in—if there were even a hint that I might never be able to get back to you, I would toss that part of my life into a fire. You come first, always. I love you endlessly. CB, your ability to put up with me and my writing dreams with nothing but love and encouragement is a miracle in itself. I am tempted to dunk you in the lake to perform a witchcraft water trial—how are you real? *hearts*

Last, but never least (especially if we're talking pounds—sorry, had to get that one in), I want to thank the Tudors themselves, particularly King Henry VIII. I joke about Henry, but the truth is that I like him, even though he made such appalling decisions at times. Without Henry's face-palming shenanigans that changed Britain forever, I'd never have fallen for this dramatic slice of history that has captivated people for centuries. The Tudor dynasty is ultimately what inspired me to write stories about charismatic kings stricken with the dart of love (Henry's words, not mine). So, without further ado, I wish to thank Henry VIII, Catherine of Aragon, Anne Boleyn, Jane Seymour, Anne of Cleves, Catherine Howard, Catherine Parr, Mary I, Elizabeth I, and Edward VI. Wherever you are, broken family, I hope your hearts are mended (and your necks, gulp!) and please know that—nearly five hundred years into the future—we still speak your names.

ABOUT THE AUTHOR

Natalie Murray is the author of Emmie and the Tudor King (June 2019) and Emmie and the Tudor Queen (August 2020). The YA time travel romance series follows a high school graduate to a reimagined Tudor England, where she meets a doomed, but utterly dreamy, Tudor king. Emmie and the Tudor King has received acclaim from Foreword Reviews, InD'Tale Magazine, YA Books Central, and popular YA authors Brigid Kemmerer (A Curse So Dark and Lonely) and CJ Flood (Infinite Sky), among others. Emmie and the Tudor King was a finalist in the 14th Annual National Indie® Excellence Awards in the category of New Adult Fiction. Natalie is currently penning her next angsty romance from beautiful Lake Macquarie on Australia's east coast, where she lives with her husband, two children, and hangry miniature schnauzer, Otto.

You can find Natalie Murray forgetting to update her website or procrastinating on social media at:
    nataliemurrayauthor.com
    instagram.com/nataliemurrayauthor
    twitter.com/natmurrayauthor
    facebook.com/nataliemurrayauthor

CPSIA information can be obtained
at www.ICGtesting.com
Printed in the USA
BVHW071930240820
587204BV00001B/108